BLACK WOLF

BLACK WOLF

Philip Caveney

HEADLINE

First published in Great Britain in 1993
by HEADLINE BOOK PUBLISHING PLC

10 9 8 7 6 5 4 3 2 1

British Library Cataloguing in Publication Data

Caveney, Philip
Black Wolf
I. Title
823.914 [F]

ISBN 0-7472-0745-3

Typeset by
CBS, Felixstowe, Suffolk

Printed and bound in Great Britain by
Mackays of Chatham PLC, Chatham, Kent

HEADLINE BOOK PUBLISHING PLC
Headline House
79 Great Titchfield Street
London W1P 7FN

With thanks to Phil Davenport
for providing the spark.
To Peter Lavery, who added some fuel.
And to Michael Milne BDS
who helped me construct the teeth.

'Beware of false prophets which come to you in sheep's clothing, but inwardly they are ravening wolves.'

Matthew 7:15

'Oh no, it wasn't the airplanes. It was Beauty killed the Beast!'

Carl Denham, *King Kong*

PART ONE

Prologue

Welcome to Leonard's room.

It is an upstairs bedroom in an old brownstone in Dennings, Pennsylvania. This is where Leonard reads his books and watches his videos. It is here that he thinks his thoughts and dreams his dreams. Sometimes, when the need for solitude is especially strong, he will even take his meals up here. Leonard is fond of his own company.

It is not a particularly big room, but there is a lot packed into it. It would look impossibly cluttered if all the items were not so rigidly organized and arranged. *A place for everything, and everything in its place*. This is one of Leonard's favourite sayings, and one that he adheres to religiously.

The room is a shrine to horror, and the creation of horror. It is Leonard's unashamed obsession. Along the entire length of one wall, galvanized steel shelves hold his collection of books: hardback and softback. Horror fiction, horror textbooks, encyclopaedias and anthologies, magazines and fanzines; they rise from floor to ceiling, a multitude of brightly-coloured spines, each book encased in a clear plastic envelope to keep it in mint condition. The books are filed in strict alphabetical and chronological order. To Leonard it would be unthinkable to put a book back in the wrong place.

The rows of shelving along the next wall, which frame the room's one small window, contain Leonard's extensive collection of memorabilia. Here are bubblegum cards and ghoulish construction kits, featuring glow-in-the-dark characters from classic horror films. Frankenstein's Monster, Dracula, the Mummy, the Phantom of the Opera – Leonard has them all. Here, too, are cardboard promotional displays for books and films; there are scores of gruesome toys, still neatly packaged in their original boxes. Here's the face-hugging beastie from *Alien*; there's a professional make-up kit for creating realistic flesh wounds and scars. But pride of place goes to Leonard's latest acquisition: a dummy severed hand, almost too realistic, the stump thick with congealed blood. Go on touch it! You see, it's only latex!

By the next wall, almost as an afterthought, there's Leonard's neatly-made single bed. A mobile hangs above it, depicting a flight of rubbery black bats; and the lamp beside the bed is a grinning translucent skull. At the foot of the bed are a television and a video-recorder set up so that Leonard can watch them in absolute comfort. The rest of the wall is taken up by Leonard's video collection, all horror films, many of them bootlegs of titles once condemned as 'video nasties'.

Against the last wall, bordered by inflatable dinosaurs and childish-seeming rubber masks of demons, werewolves and vampires, stands Leonard's writing desk, a huge construction of antique scrolled mahogany, which the salesman assured him once belonged to Bela Lugosi. Leonard has a signed document to that effect in one of the drawers of the desk, and has no misgivings about having handed over virtually his entire life savings to buy it. He knows that there are some opportunities in this world that cannot be ignored – no matter what the price.

On the wall above the desk, in a strategic place of honour, is Leonard's 'Rogues' Gallery', a collection of framed, signed photographs of horror authors. Look, here's Stephen King and James Herbert, there's Clive Barker, Dean Koontz, Ramsey Campbell and Peter Straub . . . But there's an empty space in the arrangement: a blank frame hanging there, a blank nameplate waiting to be filled in . . . as though Leonard is intending to make a new addition to his collection.

Perhaps the book on the desktop is a clue. It's a hardback novel called *Black Wolf*, and its author is a man called Mark Tyler. The pages of the book look well-thumbed, and you can see that slips of paper have been placed between some pages, as if Leonard intends to return to certain passages and read them again. There's also a brown manila folder lying on the desk. It's open and the contents are trailing out, as though Leonard was looking at them and was then interrupted by something. You can see the headlines quite clearly. MYSTERY BEAST STRIKES AGAIN and CAT FOUND SLAUGHTERED. If you examine the clippings more carefully, you discover that they all tell a similar story. Some animal has been preying on local pets. Cats and dogs have been found with their throats ripped out, their bodies horribly mangled. In one incident, a hen coop has been invaded and dozens of birds ripped to shreds. Even more bizarre is the testimony of one Earl Cooper, the owner of those chickens, a middle-aged bachelor with a smallholding out on the Four Mile Road, just north of

Dennings. Look, here's the story in his own words, cut from an edition of the *Dennings Courier*.

'I was woke in the night by noises from the hen coop, sounded like they was coming from the depths of hell. I figured there was a fox in the henhouse; it's happened before. I got up out of bed, put on my dressing-gown and boots, and grabbed my twelve-bore from the rack. It's kind of remote out here on the Four Mile Road, so I always keep it loaded. I ran out into the yard and saw the door of the coop was open. The henhouse door was open, too, and there was a terrible commotion in there: chickens flapping and squawking as they tried to escape. I yelled something and ran straight into the henhouse. It was pitch dark in there. As I came through the doorway, something sprang on me, something mean and wild, snapping and slavering at my throat. I went down on my back, and the gun slipped out of my hands. After that I just had to concentrate on covering my face. My hands and shoulders was all bit, and there was a chunk taken out of my right shoulder. Then whatever it was took off through the doorway, and I was too scared to go after it. The doctor said afterwards that the bites looked like those which would be made by a dog. Of course, I didn't catch so much as a glimpse of it, but it seemed to me to be bigger and stronger than any dog I've ever heard of. The other thing I can't figure out is how it got in there in the first place. After the last trouble, I had the fence extended to fifteen feet all round; but this thing managed to burst a padlock and walk right in through the door. Now what kind of an animal can do something like that?'

What indeed? Maybe the same animal that attacked local teenager Candy Winningham, ten days later as she walked home from her boyfriend's house in Calder Street, Dennings. Candy was walking along a deserted street, deep in thought, when something 'big and heavy' jumped her from behind, pushing her forwards on to her face and knocking her temporarily unconscious. When she came to, mere seconds later, she was aware of a terrible pain in her left thigh. Putting her fingers to the wound, she was horrified to discover that she had suffered a jagged bite that later required thirty stitches. Her mysterious assailant had vanished.

Now, look, here's an interesting article! Local businessman Ray Teale was driving along Highway 12 three weeks later, when . . .

Listen! Hear that? You can hear voices in the room next-door. One speaks in low, subdued tones. Then, every so often, there's another voice, a woman's voice rising in a shrill manic shriek and, my goodness, the language she's using! That will be Leonard's mother. We'll have to make allowances for her; she's not been well. Now a man's voice is shouting back at her. He hates it when she swears like this. It makes him so angry. And when Leonard gets angry . . .

Oh, oh! *Now* listen! The sound of Mother's door opening. Slow heavy footsteps on the landing. He's coming back. Leonard's coming back. We'd better go now. He wouldn't like it if he found us here . . .

Chapter One

When Mark Tyler collected the mail from the doormat that morning, inevitably one letter stood out from the rest. It was a white airmail envelope bearing an American stamp and postmark, and he quickly realized that it was from his US publishers. Opening it, he found that it contained only another, smaller envelope and a compliments slip. Mark examined the inner envelope. In the left-hand corner a small gold sticker, printed in an ornate Old English text, announced its sender. Mr Leonard J. Goldman of Dennings, Pennsylvania. Mark frowned. He knew few people in America other than his publishers, and so far his only personal contact with them had been regular letters from his editor, a lady with the unlikely name of Brook Dellon. She had told him how much they had enjoyed *Black Wolf* and how they were sure it was going to do great business over there and, oh, would Mark mind if they substituted the word *terrified* for the word *horrified* on page 253, since she felt it had been rather overused already in that chapter.

Mark left the bills and circulars on the hall table, and strolled through into the kitchen to complete making the two cups of coffee and toast he had been preparing when the letterbox had rattled. He put the letter on to the round wicker tray with the mugs and plates, resolving to read it in the comfort of bed. He gazed thoughtfully through the kitchen window at the bedraggled garden that backed his house, and resolved once again to get it mowed and weeded as soon as the weather improved. This morning was grey and overcast, and there was no sign of spring on the way, even though it was late April. If the second Black Wolf saga showed signs of emulating the success of the first, he might move away to the country, leaving London far behind. He had a vague idea about going to Ireland; Brendan had once told him that writers didn't have to pay tax there. He'd have to look into that sometime.

The kettle came to the boil. He poured hot water into the mugs, reflecting as he did so that he had a meeting later that day with Peter Maughan, his literary agent. He knew what it would be about, and part of him sagged. Since he was a school kid, Mark had nurtured dreams of becoming a published writer. And after many years of fervent hopes, false starts and cruel rejections, at the comparatively young age of twenty-eight, he had finally achieved that ambition. His first novel, a Celtic ghost story called *The Haunting* had been released to modest sales in Britain and considerable indifference elsewhere, which had not prompted him to give up his day job as a freelance copywriter. A year later, his vampire story, *Night Kiss* had done considerably better for him. This time round there had been translation sales to some European countries, and a bookclub deal had helped boost his royalties. But he seemed unable to crack America and it was probably with this thought in mind that he sat down to create *Black Wolf*. This story of a Sioux shaman, who possessed extraordinary occult powers, incorporated elements of Red Indian folklore and was unashamedly pitched at the American market. Part fantasy, part horror story – amongst Black Wolf's chief powers was the ability to transmogrify himself into a powerful wolflike beast – the gamble proved more successful than he could ever have anticipated. Bored by the predictability of their current programmes and excited by the freshness and authenticity of this unusual new product, several American publishers had expressed a fervent interest in adding it to their lists. Peter Maughan was able to play them off against each other, coaxing a sizable advance from the eventual victors. When it became apparent that *Black Wolf* was going to be a big seller just about everywhere, Peter suggested that Mark sign up a sequel while enthusiasm was high. At that time, Mark had been happy to ink his signature to a contract that offered him an even more lucrative advance. But now, having just finished the typescript of *Black Wolf 2*, he knew only too well why Maughan had asked to see him. Mark Tyler was going to be asked to perform the hat-trick.

The idea didn't exactly drive him wild with enthusiasm. Nobody had warned him it would be like this: married to the concept of Black Wolf and seemingly doomed to go on spinning out more tales about him *ad infinitum*. Mark told himself he ought to be happy. There were many other people who were obliged to stand beside a conveyer belt for the rest of their lives; their dreams would never come near to being fulfilled. And yet . . .

Mark sighed, berating himself for being ungrateful. He picked up the tray and carried it up the staircase and into the bedroom. Sarah lay in that transient state between sleep and wakefulness, and he stood for a moment, looking down at her fondly, and thinking how he would describe this scene if he was writing about it.

8

The woman was in her late twenties, slim, graceful, not conventionally pretty, but striking, with her large grey eyes and her full, generous mouth . . .

Mark grinned ruefully. He had actually used some of Sarah's characteristics for Connie, one of the protagonists in *Black Wolf*, and had then felt vaguely guilty when he'd written her death scene. Not that there had been anything personal in it.

'Come on, sleepyhead,' he shouted. 'Breakfast is served!'

She opened her eyes and stared at him, disorientated for an instant. Perhaps he'd interrupted a dream. Then she registered the breakfast tray and smiled. She yawned, stretched, sat up, and reached out her hands to take the tray.

'Hey, this is all right,' she observed. 'I'll have to sleep over more often.' She steadied the tray while Mark cast off his towelling robe and slipped into bed beside her. 'Oof!' she complained. 'Your feet are freezing!' She handed him a mug of coffee and then sipped gratefully at her own. 'Oh, yes,' she sighed. 'That's better. We must have really tied one on last night.'

'I lost count after eight gins,' he admitted. 'Say what you like about Brendan, but he knows how to throw a party.'

Sarah looked dubious. 'Most people provide some *food* to go with the drinks,' she said.

'Question of priorities,' he told her. He knew that Sarah wasn't fond of Brendan, who had somehow fallen into the role of being Mark's closest friend for many years. Sarah regarded him as an upper-class layabout who'd never done an honest day's work in his life. This probably wasn't so far removed from the truth, but Mark had a forgiving nature.

'What's this?' inquired Sarah, picking up the letter. She eyed its address sticker with interest. 'Didn't know you had friends in the States.'

He shrugged. 'Neither did I. It was sent to my publishers in New York, and forwarded on.'

'Really?' She smiled. 'Hey, you know, I bet it's a fan letter.'

'If it is, it's the first from that neck of the woods.'

'First of many, probably. The Americans are big on that kind of thing. I remember when *Mr Batty's Birthday* was published over there, I got dozens of letters.'

Mark tried not to smile. Sarah had a way of speaking quite seriously about the most outlandish titles. She was an illustrator of children's books and *Mr Batty's Birthday* had been one of her biggest successes. So far it was her only work to appear in the USA where it had achieved modest sales. Mark thought that Sarah secretly harboured some resentment about his own meteoric success over there, and that he was therefore treading on eggshells whenever the subject came under discussion.

He took the envelope from her and studied it for a moment.

'Well, aren't you going to open it?' she prompted.

'I suppose so.'

He ripped open the envelope and took out a single sheet of writing paper. He scanned the contents quickly.

'Well, fuck me,' he said. 'It *is* a fan letter!'

'Told you.' She studied him for a moment. 'Well, you've had them before?'

'One or two, I suppose. But this one's from *America*!'

She laughed. 'My God, it's still one big Disneyland to you, isn't it? Go on, let's hear it!'

He tried to hand her the sheet of paper, but she pushed it back.

'My eyes haven't focused yet. You read it out to me.'

He shrugged. 'All right, then.' He leaned back against his pillows.

Dear Mr Tyler,

I trust you will forgive the presumptuousness of me writing to you via your publisher, but I recently read your excellent horror novel *Black Wolf* in hardback and I feel I must comment.

Firstly let me explain that I have also read your two previous novels, which I managed to obtain through an import bookstore in New York. While they were enjoyable enough, they only hinted at your potential as a writer. *Black Wolf* however is in an entirely different league! This was a first-rate story, full of suspense and drama, and streets ahead of most other exercises in this genre. I don't mind telling you that I am a horror fanatic of the first order and this spellbinding tale had me enthralled from page one to the very end. Forgive me for not knowing if you have a fan club, but if there is one, I would be very proud to add my name to it. I have written to just about all the "masters" of the genre, and I realize that you are probably too busy to reply in person; but if I could beg from you a signed photograph to add to my "Rogues' Gallery", then I would indeed be a happy man! I already have signed photographs of all the accepted "masters" of horror fiction, and can assure you that you would be in august company.

If I may presume upon your valuable time a moment longer, may I inquire if there are to be more Black Wolf novels? I certainly hope so, because you have created an intriguing and multi-faceted horror hero who I am sure has the necessary depth to sustain many more exciting tales of dark fantasy. Thank you for sharing your wonderful talents, and let me assure you that I am only *one* of a legion of devoted fans.

> Your servant (and Black Wolf's),
> Leonard J. Goldman

Sarah brought her hands together in a burst of applause. 'Hey,' she said. 'Now that's what I call fan mail!'

Mark grinned sheepishly. 'Not bad,' he admitted.

'Not bad! God, if only the *reviews* had been that good. What was that bit about "sharing your wonderful talents"?'

'Leave it out,' he said fondly.

She chewed thoughtfully on the corner of a piece of toast.

'I wonder where this puts our little project?' she mused. 'Perhaps you'll be too busy now to spare any of your valuable time for a mere children's book.' She was referring to *The Jumblies*, her long cherished project about items of clothing in a jumble sale. Already in her mind, every item had been assigned a name and a character, and the various chapters would follow each garment to its new home. As a freelance illustrator she had usually worked to a writer's brief, but this concept was all her own. Sarah had already produced many of the pictures, but still needed somebody with the skill to put her vision into words. Mark had been her obvious choice.

'Don't be silly!' He put an arm around her and kissed her fondly on the forehead. 'Soon as I sort out this third manuscript, we'll get down to it.'

'You said that about the second one,' she reminded him.

'I know. It's just that the publishers are putting on a lot of pressure for me to . . .'

'Oh God, the pressure, the pressure!' Sarah put a hand to her forehead in a theatrical gesture.

'Well, I mean, it's crazy to pass up the opportunity. For years, nobody wanted to give me the time of day, and now they're actually begging for more.'

She patted his hand reassuringly. 'I know, love. You've worked hard for this, and you deserve it. I suppose there's no great hurry. *The Jumblies* can wait a while longer.' She tapped the sheet of paper in Mark's hand. 'I hope you're going to reply to this.'

He frowned. 'Think I should?'

'The guy's taken the trouble to write to you, so I think it's only polite.

You've still got some of those black-and-white photos left from the book shoot, haven't you?'

He nodded. 'Don't know why I bothered,' he complained. 'Nobody ever used them.'

'It's because you don't look sinister enough. You've got the face of the boy next-door.'

'Have you *seen* the boy next-door? He looks like Freddy Kruger!'

'That's cruel. He has acne, that's all.' Sarah glanced at the bedside clock and suddenly became all businesslike. 'Jesus, it's nearly ten o'clock! I'd better get home and finish up those sketches for *Mortimer Rabbit*. I'm showing them to the publishers tomorrow.'

'Mortimer can wait another hour, surely? You could look at this as research . . .' His lecherous advance was neatly thwarted when she thrust the breakfast tray into his hands.

Sarah threw aside the duvet and made for the bathroom.

'Actually, I thought you might give me a lift into town,' he called after her.

She paused at the door and glared at him. 'Did you now? Listen, mate, now that you're pulling in a good whack from this writing lark, isn't it time you booked yourself some driving lessons?'

He grimaced.

'Yeah, well I keep meaning to, but . . .'

'But it's easier if I drive you around? Listen, I sometimes like to have a drink myself, when we go out. Look at the hassle we had finding a cab at three o'clock this morning. If you could drive, we could take turns.'

'I'm not really convinced I want to learn.'

'It's sheer laziness, that's all. I can't believe you've reached the grand old age of thirty-one without even taking a driving test. Suppose one day you're in some kind of emergency? Suppose I was taken ill and you had to get me to hospital . . .'

'All right, all right, I get the message. I'll organize it. But in the meantime, are you *sure* you don't want to come back to bed?'

'Just hit the brakes, sunshine. Duty calls!'

Mark sighed, dropped back against his pillow. 'Great,' he said. 'Now I've got a couple of hours to fill and nothing to fill it with.'

'It will give you time to write back to your number-one fan, won't it?' She moved on along the hallway, smiling to herself.

Mark sighed and regarded the uneaten breakfast on the tray. 'At least it's one person who appreciates me,' he muttered to himself.

Chapter Two

After writing back to Leonard Goldman, and enclosing the signed photograph, Mark let himself out of the house and walked down to the nearest tube station. He called at the post office on route and mailed his brief reply. Then he rode in to the city, sandwiched between ranks of faceless commuters. Once upon a time, he reflected, there had been quiet periods on the tube trains, but these days there seemed to be only two modes of travel: overcrowded and just plain frantic. The sliding doors disgorged him at Warren Street and he let the crowds push him along the echoey windswept corridors and up the packed escalators on to the crowded streets. The weather had not improved. The air was icy and filled with pockets of drizzle that spat at him as he strolled along Tottenham Court Road. Cars moved fitfully along the street, horns blaring as motorists vented their frustration on the vehicle in front, and he began to wonder if learning to drive was really such a great idea. The people he saw behind the wheel all looked grey, stressed and very bad-tempered. Now if he lived in the country, that would be different, driving might actually be a pleasant experience – but in London . . .

His thoughts were interrupted by the relentless yammer of pneumatic drills. Workmen were digging up the road opposite the tube station and the noise was a violent assault on the eardrums.

He cut down a side street and arrived at the shabby, three-storey building where Peter Maughan's literary agency had its home. He buzzed the intercom, identified himself, and received a curt invitation to come on up to the first floor. Pushing open the front door he threaded his way past cartons of paperbacks piled up in the hallway. On the linoleum-covered staircase he was surprised to encounter a framed enlargement of the original cover for *Black Wolf* – a new addition since his last visit. He paused to look at it for a moment. It was a stark graphic image, a close-up of an open mouth, framed by a dark blue background. The mouth was not quite human, not quite lupine, but somehow a mixture of both. It was an image that managed to be both startling and intriguing, and Mark reckoned it had probably played a significant part in the success of his book. What was that old adage about not judging a book by its cover? The simple truth was that everyone did.

He moved on up to the first floor, and halted at the open doorway of Meg's office. She sat at a computer screen, ranks of green digits reflecting in her wire-rimmed glasses. Then she glanced up, feigning surprise though she had just invited him up.

'Oh, hey, Mark, hi!' Meg seemed a blatant Sloane Ranger, and was perhaps the only person he knew who actually said 'OK yah' without meaning it to be ironic. She was only in her early twenties, but her air of rosy-cheeked innocence masked a very astute grasp of the book business. Mark knew that she did ninety per cent of Maughan's work, without ever receiving due credit for it. Indeed, it was she who had read *Black Wolf* first and heartily recommended it to her employer. For that much at least Mark would always be grateful to her.

'How's our best-selling author today?' she asked.

'He's OK. In fact, he received his first American fan letter this morning.'

'Wow, fantastic! Who from?'

'Some guy in America.'

'First of many, I'm sure.'

'That's what Sarah said. Is his nibs at home?'

'Yah. You can go right up. By the way, I think the new manuscript's just fine. Just a couple of details to sort out. Nothing serious.'

'Peter read it?'

'Not yet. You know how it is; we've been snowed under.'

'Hmm.' Mark turned and went up the next flight of steps to his agent's office. He opened the door and found Peter Maughan at his desk, virtually hidden behind mounds of correspondence, typescripts, boxes of paperback and hardback novels, and cardboard displays for past successes and glorious failures. He beamed myopically up at Mark from behind glasses that magnified his pale blue eyes to twice their normal size.

'Ah, how's our best-selling author today?'

Mark smiled. 'I think I've already had this conversation with Meg,' he said.

'Well, sit down, sit down.' Maughan got up and came around the desk to move a pile of paperbacks off the only vacant chair. He was somewhere in his middle years, thin and rather dishevelled. His skin had already acquired the mottled tones of the habitual drinker, a legacy of too many lunchtimes spent 'entertaining' authors. Mark knew with a dread certainty that after half an hour's chat the two of them would

14

almost certainly retire to the pub next-door for some serious drinking, an unwise move given Mark's excesses of the previous night, though he also knew that he would do nothing to discourage the idea. Besides, Peter only really got himself into gear after his second drink of the day.

Mark dropped into the chair and waited for Maughan to resume his seat. They smiled at each other across the cluttered desk.

'Well,' said Peter at last. 'It's all going rather well, isn't it? You must be very pleased.'

'I'm over the moon,' said Mark unconvincingly.

'And I'm glad to say that I love the new manuscript. A bit of fine tuning is all that's needed.'

'Meg told me you hadn't read it yet.'

'Not *all* of it. Of course, I've, er . . . I've *skimmed* it.'

'Skimmed it?'

'Yes . . . and Meg's read it from beginning to end. As you know, I trust her judgement implicitly. We may ask you for a few minor alterations, and then it should be all plain sailing. Meanwhile, you can be thinking about the next novel in the series . . .'

Mark grimaced.

'I wanted to talk to you about that.'

'Mmmm?' Peter made a spire out of his hands and rested his chin on the peak. His huge, watery eyes regarded Mark blankly. 'Is there a problem?'

'Well, yes. You see, I'm not sure . . . not one hundred per cent sure, anyway . . . that I want to write another one.'

Peter frowned. 'I see.'

'It's just that I've got lots of other ideas in mind. And to tell you the truth, I never envisaged being tied to the same set of characters over and over . . .'

'Hardly "over and over",' Maughan reminded him. '*Black Wolf* was an outstanding success. It reached a much wider readership than your earlier novels – so naturally, everyone wants more. Your publishers are confident that the second in the series will do even better, and then a third . . .'

'Yes, but everybody seems to assume that *I'll* be happy to go along with it. I mean, I'd like to think I'm capable of a bit more versatility than that.'

'Versatility is a curse, Mark. Remember what old Oscar said!'

'Yes, but then, Oscar Wilde never had to write *The Importance of Being Earnest 2*, did he?'

Peter grinned.

'Joking aside,' Mark continued, 'you know that Sarah and I have been planning this joint children's book. I've already had to shelve it once, when we had that panic about a second *Black Wolf.*'

Maughan made sympathetic noises.

'I can see that must be frustrating. But, you know, you've been incredibly lucky. There aren't many writers who score a direct hit with only their third novel . . .'

'My third *published* novel, you mean. Don't forget the four other manuscripts which we never sold!'

'Finding your feet, that's what they amounted to. But listen, I'm confident that we can get the publishers to improve dramatically on their last advance.'

'It's not just the money!'

'Of course not, of course not. You must admit though, it's rather nice to have it. Still, I dare say you could always go back to copywriting to make ends meet. You still doing any?'

Mark shrugged. 'The odd bit of freelance for my old firm. Tell you the truth, I've been turning down a lot of offers now that the financial pressure's off . . .'

'Best not burn your bridges entirely, if you're going to have to live on the earnings from a *children's book.*' He pronounced the last two words with evident distaste, as though describing some repulsive lower life form. Mark noted that Maughan always employed a similar tone when using the word *poetry.*

'I know what you're trying to do, Peter.'

'What, *moi?*' Maughan looked vaguely insulted. 'My dear chap, I'm merely trying to look after your interests. We're living in the age of the sequel. And now that some powerful new players have entered our arena . . .'

Mark studied him suspiciously. 'Come again?' he murmured.

'Well, I wasn't going to mention this until it was more definite . . . but I took a call this morning from Tom McBride of Ventona Productions.'

Mark held up a hand to interrupt. 'Ventona Productions? Who are they – the manufacturers of some powerful new decongestant?'

Peter chuckled. 'No. Ventona Productions of Hollywood is an independent film production company with considerable success in the horror genre.'

'Yeah?' Mark was doubtful. 'Name one.'

'I'll do better than that. I'll name *three.*' He referred to a sheet of paper in his intray. 'Ah, yes, *The Thirst,* then *Grind House* . . . and a charmingly titled item called *Bug Hutch.*'

Mark was somewhat taken aback by the information.

16

'Christ,' he said. 'I've actually heard of those. In fact, I've seen *Grind House* on video. It was pretty good.'

'Well, Ventona are now interested in acquiring film rights to the Black Wolf series. Even if it's just an option, we're talking considerable spondulicks. But McBride pointed out that they see this as a project with *legs*. In other words, they're thinking in terms of sequels. So I mentioned that there was a third book in the pipeline. Think about it, Mark. Movies. That's a whole new ball game. You'd have money coming out of your ears. And then you'd be able to pursue any project you like.'

'Would I get the chance to write the screenplays?'

Maughan considered for a moment. 'That's not totally out of the question . . . and I'd do my damnedest to get you the opportunity. But let's face it, if they talk the required number of digits, you'll probably be happy to hand it to the studio janitor for adaptation.'

Mark scowled. 'I already told you, it's—'

'"Not just the money." I know, I know.' Maughan sighed, and leaned back in his leather chair. 'Mind you, it beats the shit out of whatever's second best.' He lifted an arm and glanced at his wristwatch. 'I don't know about you, but all this talking's given me a thirst. Perhaps we should nip over to The Crown and discuss this further over a few snifters.'

Mark looked doubtful. 'I know exactly what will happen. You'll get me shit-faced, and then I'll agree to write that sodding third book for you.'

Peter spread his hands in an expansive gesture.

'Mark, really! Remember, I'm just Mr Ten Per Cent. Whatever's good for me is ninety per cent better for you.' He got up from his seat and moved towards the door.

They went down the stairs to the next landing and paused at the door of Meg's office.

'Meg, love, we're just popping out for lunch. Hold the fort, will you?'

Meg smiled knowingly. 'I'll make sure there's plenty of black coffee on the boil.'

'Can't imagine *what* she meant by that,' muttered Maughan, heading down the next flight of stairs. He paused under the framed *Black Wolf* poster. 'How's about this, then? That's the first thing anybody sees when they enter these hallowed portals.'

Mark studied the poster again, the distended sub-human jaws bristling with teeth. He was seized by an abrupt sense of foreboding, a chill that tickled along the length of his spine. Something bad was coming. His luck had been too exceptional lately. Something had to go wrong, spoil things for him . . .

He shrugged off the sensation and almost laughed out loud at his uncharacteristic fears. He had never believed in premonitions.

Maughan opened the front door and they stepped out on to the street. They turned right and strolled along to the pub.

Before heading home that night, Mark had predictably agreed to write the third instalment of *Black Wolf*, and had drunk six pints of Belgian lager; though these events did not, of course, happen strictly in that order.

Chapter Three

Leonard started downstairs in his silk dressing-gown when he heard the mailman's heavy tread on the front porch. He hadn't fallen off to sleep until four a.m., and had woken again at seven on the dot. These days he didn't seem to need much sleep, and when he did close his eyes, he was bothered by the bad dreams.

A bundle of letters lay on the doormat, and he moved quickly and quietly down the last few steps, hoping not to wake Mother, who was also a light sleeper. He bent to pick up the mail and as he straightened, he caught sight of himself in the hall mirror. He examined his reflection, trying to see himself as others saw him, looking perhaps for a reason why most people chose to shun him. His wasn't a handsome face by any stretch of the imagination, but neither was it particularly ugly. It was squarish and uninteresting: a block of impassive tanned flesh with little to distinguish it other than the small, tawny-brown eyes which peered suspiciously out at a world with which he had little in common. Leonard didn't much care for the face, and had done his best to obscure it beneath layers of wiry black beard and thick centre-parted hair that hung to his collar. He smiled at his reflection, and revealed his one saving grace: two rows of even, white teeth – a movie star's grin. Leonard's father had been a dentist, so, throughout his childhood and teens, treatment had been regular and free, had only stopped with his father's unfortunate death when Leonard was fourteen. A new piece of equipment his father had been testing out had been incorrectly wired at the plug. The resulting shock had stopped his heart, killing him as effectively as if he had been hit by a runaway truck. Nobody could understand how Mr Goldman, a precise and meticulous sort, could have made such a careless mistake.

Leonard flicked through the pile of mail and came to the one he'd been anticipating for over a week. He studied the British stamp and postmark and suddenly, he wished he had dressed before coming downstairs. He felt as though the author of the letter could somehow see him standing there half clothed in the gloomy hallway of that

Victorian brownstone in Dennings, Pennsylvania. Instinctively, he pulled his Father's old dressing-gown tighter around him. Dad had been a smaller, more slender man and on Leonard the garment was barely decent. But Brenda, the home help wasn't due till eight-thirty. Mother seemed to be asleep still, so there was nobody else to see him. He was glad of that.

He moved slowly back up the big, ornate staircase, placing his bare feet carefully, because he had learned over the years where the worst creaks were situated. If he woke Mother up, she would start to pester him. It wasn't that he minded, not really. He loved his Mother and wanted only to please her. But now this special letter had come and he needed a little time to enjoy it, undisturbed. He gained the landing and paused for a moment at Mother's open door. He listened carefully, and after a few moments he could hear her regular breathing, a slight snore mingled with each intake of breath. Smiling, he slipped along to his own room, right beside Mother's. He went in and closed the door gently behind him, feeling safe and secure now in his sanctuary of horrors.

Sitting down at Bela Lugosi's desk, he extracted the envelope from his pocket. First he examined the outside carefully, looking for clues. Mark Tyler's handwriting – if indeed it was his and not that of some secretary or press agent – was neat and precise, and sloped gently to the right, which suggested a hint of ambition. Leonard lifted the envelope to his nose and sniffed it gently. No traces of perfume or aftershave, but he did detect the faintest odour of tobacco. That told him that his hero had probably been smoking a cigarette when he wrote this letter. Leonard's sense of smell seemed to have become highly sensitive lately, a development he perceived as inevitable. Next he inspected the postmark and noted, with a twinge of satisfaction, that his own letter must have been answered almost immediately. In the past, with other heros, he'd been obliged to wait months for a reply.

Now Leonard picked up a decorative silver knife, its handle worked into a representation of a demon's head. He slit the envelope open carefully, wanting to preserve it precisely in its original form to store the precious contents. At last he withdrew the single sheet of notepaper, and felt a jolt of disappointment when he saw how brief the reply was. But then he located the enclosed photograph, and found himself looking at a handsome young man, probably in his late twenties or early thirties, with exquisitely groomed dark hair, soulful eyes – what a pity this was only black and white, he'd love to know what colour those eyes were – a nicely proportioned face, the nose proud, the mouth authoritative. The photograph had been signed, '*To Leonard, my first*

20

and foremost American fan. Best wishes, Mark Tyler.'

Leonard felt a glow of pleasure spread through him. *'First and foremost!'* He'd never hoped for such an honour.

Now he turned his attention to the letter itself, written in that same neat hand.

Dear Leonard,

(Leonard, mark you! Not Mr Goldman or L. Goldman, but *Leonard!*)

Thanks very much for your warm and appreciative remarks concerning *Black Wolf*. I have to admit that yours is my very first American fan letter and I feel honoured that you have lavished my novel with such generous praise.

In answer to your question, yes, there is another novel, *Black Wolf 2: Night Feast*, already written, which will be released in Britain in September. (I apologise for not knowing the American release date, but I'm sure my publishers there can advise you.)

There is currently some talk of a *Black Wolf 3*, but at this early stage, I have not decided whether I want to undertake it. I wouldn't want my lycanthropic hero to outstay his welcome!

Well, I guess that about answers your question. Thanks once again for your kind remarks about my book. I really do appreciate it. If you're ever in London, look me up, and I'll buy you a drink. I've enclosed the photo you asked for, and I apologise in advance for any nightmares it might cause!

All for now,
Best wishes,
Mark Tyler

Leonard read the letter through several times, feeling his sense of elation mounting by the moment. This was more than he could have hoped for, such an agreeable and personal letter, far better than the stereotyped, standard printout that he usually received. And it said that Leonard's was the *first* American fan letter that his new hero had received! Well, he really shouldn't be surprised about that. After all, he'd bought a copy on the day of its first release in the States; he'd even put in an advance order for it. It had been exciting following Mark Tyler's developing career from the beginning, seeing his writing mature, noting the increasing inventiveness of his ideas, the added depth of his characterisations. A soul-mate in the making. And then, like a bolt from the blue, there had been *Black Wolf* and Leonard knew that Mark had finally earned his place in the 'Rogues' Gallery'.

Black Wolf had become a very special book for Leonard. The moment he'd seen that cover he'd known it would be special. For Mark Tyler had somehow seen into his mind; read his thoughts, registered the unstoppable power of his emotions – because Leonard and Black Wolf were *the same*. How he had trembled and sweated when he read that amazing book for the first time! He had since read it a dozen times over. He, too, *knew* the fears and terrors that the Red Indian lycanthrope had suffered; for just like Black Wolf, Leonard was afraid to give rein to the sexual side of his nature, knowing that he also could so easily lose control – turn into a raging, blood-lusting animal. Too many times now he had been close to abandoning himself outright to the beast that sheltered within him. It was clear that Mark Tyler understood his situation perfectly. He *must* do, for, after all, Black Wolf was Tyler's creation. His *child*. If anybody in the world really understood Leonard, Mark Tyler was that man. The two of them were truly kindred spirits now . . .

Leonard slipped suddenly into a favourite infantile fantasy. He pictured himself in the front row of a prestigious Hollywood theatre. Veronica from Checkout 4 was sitting beside him, her arm linked with his. Mark Tyler was up on stage, dressed in a tuxedo, giving an address at the microphone, as he clutched a glittering golden trophy.

His voice echoed around the auditorium. 'I, er, just want to say that there's somebody out there in the audience tonight – someone without whom this book would not have been possible.'

Bursts of applause, heads turning to stare enviously. Veronica squeezing his hand excitedly, gazing lovingly up at him.

'He'll hate me for mentioning this, because he's a very modest guy; but it was his phenomenal vision and insight that guided and instructed me in fulfilling this project. Ladies and Gentlemen, I give you my very good friend . . . my *brother* . . . Leonard Goldman!'

And Leonard was standing now, bowing to the crowd, his eyes filling with tears. Flashbulbs crackled as the press scrambled for their shots. The applause rang in his ears. Now he was stumbling towards the stage, where Mark Tyler waited, open-armed to embrace him . . .

Unconsciously, he had slipped a hand beneath the folds of the silk robe, his fingertips brushing against the shaft of his erect penis. He could feel *Black Wolf* rising within him like a cloud of warm energy, filling him with unnatural power, making him feel potent, confident, articulate, *alive*. He tilted back his head to stare at the ceiling and felt the howl begin to build from somewhere deep inside him. He squeezed his eyes shut . . . opened his mouth to shape the sound . . .

The front door opened and closed. He snapped upright in his seat, his face reddening with shame. He could hear Brenda's heavy footfalls on the stairs, climbing slowly towards his room. He waited in silence. Knuckles rapped the ancient wood of the door.

'Leonard? You 'wake?'

He said nothing. He sat there, glaring at the door, waiting for her to go.

She knocked again a couple of times. Then the sound of her footsteps padding slowly towards Mother's room. Leonard breathed a sigh of relief.

She had killed his sense of excitement as effectively as if she had doused him with a bucket of cold water. His penis was flaccid now and the fantasy had slipped beyond his reach. He needed something to occupy himself. He opened a drawer of the desk and took out a stack of high-quality writing paper. He would waste no time in developing this new friendship. Now he had assured himself that Mark Tyler really was his soul-mate, he would show the man the full extent of his talents. Theirs would be an intellectual friendship, an open exchange of ideas, a *partnership* of equals – not, as he had expected, a relationship of master and servant. Leonard had plenty of ideas for stories, he'd tried to write them himself many times, but somehow they never turned out quite as he intended. Mark could write beautifully though, and he would recognise the vital essence of those ideas, would utilise them. Working together they could take *Black Wolf* in exciting new directions . . .

'So you *are* awake! I thought I heard somethin'!'

Leonard turned to find Brenda peering in the doorway, her lank, greasy hair hanging in her eyes. She was a woman in her mid-forties but looked much older. She was stout and shapeless, given to wearing thrift-store clothing mottled with foodstains. When she grinned, it was to reveal teeth stained with nicotine. She was holding Mother's bedpan, and the room was already rapidly filling up with the stink of it.

'I just got up to take a pill,' muttered Leonard. 'I'm going straight back to bed.'

'Oh, yeah?' She fluttered her eyelids at him, a ghastly parody of a *femme fatale*. 'Want some company?'

He didn't even bother to mask the repugnance that came to his face.

'No, thank you,' he said coldly.

She shrugged. 'Suit yourself, sugar. I'll keep it hot for you.' She closed the door behind her and he heard her cackling laughter as she moved off in the direction of the bathroom. The smell of the bedpan lingered in the room, and Leonard felt nauseous. He got up and opened a window. The filthy old scut! He'd have to be desperate to envisage laying so much as a finger on her stinking body.

Returning to his desk, he made a mental effort to dismiss the interruption and directed his attention back to the letter. He picked up his favourite fountain pen, uncapped it with a flourish, and began to write, making himself take his own good time – because if he didn't, he knew his handwriting would quickly become illegible. He wrote for the best part of an hour, and when he felt he had said enough for one letter, he found he had four pages. He read them through, correcting the odd word here and there with typing fluid, striking out any spelling mistakes and going painstakingly over them, until he was sure it was all word-perfect. Then he decided that, to sound really smart, the letter needed a postscript. An idea came to him, so he wrote:

Thought you would like to know what your number-one fan looks like. I enclose a recent signed photograph of *myself*. Now we're even!

Instantly, he regretted the decision. He imagined handsome Mark Tyler looking at Leonard Goldman's homely, bearded face and recoiling in disgust – worse still, *laughing* at him! This was simply not the face he wanted to show to his hero. He required one that went with the superior impressions conveyed by his writing. He considered painting the PS out, but realized that Tyler would then be curious about what had been there before. Perhaps he should write out the last page all over again? Then he had a better idea. He went to one of his shelves and rooted out an old cigar box containing a series of pictures taken at high-school. He found a portrait of George Stevens, a former teacher of Leonard's, and a conventionally handsome guy. The picture had been taken at one of the school functions. George wore a plain red T-shirt, and he had one arm flung around Laura Bishop, one of Leonard's old classmates. George was grinning knowingly at the camera, and was in the act of raising a can of Shlitz in a mock toast. Leonard had often wondered if old Georgie boy had been poking Laura all those years ago; the covetous, sidelong glance that Laura was giving George suggested it was a distinct possibility. More importantly, though, in the photo, George had then been around the same age that Leonard was now, somewhere in his early-thirties; and he looked like everybody's favourite pal, the kind of guy who always had a girl on his arm and a beer in his hand. Judging from the letter he'd just written, this was probably the kind of person that Tyler would expect to see.

Leonard went back to the desk, raised his pen and wrote across the base of the photo, *To Mark, with all best wishes. Leonard.* Then another thought occurred to him, and he added a P.P.S. He smiled, gave a nod of satisfaction. He felt the letter was now complete. He folded it neatly and slid it into an envelope, together with the photograph. Brenda could post it for him on her way home. And, look, even to Mark's personal address, as displayed right at the top of his letter. A rare show of trust, thought Leonard. Most writers were cagey about releasing that kind of information, preferring to correspond care of their agent or publisher. But here was a man who went beyond such petty considerations. A soul-mate indeed!

Oh and what else was that he'd said in his letter? *If you're ever in London, look me up.* Leonard smiled. Maybe one day he'd take Mark Tyler up on that offer. Yes, maybe he would, at that.

Chapter Four

Late that afternoon, Leonard got the dun-coloured Camaro out of the garage and drove slowly to work. He had dressed himself in the regulation white shirt, black bow-tie and black slacks that were the required wear for all male employees of Olsen's.

Olsen's was a twenty-four-hour shopping mart on the outskirts of Dennings, and Leonard had now been working there for around eight months. Mother had been insistent that he take a job, something to get him out of the house – to give him an interest.

He had spent too many years in isolation with his books and his videos, she told him. He needed to get out more, meet people, start making some friends; why, did he realize that apart from Brenda and the occasional tradesman, nobody else ever came to the house? It wasn't good for a body to spend so much time alone. It wasn't *natural*! He had argued that he didn't like the idea of leaving her alone for so long, especially at night, but they'd come up with a workable solution. Leonard had bought a radio alarm system. Mother would keep a pager right beside her bed, which would send a signal to a small bleeper that Leonard wore on his belt. Though she'd never yet had the occasion to use it, this gave Leonard peace of mind, especially now that he always seemed to be working the graveyard shift.

When he had first started at Olsen's, he had been expected to take the late shift only on rotation, like everyone else, every fourth week. But, as time passed, he found people asking him if he'd mind exchanging with them, and he never refused such a request because really he preferred working at night. It was quieter then, and there was less pressure. So, pretty soon, he found the 6 p.m.-till-2 a.m. shift had become his regular fixture. That had suited him fine until three months ago, when old Mr Baxter had retired and Olsen's had acquired a new night manager.

Leonard pulled into a vacant slot in the car park immediately outside the large, squat brick-and-glass building. A few shoppers drifted in and out of the entrance doors, pushing their battered trolleys in front of

27

them, some of the older shoppers clearly using them to support their infirm bodies rather than carry purchases. Beyond the mart, the rooftops of Dennings' houses appeared a uniform grey, rising in steep ranks to the distant outline of the steel-processing mill, once the very lifeblood of the town but now rapidly winding down its production. Beyond that, hills dotted with sorry-looking cottonwoods threatened to merge with an overcast sky. The air was hazy, and shot through with an acrid, metallic smell that was always present in this dingy little town. The sunlight barely made it through the intervening screen of pollution, so it seemed somehow much later in the day than it really was.

Leonard stepped out of the vehicle, reached in for the Tupperware container that housed his lunch, and locked the car securely after him. There'd been a recent surge in car thefts in the area, and many blamed redundancies at the steel mill for the problem. Leonard figured it was more probably a result of boredom. There wasn't much for young people to do around here. Most of them soon took the hint and headed for Pittsburgh. There'd even been a time when Leonard had nurtured the same aspiration, but when his Mother had fallen sick, he had never found the heart to leave her alone in that big empty house. She was his focus.

He strolled across the parking lot, ignoring the shoppers who occasionally moved around him, as insubstantial as grey phantoms. The sliding doors parted in front of him with a hiss of warm, stale air. The fluorescent ceiling lights gave the interior of the mart a clinical, soulless ambience. Muzak pulsed from hidden speakers, like warm oil.

He moved along the rows of checkouts, only some of which were currently in use. Eventually he raised his eyes from the tiled floor and gazed hopefully towards Checkout 4. Sure enough, Veronica was there. He halted beside her till and stood absolutely still, waiting for her to notice him.

Veronica was about the most beautiful girl he had ever seen. She was slim, rather frail-looking, with straight blonde hair that would have hung to her shoulders if regulations did not insist that she wear it tied back in a pony-tail. Leonard had never yet seen her with her hair loose, but he figured she would look like the painting of Shakespeare's Ophelia he had once seen in an art magazine. She had beautiful hazel eyes and the prettiest smile, her teeth white and even. Whenever she turned her gaze in his direction, Leonard felt hot and dizzy and tongue-tied. And yet, despite his confusion, he lived for those special nights every few weeks when it was her turn to work this shift. He had her rota marked down in his calendar at home – the one that hung beside the *Dawn Of The Dead* poster. Leonard stood there, savouring the smell of her. She used an apple-scented soap and a spray cologne that had the unmistakable aroma of dewberries. To him, she smelled good enough to eat.

Veronica eventually became aware of his presence, at her side. She had no customers at her till, and was surreptitiously glancing through a copy of *National Enquirer*. She glanced up in alarm, then relaxed when she saw it was only Leonard. She smiled dazzlingly.

'Hi, Leonard. How's it going?'

He felt his cheeks burning, but struggled to make a reply, terrified of the occasional stutter that lurked somewhere at the back of his head, waiting to trip him up, make him look stupid. The stutter that had once bedeviled his adolescence.

'I'm . . . I'm fine, thank you. And yourself?'

'Oh, I'm OK, I guess. Little tired though, and this is my first night on lates. I was out partying last night. I'll be bushed by tomorrow. What's your secret, Len?'

He was startled by the question. 'My . . . my secret?'

'Yeah, y'know, always looking so wide awake.'

'Oh, you get used to it.'

'But you do this shift full-time, don't you? Don't you miss out on a lot of fun? You know, going out with friends and stuff? Concerts, parties . . .'

Leonard shrugged. He was about to say that he didn't have any friends, in fact didn't *need* any, but realized that sounded pathetic, even though it was true. He cast around for something else to say and a sudden inspiration struck him.

'Well, I like to keep the days free to work on my writing.'

Her eyes widened slightly.

'You're a writer?' she asked him.

He nodded.

'Cool. What kind of stuff do you write?'

'H . . . H . . . H . . .' The word somehow stuck in his throat, and it took an effort to spit it out. 'Horror stories!'

'Hey, that's really neat. Maybe you'll get famous one day and I'll be able to say, "I used to know that guy when we worked together at Olsen's!"'

Leonard smiled, encouraged. He was warming to his theme. He was even beginning to picture it, another little movie unfolding in his mind's eye: him driving up to Olsen's in a big, expensive foreign car, but no longer working there – he'd just dropped by to pick up a few things. Naturally he would stop at Veronica's checkout, and she'd ask him how he was getting on. He'd tell her fine, he'd been busy just at the moment, he'd been on the set at Universal helping Clive Barker with a few problems on the script of his latest movie. And then he'd ask her, just kind of casual, if maybe she'd like to stop by his place later on and have dinner with him . . .

'So, what are you working on at the moment?'

'Huh?' He stared at her a moment, his fantasy rudely disrupted by the necessity of creating a convincing lie. 'Er, actually, I'm working with a successful writer at the moment. Guy called Mark Tyler. Don't know if you've heard of him. He's English . . .'

Veronica shook her head.

'The Black Wolf stories?'

She was looking up at him blankly, but he pushed on anyway. 'I'm kind of helping him with his books. We work through our ideas together, and sometimes, when he's stuck, he phones me and the two of us—'

'Hey, Goldman! You on vacation today?'

Leonard broke off as the night manager, Rick Devereaux came swaggering along the line of checkouts. Rick was tall and wiry, and the proud possessor of more than his fair share of arrogance. He sported an aggressive-looking crewcut and a discreet smattering of acne pits on his sallow cheeks. He habitually kept a sharpened pencil behind one ear, and a large bunch of keys hung ostentatiously from his metal-studded leather belt. Rick was barely out of his teens and there were many people at Olsen's who thought him insufficiently mature to handle a position of authority; but since he was the managing director's nephew, nobody had been too surprised by his appointment three months back. One thing was certain. He didn't like Leonard Goldman one little bit, and seemed to take every opportunity to bait him. Perhaps something about the big man's impenetrability rankled him. Or maybe he just didn't like his face.

Rick strolled over to Veronica's checkout and lolled against the counter, his arms crossed as he stared intently at Leonard.

'You bothering Miss Nelson?' he asked.

'We were just chatting,' murmured Leonard, staring back.

Rick grinned, nodded. 'Just chatting, huh? And do we pay you to stand around, passing the time of day with people? Was that mentioned in the contract?'

'Oh, come on, Rick,' interrupted Veronica. 'It's not exactly busy, is it? And Leonard doesn't officially start work for another ten minutes . . .'

'Leonard?' Rick feigned a puzzled expression. 'Leonard? I don't know any . . .' Then exaggerated enlightenment spread across his thin face. 'Oh, you mean *Creepy* here!'

'Don't call him that,' protested Veronica; but she could not help grinning as she said it, her hazel eyes glinting with devilment as they flicked between the two men, enjoying the spectacle. Suddenly Leonard felt a terrible sense of betrayal. He had thought she was different to the others, that he was beginning to communicate with her. He had thought she *understood* him. He struggled to find a suitable reply.

'Mr Devereaux, I don't think that's very respectful!'

'Oh, no?' Rick was still grinning at him, contempt flickering spitefully in his snakelike eyes. 'What would you like me to call you, then? What's a good name for a guy who's thirty-five years old and still lives with his mom? Guy who's never had a girlfriend and spends all his money on horror comics and kids' toys? You don't think that's kind of creepy? Shit, I think it's *weird*.'

'Rick, you *shouldn't*!' Veronica was desperately trying not to laugh out loud, and her outraged expression was a poor disguise.

'I know,' purred Rick, turning now and leaning across the counter towards her. 'But that's not what you said last night, remember?' He ostentatiously slipped an arm around her waist.

Veronica's face suddenly became a mask of indignation.

'Rick, shut up!' she snapped; and this time there was no humour in her tone. It was enough to silence him, but the damage had been done. Leonard had seen the conspiratorial glance that passed between them. He stood there impassively, staring at Veronica in concealed anger and dismay. He had thought she was pure, special, an enlightened being above all that. But now he knew she was like all the rest, hungry for the taste of a corrupt world, willing to open her legs for any man. And for *him*, Rick Devereaux, his tormentor, the man Leonard despised most in the world.

'What are you staring at, Creepy?' demanded Rick, but now he didn't sound quite so sure of himself.

Leonard glared at him for another moment, sensing the beast in himself now clawing its way to the surface. He must make a titanic effort to leash Black Wolf and drag him back down again. This was neither the time nor the place.

'You got some kind of problem?'

Leonard shook his head, and turned his attention back to the tiled floor as if in submission. He couldn't afford any longer to look into Devereaux's pale eyes. To do so was to invite the beast to rise again.

'All right, then. Suppose you move your ass to the storeroom?

There's some crates of melons there need unpacking. And be careful, they bruise real easy.'

'Yes, Mr Devereaux.' Leonard walked silently along the line of checkouts, turned along a vacant aisle and headed into the main area.

'Dumb motherfucker,' he heard Rick mutter. Leonard flinched inwardly with the outrage of this, but kept his outward composure, his face impassive. Inside was a cauldron coming rapidly to the boil. He quickened his step towards the storeroom, feeling once again the hot surge of anger beginning to rise within him.

He made it to the storeroom with seconds to spare, passing through into the cool semi-darkness, and allowing the swing doors to close behind him. He glanced quickly around to assure himself that he was alone. A wooden crate of melons stood on the floor, already opened, the round yellow spheres neatly packed in straw. He bent over and picked up the largest of them: roughly the size of a man's head. He lifted it to chest height and stared down at it, visualizing a startled face gazing helplessly up at him. Now he let Black Wolf slip the leash, felt him claw upwards again, lending him power, lending him rage.

'You scum!' he whispered. 'You insulted me! And you touched her with your filthy hands . . .'

Black Wolf reached into his arms, and together they began to exert a steady pressure with their hands, crushing Devereaux's head between them. He saw Devereaux's expression turning from fear to panic to pain.

'Who's the creep now?' he growled triumphantly. 'Who's the fucking creep now?'

The melon exploded suddenly, splattering him with sticky pulp. His big hands now contained little more than fragments of limp yellow skin. Breathing heavily, he waited for calm to return to him, for the rhythmic throbbing in his temples to recede. As he stood there, his mind worked over an explanation for his spattered appearance. He'd tell them he just dropped a melon on to the concrete floor, they'd laugh at his ineptitude. But, then, what else could you expect from a creep?

He smiled. One day they'd talk of him with respect in their voices. One day when they knew who he really was.

Calm again, he turned back to the crate and started unpacking the melons, taking care not to bruise them.

Cora Starkey came abruptly awake in the small hours of the morning, with the distinct impression that something was wrong. She lay in her single bed in the small ground-floor apartment, trying to gather her scattered thoughts. A glance at the illuminated face of the bedside clock told her it was three-fourteen a.m.

A middle-aged spinster who worked part-time behind the counter of Dennings' main post office, Cora was generally a sound sleeper but just lately her tabby cat, Arabella, had been causing trouble. She was nearing that sensitive period when female cats always gave trouble, and had developed a liking for wandering off till all hours of the morning. It had been in Cora's mind for some time now to take Arabella up to old Doctor Hotchkis, the town vet, and get her fixed. But month after month, when it came to the crunch, Cora didn't have the heart to do that. The truth was, she loved rearing kittens; she'd already taken care of three litters, nursing them, feeding them, and finally finding them suitable homes. At forty-eight years old, a plain-looking and even plainer-speaking woman, she'd long since given up any hopes for romance in her life. The kittens filled an empty space, gave her something to lavish attention on, so who was going to convince her that she should put an end to it? Of course, there would always be this couple of weeks of inconvenience when Arabella's urge to mate kept her out on the tiles with a motley collection of male admirers; but she always returned in the early hours, mewling, shamefaced and slightly dishevelled, wanting the dinner she had been too agitated to contemplate earlier.

Sure enough, Cora could hear the cat now, calling urgently from the vicinity of the apartment's back entrance, a prolonged mewling that sounded almost like the crying of a human baby. Cora tutted to herself in a pretence of irritation, though deep down she was relieved that her old girl had made it back safely. Cora always slept more soundly once she knew Arabella was home.

Cora switched on the reading lamp, got out of bed, and put on her bathrobe and slippers. It was chilly and she wrapped her arms around her lean body as though trying to cling on to its warmth. She was almost at the bedroom door when a sudden wailing shriek stopped her in her tracks. The noise was so ominous that she lifted a hand to her mouth to stifle a gasp. That was Arabella, she was sure, but sounding so unlike herself that she must surely be in pain, or terrified, or both. If one of those filthy toms had injured her darling in some way . . .!

Cora hurried out of the bedroom, down the short hallway and into the kitchen. She flicked on the light and stepped fearfully over to the window. From there she stared out into the back garden. There wasn't much moonlight tonight, and at first she couldn't make out anything at all. She moved even closer to the glass, peering myopically out at the night, telling herself that she should have collected her glasses from the bedside table. Cora was just considering going back to fetch them when she realized, with a jolt of absolute terror, that something had just approached from out of the darkness. Now a face appeared on the other side of the glass, and was staring in at her. She gave a small, involuntary shriek of terror, and shrank back from the window.

She saw it for only an instant, but it gave an impression of absolute malignance. Later, she would remember only a pair of blazing, feral eyes and twin rows of jagged, dog-like teeth. They seemed to be grinning at her, as though enjoying her fear.

When she dared approach the window again, the devilish face was gone, as though it had simply dissolved into the texture of the surrounding darkness. Cora remembered to breathe again. She had seen the horror so briefly that she could not be sure whether it was real or the product of an overworked imagination.

Now the sound of mewling started again, reminding her of her reason for climbing out of bed in the first place. Fearfully, she unlatched the back door, to peer through the screen beyond. On the short stretch of path leading from the gate, she could see a small, dark shape moving slowly towards her. Could that be Arabella?

Cora hesitated – remembering that thing she had seen – or thought she had seen. She reached out tentatively to push the outer screen open a fraction. It *was* Arabella out there on the path, mewling pitifully, but making only slow, awkward progress. Something was wrong with her, she was injured in some way . . . Her former terror instantly dissolved in the realization that her beloved was hurt. Cora opened wide the screen and stepped out on to the path.

Over to her left, something moved through the bushes at the end of the garden, something big and powerful, but thankfully moving away from her. A dark shape swept over the pale stretch of the picket fence, and was gone. A big dog, Cora decided; a dog or maybe a coyote, though that face she had glimpsed hadn't put her in mind of either.

Another feeble cry from the cat concentrated Cora's attention, and she hurried further along the path towards her stricken pet. She stopped and stared in disbelief. Arabella was very nearly dead, but still attempting to drag herself towards the house. She left a thick shiny trail behind her, showing black in the moonlight. The poor creature's back legs were splayed limply on the concrete. Suddenly she gave a last despairing cry, and flopped over on to her side.

Something vicious had bitten her almost in half. The cat's belly was a gaping wound, from which viscera trailed like strands of bloody spaghetti.

Cora opened her mouth to scream, but felt her supper rising into her throat instead. With a groan, she twisted sideways, and was violently sick on the lawn. Then, her eyes streaming with tears, she ran back into the house to phone the police.

Chapter Five

Dear Mark

What a wonderful surprise this morning when I picked up my mail and found, not only the signed photograph I requested, but also a letter from the hand of the author himself! Thank you, thank you. It is something I shall treasure forever.

I was astonished to learn that mine was the first American fan letter you have received. I must say I find this very hard to believe. Rest assured, many more will soon follow my example. But I shall always remember that I was the first, and shall do my best not to abuse the honour.

I thought I should tell you a little bit about myself. You may actually wish to know more about the impulsive stranger who has chosen to write to you. First of all, let me explain about the name. You've probably already assumed that I'm Jewish (everybody does, for obvious reasons!). Actually, nothing could be further from the truth. I originate from Polish, Roman Catholic stock. The family legend relates that my great-great-grandfather, an illiterate farmer who rejoiced in the name of Edek Jeziorski, arrived at Ellis Island with his wife Katya sometime back in the 1800s and, not surprisingly, couldn't get anybody to understand what he was saying, or even how to pronounce and spell his name! It seemed that Edek had bought all the family heirlooms across with him in the form of gold ornaments and several large ingots, which he wore around his neck on a loop of rawhide. The harassed immigration officials thus issued papers in the name of Gold-Man, presumably to differentiate him from all the other unpronounceable Poles who were disembarking at the same time.

Anyhow, the name stuck. At one time there was a move to change back to Jeziorski, but my father found it advantageous to keep the name of Goldman when he set up his dental practice back in the 1950s, since most of the competition had names like Cohen and Goldberg. So this, I hope, explains why I am not quite what I seem.

Please don't get me wrong, I am in no way anti-Semitic. I'm simply tired of people making wrong assumptions about me. Actually, I don't exactly embrace the Roman Catholic faith either. If pushed I would describe myself as a devout agnostic!

Anyway, back to more important matters . . . I am so pleased to hear that you have already written another Black Wolf novel, which I feel sure will take the characters in interesting new directions. I must confess that when I read the advance review in *Kirkus*, I had grave doubts (forgive the unintentional pun) about the central premise. And yet, somehow, you have managed to create something challenging and entirely original. I think making Black Wolf a *shaman* was a masterstroke. It enabled you to draw on elements of native American folklore which you have cleverly adapted to the needs of your story.

You say you are undecided about a third tale; but it seems to me that the possibilities are endless! Black Wolf could feature in a whole series of these stories, set against the changing face of the American west, right up to contemporary times. (He's immortal, don't forget!) And imagine him having to eventually adapt to life on a reservation! Wow, wouldn't that be something?

I appreciate that what I have in mind here is a massive multi-volumed saga, and that it may be difficult for you to come up with all those stories; but if I might make a suggestion (and forgive my impetuous nature) I may be able to help you there. I'm something of a writer myself, though I would be the first to admit I lack your unsurpassed skill in threading together a narrative. What I *do* excel at, however, are ideas. If you were interested in seeing some notes I've been working on, I would be more than happy to forward them to you. I would not be looking for any payment for these ideas; incorporation of them into one of your magnificent books would be reward enough – though you might wish to give me a mention in the book's dedication. That of course, would be up to you.

Forgive me for galloping on in this unseemly fashion. I'm still quite intoxicated at the thought of such a gifted author sparing me valuable time. I know you must have a busy schedule and, at the risk of boring you into a coma, I should like to share with you my impressions of Black Wolf the character. It seems to me that he's timeless; as old, if you will, as time itself. He's the dark side that bubbles and seethes behind the facade of contemporary man. He's essentially pagan, yet encompasses all known religions, he's a god, he's a devil, a sinner and a saint, a mage, a poet and yet, somehow, he embodies the common man, the salt of the earth. More importantly, perhaps, he's *me*. I feel a sense of recognition when I read about his exploits. I see him as my blood brother, my personal guru, my mentor. The sensations we readers share with him; the thrill of the hunt, the all-powerful lust for blood . . . who among us can truthfully claim that we have not, at one time or another, experienced the same sensations? For do our fantasies not show us our true nature? And do we not constantly strive to make flesh of our fantasies?

Forgive me. I cannot help but be excited when I write about Black Wolf, because somehow you have reached across distance, across cultures, across a black screaming void and *touched* me. When I read your words, I feel you know everything about me, that you can see into my soul. I have read somewhere that the act of writing opens up the mind to some kind of collective unconscious, a kind of shared reality. Could it be, Mark, that in creating Black Wolf, you have made just such a psychic exchange with me? Was I unconsciously guiding your hand when you wrote the story? Are we in reality the joint authors of the book?

I am aware that I may have already overstepped the bounds of our newly forged friendship, but I do feel from close perusal of your work that I know you better than you might imagine. They say that any story contains elements of the author's character and life. Black Wolf's mate, Star Child, may, I suspect, be based on a special lady in your life. His friend and ally, Leaping Horse, may have characteristics that correspond to a particular 'blood brother' of your own; and perhaps Thunder Heart, the wise old medicine man who advises Black Wolf, corresponds to a similar figure in your own world. But who, I wonder, has inspired the demonic bounty hunter, Thaddeus Moon, the man pledged to destroy Black Wolf and all his family? Could it be that somewhere in your background, a man not a million miles unlike Moon might be unearthed by those who know what to look for? I have made a science of reading horror literature, and I pride myself on knowing how to search out the seeds of reality that, when nurtured by an accomplished hand, will blossom into inspired fiction.

I could go on in this (jugular) vein for pages and pages, but I am loathe to intrude too long on your precious time. Suffice it to say that I honour the rare privilege you have extended to me, and will strive not to abuse the responsibility. Meanwhile, if there is anything I can do to assist you – if you need a mentor, an advisor or even just a spy here in America – I would consider it an honour to undertake anything that will aid you in further realizing your great work.

Till I hear from you next, I remain your humble servant and fervent admirer.

Yours (and Black Wolf's)
Leonard J. Goldman

P.S. Thought you would like to know what your number-one fan looks like, so I enclose a recent, signed photograph of myself. Now we're even!

P.P.S. Do you honestly feel you are being well served by your publishers? I have now read *Black Wolf* a dozen times in total, and have found no less than *fourteen* typesetting errors. Perhaps you should take the matter up with them? I would be happy to travel to New York and discuss it with them on your behalf. Just say the word.

Sarah set down the letter and looked at Mark across the restaurant table. She grimaced.

'Bloody hell,' she murmured. 'This guy's several bricks short of a full load!' She studied the photograph for a few moments, then shook her head. 'He certainly doesn't *look* like he sounds. He looks so . . . well, *normal.*'

'And he sounds like Vincent Price crossed with Uriah Heep,' observed Mark glumly. He presided over the remains of a barely touched steak-au-poivre, and lit his fourth cigarette of the evening. He was feeling distinctly edgy, a dissatisfaction fuelled by his seeming inability to make any headway with *Black Wolf 3*. Goldman's letter, which had arrived that morning, had simply compounded his anxiety. His first note had seemed so polite, so *reasonable.* Now the guy was coming on like *The Times Literary Supplement* with the 'pretentious' pedal pushed to the floorboards. Worse than that were the elements that struck Mark as distinctly creepy; all that stuff about 'being' Black Wolf, for Christ's sake! Who in their right mind would want to seek identification with a fictional character who occasionally transformed himself into a drooling beast and ate people's faces off?

Mark topped up their glasses with Burgundy, then glanced moodily around the interior of the bistro. This used to be his favourite place to eat, an intimate local venue featuring stripped-pine floors, chairs and tables, simply framed Impressionist prints on white stucco walls, a chalked-up menu that changed daily, and a selection of 1940s jazz favourites tinkling soothingly away in the background. Tonight, however, everything seemed wrong for him. The table they'd been assigned was too near the swing doors of the kitchen, there was a large party of boorish drunks singing football songs close by, and even the food seemed unpalatable. Mark had ordered his steak well done but, when he had first sliced into it, it oozed blood. Any other time, he would have shrugged that off, realising that his present frame of mind stemmed from having to work on a book he had no real interest in. But somehow, he couldn't seem to lift himself out of his depression.

A young waitress approached the table. She had permed blonde hair sticking out from under a red baseball cap, and was wearing a pair of red overalls with the word 'SCOFF' emblazoned on the bib front (the name of the restaurant). She eyed Mark's plate dubiously.

'Was everything all right?' she asked hopefully.

'No, it wasn't,' snapped Mark. 'Listen, if I want a blood transfusion, I'll head down to casualty, OK?'

The girl looked crestfallen.

'Oh, gosh, I'm sorry. Was it a little rare?'

'Rare. It was virtually an endangered species!'

'Perhaps I could bring you something else, sir?'

'Don't bother. Another bottle of wine will suffice.'

The waitress began to gather up the plates. Sarah reached out and put a comforting hand on the girl's arm.

'Take no notice,' Sarah advised. 'He's just in a bad mood. My meal was lovely, thanks very much.'

The girl smiled gratefully and headed back for the swing doors to the kitchen. Sarah levelled an accusing glare at Mark.

'There's no need to take it out on her,' she said.

'Maybe it's *you* I should blame.'

'Me?' She stared at him. 'How do you make that out?'

'Well, you were the bright spark who said I should write back to that fruitcake.' He tapped the letter on the table.

'Oh, and I suppose you wouldn't have done that anyway?'

He shrugged. 'I might not have.'

''Course you bloody well would! You were *thrilled*. Besides, I assumed then you'd have the sense not to enclose your own address, you gibbon!' She sipped contemplatively at her wine. 'Anyway, I don't see that it's such a problem.'

'No?'

'Well, it's not as if he's exactly handy, is it? He's over there in far-off Philadelphia . . .'

'Pennsylvania,' he corrected her.

'Pennsylvania, Transylvania, wherever. It's not as if you're likely to bump into him at the corner shop, is it?'

'No, I suppose not.' Mark looked doubtful. 'Only . . .'

'Only what?'

'It's just that I think I said something about him looking me up sometime – if he was in the neighbourhood.'

She stared at him. 'You did what?'

He spread his hands in a gesture of helplessness.

'Like you do,' he said. 'You know, thinking that you'll never be taken up on the offer.'

'Christ. Imagine somebody who sounds like this turning up on your doorstep. The fan from hell!'

'Don't.' Mark gulped at his wine, then topped up their glasses with the last of the bottle. He glanced impatiently around the room. 'Where's that other bottle got to?' he wondered irritably.

'Take it easy,' Sarah advised him. 'Or they'll be carrying you out of here on a stretcher. If this is how success is going to affect you . . .'

'What do you mean?' he said irritably.

'It's just that you haven't been quite the same since the first big advance payment rolled in. You're becoming a right little prima-donna.'

'That's ridiculous. I've always enjoyed a drink.'

'That's just the point. These days you don't seem to be *enjoying* it. You've been in a stinking mood for the last two weeks.' She turned her attention back to the letter. 'I tell you one thing. He's pretty astute, your Leonard.'

Mark grimaced. 'Not *my* Leonard. I'm taking no responsibility for him. What do you mean, "astute"?'

'He's sussed out a couple of things correctly, here, where he's wondering which of your characters are based on real people. Has your agent ever clicked that he's the inspiration for Thunder Heart?'

Mark stared at Sarah in surprise. 'What makes you say that?'

'Oh, come on, it's obvious. Black Wolf's advisor, the wise old medicine man who's addicted to whisky.'

Mark waved her to silence.

'Yes, all right, all right. You get the gold star. But don't, whatever you do, suggest that to him. He might not feel exactly flattered.'

'I can't think why not. Then, of course, there's Black Wolf's old friend, Leaping Horse. Or Brendan – whichever name you prefer.'

'Well that's no great secret. Brendan was quite chuffed about it. Said he'd return the favour sometime.'

Sarah made a wry face. 'If he'll ever get around to finishing anything! How long's he been working on his novel? Six years?'

'I suppose . . .'

Sarah leaned across the table and fixed him with a searching look.

42

'Of course, the great mystery is this. If Black Wolf is you – and they say that every book's hero is to some degree based on its writer – then who is Star Child?'

He gazed back blankly.

'Well . . . nobody, really. She's just pure invention. A lot of fictional characters are, you know.'

'But not with you, Mark. I know how you work. I've watched you observing people, making mental notes . . .' She moistened her index finger and began to push it slowly around the rim of her empty glass, until she managed to produce a shrill, oscillating whine. 'It's funny, because she reminded me of that woman you were seeing before I came along. Nancy, or Gladys, or something . . .'

Mark grinned despite himself.

'You know perfectly well she was called Natasha.'

'Oh, yes, Natasha. Stuck-up little cow. Used to strut about in stilettos like she had a fifty-pence piece clenched between her buttocks. I believe she sold timeshare accommodation or something equally suspect.'

Mark shook his head. Sarah mostly looked like butter wouldn't melt in her mouth, but she could be truly bitchy when she wanted.

'What's Natasha got to do with Star Child, for God's sake?'

'There are certain distinct similarities. And I just think it's strange that you didn't base the character on *me*.'

'I *did* base a character on you. Connie.'

'The town whore who got ripped to pieces by Black Wolf in Chapter Seven! Oh well, thanks very much. Nice of you to remember me.'

Mark glared at her.

'Come on, that's ridiculous! Fictional characters are composites, that's all. There were just a few of your qualities that I wanted to incorporate in Connie, so . . .'

'What qualities?'

'Well, an earthiness I suppose. And some physical characteristics . . .' He shook his head, laughed. 'This is dumb. I shouldn't need to defend myself like this. We're only talking about words on paper.' He turned as the waitress moved past, laden with plates of food. 'Hey, where's that bottle of wine?' he asked.

'It's on its way,' she assured him in a harassed tone.

He turned back to find Sarah lighting up one of his cigarettes. A bad sign, she only ever smoked if she was annoyed about something. She inhaled inexpertly and blew a large cloud of smoke in his face.

'I just think there's something funny when I get to be the town whore, and you base the main love interest on your *ex*.' She managed to make ex sound like a dirty word.

'She's *not* based on Natasha. She's not based on anybody! For goodness sake, she's a bloodlusting bitch who goes around castrating her male victims . . .'

'There you are, then!' Sarah waved a hand dismissively. 'Natasha to a T. And there's no need to raise your voice.'

'I'm not raising my voice!' he shouted. Heads turned at the surrounding tables. Happily, the blonde waitress chose this moment to deliver the second bottle. Mark nodded his thanks and replenished the glasses. Then he glanced defensively around the bistro, and was suddenly struck by how weird everybody looked. That couple over to his left, obviously out for a romantic tête-à-tête, but now tearing ravenously into bowls of spare ribs, their mouths streaked with red barbecue sauce. Or that noisy party along the far wall, a collection of office workers by the look of them. The women were gathered at one end of the long table, leaning forward in a conspiratorial huddle to gossip madly about something or somebody. They all sported loose perms and had cigarettes on the go, holding them at arm's length above their heads, thick coils of smoke ascending to the low ceiling. The men, drunker and less coherent, had divided themselves into groups and were now singing rival football chants, trying to overwhelm the opposition by sheer lung power. To Mark's right, a lone diner, a thin, seedy-looking man with a toothbrush moustache, was picking half-heartedly at a bowl of pasta, whilst apparently holding an engaging conversation with a large rubber plant that stood next to his table. When he noticed Mark looking at him, he grinned sheepishly, displaying the bits of spinach lodged in his teeth.

Jesus, thought Mark, *Creep City*!

Sarah had picked up Leonard's letter. 'What do you intend to do with this?'

He frowned. 'I haven't decided,' he admitted. 'I'm certainly not going to continue the correspondence. You see that bit where he wonders if he might actually be the joint author. The bastard will be asking me for royalties next!'

Sarah grinned. 'Well, at least he offers to help you write the next twenty-five volumes. Now there's a prospect!'

Mark scowled. 'Just *one* volume is bad enough. I sat for hours today just staring at a blank screen. Nothing came to me – not a damn notion. I'm suffering from a massive dose of writer's block.'

'And that's why you're in such a filthy mood?'

'It may have something to do with it.'

She reached out a hand and put it on his.

'So, just say no,' she urged him. 'Tell them you want to develop one of your other ideas. You could always send back the advance.'

He shook his head.

'It's not quite as easy as that, I'm afraid. I signed a contract, agreed to deliver it by next February.'

'Well, what if you did? They can't *make* you write it, can they? Or you could just deliver three pages and say, 'Okay, there's your book!'

Mark laughed hollowly.

'Oh, that would be an inspired move, wouldn't it? I'm hoping to maintain a good relationship with my publishers. I'm still hoping that they'll handle some of my other projects in the future.' He thought for a moment and took the letter from Sarah. 'That's something else that worries me. This bit in the P.P.S. where he's threatening to go and talk to my New York publishers about misprints, for Christ's sake! That would be really useful, wouldn't it?'

'Relax,' Sarah advised him. 'You're getting a little paranoid about this. He's not really going to do that – not unless you ask him to. Tell you the truth, I get the impression this guy would stick his head in a bucket of shit if you requested it.'

'Maybe his fingers in a light socket would be more appropriate.'

'Oh, that's unfair.' Sarah gazed at him reproachfully. 'When all's said and done, Leonard is just a fan. He worships the ground you walk on, sunshine. I'm sure he'd never wish you any harm.'

'I suppose not.'

'Here's what I think you should do. Just write him another letter.'

'You're joking, I trust!'

'No, hear me out. Just a short, polite note saying that you regret that you're now too busy to answer any further personal correspondence. Tell him you're now getting tons of the stuff. Since he already seems to believe that you have this incredibly busy schedule, you'll simply be reinforcing his belief. Tell him that *Black Wolf 3* is taking up every minute of your time.'

'That's not so far from the truth,' muttered Mark. 'Think that'll do the trick?'

'Sure. Your initial letter encouraged him too much, that's all. Now you've got to let him down gently.'

Mark grinned.

'You sound like Claire Rayner,' he observed.

'Trust me,' she told him. 'I've read every advice column the woman's ever written.'

Eventually they came to the end of the second bottle. Mark's mood had lightened considerably and he was feeling pleasantly woozy. He called for the bill, and left a generous tip in a sheepish attempt to make up for his previous remarks to the waitress. They collected their coats and went out into the street. The weather had improved a little, though there was still a chill wind in the air. Mark hailed a passing cab, and it pulled to a halt beside them. They climbed in the back and Mark slipped an arm around Sarah's shoulders.

'Sorry I've been a grouch,' he said. 'I'll try harder.'

'Can I have that in writing?'

'I'll slot it in after the next novel.'

'And you'll write back to him?' she asked sleepily.

'OK. Polite but dismissive, right?'

'Uh-huh. Should . . . do the trick . . .'

'And supposing it doesn't? Supposing he just insists on writing more letters?'

She didn't answer that one. Glancing down, Mark realized that she had fallen asleep in his arms. He leaned forward and kissed her gently on the forehead. He'd have to save that question for another time.

The cab sped onwards in the direction of home.

Chapter Six

Dear Mr Goldman,

Thank you for your recent letter concerning my work. I regret that due to my current busy schedule and an unprecedented amount of mail, I shall be unable to reply to any more letters in person. I would therefore ask you to direct any further correspondence to my agent at the address indicated separately.

Thanking you once again for your interest.

Yours Sincerely,
Mark Tyler

Leonard sat at Bela Lugosi's desk, staring at the letter in disbelief. He had just gone down to check the mail, and was still wearing his dressing-gown. He felt a little groggy after a poor night's sleep and had been ill prepared for the shock of such an abrupt reply to his last communication. He turned the single sheet of paper over in his hands, as though expecting to find more words written on the reverse side. But there was nothing. He picked up the envelope and opened it with his fingers, but that too was depressingly empty. He could not quite believe what had happened. The letter seemed cold and formal. '*Dear Leonard*' had been replaced by a horridly businesslike '*Dear Mr Goldman*'. The pages of chatty anecdotes he had eagerly anticipated had come down to one brief paragraph. It didn't actually say 'get off my back' – not in so many words – but the message was there, loud and clear. Mark Tyler wanted out of this vital dialogue. But why?

Leonard sat there stunned, trying to think back to his last letter, trying to remember if he'd said anything at all that might have offended Mark. Perhaps he'd seemed too pushy, too arrogant. Was there some fault he was unaware of, something he should try hard to keep in check? He'd been so excited about this meeting of minds, but maybe he'd been too eager to make a first impression.

Well, it wasn't too late. It couldn't be! Leonard's hands fumbled at the desk drawer, and he pulled out his writing pad and pen, his pack of airmail envelopes. If he wrote straight back, explained how very sorry he was . . . He'd promise not to presume too much, he'd restrict himself to observations about Mark's writing, no more premature offers of help or advice . . .

Despair welled up inside him, black, impenetrable, overpowering. He groaned, closed his eyes, then brought his head down abruptly on to the desk top. His forehead struck the smooth surface with a dull clunk. He straightened again, sat still for a moment, feeling the pain throbbing through him. Then he repeated the action, harder this time, so that little fizzing sparks of light danced beneath his eyelids. It was a self-punishment he'd used ever since childhood, a device he employed whenever he miscalculated a move. He'd just made a stupid mistake; he'd nearly gone and blown his chance to be involved with the creator of Black Wolf. He'd somehow managed to frighten him away.

Leonard brought his head down a third time, and the pain seemed to blossom like fire across the whole of his face. Everything receded into a grey, insubstantial blur. For an instant he drifted, reassuringly lost somewhere between reality and dreams. Then the world broke back into his thoughts, a shattered jigsaw reassembling itself at the edges of his vision. He slumped back in his chair with a moan, aware now of the tickle of a line of blood running down his forehead and into one eye. He took a paper handkerchief from a box on the desk and held it to his head, while he sat there waiting to recover his senses.

Fool, he thought. *What did that solve?* He would have to salvage the situation the only way he knew how. He would have to win Mark's confidence with cunning. He would write and say how sorry he was. He would beg Mark for a second chance. He'd *prove* to him that he could be worthy of his trust . . .

'Leonard? Leonard, you there?'

Mother's voice reached him faintly from the next room, cutting into his dazed senses. He rose obediently to his feet and stood swaying for a moment. He had to throw out one arm to the desk in order to support himself. He shook his head and his blurred vision redefined itself. For a moment he stared at the blood on the tissue, feeling a surge of the old excitement.

'Leonard, *please!*'

'Coming, Mother!' Reacting now to the urgency in her voice, he swayed towards the door of his room and fumbled out on to the landing. He made his way carefully along to Mother's room and opened the door. He stepped inside, trying not to flinch at the overpowering stench of soiled bedding.

Mother lay in the big four-poster, propped against mounds of yellowed lace pillows. She looked tiny and inconsequential beneath the layers of sheets, as though her body consisted of nothing more than a bundle of dry sticks. Her wizened face was powder-white, etched with deep lines around the eyes and mouth; but, as ever, she wore her blonde, shoulder-length wig, and her cracked lips were painted a garish shade of red. There were exotic smudges of turquoise around her eyes, and her plucked brows had been repainted as two dramatic black arches. One of Brenda's daily jobs was to 'fix' the old woman's face, and Mother was very particular about how that was done.

'What's wrong, Mother?' asked Leonard wearily. He moved closer to the bed, dabbing at his forehead with the bloodied Kleenex.

She turned her big, mournful eyes on him and, as always, he was reminded of Bette Davis, an old favourite of his video collection. But this was Bette as Baby Jane, one of the most grotesque roles of her illustrious career.

'It's your father,' she told him. 'He was here again. Keeps pestering me for sexual favours. How's a girl supposed to get any sleep around here?'

She had been having this delusion a lot lately, Leonard reflected. He settled himself into the seat at the head of her bed, and he put a large hand over one of hers.

'Now, you know Daddy's dead,' he told her sadly. 'He's been gone these twenty years and more.'

'Can't help that,' she told him, grinning wildly. 'That man always did demand his conjugal rights, didn't matter what time of the day or night it was . . . *never* saw a man with such appetites! I used to say, "Jerry, you've a permanent case o' the hots."' She looked confused for a moment as though trying to remember something. Then her eyes seemed to focus, and she was abruptly rational again. Leonard was reminded of himself only a few minutes earlier, first dizzy from butting his head, then emerging from a mist back into the real world. Mother seemed to slip in and out of reality with astonishing ease, twenty or thirty times a day. She was seventy-two years old, deeply affected by Alzheimer's disease, but despite it all she did have her lucid moments. She was staring fixedly at him now, as though noticing him for the first time.

'Leonard, for goodness sake, what you done to yourself? There's blood on your forehead.'

He dabbed at the wound ruefully.

'Aww, I just bumped it on a cupboard door, that's all.'

She smiled, patted his hand fondly.

'Clumsy,' she chided him. 'You ought to take more care.'

'Yes, mam. Now, what say you get some sleep?'

'I ain't particularly tired. Stay and talk to me a spell, will ya? Jus' till Brenda gets here.'

He sighed, nodded.

'OK, Mother. What shall we talk about?'

'Do one of your impressions for me! Do Johnny Carson!'

'Oh no, Mother, I really don't feel up to it.' Leonard was a good mimic and, when he was in the mood, he would sometimes keep her amused for hours with his performances. She always asked for Johnny Carson or Jack Benny, but he felt happier doing the current crowd from 'Saturday Night Live'.

'Oh, shoot, go on, Leonard. Don't be such a sourpuss!'

'Really, Mother.' He dabbed at his forehead again with the tissue. 'I'm not feeling so good. Maybe tonight.'

She sighed, clearly disappointed, and cast about for something else to occupy her. 'Well, then, tell me . . . tell me about work.'

He shrugged. 'There's not much to tell. It's a job, I guess.'

'You don't enjoy it much at Olsen's, do you?'

He shook his head. 'No, mam.'

She studied him for a moment, looking perhaps at the dark bruise that was spreading gradually across his forehead.

'Still, I think it's real important, Leonard. It gets you out of the house. It ain't healthy for a boy your age to be stuck inside till all hours. Lord knows, it ain't that we need the money. Your Daddy left us well provided for, Lord rest him. But he would have approved of you working, wouldn't he? He never much liked the thought of you gettin' it all on a plate. Work makes the man – ain't that what he used to say?'

Leonard nodded, sending waves of dizziness through himself.

'That's right,' he agreed. 'That's exactly what he used to s . . . say.' *Oh, Daddy was a stickler for work all right*, thought Leonard bitterly. *Mother, if you only knew the half of it.*

'Maybe . . . maybe you could find something more agreeable, Leonard. Something where you could work in the daylight, come home evenin's like any normal human being.'

'There's not much else around Dennings, Mother. I'm lucky to have any kind of work, what with this world recession and all.'

She scowled, which etched the lines around her eyes deeper still.

'But you're such an *intelligent* boy, Leonard! And you write beautifully. If only you didn't have to leave school before taking your exams. If only you hadn't been ill that one time . . .'

Leonard laughed bitterly.

'Ill,' he murmured. It was an interesting word for what had been wrong with him. The truth was, he'd been thoroughly bullied at high-school, systematically picked on, mocked, humiliated for his strangeness, until he'd finally been unable to take any more. There was one particular kid called Ritchie Burke who had been the ringleader. It hadn't been so bad in the first couple of years, because Leonard was big for his age and Ritchie was kind of scrawny. But as time went on, and the boys moved steadily through the grades, Ritchie acquired height and muscle, and it was then that he began to play pranks on the class loner, Leonard – putting chilli powder in his sandwiches, tying his laces together, sandwiching a dog turd in the middle of his exercise book.

That final year, Ritchie had come down on Leonard with a vengeance. Ritchie was a lazy kid with little aptitude for learning, and not a hope in hell of getting his grades. But he did have one ability: he was good at manipulating his classmates. Suddenly, it wasn't just one boy who habitually picked on Leonard; it was the whole damned class. Tall, slow of speech and movement, solitary and friendless he was an easy target. Leonard's life now became an endless parade of misery. From the moment he arrived in the morning to the moment he left for home, he was subjected to a relentless series of put-downs, practical jokes, even physical beatings. With Ritchie's active encouragement, every member of the class, right down to the smallest, weediest kid, eagerly joined in the fun.

A few weeks before the final exams, Ritchie somehow discovered that Leonard was terrified of spiders. This was too good an opportunity to miss. So Ritchie and a bunch of friends jumped Leonard one afternoon as he was walking home from school. They pushed, dragged, manhandled him along to the old Harris place, a derelict mansion on the edge of town. They had long since cut a secret entrance through the tall railings that surrounded the place, and they carried Leonard inside and tied him to a bentwood chair so he couldn't move. Then Ritchie produced an old football helmet, its visor covered with strips of masking tape. He tilted it carefully so that Leonard could see what swarmed inside it. Spiders: small, average-size and large. It must have taken those kids days to collect so many.

Then slowly, savouring his victim's growing terror, Ritchie placed the helmet over Leonard's head – then all settled down to watch the entertainment. After just a few seconds, Leonard had wet himself, which gave everybody a real good laugh. From time to time, one of the spiders would struggle out from under the helmet and go skittering down Leonard's shoulder to the floor, where somebody would stamp on it; but after that, there wasn't much to see. Leonard would just twitch occasionally and give a muffled groan, which was disappointing. The kids didn't realize it, but he was actually near to suffocating in there. After a while they began to get bored, and wandered off. Leonard was left sitting there all night long in the crawling, breathless dark.

Luckily, some of the younger kids excitedly told their parents what had happened. When the police finally got to Leonard and removed the helmet, he was near catatonic – making noises that could hardly be interpreted as words. Occasionally he would throw back his head and howl at the top of his lungs. Once they untied him, he immediately began to claw madly at his own cheeks and neck, as though trying to tear some pestilence from his skin.

They brought him home, but he was unable to speak for a full six months. And even when the psychologists and counsellors finally coaxed him back into using his tongue, they found that he had developed a pronounced stutter, which took years of therapy to get under control. But the horrific events in the Harris place had totally slipped from his mind. He had blanked it out, and it wasn't till years later that he could recall that terrible moment when the tight-fitting helmet slid over his head and he'd felt those awful, skittering, hairy *things*, tangling in his hair and trapped against his skin. In that moment, he'd prayed for death to take him – because it would have been preferable to the reality of what was happening.

By the time he recovered, any hope of sitting his exams had long gone. Ritchie was gone too, but there were bound to be others to take his place – sooner or later. Better to retreat further into himself, to confine himself in his room with his beloved books and videos, where the horrors around him were all explicable and self-contained – and could never turn themselves in his direction.

Years later, when he read about Ritchie Burke's death in the local newspaper, he didn't know quite what to think. Ritchie had been apprehended by a couple of highway patrolmen as he attempted to flee the scene of a bungled robbery. He'd tried to hold up a liquor store in Pittsburgh and the cops had pulled up outside by coincidence. Ritchie had lost his nerve and had run out of the store, brandishing a pistol. The cops, who were jumpy types, had shouted for him to throw down his weapon, whilst simultaneously pumping bullets into him. Later, it was discovered that Ritchie's 'gun' was nothing more than a child's plastic toy. Leonard might have been expected to feel happy at such news, but despite everything that had happened to him, in fact he didn't feel anything at all.

'When you bringin' your young lady over for a visit?'

Mother's voice broke into his thoughts, jerking him abruptly back to the present. He frowned, aware that he might have exaggerated somewhat when he had spoken to Mother about Veronica.

As he so often did, he had allowed his hopes and aspirations to become something more solid. He had told Mother that his workmate was rapidly becoming more than just a friend; that she was devoted to him and took every opportunity to be at his side. Rashly, he had even hinted at marriage, giving her the impression that it was just a matter of time before they named the day. He should have thought more carefully before shooting his mouth off.

'W . . . well now, Mother, that's k . . . kind of difficult,' he explained, aware of the stutter which always seemed to plague him when he was trying to be devious with her. 'See, we mostly work on different shifts and . . .'

'You could bring her over sometime, just for an hour or so. I'd like to meet her – unless, of course, you'd be ashamed of me.'

He shook his head.

'It's not that, Mother, honestly. I'd be *p* . . . *proud*. It's just . . .' He sagged inwardly, realising that he'd now have to level with her. She would already be planning the wedding reception in her crazy old head. 'Tell you the truth, Ma, we're not getting on as well as we used to.'

He saw the sudden disappointment clawing at her face. He wanted to put his arms around her and beg her forgiveness.

'Damn it,' she growled. 'I really hoped . . .'

'I know, Mother, I'm sorry. It just wasn't working out. You know how particular I am . . .'

'A mite too particular, I reckon! It's a vexation to me, boy. You know I ain't goin' to be here for very much longer. I want to see you settled afore I go. Who's going to look after you when I'm gone?'

'Don't talk that way, Mother!'

'I got to, boy! You ain't fit to fend for yourself. What happens when I pass over?'

'That'll be years yet.'

'No, it won't! How can I go on to glory, knowin' you're all alone in the world? Now, listen, I'm goin' to suggest somethin', and I want you to consider it real careful. There's always Brenda.

He turned away from her in disgust. 'No, Mother. I couldn't!'

'Hear me out one minute! I know she's no great looker . . . and she ain't the cleanest creature in the world . . . but she's a tough old bird, already worn out one husband. She'd look after you, Leonard – make sure you stayed out of trouble. There's a considerable dowry waitin' there in my account. It'll all be yours the day you tie the knot.'

'With Brenda? Mother, she's ten years older than me.'

'So? She's steady, she has experience o' life. Damn sight more'n that little flibbertigibbet over at the mart, anyways. Young gal like that would spend all your money and go out chasing young beaus every time your back was turned. And I happen to know Brenda would be willin'.'

'You . . . you've discussed this with her?'

'Didn't have to. I can tell by just lookin'. The way her eyes follow you. The way she talks to you. There's plenty of fire left in *them* coals, you take it from me.'

'Mother, she disgusts me. Why, I wouldn't marry her if she—'

'And your Daddy thinks it's a good idea too. We was just talking about it – wasn't we, hon?'

Leonard stared at her. Just like that, she'd gone back into her crazy world where the dead lived on and she was a young, lusty bride again.

'No, you weren't, Mother. I told you, Daddy's dead . . .'

'Said to me, "Cora, I do believe I want to go to it again!" And I sez to him, "If you must have it, then who am I to argue?" And he's gruntin' and strainin' at me like a prize bull.'

'Mother, please!' Leonard shook his head in dismay. She was quite beyond his reach, her eyes rolling, her tongue lolling obscenely. She could slip back so suddenly, even in mid-sentence, and at times she'd give vent to the kind of language she'd never tolerate from others when she was herself. It was like she was possessed, taken over by some foul-tempered demon. Now her body was jerking convulsively beneath the sheets.

'He wanted me to take him in my mouth, the whole length of him! I knew it was a sin, but I couldn't refuse that man anything, you hear? Not a goddamned thing!'

He retreated from the bed, and her rising voice followed him out on to the landing. He pulled the door shut behind him and moved to the top of the stairs. Brenda was standing down by the front door, sifting through the mail. Due to Mother's shouting, Leonard hadn't heard her come in. Brenda was wearing her usual coat, a shapeless brown tweed and she was staring expectantly up at him, a twisted smile on her face.

'Old girl ravin' again?' she asked him.

'My Mother is having one of her little turns,' he informed her, primly. She remained where she was, gazing up at him. 'Well,' he demanded. 'Haven't you got some work to attend to?'

'Sure,' she said. 'I was just enjoying the view.'

He hadn't realized that the front of his robe was hanging open. He turned away from the stairs, pulling the robe tighter around him, his face reddening.

'I'll be in my room,' he muttered. 'I don't want to be disturbed.'

But she was climbing the stairs in pursuit, shouting up after him.

'You spend an awful amount of time up in that room, don'tcha? What exactly do you get up to in there?'

'That's none of your business!'

'Won't even let me come in to clean the place! What is it you do in there you're so ashamed of? You spend all your time whacking off? You beating the old meat, Leonard? I could help you with that, you know!'

He wheeled around to face her.

'You're disgusting! Do you know that?'

She gave her cackling little laugh.

'I have my moments,' she admitted. Then she noticed the bruise on his forehead. 'Hey, what you done to yourself? Want me to come in and rub somethin' on that?' She reached out a hand to touch his thigh. 'Want me to rub anythin' else?' He slapped her hand away with a grunt of irritation.

'I want to be left alone,' he told her bluntly.

'Yeah? Who do you think you are, Greta fuckin' Garbo? Come on, Leonard, why are you so stubborn? We could go to it right now, in that room of yours. Ain't nobody to hear us but the old lady, and she's past carin'.'

'Don't you dare speak about Mother that way!' he snapped. 'Don't you dare!'

She seemed to realize that she'd overstepped the mark. She moved back a little, planting her feet slightly apart, her hands resting on her well-upholstered hips.

'Aww, Leonard, I'm just curious, that's all. What do you do in there all these hours? Just a' readin' them creepy books of yours?'

He pursed his lips.

'No,' he said. 'Actually, I'm writing one.'

She studied him for a moment, her eyes narrowed down to shrewd little slits.

'You're kidding me,' she said.

'It's t . . . true. I'm writing a horror novel. It's nearly finished. It's going to be the first of a whole series.'

She sneered. 'You figure you're gonna get it made into a book or somethin'?'

'Of course. That's already taken care of. The book's a c . . . commission.'

She stared at him, uncomprehending. 'Huh?' she grunted.

'It's already sold to a publisher. I have just a few months to deliver the finished manuscript. Yes, that's why I mustn't be d . . . disturbed, you see?' He turned away from her and walked the last few steps to his bedroom.

'B . . . b . . . bullshit,' she sneered. She was grinning, displaying those mud-coloured teeth. But she was moving off now, heading for Mother's room, responding to the muffled sounds of the old woman's yelling. Leonard opened the door of his room and went inside, slamming it behind him. He stood for a moment with his back to the door, breathing heavily, listening to the distant sound of Mother's voice. He turned his attention to the Lugosi desk. Mark's unanswered letter lay waiting for him on its surface. Leonard saw that there was a small bloodstain on the corner of it.

For a moment he was puzzled, but then he touched his forehead and winced as his fingertips rekindled the dull pain. He sat down at the desk and tried wiping the stain off the letter with a Kleenex, but the blood had already congealed. He frowned, pushed the letter aside, then took up his pen and writing paper. He thought for a moment, wondering how best to start.

Dear Mark, he thought. *Please forgive me. I am so desperately sorry that I offended you* . . . He set down the first sentence and appraised it for a moment. He nodded. He thought it had the necessary tone.

Then he began to write, as if his life depended upon it . . .

Chapter Seven

Mr Tyler,

I thought you were different ~~than~~ FROM all the others. I thought that we had a special bond. But clearly I was mistaken. Over the past month I have written fourteen letters, not one of which you have had the decency to answer. You did not comment on the Black Wolf notes I sent you, nor did you bother to even thank me for the illustrations, which took me some considerable time to produce.

Whilst I appreciate that you have a busy schedule, it seems most impolite not to take the time to communicate with your fans. Don't forget, Mr Tyler, we are the ones who put you where you are today. If we all decided to boycott *Black Wolf 2*, you'd soon find a lot more time to answer your correspondence, wouldn't you? Such boycotts have been organized in the past. Not that I'm suggesting I would personally stoop so low, but look behind the cosy facade of most so-called celebrities these days, and you'll find some unsavoury skeletons rattling away in their closets. A word to the newspapers is all it would take.

I'm sorry, but this situation is beginning to make me rather angry and, for better or for worse, I am going to speak my mind. I know Black Wolf would adopt the same attitude, but then he's an honourable, higher being, the kind who would never turn his back on a true friend.

Betrayal – that's what it comes down to. An absolute betrayal of trust. I wrote to you initially out of the blue, with no expectation of receiving a reply. It would have been kinder never to have offered me that first encouragement to reveal myself, never to have led me to believe that you were someone to be trusted with my most intimate thoughts. But I think I am beginning to see now what your ploy is: the typical approach of a lesser talent seeking to leech on to the ideas of a more original mind. It worked very well for you on the face of it. You now have all my notes and drawings. How stupidly trusting of me not to have ensured copyright before I sent them!

57

More importantly, you have my recommendations on the development of the Black Wolf series, so no doubt we'll see them pirated and incorporated into subsequent books. Now I think of it, in fact, how much of *Black Wolf 1* actually arose from your own imagination, and how much from mine? Little wonder I was so enamoured of it in the first place! Black Wolf was obviously my creation. Somehow, I'll never know exactly how you managed it, how you crept into my mind and stole my ideas. Of course, I shall never be able to prove it to the world. You've covered your tracks too well. But *you* and *I* will know the truth, won't we?

You must see, Mr Tyler, how this affects my view of the unsavoury, unsatisfactory world in which we exist. There are only a very few true shamens left alive, we special people with great minds, blessed with original ideas and profound thoughts, though lacking the shrewd, dishonourable nature to capitalise on them. And then there are people like you, gifted only with a low, animal cunning. If I may use an analogy, it's like that first dawn of time when great, lordly dinosaurs prowled the earth but were eventually brought down by the sneaking, cowardly little rats that stole their eggs, sucking out the mighty yoke of originality in order to thrive and multiply themselves.

I can only feel sorry for you, Tyler. You now have undeserved success in your hands. You doubtless have material wealth accumulating in a bank vault somewhere, yet you have no real talent of your own – only that which you can appropriate from others. How hollow such success must seem! How worthless!

Incidentally, I went through *Black Wolf 1* again last night and I have to tell you that it now begins to seem an extraordinarily clumsy book. If you discount the brilliant central premise (which is mine) you are left merely with some sketchily drawn characters, some rather hackneyed dialogue, and a poor story development. If I had bothered to write it myself, the result would have been far more elegant, more assured. What we actually have there is a crudely drawn caricature that barely passes muster – a pale reflection of its potential glory.

Yet we could *still* work together on this life-work. This may seem an overly generous offer on my part, and there are many higher souls who would express disbelief at my forgiving nature. But I am a pragmatist above all. I realize that thanks to your deviousness I could never prove myself the true inspirer of the Black Wolf concept. But *you* do not possess the kind of talent necessary to extend this story further, while I on the other hand have the insight to take him into the twenty-first century and well beyond! It is with this higher purpose in mind that I offer you this one last chance to salvage our relationship. I am willing to talk the matter over with you intelligently and calmly, but I must emphasise that this is *MY FINAL OFFER*. If I have not heard back from you personally in ten days' time, then all deals are off, and you will be eternally branded as a scum-licking, shit-holing cocksucker of the lowest order. And I shall personally take steps to ensure that the whole world knows it.

Leonard J. Goldman

P.S. I saw that interview with you in *Esquire*. Very clever. All that wide-eyed innocence crap! 'I'm really delighted and astonished that my little book is doing so well!' *Your* little book indeed! If you are ready to re-establish the bond between us, I think maybe we should talk about some financial compensation for me, don't you?

Brendan laid the letter aside and reached for his gin and tonic. He took a contemplative sip, then smiled quizzically at Mark.

'You know, I can't quite put my finger on it, but there's something in that chap's tone that's ever so slightly off.'

Mark feigned a look of surprise. 'Why, Brendan, whatever makes you say that?'

'Well, you notice he didn't put "*Dear* Mr Tyler". Now that's just bloody rude, if you ask me.'

He was sitting on the sofa in Mark's study, his feet up on the oak coffee-table, seemingly oblivious to the fact that his size-nine Dr Marten's wouldn't be doing the glossy wood-grain any favours. He was also smoking a hand-rolled cigarette, and flicking its ash on to the carpet.

Mark knew he should have been annoyed about this, but he somehow couldn't work up the necessary energy for that. He knew only too well that Brendan had no appreciation of either money or the things it could buy. To look at him, a stranger would probably take Brendan for an out of work ex-student. He habitually wore a torn, mottled suede jacket of indeterminate age, dirt-crusted Levis that were scuffed and ragged at the knees, and a crumpled T-shirt that invited onlookers to 'Stuff the Poll Tax'. It required a more careful eye to discern that the short blond hair, worn in a playful schoolboyish fringe, had actually been cut at Vidal Sassoon's; that the tasteful little watch on his left wrist was a genuine Rolex; and that the discreet bulge in his back jeans' pocket was made by a wallet containing an almost indecent collection of credit cards. And when Brendan spoke, it was there too in the refined accent that he vainly tried to smother beneath a streetwise sneer and a mouthful of expletives.

In short, Brendan was no stranger to privilege. He was a poor little rich kid, with a wealthy industrialist for a father, a mother who regularly got her photograph in *Harpers & Queen*, and a palatial home in Buckinghamshire that he was free to visit any old time he liked. Brendan, however, insisted on maintaining an outward show of working-class solidarity. He refused to own a car, and went everywhere by bus or tube (unless of course, he was in a hurry, when he would shamefacedly creep into a taxi). He lived in a single room in a malodorous squat in Islington, along with a bunch of genuine hard-timers, only his room was the one with an answerphone, fax machine, and a regular supply of hampers from Fortnum & Mason. He handrolled his own cigarettes, keeping the tobacco and papers in a scuffed Golden Virginia tin, and he was one of the few people that Mark knew who actually read every issue of *Socialist Worker* from cover to cover. This would all have been more convincing, of course, if he'd also turned down the generous monthly allowance his parents sent him to 'supplement' his earnings as a writer; but evidently, Brendan's principles didn't extend to their money. This he seemed to feel duty-bound to spend as quickly and as recklessly as possible.

Mark sat at his desk. He, too, was drinking gin and tonic. His word-processor squatted accusingly on the desk top, displaying the two paragraphs he had committed to memory just before Brendan came calling. When Mark had gone down to answer the door, Brendan had slouched past him into the hallway, announcing that he was bored and thirsty, and demanding to know what Mark intended doing about it.

So that was an end to any further progress on *Black Wolf 3* for that afternoon. Mark didn't really need much encouragement to down tools. He broke open a large bottle of Gordons and they settled down for a chat. Talk had quickly turned to the subject of Leonard Goldman and his nutty letters. Brendan was new to the subject and expressed disbelief, whereupon Mark produced the latest offering for his perusal, explaining how these letters had been arriving in a steady torrent, one every few days, for the last month. At first, the tone of them had been meek, apologetic, Leonard desperate to make friends with his hero. When these attempts had failed to prompt a response, the tone of the letters became steadily more bitter, more resentful, till the last few had bordered on out-and-out abuse. Now, finally, what Mark had once jokingly predicted: Leonard was pushing for a share of the proceeds – his 'fee' for co-writing *Black Wolf*. He had somehow convinced himself that it was his own creation.

'Weird bastard,' muttered Brendan, flicking the fringe out of his eyes with a delicate motion of one hand. 'I don't know why you bother to read them any more. You should put the fuckers straight in the bin, where they belong.'

'I always intend to,' Mark assured him. 'Then – I don't know – I get *curious*. I want to see what the poor mad bugger's saying about me now.'

'Ever thought about going to the pigs? To get a restraining order put on him, or something?'

'I wouldn't like to do that to anybody. He's causing no real harm. And, like you say, I don't *have* to read them, do I?'

'It's like he's trying moral blackmail, just to get you to write to him. He's craving attention. I bet if you did write, he'd be as nice as pie again. What's all that stuff about notes and drawings?'

Mark sighed. He opened a drawer of his desk and took out a single sheet of paper. 'Notes,' he announced, handing it across to Brendan. On the sheet were five handwritten lines.

BLACK WOLF NOTES

1. Encounters extinct tribe. Visions destroy army attackers.
2. Discovery of monsters in desert. Lizards?
3. B.W. undergoes trial by torture.
4. Reservation. Impact of modern drugs. Man with binoculars.
5. Trains.

Leonard J. Goldman, 1993

Brendan looked puzzled. He turned the paper over, but its other side was blank.

'That's it?' he asked. 'They're a bit sketchy, aren't they?'

'Indeed. Can you believe the guy being worried about copyright?' Mark rummaged in the same drawer. 'Ah, yes, now the drawings.'

He handed over several sheets of paper. They contained a series of crude pencil drawings. A misshapen creature surrounded by capering stick men in oversize cowboy hats. Some animal (possibly a wolf?) with something (a hand or perhaps a bunch of bananas) clutched in its mouth. Here, a pathetically executed title design in loopy, Sixties-style lettering. And, there, what was intended obviously to depict a Red Indian village, triangular tipis all out of scale, with a soldier seated on a dog – or was it supposed to be a horse? To Brendan, it looked like the work of a singularly untalented ten-year-old, but an accompanying note, written by Leonard in a friendlier mood, invited Mark to use these drawings as illustrations in the next *Black Wolf* novel.

'Oh my giddy aunt,' murmured Brendan. 'It's a bit bloody sad, isn't it? The poor sod's clearly got no talent for anything whatsoever.' He handed the papers back to Mark. 'And he's convinced you want to steal *this* stuff! Christ, you'd have to be pretty desperate.'

Mark shrugged.

'I'll get my agent to send them back to him,' he said, 'together with a carefully worded invitation to get off my case. I've about had it with this loony.'

'I bet you have. How's the book coming along, anyway?'

'Fitfully. I've blocked in a couple of chapters, and I'm now beginning to get an idea of where it's all going. But I really don't like working this way. I'd much rather have a clear idea of the whole thing before I even start.'

Brendan nodded. 'The price of fame, dear boy. You're on the old treadmill now, I fear.'

'What about your own *Magnum Opus*?'

'Magnum Hopeless, more like. Actually, I've shelved it for a while. As far as I'm concerned, the novel, as a valid art form, has had its day. I've decided that the screenplay is where it's at.' He glanced at his watch. 'Anyway, why don't we forget about all that bilge for tonight? Let me take you away from it all.'

Mark looked doubtful.

'I don't know, mate. I really ought to spend the evening working. This book isn't going to write itself, you know.'

'You've plenty of time for that. Come on, it'll do you good to get out for a change. Besides, in the immortal words of the Rolling Stones, I've somebody who's just *dying* to meet you.'

'Oh?' Mark glanced at him suspiciously. 'Who would that be, I wonder?'

'Bloke called Winston Short. He's a film producer, and he's interested in my screenplay.'

Mark tried not to wince. He was well aware that Brendan's 'screenplay', like his novel, had been several years in gestation and existed, so far as Mark was aware, only as an outline on a few sheets of paper. From what he remembered of its subject matter, it revolved around the adventures of a young, ex-convent girl 'finding' herself in the London of the Swinging Sixties. The whole '60s sex, drugs and bonking angle might have some potential. But Brendan, true to form, had never actually got around to *writing* much.

'Well, that's great,' said Mark unconvincingly. 'But I don't see what it's got to do with me.'

'I need somebody to hold my hand,' explained Brendan. 'I mean, this could be my shot at the big one, and I'm a little bit nervous. All this stuff must be second nature to you . . .'

'Well, hardly.'

'When I was discussing it with Mr Short, I got a bit excited and I . . .' He fidgeted nervously with his glass. 'Well, I sort of told him that I had this . . . this best selling author earmarked to write the screenplay.'

Mark glared at him. 'You what?'

'Now, don't get your knickers in a twist! It just sort of came out.'

'For God's sake! What were you thinking of? I haven't got time to take on another project. You should have consulted me.'

'Yeah, I suppose so. But, listen, it's no big deal. I mean, these things rarely come off anyway. And even if it does, there's nothing to say that you actually have to *write* anything, is there? You could just put your name to it, and I'd do the writing.'

Mark buried his face in his hands.

'Brendan,' he muttered, 'we need to talk about this.'

'Sure. In the taxi.'

Mark removed his hands. 'What taxi?'

'The one I'm about to order. I told Winston I'd meet him at seven in this pub off Wardour Street. OK if I use your phone?' He got up and went across to the desk. 'This is the first time I've met the guy face-to-face, so I'm anxious to make a good impression. Have you got a nice jacket I can borrow?'

'Brendan,' said Mark quietly, 'this really isn't on. I'm not going with you, and that's absolutely final.'

Chapter Eight

The Gryphon was a poky spit-and-sawdust pub located in one of the shabbier side streets of the West End. Apparently it was Winston Short's favourite watering hole. He had joked to Brendan on the phone that the Gryphon was his unofficial office, that he conducted a good deal of his business there.

There were only a few punters in evidence when Mark and Brendan made their entrance, a good fifteen minutes later than arranged. Brendan had somehow talked Mark into putting on his best suit, and lending Brendan his second best. Mark had, of course, never met Winston Short before, but the moment he clapped eyes on the two individuals seated at a small corner table, he just knew, with a slow, sinking feeling deep inside, that these must be the people Brendan had arranged to meet. They looked like a pair of villains.

The first was a small, wiry man dressed in a crombie overcoat that seemed to be several sizes too big for him. He had a cropped 'skinhead' haircut and, despite the gloom of the pub interior, he was wearing wrap-around shades. He grinned up at the newcomers to reveal a tiny, glittering diamond mounted in one of his front teeth, then he held out a hand that literally bristled with chunky rings. 'Winston Short,' he announced in a gruff voice with more than a touch of cockney in it. 'This is my business associate, Mr Springer.'

Mark studied Mr Springer doubtfully, noticing that the man looked big and mean and ugly. Like his companion, he sported a skinhead cut, and he also had some rather fetching tattoos on his neck and on the knuckles of each hand. His pale brown eyes examined Mark indifferently, and he possessed a nose that had been spectacularly flattened at some point in his career, so it lay almost parallel to the contours of his face. He, too, favoured a crombie overcoat, but in his case the effect was finished off by a pair of steel-capped Dr Marten's boots. Mark reflected that these men looked more like a pair of National Front rabble-rousers than a film producer and his assistant.

Everybody shook hands as introductions were made.

'Can I get anyone a drink?' asked Brendan chirpily.

'Very kind, squire!' exclaimed Winston, flashing that dazzling grin. 'Mr Springer, if memory serves correctly, will have bitter, one pint of! I, on the other hand, will have a rum and Pepsi, tall glass, no ice.'

'Er . . . yes, of course. Lager, Mark?'

'Yes, please. One pint of,' said Mark, not without a touch of sarcasm but nobody seemed to notice.

Brendan headed off in the direction of the bar. Winston Short was still grinning up at Mark. He patted a vacant stool beside him.

'So, Mr Tyler, please sit down. I must say, when Brendan told me of your involvement in our little project, I was most pleasantly surprised. We both were, weren't we, Mr Springer?'

Springer retained a kind of sneer on his face, but he moved his bony head up and down in the affirmative.

'I've seen your book in the shops,' added Winston. 'I must make a point of reading it one of these days. Never seem to get the time lately. Busy, busy, busy!'

There was an uncomfortable silence. Mark decided he'd better make an attempt at polite conversation, at least until Brendan returned.

'So, er, what films have you made, then?'

'Oh, I've made many films, Mr Tyler. Titles too numerous to mention without running the risk of boring you rigid.'

'Would I have seen any of them?'

Winston reached up and removed his shades. He stared at Mark for a moment. He had tiny black eyes, like a bird. 'You might,' he said.

Mark considered this for a moment.

'Have any been showing recently?' he ventured.

'Oh, my films are *always* showing, Mr Tyler. Made directly for the video market, you see. So I'm unencumbered by the petty restrictions imposed by distributors and theatrical outlets. I like to think of myself as one of the great maverick film directors, don't I, Mr Springer?'

Mr Springer's head jerked up and down again, indicating agreement.

'Video, eh?' Mark was gradually putting two and two together. He wished Brendan would hurry back with those drinks.

'Ah, I see you looking dubious, young sir! But believe me, the cinema is an outmoded concept, doomed to die within the decade. All these multiplexes springing up like cancers across the land, they're simply the last gasp of a doomed empire. People prefer to watch their films at home, Mr Tyler, in the comfort of their favourite chair, where they can take a quick break for a nice cup of Rosie Lee. And naturally, if they have specialized tastes, it's so much easier to . . .'

Brendan appeared, carrying a tray of drinks.

'Sorry I was so long,' he apologised. 'I only had a fifty-pound note and they couldn't find any change.' He set down the tray and pulled up another stool. 'So . . . Winston. Do you mind if I call you Winston?'

'Not at all, dear boy, not at all!'

'I trust you've had the opportunity to take another look at my outline?'

'I have, Brendan, and I don't mind telling you I'm terribly excited about this project. In fact, we're both terribly excited, aren't we, Mr Springer?'

'Yeah,' said Springer. Mark was vaguely surprised, he'd assumed by this point that Mr Springer didn't actually possess anything as mundane as a voice. He then watched as Springer tilted a pint of bitter to his mouth and demolished half of its contents in one mighty gulp.

'Great!' enthused Brendan. 'So you're saying we've got a green light?'

'We've got an amber light,' Winston corrected him. 'You see, I feel that the story has great potential. But I also feel that there are certain revisions needed that would help tailor it more closely to our requirements.'

'Oh, sure,' said Brendan good-naturedly.

Mark threw him a cautionary glance, but he didn't seem to notice. Brendan was so excited by all this that he'd agree to just about anything.

Mark decided to pitch in. 'Since I'd be the one making these changes—'

'Revisions,' Winston corrected him.

'Since I'll be the one making them, could you give us an idea how extensive they'll be?'

'Oh, not much at all, really.' He held out a hand and Mr Springer produced a slim leather portfolio from under his coat. Winston took it, unzipped it with a flourish, and pulled out a couple of crumpled sheets of manuscript paper. 'What we have here at present,' he announced, 'is a charming, slightly vulgar story of lost innocence.' He read from the text on the page. 'An eighteen-year-old girl's first halting steps towards womanhood, set against the turbulent backdrop of the 1960s.' He paused to take a delicate sip of his drink, then he put down the paper and continued. 'But markets have moved on a little since this project was first conceived. Audiences have become jaded, harder to shock. So, first of all, I think we might need to, er, spice it up a bit.'

Here we go, thought Mark. *He only makes films for the video market.*

'I think that's no problem,'said Brendan. 'Tell you the truth, I've toned it down a bit from the original version. I thought it might frighten some people off.'

'Not a bit of it, dear boy!' Winston seemed positively outraged by the idea. 'That only applies to the *majors*, those organisations shackled by outmoded concepts of morality. We needn't concern ourselves with their restrictions. *We* are free agents!'

'Thas' right,' growled Mr Springer. He grinned, displaying rows of misshapen teeth which appeared to be jostling each other for a prime position in his mouth. Mark found something vaguely chilling about that grin.

'OK,' he said quietly. 'So you want it to be more daring?'

'And more *often*,' Winston added. 'In this outline, there's what — three sex scenes? We could easily squeeze in seven or eight, without changing the film's message in any way.'

Mark and Brendan exchanged glances. Even Brendan was beginning to come out of his initial euphoric reverie.

'Isn't that rather a lot of sex?' he asked. 'I mean, this story is—'

'Magnificent!' interrupted Winston. 'Moving, funny, heartwarming — all of these things. But there's no reason why those qualities should be lost just because there's a lot of *boffing*, now is there?'

'I suppose not,' mumbled Brendan.

'Then, of course, we'd like to lose the Sixties setting.'

This was enough of a bombshell to shake up even Brendan. 'What?' he cried. 'But that's the whole point of it!'

'My dear boy, don't underestimate this project. Your story has a universal message, it has relevance to *any* time sphere. Why not bring it smack up to date, here and now? Besides, with a historical setting you're opening a whole can of worms. Costumes, hair-styles, locations, research. A contemporary setting would make it . . .'

'Cheaper?' offered Mark caustically.

'. . . less problematic,' finished Winston.

'Well, I don't know,' said Brendan. 'That's rather a lot to think about. I assume that's all your suggestions?'

Winston shook his head. 'There's one other revision, actually. Mr Springer and I both feel it's the most important of all. The age of the heroine.'

'What, you think she's not old enough?' asked Brendan.

'On the contrary, we feel she should be *younger*.'

'How much younger?' cried Brendan.

'Sixteen?' suggested Mark, trying to be helpful.

Winston shook his head.

'That would make her a veritable *grandmother* in these liberated times.' He leaned forward across the table and Mark could see tiny beads of sweat glittering on his upper lip. 'We thought somewhere about twelve.'

There was a long moment of shocked silence.

'Christ, isn't that a bit young?' asked Brendan innocently.

'Oh, yes,' agreed Winston. 'The golden age.'

'You'd . . . you'd never find an actress who could carry it off,' argued Mark.

But Winston was shaking his head.

'Gentlemen, gentlemen, this coy facade is all very touching, but it doesn't convince for one moment. We all know you wouldn't have contacted me unless you had a taste for chicken. Of course I can get you the right girl. I can get any number of them.' He opened the portfolio again and took out a series of large colour prints. He spread them out on the table in front of Mark and Brendan. They stared down at them in mute disbelief. 'These kids range from around eight to twelve years,' Winston explained quietly. 'This boy is only seven but, as you can see from the attention he's showing the elderly gentleman, he's quite experienced for his tender years. Now, I had *this* girl in mind for the lead role. She's eleven, but she has the most soulful eyes I've ever seen.'

At first Mark was stunned; then he felt profound disgust. He had sniffed out the hint of pornography pretty quickly, but had assumed it would be of an adult nature. He could never have anticipated anything like this. Turning to look at Brendan, he was relieved to see that his friend also seemed horrified.

'Brendan,' he said quietly. 'This may be an odd time to ask the question, but *how* did you happen to get in touch with these people?'

'An advert in a contact magazine.' Brendan's voice sounded slow, clumsy, as though he was suffering from shellshock. 'They were soliciting for scripts, and I thought—'

'You idiot!' snapped Mark. 'Didn't it occur to you that there might be something dodgy about all this?'

'Here, just a minute!' protested Winston. 'There's nothing dodgy about our outfit. I can assure you!' He glanced at Brendan. 'What are you trying to pull here? I told you over the phone that we made chicken movies. You said that was fine by you, and that Mr Tyler would also be interested.'

'Well, yes, but . . . I thought you just meant movies with . . . with chicks in them. You know, young women? Not *little girls*.'

Winston gave him a look of sheer disbelief.

'Either you're incredibly naive or unbelievably stupid,' he observed.

'I'd plump for the latter,' said Mark grimly.

Now Winston began to gather up the photographs from the table top.

'Clearly there's been a serious misunderstanding,' he said primly. 'I suggest we all go home and forget this ever happened.'

'Hang on a minute!' snapped Brendan, fired by disappointment. He put a restraining hand on Winston's arm. 'You can't just leave it like that!'

'Yes, we can,' Mark assured him. He had seen the furious scowl coming from Mr Springer, and decided that discretion was the better part of valour. He put an arm around Brendan's shoulders. 'What say we just walk out of here, right now?'

'No fucking way! This kind of garbage is illegal!'

Winston rolled his eyes towards the ceiling. 'You don't say?' he murmured. 'Listen, there's nothing you can do about that. Winston Short isn't my real name, and five minutes from now I'll have a new one . . .'

'If you get out of here *alive!*' snarled Brendan. 'If you think we're just going to forget about this, you must be crazy!'

'Oh dear,' said Winston Short. 'Mr Springer?'

The big man was aptly named. Before Brendan even had time to react Mr Springer sprang. The meaty splat as his fist connected with Brendan's nose seemed to fill the entire pub. Brendan's stool pivoted backwards and he went sprawling to the floor. Mark, who still had an arm around his friend's shoulders, went unhappily along for the ride. They landed heavily, and lay there for an instant, stunned. Brendan's nose was pumping blood down the front of Mark's second-best suit, and he was making a kind of groaning sound. Mark sat up quickly, and began to help Brendan to his feet.

OK, he thought, *We'll just leave quietly and . . .*

But Brendan came suddenly awake and started mouthing off, his blocked nose making him sound doubly aggressive.

'You fuggin perverts! You dirty fuggers! I gonna ged the police on to you!'

Things seemed to accelerate further from that point. Springer grabbed an empty pint glass and smashed its top against the edge of the table, leaving a jagged, stabbing weapon clutched in one huge hand. Winston meanwhile, continued carefully tucking the photographs back into his portfolio, seemingly unconcerned by the disturbance around him. He was humming a businesslike little tune to himself.

'Oh *shit!*' said Brendan bleakly, as Springer advanced on him.

'Come on, for Chrissakes, let's *go*!' Mark pulled at Brendan's arm and dragged him towards the exit, aware, out of the corner of his eye, that the landlord and the few other punters present were watching the proceedings with passive interest. Brendan, though, was in that risky frame of mind where he was determined to get the last word in.

'You *scumbags*!' he screamed.

Mr Springer was evidently now on a short fuse. With a roaring noise he charged at Brendan just as Mark managed to pull his friend out through the swing doors of the entrance. When Mr Springer lashed out with his improvised weapon, it caught the door-frame and shattered into fragments. The door slammed shut behind the fugitives and they heard a bellow of mingled pain and rage from the other side.

'If we both jump on him, we've god a good chance!' snorted Brendan bloodily.

'Fuck that!' snapped Mark.

He turned and fled along the street. Brendan stood for a moment, staring after him in surprise, then followed suit. Behind them, the swing door burst open again, and the huge, crombie-clad figure came lumbering in pursuit. It was clutching one bleeding hand against its massive chest.

'Oy!' he roared. 'Come 'ere, you two!'

This struck Mark as a particularly stupid request. He hurried on along the high street, weaving in and out of the pedestrians and tourists, desperately looking around for some avenue of escape. He glanced over his shoulder to see Brendan toiling along in pursuit, one hand still clutched to his bleeding nose. Springer was only a short distance behind him, and making ground fast.

'Come on!' yelled Mark.

He nearly collided headlong with a plump woman shopper. He weaved to one side at the last instant and was just congratulating himself on his good reactions when he tripped over the tartan shopping trolley she was dragging behind her. He fell heavily to the pavement amidst a jumble of spilled shopping. He rolled awkwardly on the concrete, skinning his knees and elbows, tried to scramble to his feet but was hit by the hurtling figure of Brendan, who was going too fast to take evasive action. They went sprawling again, crushing most of the woman's shopping beneath them. Mark felt a tomato squash under his hand. He groaned, raised himself on to his hands and knees. The woman started shouting incoherently at him but he was aware only of Mr Springer closing in for the kill, a triumphant grin on his face. Mark saw to his horror that Springer now had an old-fashioned cut-throat razor in his uninjured hand. It was the sight of this that galvanised him into action. Clambering to his feet, his hands closed instinctively on the metal handles of the shopping trolley. As Springer flew towards him, he swung the contraption at the man's cropped head, striking him square in the face. One of the metal rails clanged against his clenched teeth. Springer reeled back with an oath, stepped on a fallen soft drink's can and skidded on to his backside, blood oozing from his broken mouth. Mark turned back, stooped to help Brendan to his feet. He spotted a black cab some thirty yards away, on the other side of the busy street, just dropping off two passengers outside an Italian restaurant.

'Taxi!' He saw a gap in the traffic and plunged across the road, waving his arms like a madman. The cab was revving up to leave, but the driver must have glimpsed Mark in the rear-view mirror. He made it to the rear door, flung it open and dived inside. Brendan was still stuck on the other side of the street, waiting for a gap in the traffic – running to and fro in blind panic. Mark saw that Mr Springer was back on his feet, still holding the vicious razor in his left hand.

'Move it! He'll cut you!' yelled Mark, beckoning.

Brendan stared back at him helplessly, looking like a doomed rabbit caught in the headlights of an oncoming car. Then he seemed to realize that it was now or never. He closed his eyes and lunged out into the traffic. Cars screeched to a halt only inches away from him, but he kept running. Mr Springer went after him, only a short distance behind. Mark glanced forwards at the taxi driver, now looking back over his shoulder in consternation.

'Start moving slowly,' Mark advised him.

'Look, guv, I don't know about this.'

'Ten quid bonus.'

The man looked thoughtful. 'Make it twenty?' he suggested.

'*Done!*' said Mark. 'Now *please* . . .'

The cabbie put the vehicle into gear, and started to move slowly forward. Brendan was sprinting up the road like a champion nearing the winning tape. He threw himself into the cab and attempted to slam the door closed, but it was intercepted by a large hand that left a bloody paw-print on the glass. Springer then reached in with the razor and slashed at Brendan's face. Brendan squawked, threw up an arm to try and protect himself. The razor sliced through the fabric of his jacket sleeve and shirt, and found the flesh beneath. He gave a yelp of mingled pain and fear.

Mark leaned across and aimed a desperate punch at Springer's face. His knuckles found the big man's recently broken teeth, and Springer grunted, dropping the razor to the floor of the cab. He threw a retaliatory punch at Mark, catching him on the side of the head, making sparks dance in front of his eyes. Then his left hand grabbed a handful of Brendan's hair.

For a few moments it was anybody's fight. The taxi was picking up speed, Mr Springer was galloping determinedly alongside, a flurry of punches, kicks and curses being exchanged through the still open door.

Then Springer stumbled, lost a few paces, and at last Mark was able to pull the door shut. Springer had to content himself with a final kick at the vehicle's rear bumper with his steel-capped Doc's – then the taxi was accelerating away.

They stared fearfully back at his dwindling figure through the rear window, as he stood in the middle of the road, waving his fists above his head and shouting at the top of his prodigious lungs. For some reason, Mark was reminded of *King Kong*.

'Jesus,' he muttered. They sank down into the back seat with relief. 'That was close.'

'Fuggin' perverts,' muttered Brendan. He took out a handkerchief and dabbed gingerly at his mashed nose. 'If that's the film business, they can keep it!'

Mark shook his head. 'Why is it, Brendan, that I never learn by my mistakes?'

'Whad'ya mean?'

'Time after time I let you talk me into these stupid situations, and time after time we end up in the shit. Somehow, I never have the sense to say no.'

Brendan shrugged, wiping a clot of blood from his left nostril. 'Hey, maybe we should stop at the next pub? I need a couple of brandies.'

'No, we'll have them back at my place. You're not safe to be out.' He leaned forward to instruct the driver. Then he sat back again and studied Brendan thoughtfully, assessing the remains of his second-best suit. The right sleeve was torn and bloody, the trouser knees were scuffed and grimy where Brendan had fallen.

'How's your arm?'

Brendan inspected it gingerly.

'It's not so bad. The sleeve took the worst of it.' He leaned forward and picked up the cut-throat razor. He inspected it curiously. 'Jesus, it's got my blood on it.' He folded it carefully and slipped it into his pocket. 'Little souvenir,' he announced.

Mark stared at him in disbelief. Already Brendan was turning this sorry disaster into an adventure. He'd soon be regaling his friends with the story in his favourite pub, the razor produced as evidence. 'Look,' he'd say brightly. 'It's still got my blood on it!' Then he'd roll up his sleeve and proudly display the scar on his arm.

'You're mad,' observed Mark. 'Absolutely bloody barking!'

Chapter Nine

It was 2.45 a.m. and Leonard was standing in aisle D, stacking the shelves with cans of Campbell's soup. *Very Andy Warhol*, he thought, and allowed himself a little smile of satisfaction. That was an intelligent thought – the kind of thing he came up with every day of his life. Few people appreciated his intelligence and that was sad for them. In fact, now he came to consider it, only Mother really had any idea of his intellectual capacity. Only Mother. He didn't like to think of a time when she was no longer there close by, because *then* there would be nobody to appreciate him fully.

He had really thought that Mark Tyler would be in tune with him. He had looked forward to them trading thoughts, discussing their joint passions. Leonard had once had it all planned. But that bastard hadn't given him a chance. Godamned stuck-up Brit, frightened of making a genuine commitment to somebody who would have been a true friend. Well, Leonard would show *him*, too. He'd show them all. The rage bubbled deep inside him. His emotions were stirring. He raised a hand to wipe his sleeve across his brow. All night he had felt oddly excited, hot and sweaty, despite the air-conditioning in the mart. It had been a long, slow shift, but in less than fifteen minutes he was free to go.

Rick Devereaux appeared at the far end of the aisle, but Leonard went on with his stacking. Devereaux strode on, a brief mocking grin on his face, but for once he wasn't interested in baiting Leonard. Instead he made for Checkout 4, where Veronica was ringing up some four-packs of beer for a couple of grungy-looking youths in leather jackets. Out of the corner of his eye, Leonard watched as Devereaux leaned in behind Veronica and opened the drawer of her till, doing his routine last check before Bill Fernly came in to replace him. Rick slyly placed a hand on Veronica's butt and she wriggled, and brushed him off, trying not to laugh. The leather boys exchanged knowing glances, paid for their beers, and left.

Leonard smiled grimly. Over the last few weeks, Rick and Veronica had become increasingly blatant about their relationship. Everybody in the store was commenting on it, behind their backs of course. Nobody had much love for Rick, but there were quite a few who had liked Veronica and were sorry that she had got herself mixed up with that greaseball. But there was no accounting for some people's taste.

'Yo, Leonard.'

He cringed instinctively and a can of tomato soup fell sideways and rolled off the shelf. Before it could hit the ground, it was neatly caught by Wayne Hopkins, a skinny, hyperactive youth who normally replaced Leonard after his shift.

'Good reactions,' observed Leonard gratefully. He didn't mind Wayne, who was one of the few people who never avoided him, probably because Wayne was a runty little guy, who was a bit of a misfit himself and got more than his fair share of strife from bullies like Rick Devereaux. More important, Wayne was also an avid Stephen King fan, which at least made him interesting to talk to, even if in a somewhat limited way. Wayne stepped up to the shelf to replace the rescued can.

'What's going down?' he enquired.

Leonard shrugged. 'Not much. Very quiet. Just restocking these shelves. Then there's some cheese to be cut in the storeroom.'

'Wild.' Wayne pulled a face. 'Another few days of this and I'm liable to wrap that cheese-wire around somebody's neck.' He made a bug-eyed expression and glanced down the aisle towards Checkout 4. 'And there's my *numero uno* choice. Jeez, I hate that fuck. Look at him pawing that blonde babe. What I wouldn't give for a slice of that pepperoni!'

Leonard pulled a disapproving face.

'That's not a nice way to talk, Wayne.'

Wayne grinned. 'Well, wash my mouth out with soap and water! Read anything good lately? Hey, any chance of borrowing that *Black Wolf* you was telling me about? I see it's kind of pricey in hardback.'

Leonard shook his head.

'You know I never lend out my books, Wayne. They always come back all dog-eared and grubby.'

'Aww, come on, Leonard. I promise I'll take care of it.'

'Sorry. You'll just have to wait for the p . . . paperback. I don't ever see you lending out your Stephen King's.'

'That's different, man. There, we're talking about my *religion* – if you know what I mean.'

Leonard smiled. 'I know what you mean.' He glanced at his watch.

'Well, I'd better shake a leg. Mother's not feeling too well lately. I promised I'd hurry straight back.'

'You're a reg'lar saint, Leonard. Anybody ever tell you that?'

'All the time. See you, Wayne.'

'Yeah. Same time, same place. Jesus, it's the inevitability that gets to you!'

Wayne picked up on stacking the soup tins as Leonard headed to the back of the store to collect his jacket and sandwich box from the staff room.

'G'night, Leonard!' somebody shouted over.

'Night!' He slipped into his jacket and then walked slowly back out into the main area. He then angled left towards the exit doors, passing a few stragglers coming in for the next shift. As he moved past Checkout 4, Rick was still leaning over Veronica, making a show of helping her bag up her change. He glanced up at Leonard and whispered to her.

'Hey, lookit, the creep's going home to his itsie-bitsie bed.'

'Leave it alone, Rick.' Veronica hissed, flashing Leonard that dazzling smile. But her eyes mocked him.

'Goodnight, Leonard,' she said.

'G . . . goodnight, Veronica.' He moved on to the exit.

'Goodnight, Creepy!' He heard Rick call out, after he had passed through the door. Leonard just smiled. It didn't matter any more. He knew who would have the last laugh.

Leonard stepped out into the muggy morning air and walked across to his parked Camaro, standing in shadow on the edge of the forecourt, beyond the glare of the arc-lamps. He opened up and climbed behind the wheel. He didn't switch on the lights or the engine, but sat there and waited patiently, sweating gradually in the warm interior. Up above the dark silhouette of the mall roof, a full moon hung in the night sky, lightly veined with blue like a ripe, sweaty sphere of Danish cheese. Leonard had read how, in the Middle Ages, people believed that the moon affected people dramatically: turned them mad or changed them into raving beasts. He was beginning to think there might be something in all that.

He gave the ignition a half turn and flicked on the radio, keeping the volume low. In one of those rare flashes of sublime coincidence he heard Screaming Jay Hawkins singing 'I Put A Spell On You'. He sang along with it softly, stressing the line that said 'because you're *mine*'. That's how it was, in a nutshell. Veronica *belonged* to Leonard. She was one of his people – one of his tribe. She might not realise it yet, but Devereaux was entirely the wrong choice for her. He was exploiting some weakness she had, a flaw in her personality, that currently left her open to the approaches of white trash like that. Three nights now, he had watched them grunting and struggling in the back of Rick's Pontiac, unaware that they were being observed. Their liaison was all wrong, but maybe she couldn't yet see that. Leonard would make her see it. He would explain it all to her in time. When she appreciated the depth of his importance for her, she would finally understand.

Veronica linked her arm through Rick's as they strolled out of the exit door. She had thought that shift would never end. Now here it was, the small hours of Saturday morning – and she knew what would happen next. Her body was tingling with excitement. She realized that most of the staff at Olsen's didn't much care for Rick. There were many who bad-mouthed him behind his back, but she didn't worry about that. She knew how he made her *feel* – like she was suddenly alive for the first time in her nineteen years of existence.

Up till now it had been always that same grim ritual of sitting at home each night with her brothers and sisters, watching television, playing some dumb board-game, maybe, if she was lucky, being allowed to go to the local youth centre with some girlfriends, so long as she was back by eleven. Jesus! Her parents were OK, she supposed, but they were living in the Stone Age. Dad was the worst: he could still only think of her as his little girl, even though she was the eldest. And it was Dad who was responsible for her silly name, Veronica. How she hated it! He had explained how she'd been named after some old movie actress called Veronica Lake – he'd had a thing about her back when he was a teenager himself. Veronica had seen one of her old movies on the late show once, and that woman was *unreal*. She had this hair that came down over one eye and a *totally* dorky voice, sounding like she was half asleep. This dumb name was supposed to be a compliment?

The night shifts at Olsen's had proved a boon; even Mom and Dad couldn't complain about her being out late when she was *working*. And everybody had to take their turn at it; it was one of the conditions of their employment. Dad had hummed and hawed about that, pulled a few faces, but in the end he'd had to give permission. Another income was needed to sustain the family, and jobs were hard to find these days. So she'd gone off to Olsen's, and just a few months later along came Rick, and she'd known from that first sly wink that her luck was finally going to change. Oh, sure, he was rough and ready, and he had a mouth on him could cut to the bone when he wanted to, but she admired that confident quality in him, wished that a little would rub off on her. All her life she'd held back from what she really wanted to say to people.

Halfway across the car park, Rick slipped an arm around her shoulders and leaned in to kiss her. She stood with head tilted back, her mouth open to take his tongue, feeling a tingle of excitement rippling through her whole body, coaxing a sick feeling of anticipation from the pit of her stomach. Now his hand was exploring the buttons of her blouse, but she pushed him away, giggling. 'Not here!' she reproached him.

'Why not?' he asked her. 'Why not across the hood of my car, where everyone can see us.'

'It's too cold,' she protested, and he just laughed.

They reached the big, maroon Pontiac. Rick unlocked the door, climbed in behind the wheel. He then threw open the passenger door, and she slid in beside him. Rick started up the engine and clicked on the headlights. The Pontiac glided towards the car-park exit.

He turned left on to the main highway and drove slowly onwards, making the turn that would take them on to the road that skirted the edge of town and went out towards the Marsh. This was little more than an area of wasteland, too swampy for cultivation, and left to run wild. In the daytime the kids of Dennings used it to make hideaways and tree houses, or they dammed streams and went skinny-dipping in the one serviceable swimming hole. At night it became the haunt of courting couples. There were plenty of places amongst the trees where cars could pull in, unobserved from the dirt-track road that bisected the area. It was a popular myth in Dennings that more children had been conceived there than in all the beds in town put together. With this myth firmly in mind, Veronica always insisted on Rick wearing a rubber when they were doing it. She aimed to get herself on the pill just as soon as she could organize it, but that was tricky. If her parents ever found out, there'd be hell to pay. Being staunch Catholics, they believed that sex was something only married people did, and then only to make more kids. Veronica thought of them now, long since tucked up in their bed and dreaming sweet dreams. They wouldn't even wake when she got home, oblivious to whether she came in at two, three or four a.m.

Rick flicked on the radio, but encountered an advertisement for a haemorrhoid cream, some dude asking in a confidential whisper if any of the listeners out there suffered from an 'embarrassing personal problem'. Now, it seemed, help was at hand: 'new improved Preparation H will provide instant relief, and make that maddening itch a thing of the past!'

Rick and Veronica exchanged glances, then burst out laughing.

He fiddled with the dial and eventually found an oldies station,

Sinatra singing 'The Summer Wind'. Rick started miming to it, singing out the side of his mouth, shimmying in his seat. He always made her laugh, and she couldn't remember when she had last had so much fun.

Now Rick was turning off the highway on to the cinder track road that climbed through an avenue of stunted trees. After a few hundred yards he nosed the car into its regular spot, under the cover of a big white oak. There he cut the engine and the lights, and Sinatra's voice vanished along with them. They sat still for a moment, letting their eyes adjust to the darkness, listening to the sounds of the night all around. Through the half-open windows they could hear the occasional whine of insects. Somewhere off to the right, an owl hooted.

Rick turned to smile at her. He pulled a lever and the seats reclined until almost horizontal. Rick had once explained that this was the main reason he'd bought the car, as if wanting her to appreciate that she wasn't the first girl he'd shared this experience with. She didn't worry about that; the thought of him having lots of girls out here in the darkness made all of it even more exciting for her. Suddenly he reached out and pulled her close, crushing her lips beneath his as she returned his embrace, wanting to bury herself in the warm, manly smell of him.

At the back of Veronica's mind was always the hope that he might take her away from her parents' home, and let her move into the bachelor apartment he rented on the other side of Dennings. She knew that was a long shot, but she figured that if she did enough to please him, and got him so he depended on her above all his other girlfriends, he might just be tempted. And she wanted *nothing* more than to get out of her parents' ever-vigilant clutches. She pulled away from him now, and reached out a hand to untie her hair, letting it fall across her shoulders. She knew how he liked to look at her hair, how it turned him on to touch, to smell . . .

Rick pulled her towards him again, his hungry mouth devouring her moist tongue. She reached down a hand and began to unbutton his trousers, taking her own sweet time, not wanting to fumble like she had the first couple of times. Her best friend Amy had told her that this was what men liked best in the world.

Now Rick was guiding her face down into his lap, and she went to it eagerly, wanting to master the technique, wanting to be the best he had ever had. She heard him groan as her mouth engulfed him and, glancing up, she could see him stretch out above her, his head tilted back on the seat, his white throat stretched taut, Adam's apple moving up and down in a steady rhythm that matched her own . . .

And then they heard the howl.

80

Veronica stopped what she was doing. She lifted her head to stare at Rick.

'What was that?' she gasped.

He looked puzzled.

'I don't know. Maybe just a dog . . .'

It sounded again, quite close, a long, drawn-out wail like some mad beast howling at the moon. Veronica sat up, frightened now.

'Sounds more like a wolf!' she said.

Rick frowned. 'A coyote maybe.' But he looked a little worried himself. 'You get them out here sometimes. They come down from the hills, hunting for food.'

'Uh . . . are they dangerous?'

He glanced at her slyly. 'They can be,' he admitted. 'I've heard cases of a bunch of 'em chewin' on some drunk they found . . .'

Veronica muttered an oath and pressed secure the lock on the passenger door. She looked over at Rick imploringly. 'Maybe you better lock yours, too,' she told him.

He reached out a hand as if to do so, then stopped. Then he began to laugh, his eyes mocking. 'Hoo boy, you fell for that one, didn't'cha! Coyotes!' He threw back his head and laughed out loud, delighted at her panic. 'Oh boy!' He slapped his leg. 'Oh Rick, it sounds like a wolf!' he mimicked.

'You bastard!' she shrieked, aiming a playful slap at his face.

And then they both froze in their seats. There had been another sound, just beside the driver's door. A low, guttural growl that seemed to reverberate even inside the car.

In the darkness, Rick's face suddenly turned startlingly white. He opened his mouth to say something and then, with heart-stopping suddenness, his door was wrenched open and something grabbed him by the collar of his jacket, pulling him out into the blackness.

Veronica sat stunned, her heart hammering in her throat. Through the open door, she could see Rick struggling to stand upright. But it was much too dark to see anything beyond.

'What the fuck?' she heard him mutter.

Again, that deep resonant growling. Rick gave an exclamation and took a quick step backwards, slamming up against the car so hard that it quivered on its wheels.

'What is it, Rick?' cried the girl desperately.

Rick glanced in at her. 'Nothing, honey. Just some asshole thinks it's Halloween night.' But his fright was evident behind the show of bluster. He suddenly turned round as a figure approached him. 'You basketcase!' he yelled. 'Get the fuck away from here!'

A long silence now. Veronica could hear the buzzing of insects by her window.

Then Rick shouted out again, his voice rising several octaves. 'I fuckin' warned you, man. Now, I'm gonna count to three, right – and if you're still here . . . Well, you've had it. One . . . two . . .'

Rick's next word sounded something like 'Gak!'

Veronica could only sit in terror, desperately listening for the reassuring sound of his voice. Instead she heard a sudden spattering like liquid hitting the dry earth. He must be taking a leak out there. Maybe this was some stunt he'd organized to freak her out, getting one of his pals to wait for them out here in the darkness. Sure. Any second now he would lean back in at the door, laughing his guts out at her consternation. 'Hoo boy, Veronica, you sure fell for that one, didn'tcha?'

She began shifting in her seat so she could peer out the open driver's door – see what the hell he was *doing* out there.

Suddenly, something heavy struck the car's bonnet, making the Pontiac dip on its front axle.

Veronica screamed as a face thudded into the windscreen, its features distorted as it pressed up against the glass. It was Rick, his eyes bulging in shock, his open mouth working spasmodically, as though he was trying to speak to her. His teeth made a squeaking noise as they ground against the windscreen and his hands came up to claw at it, as though he was trying to tunnel his way through. His hands were wet with blood, and when his position shifted slightly, a jet of red squirted upwards across the glass, half obscuring the bulging face. The liquid was pumping out of a ragged hole in his throat.

She tried desperately to scream then, but at that moment a gloved hand came curling around the frame of the open door. Then she saw the face looking in at her: dark and hairy, with an open mouth framed by rows of jagged, bloody teeth.

Veronica shrank back against the passenger door, staring in voiceless horror at the thing that was crawling into the car beside her – creeping in on hands and knees. And all the time, Rick continued staring in at her through the windscreen, the car thudding as his body bucked and kicked on the hood . . . as he gasped and choked his life away.

Veronica fumbled behind her and her fingers found the door handle, but it wouldn't open. In her panic she forgot that she had locked it minutes earlier. She panted; unable to control her breathing. Now a gloved hand extended towards her face; it was stroking her hair with its leather fingertips, the face was pressing up against hers, its warm coppery breath gusting over her. The thing began to speak to her in its deep guttural voice, the words made clumsy by the huge teeth that distended its lips.

'Dob be afraid. I ony wad to lub you!'

That was when at last she found her scream. Closing her eyes she threw back her head, so that her white throat stretched out straight to show the vein where her life blood slowly pulsed . . .

Chapter Ten

Leonard let himself in the front door, and stood for several minutes in the darkened hallway, waiting for his harsh breathing and the sledgehammer beat of his heart to subside.

The house slept fitfully, ancient brick and wood creaking mournfully beneath the assault of the night winds. After a while, he could hear Mother's resonant snore, up there in her room. Turning, he closed and locked the door behind him. He took off his shoes and ascended the staircase. Reaching the landing, he crept down the hallway to the bathroom. He went in, locked the door and switched on the light.

The face that scowled at him from the washstand mirror was a fright, its beard stiff with coagulated blood, no longer red but a deep nut-brown. The shirt front was also spattered with blood, the leather gloves soaked with it. Already the violent incident had the vague, shadowy quality of a half-remembered dream.

Leonard pulled the curtain across the bathtub and turned on the shower. He usually showered once he got home from work, so Mother wouldn't think it odd if she woke now. He stripped off all his clothes and laid them out on the tiled floor, inspecting each item carefully for traces of blood. Finding a smear on the heel of his left shoe, he wiped it away with a damp flannel. He bundled the shirt up tightly, for disposal at the earliest opportunity. His other garments would be fine after a wash, he decided.

He stepped beneath the shower flow now and began to soap away the blood from his face and hands, paying particular attention to beneath his fingernails. He hadn't planned to hurt Veronica, only to hold her, kiss her, persuade her . . . In the end it had been necessary to shut her up. Oh, he'd always meant to bite Rick. But not Veronica. He loved her, could never have dreamed of hurting her. But however much he coaxed her, she would not stop screaming . . . Somehow, it had simply become necessary. Then, as he'd bitten into the taut white curve of her throat, as his teeth had locked together deep in her flesh, and he'd felt the abrupt pulsing of hot, coppery-tasting blood in his mouth . . . then an exquisite, orgasmic shudder had rippled through him, and he'd lain there, stroking Veronica's beautiful hair and whispering her name, over and over . . . wishing that she would speak to him . . .

Abruptly, he had come back to reality. He was sprawled in a strange car, lying atop a still, silent woman – both of them covered in her blood. Panic rose within him as he imagined being discovered out there, perhaps another courting couple happening along and seeing him, picked out like a ghoul in the glare of their headlights. He had leapt out and run back to his car like a frightened animal.

Standing in the shower, he cast his mind back, moment by moment, to try and recall anything he might have forgotten. No, nothing occurred to him. Finally he reached up a hand and took out his false teeth. He gulped a mouthful of water and swilled it around, before spitting it out. He noticed how the water came out pink. Then, he crouched over the edge of the bath-tub to his trousers, and extracted the round wooden box from the pocket. He opened it to remove his killing teeth, gripping them in the palm of one hand while he scrubbed at them with a nailbrush to remove those stubborn shreds of flesh lodged between the tightly-spaced fangs. He continued scrubbing till they sparkled, the long sharp canines and jagged incisors glittering hungrily.

Leonard had lost nearly all his teeth by the age of fourteen; or, rather, he'd had them *taken*. His father had been a little too zealous with his son's dental treatment. From an early age he had instigated regular monthly check-ups for Leonard, and was proud of the fact that his boy's teeth were in perfect condition. But then one day, when he was around ten years old, Leonard had got into a baseball game with some neighbourhood kids and had caught a careless backswing full in the mouth. His front teeth had exploded like firecrackers, and he was carried back to the house, bloodied and groaning, for his father to tend to. He had been obliged to sit there snivelling in the big leather chair while Dad probed and prodded at the broken stumps, digging for the nerves, his stern eyes cold behind the frames of his spectacles, the round metal reflector shining like an alien moon on his forehead.

'Now, don't be a baby, Leonard. I'll make you replacements that will be just as good as your own teeth. Better! They'll never hurt you, never go bad. They'll last you a lifetime.'

Dad loved making dentures. He had always hankered after being a dental technician, and had often expressed regrets that he'd spent so much time training to be a mere dentist. He was not yet really qualified to do the job, he could only take impressions and send them off to a

86

laboratory, but it was a craft that he was determined to gain mastery of. He was doing a correspondence course on the subject, had all the equipment he needed, and for the first time in his life he had a live subject to work on.

Dad was also a perfectionist. He wasn't happy with the first set he made for Leonard, nor the second, nor the third. Finally he announced himself satisfied with the results. Leonard was just congratulating himself on having survived an unpleasant ordeal, when his next monthly check-up revealed that he needed another extraction . . .

He couldn't believe it. He sat there in the chair, trying to protest, knowing that he felt no pain from the tooth, that he had eaten no sweets for a whole month, scrubbed and soaked his teeth religiously after every meal. The tooth *couldn't* be bad, it just couldn't! But Dad was adamant, already preparing his needles and cutting tools.

'What's a little discomfort, Leonard? With modern technology, we can improve on nature. Now, open wide . . .'

Leonard wanted to say, 'But Daddy, the tooth doesn't hurt, how can it be bad if it doesn't hurt?'

But already the needles were spiking the inside of his mouth with Novacaine, turning it into a clumsy dead thing that no longer obeyed him. And then Dad was filling it with all that metal junk, cranking the jaws wider and wider until Leonard thought his face would split across the middle. And now Dad had the tooth in his grip and he was pulling, heaving with a force that threatened to lift Leonard clear out of the chair, tear his whole skeleton out of his skin and leave him curled up like a discarded flesh-coloured balloon on the leather upholstery. And, for the first time, Leonard noticed how excited his father looked, his face red, his breathing hard, small beads of sweat on his top lip. Then, worst of all, there was the awful sound of the tooth breaking up inside his head, bits of enamel bouncing off the roof of his mouth, the roots being dug out of the possessive gums, and his mouth filling with the thick, sweet taste of his own blood. As the months rolled by, it was a taste he grew well used to.

It was around this time too that Dad started coming to his room at night. Leonard would be roused from sleep in the early hours to find Dad standing beside his bed, gazing down at the boy with the same wild look he had when he was extracting teeth. He would take hold of Leonard's hair with one hand, pulling him roughly up out of the bed, while his other hand fumbled with the cord of his pyjamas. He always said the same thing, in a voice that was hoarse with excitement.

'Leonard, take them out. Take out your teeth.'

Leonard did what his father made him do, enduring the humiliating ordeal, the same way he endured those monthly torture sessions in the chair. And he began to nurture a fierce, cold hatred deep in his heart and he was calmly waiting for an opportunity to revenge himself.

By the age of fourteen, the few real teeth that Leonard had left were needed to anchor his false ones in position. Dad seemed to take solace by stepping up the levels of abuse. He started coming to Leonard's room more regularly, every few weeks now. The boy was too frightened to sleep, he would lie awake waiting for the old man's step on the landing. Finally, he could stand it no more. When Dad purchased a powerful new electric drill, Leonard saw his opportunity. He crept down to the surgery that night and rewired the mains plug, using Dad's *Home Handyman* book for reference, with special regard to the page labelled 'How *Not* to Wire A Plug!' The next morning, Dad switched on the apparatus to test it out – and was dead seconds later. That same night, Leonard slept sounder than he had done in years.

It never really occurred to him that he was now a murderer. All these years later he could still vividly remember walking slowly behind his father's coffin, keeping that sober expression on his face, his hands clasped devoutly in front of him, when what he really wanted to do was dance with joy. He was *dead*! The old plunderer was dead. And if there really was a hell, he was down there right now, maybe having his own teeth pulled out one by one by some vengeful demon with a pair of red-hot pincers.

Once exercised, Leonard's capacity for cruelty seemed to lie dormant for many years, only surfacing in quiet moments when he found himself alone with some luckless cat that he could torture. It was his horrifying ordeal at the hands of Ritchie Burke and crew which seemed to rekindle the hatred, perhaps because in that case he was never allowed the satisfaction of direct revenge. In an attempt to make her son's life less lonely, his well-meaning mother provided him with a puppy. But after a few days, it went missing. When it became evident that the dog was never going to show up again, another one was purchased to replace it. That, too, vanished inside of a couple of weeks. Over the years, a whole string of Leonard's pets disappeared without trace, or else died of some mysterious ailment. Though adept at looking suitably mystified by it all, he knew only too well what had happened to the wretched creatures, and if his mother had managed better on her feet, she might have discovered the spot at the bottom of the garden where her son buried what was left of them after he had finished his experiments.

Then, years later, in his early twenties, Leonard found himself by chance in the cellar where his father's textbooks and equipment were still stored under white dustsheets. And as he ran his fingers over the familiar equipment, an intriguing idea shaped itself in his mind.

During the ensuing years, by studying his father's textbooks, he taught himself to construct spare dentures. At first he was simply seeking to spare himself the horror of further visits to the local dentist for replacements – visits that still recalled his worst nightmares. But as he grew more experienced with the techniques, he began to enjoy experimenting – making up plates with bigger teeth or unusual formations, noting how they changed his looks, even his personality, and made him feel more confident, more virile.

Eventually, and inevitably considering his long-term obsession with horror he made himself a set of vampire fangs, and spent hours studying his reflection in the mirror, noting how potent these made him feel – more powerful than he could ever remember. And then, one day, he knew exactly what he needed: a set of teeth that were capable of rending and tearing and vanquishing his enemies. So he set about designing and constructing them, taking months of trial and error to get them just right. These teeth were porcelain, not the softer plastic used for modern dentures. He'd chosen the very largest from his Dad's selections, then filed and polished them gradually into shape, fixing the plates on to a metal articulator so that he could get the teeth to interlock correctly. After much experimentation, he had achieved a set of dentures that nestled comfortably inside his mouth, while allowing his lips to close over them. But there was no real strength in them. Even biting into a sandwich, he found that they slipped about alarmingly. That's when he added a couple of refinements: cast metal frames with strong loops that clicked into place around his back molars, and ingenious gold hinges that linked the upper and lower plates together to make them rigid and powerful. Now he found that he could bite into a tough apple without problems.

At last he had created the perfect killing teeth, but how could he test them out? Smouldering at the back of his mind like a dull ache, the urge grew and prodded at him. First it had been the animals. After all, they were already his regular victims. Birds, cats, the occasional small dog soon fell prey to his attentions. He quickly learned to relish the sweet taste of warm blood flooding his mouth, the sense of power that came only from ending a life. For a while he had been merely a willing prey to these patternless urges and cravings. But then came the day when he first picked up *Black Wolf*, that guiding masterpiece created by a soul-mate to put into focus all his churning emotions and deepest instincts – to reveal to him his true self. His previous toyings with human kind had been half-hearted: something had made him shy away. The old chicken farmer . . . the young girl he had stumbled across that night. As she had lain unconscious beneath him, and he had leaned over to bite into the bare flesh of her thigh, it was like suddenly he was a god – he had the power of life and death over her. In retrospect he realised that had been Black Wolf rising up within him, filling him with his new power.

But tonight had been different. Tonight he had been totally in control, and his killing teeth had at last claimed their first human victims. Now he *truly* was Black Wolf made flesh! Yet Veronica's death had been an oversight. If she had only stayed calm, listened to him. If only she had understood what he could offer her . . .

As Leonard continued to scrub the special dentures clean of Veronica's life blood, a powerful sadness filled him. His broad shoulders began to move, shaking with increasing violence as grief overpowered him. His eyes filled with stinging tears that were dashed away by the stream of hot water that kept falling on to his bowed head.

He realized that he was crying for Veronica; crying because she had been his blood sister, his soul-mate too, and he would never see her again . . .

Chapter Eleven

Summer had finally kicked in with a vengeance. Covent Garden sweltered in the June heat, and crowds of eager tourists milled around its cobbled walkways, swarmed in and out of its shops. Here they mingled, Japanese, Americans, and even the occasional Brit, many of them dressed in the garish shorts and T-shirt combinations that were seemingly approved dress whenever the thermometer lifted those few magical degrees.

Mark wouldn't have been seen dead in a pair of shorts, but he reflected that he should have worn something cooler than the jeans, sweatshirt and trainers he was currently sporting. He was sitting on a wooden bench in Neals Yard, waiting for Sarah. She had suggested this was a good place to meet for lunch. Mark remained doubtful. The converted red-brick warehouses flanking the yard featured a half-dozen takeaway counters where food was dispensed soup-kitchen style. But all of them boasted impressive queues, waiting for service. And the menus chalked up on boards by the open doorways appeared to feature just the same three ingredients: mung beans, aduke beans and lentils. The cooks employed by the various establishments had managed to coax them into a bewildering variety of casseroles, curries and quiches, but to Mark's mind a lentil was still a lentil, when all was said and done. Sarah was far from being a vegetarian, but she had been indulging in a health kick lately. Mark wondered if it was an appropriate time to put his foot down and demand something more carnivorous.

He glanced up, to see Sarah approaching through the crowds. She was dressed in a sober two-piece suit in a classic houndstooth check, having just come from an important meeting with her publishers. Lugging a large portfolio, she looked hot and harassed, and not as glad to see him as he would have liked. Sarah collapsed on to the bench beside him with a groan of relief and stowed the portfolio to one side.

'What a bloody awful morning!' she exclaimed. 'Got a fag to spare?'

Mark frowned. She'd been cadging a lot of cigarettes off him lately, yet steadfastly refused to admit she had acquired a habit. Her argument seemed to be that so long as she wasn't actually *buying* the things, she wasn't really a smoker. Mark fished out his Marlboros and offered her one, then took one himself.

'It's customary to greet your beloved with a kiss,' he told her reproachfully.

She grimaced, but gave him a grudging peck on the cheek. Then she leaned forward and accepted a light, puffing out clouds of smoke that briefly surrounded her in a hazy grey halo.

'Bloody publishers!' she growled.

Mark tried not to smile. 'I take it your meeting wasn't as fruitful as you'd hoped.'

'You take it correctly. That bloody Moran woman! I could pull her fucking ears off!'

She was referring to the commissioning editor at Sackville's, the publishers who had engaged Sarah to illustrate *Mortimer Rabbit*.

'But I thought you *loved* her!'

'That was last month, when she loved me! Oh, last time I talked to Ms Moran, she was over the moon with my sketches for Mortimer. I was her blue-eyed girl. I was the next Beatrix bloody Potter! She was looking forward to a long and fruitful relationship . . .'

Mark waggled his eyebrows. 'I didn't realize it was that kind of deal!'

'Oh, har-de-har-har!' She shot him a look of profound irritation and ploughed on with her tirade. 'Now all of a sudden, she's reconsidered. Perhaps the conception of the characters is a little too stylized, a little too childlike.'

'But isn't that the point? It *is* a children's book.'

'Quite. But Ms Moran doesn't see it that way. Children are more sophisticated nowadays, she tells me. They'll want to see characters that are based on observation. Characters that stem from reality.'

'Sounds reasonable,' observed Mark.

'Whose side are you on?' she demanded.

'Yours!' he assured her.

Sarah gave him a sarcastic smile, but continued unfazed.

'Why not go back to the basics? Go to the wild-life parks and zoos, watch David Attenborough on the telly! Make sketches from what you see, search for the ultimate truth of the animals. Then we'll see how to adapt them to the demands of the story.'

Mark frowned. 'Which means?'

'Which means that I've just wasted a month preparing all that bloody work! It's back to the drawing-board, and I mean that in the most literal sense.'

'Oh, that's a shame.'

'A shame?' Sarah puffed out smoke grumpily. 'It's a disaster! I put in all that time – and you saw those drawings; they were really *sweet*. Now I've got to make Mortimer all *realistic*.'

Mark considered for a moment.

'Give him a good dose of myxomatosis,' he suggested. 'Have his cutesy little eyes dripping pus all over his cutesy little face. She'll be begging for your old drawings in five minutes flat.'

Sarah ground the half-finished cigarette under her foot. 'You're gross,' she told him. 'You want to eat now?'

'Well, that's what we're here for.' He glanced at her doubtfully. 'But maybe we should go somewhere with a licence. You look like you could use a couple of drinks. Maybe pizza or pasta and a nice bottle of vino collapso?'

'No way, José! I told you, no more alcohol before six p.m. It's my new regime. And I intend to eat better too.' She cast a critical eye over a menu directly in front of her. 'This mung bean casserole sounds interesting . . .'

'Oh joy,' muttered Mark. He got reluctantly to his feet and followed her to join the queue. 'So, is that it, then?' he asked her.

'Is what it?'

'Is that the extent of your indignation? A couple of moans about Ms Moran and the odd swear word. Aren't you going to fly into a rage and smash up a phonebox, or something like that?'

She shook her head. 'I leave that kind of behaviour to you. Actually, it makes a change for *me* to have a moan. Do you realize, you haven't mentioned your sodding book for over ten minutes?'

He grinned. 'Only because I couldn't get a word in edgeways. But I've made a bit of a breakthrough today.'

'Oh? Worked out how to switch on the word-processor, did we?'

He ignored the dig.

'No, I finally decided which direction to take with *Black Wolf 3*. It's so simple.'

'So what's this great revelation?'

'I'm going to kill the fuckers off. Black Wolf, Star Child, his family, his friends, the whole kit and caboodle. Let them try and demand another instalment after that!'

She studied him for a moment. 'You serious?'

He nodded. 'Never been more serious in my life.'

'You're not even going to leave one teensie-weensie little loophole . . . like Star Child gives birth to a cuddly little puppy at the end – something like that? Leave the door open for *Benji, Son of Black Wolf*?'

'It's tempting, but no. Listen, I decided it was the only way I was

93

going to enjoy writing this damn thing. Inventing ever more unusual ways of wiping them all off the face of the planet. The author's ultimate revenge.'

'Leonard isn't going to like it.'

'Stuff Leonard,' he said coldly.

They were in the doorway now, and gradually nearing the tiled counter. Behind it, a man and a woman stood dispensing food from large metal trays, which they occasionally replenished from ovens behind them. The young man had a cropped head, save for one long blond pigtail which hung straight down the back of his *Friends of the Earth* T-shirt. The woman had curly henna-red hair, the obligatory nose-ring, and was wearing a dress that might have been made out of a potato sack. Both of them were scowling intently at their queue of customers.

'Christ,' muttered Mark, 'whatever happened to service with a smile!'

The people in front moved away, clutching their provisions, and Mark and Sarah stepped up to the counter.

'Mung bean casserole and salad, please,' said Sarah.

The woman began to serve this, slopping a dollop of what looked like lumpy gravy into one polystyrene tub, then scooping a portion of chopped, mixed salad into another.

The man looked inquiringly at Mark.

'*Yes?*' he demanded irritably, as though he'd already been kept waiting for several minutes.

Mark scanned the trays on the hotplate doubtfully, but saw absolutely nothing that inspired him. He ordered pizza and salad and was handed a paper plate.

'What's this?' he asked innocently.

'Lentil and spinach pizza,' said the man behind the counter; and turned his attention to the next in the queue. Glumly, Mark paid for all the food, then followed Sarah back out to the bench which miraculously was still empty. He sat down beside her and poked gingerly in his polystyrene tub with a plastic fork.

He set the pot down and swallowed with difficulty.

'You don't like it, do you?' observed Sarah. 'You've got this thing about vegetarian food . . .'

'I've got nothing against it so long as it's edible!' he protested. 'But this stuff is yuk . . . And why are those people always so hostile?'

She declined to answer, but was now looking pretty hostile herself. He could see irritation glittering in her eyes and realized that they were in that dangerous territory that bordered on having an argument. He should really steer the conversation around to less confrontational topics, but for some reason he didn't feel inclined to.

'How's your casserole?' he asked slyly.

She chewed on a mouthful for some time before answering. 'It's . . . it's really nice,' she said defensively.

'It's horrible. Admit it! Tell you what, let's dump this stuff and go find a nice trattoria. I could murder a *carbonara* . . .'

'No! Look, you're going to have to learn to hold those dodgy appetites in check. Before you know it, you'll be fat and forty with a heart condition. Your trouble, Mark, is you've got a hedonistic streak a mile wide, and it's growing all the time. I blame Brendan for encouraging you.'

Mark glared at her. 'What's it got to do with him?'

'Everything!' She pointed at Mark's face with her fork, as though making a hex sign. 'Basically, he's a rich, spoiled brat who's had every whim indulged since he was old enough to breathe. He kids himself that he's a creative writer, and expects his friends to bail him out of trouble whenever he's in it. Look at that mess he got you into with those perverts in that pub.'

Mark chuckled: 'Actually, it was quite funny.'

'With hindsight, perhaps. But it could have got very ugly. Christ, that bloke had a razor! You could have been seriously injured. And supposing the police had then investigated why you were mixing with villains like that. What would it have done for your credibility as a writer?'

'Fuck that,' he said dismissively. 'Brendan's a mate.'

'Oh, well, that makes everything all right, I suppose. If you can't see when people are *using* you . . .'

'Using me?'

'Yes.' Sarah set down her unfinished plate. Her mood seemed to be slipping rapidly. 'Let's face it, what did the little shit do? Only proposed you as the author of some dodgy project without even getting your OK. I mean, that's such a slimy thing to do. But he knew full well that you'd just sit there and let him get away with it!'

'Sarah, that's just Brendan. He . . .'

'Oh, you're unbelievable! Can't you see that's exactly how he always gets away with it? Because idiots like you let him. It makes me want to vomit.'

Mark watched her warily for a moment, wondering why she was so het up.

'Calm down,' he advised her at last. 'What's all this about?'

'You know what it's about! I hate to see you being *exploited*!'

He shook his head. 'No, that's not it. I mean, you've never been particularly fond of Brendan. I know that. But this is different. You're angry about something else, and you're projecting it on to him.'

'Perhaps you could tell me how it is that, despite the fact that you're so busy working on your wretched book, you can still find time to go along with Brendan's crazy stunts . . . And yet you somehow can't find any time to work on our project.'

Mark winced. He should have seen that one coming.

'That's not really fair,' he protested. 'Brendan didn't leave me much choice, did he?'

'Oh, then perhaps that's what I should do? Go to some publishers and tell them that I've got you all signed up to work on *The Jumblies* with me? You'd be furious if I did.'

'Well, of course I would! I was bloody annoyed with Brendan, too. But I don't understand what all the fuss is about. I've already promised I'll do the book as soon as I've got more time.'

'Well, thanks a million! Nice of you to find time eventually for my humble little project. So I'll just hang around, shall I, till you've got a spare weekend?'

Mark glared at her.

'You're being unreasonable,' he observed. 'All I'm saying is I'm committed to this project first, and—'

'And you can't be bothered wasting time on anything to do with me.'

'Sarah, nobody's saying that!' He was beginning to lose his grip on his own temper now. He could feel it slipping through his hands like a strand of frayed rope. 'I'll do your bloody book when I've got the time, OK?'

'No, it's not OK!' she retorted. 'You've never rated what I do, have you? You've always thought of my work as trivial.'

'What the fuck is this?' he snarled. 'Feel-sorry-for-yourself week?' She laughed bitterly.

'Oh, that's rich, coming from you! The man who's been griping about his misfortune for a solid month, sitting there whining about the shitty deal you've landed yourself. Listen, sunshine, there are some writers who'd kill for the opportunities you've got!'

'If you don't like listening to me, Sarah, you know what you can do.'

Her eyes blazed cold fire for a moment, and he realized that he'd pushed her a little too far.

'Yes,' she snapped. She got to her feet and grabbed the handle of her portfolio. 'Yes, I know exactly what to do. Perhaps it's best if we don't see each other any more.'

'Sarah, wait a minute.' He reached out a hand to touch her arm, but she shook him off with a ferocity that shocked him.

'I'll find another writer,' she told him, as she turned away. 'Somebody who needs the work.'

'Oh, come on now, this is ridiculous.'

But she was stalking off across the crowded square, dragging the unwieldy portfolio with her.

'Sarah!' shouted Mark helplessly, turning quite a few heads in his direction. He stared challengingly around for a moment, then turned his attention to the untouched pot of salad beside him. He picked it up and threw it hard at the nearest litter-bin. It hit the metal rim, deflected, and fell to the ground, scattering oily salad leaves across the cobbles. There was a drumming of wings as the ever watchful pigeons swooped, pecking frantically at the scattered greens.

He threw a glance in the direction that Sarah had taken and considered running after her, but stubbornly he resisted it. *Bugger it*, he thought. *Bloody woman always has some kind of bee in her bonnet . . .*

Mark set off for the nearest underground station, but on the way he stopped at a conveniently placed McDonald's. There he ordered two Big Macs, a large fries, and a thick chocolate shake. He carried the food to a table and sat down. He ate wolfishly, gobbling it all down in less than fifteen minutes. Every bite tasted to him like sheer heaven.

Chapter Twelve

It was just after midday, hot and humid, slowly settling into the long, listless torpor of another Sunday afternoon.

Leonard sat at his writing desk, reading the front pages of Saturday evening's edition of the *Dennings Courier*. Veronica and Rick had died in the early hours of Saturday morning, too late for the early papers to make anything of it. The *Courier*, though, had enjoyed a field day.

TWO SLAIN IN WOLFMAN MURDERS blared the headline in large black print, and beneath it, slightly smaller, *Local sweethearts slain in popular courting spot*. There were prominent photographs of the deceased. Veronica, looking young and fresh, was smiling bewitchingly at the camera. The photograph had almost certainly been taken at her high-school prom, a year ago. Leonard felt a wave of sadness flow through him as he looked at the picture. He would cut it out and keep it in a file somewhere, he decided, so that he'd be able to look at it again whenever he wanted.

The photograph of Rick was less flattering. Taken outside Olsen's, the day he had started as night manager there, it was slightly blurred and gave him a cross-eyed look. He was grinning at the camera, with that odd sneering expression that Leonard remembered so well. But Leonard preferred to remember Rick lying helpless beside his car, his body shuddering as blood sprayed from his ruptured throat.

The article made compelling reading, especially the eyewitness account of one Lester Bodean, who had discovered the lifeless bodies in the early hours of the morning.

'I could see straight off they was all chewed up,' said Lester, nineteen, a mechanic at the *E-Z-Fit* garage in Grover Street, Dennings. 'I called to Betty, my girlfriend, to stay back and not look. It appeared to me like a rabid dog or a wolf had been at them. I'll never forget this if I live to be a hundred!'

Lester and Betty – who neglected to mention just what exactly they were doing out at the Marsh at three a.m. – drove straight back to Dennings and the office of Sheriff Sam Wade, where they promptly raised the alarm. The night deputy, realizing that this was a serious case, phoned Wade's home and told him to get out of bed and hurry on over.

Sheriff Wade, known around Dennings as a plain-spoken man who enjoyed the occasional beer and who had a soft spot for hunting deer in season, was clearly shocked to the core by the savagery of the killings.

'In twenty-three years of police work, I've never seen anything like it,' he told the *Courier*'s crime reporter, Andy Dodd (an old drinking buddy of Sam's, who had thus managed to get more out of him than a complete stranger might have). 'It appears the victims were savagely *bitten*. In both cases a bite to the throat caused the deaths, but the young girl was bitten literally all over her body, as though by some mad beast. Our first thought was that the killings had been caused by some kind of animal. But, after forensic examination, we feel confident we're looking for a man, somebody with prodigious strength who is quite clearly deranged.'

Leonard felt a glow of pride when he read this. It suggested power. Nobody had ever talked about him in those terms before. He had always been regarded as a silent, oversized nobody, with no special abilities whatsoever. Now, it was impossible to mistake the respect in which Sheriff Wade held this unknown killer – whom the *Courier* had already dubbed 'The Wolfman'. There was definitely respect there, and fear too. Yes, *fear*. Leonard wondered how Mark Tyler would react if he knew the truth. He would never have dared dismiss Leonard's friendship so casually, that was for sure.

The sound of a car engine easing down interrupted Leonard's thoughts. He got to his feet and walked across to the window. There was a big grey Plymouth parked out in front of the house. As Leonard calmly watched, two men wearing sober-coloured clothing climbed out of the car and stood for a moment, looking up at the house. Police, Leonard decided, but not local men, otherwise he would have recognized their faces. Probably sent down from Pittsburgh to handle the investigation. It figured, after all. This was the biggest thing to happen in these parts for years. Leonard smiled. He had been expecting this call, and he knew exactly how he would handle it. It was kind of strange, but since the incident at the Marsh he had found a new confidence. Even his stutter seemed fully under control.

He turned away from the window and went out of his den, padding quietly down the stairs. As he reached the bottom step, the bell clanged mournfully in the gloomy hallway. He stepped to the front door and opened it. He wore a smile, showing his perfect teeth.

'Yes?'

'Mr Goldman?' The man who spoke was the older of the two, maybe somewhere in his mid-fifties. He had a grizzled, dark-complexioned face with thick rubbery lips and pronounced bags under his pure blue eyes. His crinkly black hair was plastered to his skull with some kind of cream. The man fished a wallet from the breast pocket of his charcoal suit and flipped it open to display his ID.

'Lieutenant Chapman, Homicide.' He jerked a thumb in the direction of his companion, a younger, sallow-skinned guy in a navy herringbone jacket and off-white chinos. 'This is my partner, Detective Corelli. I understand you work at Olsen's?'

Leonard nodded.

'My goodness,' he said. 'The p . . . police.'

'Nothing to get excited about, sir. Naturally we're keen to talk to everybody who worked alongside Miss Nelson and Mr Devereaux. I wonder if we could step inside for a few moments?'

'Oh, of course.' Leonard stood back and ushered them inside. He caught the individual smells of them as they moved past him. Chapman reeked of a mixture of stale cigarettes and Old Spice. Corelli wore a less traditional aftershave that Leonard couldn't put a name to, and he had recently eaten a hotdog or burger with raw onions.

'We can sit in the lounge, but I'll have to apologize about the state of the place. We don't get an awful lot of visitors. Perhaps I can offer you gentlemen coffee. Or a soda?'

'Not necessary,' Corelli assured him. 'This won't take long.' Corelli was probably in his late twenties, Leonard decided, good-looking in a boyish sort of way.

Leonard closed the front door and led them along the hallway. He pushed into the lounge, wrinkling his nose at the musty smell in there. Brenda was supposed to clean it once a week, but Leonard knew that she hadn't bothered with it for months now. Chapman and Corelli followed him inside, their gazes flicking restlessly around the room, appraising the place, weighing it up. Leonard had to work hard to suppress a smile.

'Please,' he said and waved them towards the old leather Chesterfield. They sank into it in one fluid motion, as though attached to each other with invisible strings. Leonard took a matching armchair and sat watching the two men expectantly. Chapman was studying a framed piece of embroidered text on the wall above the fireplace, an old piece of Mother's, mottled and yellow with age.

I complained because I had no shoes
Until I met a man, who had no legs.

Corelli seemed more interested in inspecting his nails which, Leonard noted, had been beautifully manicured, almost certainly by a professional.

A long silence ensued. Leonard wondered if they were trying to make him nervous. Eventually, he was obliged to prompt them.

'So, Lieutenant, er, Chapman? How can I help you?'

Chapman seemed vaguely startled by the question, as though he'd been musing on the full significance of that yellowed inscription. He smiled at Leonard, displaying large, horse-like teeth that were stained with nicotine.

'I understand you were working the late shift last night? That would be . . . six till two a.m.?'

'Yes, sir, that's right. Of course, I won't be going in tomorrow night. I got a call from head office this morning saying that Olsen's would stay closed all day Monday, as a mark of respect. I guess that's a nice gesture, wouldn't you say?'

'Uh-huh. But about Friday night . . . or rather, Saturday morning. Did you leave on time?'

Leonard frowned as though trying to remember.

'Gee, let me see now. I usually come straight home to make sure Mother's all right . . .'

'Mother?' grunted Chapman.

'She lives here,' explained Leonard. 'Only she's not very well lately. She's confined to bed.'

'I see.' Chapman considered this for a moment.

'So you were telling us,' prompted Corelli, 'that you usually come straight home.' His apparent indifference was a front, Leonard decided. He was every bit as alert as his partner, maybe more so.

'Well, yes. And Saturday morning was no exception. I seem to recall that I particularly wanted to hurry home. Mother hasn't been feeling so good lately. We have a radio pager, but she never likes to bother me when I'm at work.'

'And how long does it take you to drive home?' asked Corelli.

'Oh, fifteen, maybe twenty minutes. No more than that. Veronica and Rick were still there when I went out. I remember saying goodnight to them.' He adopted a wistful expression. 'I had no idea then that they . . . well, how *could* I have? How could anyone?' He shook his head. 'I was just reading about it in the *Courier*. It said something about bites. My God, what kind of sick animal could do something like that?'

The cops looked at him blankly, like they didn't have the first idea.

'And I'll t . . . tell you something else,' continued Leonard, enjoying himself now. 'They catch this fellow, they won't punish him, oh no!

They'll say he's *insane* and put him in some kind of institution, place like a luxury hotel! That's what they'll do, you mark my words. They'll all but pin a medal on his chest.'

Chapman sighed. He looked kind of tired.

'I think everybody has been shaken up by this thing,' he said.

'Yes, but . . .' Leonard gestured ineffectually with his hands. 'Gee, I'm sorry. It just makes me feel so *mad*. Why is it nice people like Veronica and Rick who have to suffer? I mean, what did they do to deserve it?'

Corelli shrugged.

'Just unlucky, I guess. Mr Goldman, what time did you get home, Saturday morning?'

'Umm . . . around 2.30, or 2.35 at the very latest. Yes, now I come to th . . . think of it, I looked in on Mother as soon as I got home. She was still awake and she asked me what time it was.'

'Your mother can corroborate this?' asked Chapman.

Leonard frowned. 'Lieutenant, my mother suffers from Alzheimer's disease. In other words, she's senile. Ask her and you might get a rational answer. Or she might tell you she saw me riding a unicycle across the ceiling dressed as M . . . Mary Poppins! Fact is, you never can tell what she'll say from one moment to the next. Of course, you're welcome to try.'

'Hmm.' A pause while Chapman digested this information. Then he seemed to decide on another tack. 'What did you think of Rick Devereaux?' he asked. 'We've talked to a lot of employees and I get the impression that he wasn't well liked.'

Leonard smiled. 'Well, I think there was a lot of jealousy, you know, what with him being old Mr Olsen's nephew and all.'

'We heard you two men didn't get on,' said Corelli slyly. 'Heard he picked on you quite a lot. Called you names, that kind of thing.'

Careful now, thought Leonard.

He allowed himself a little time to ponder that one.

'Well, Rick wasn't exactly Mother Teresa, you know? He was a rough diamond. He had an abrasive personality. He liked to get a rise out of some people, and I'd be a liar if I said otherwise. But it wasn't just me; he had a dig at most of us at one time or another. Then, I don't know, after he started hanging around with Veronica, he seemed to calm down a great deal. Mellowing out, that's the effect she had on him. Of course, he still liked to h . . . horse around. And those things work both ways: there were lots of people who bad-mouthed him behind his back, said that they'd like to get him . . . but nobody ever meant any of that stuff.'

Chapman and Corelli had perked up dramatically. They tried desperately to mask it with blank expressions; but Leonard could read it in their eyes and in the almost imperceptible way they craned forwards on the sofa. He nearly laughed out loud at their gullibility.

'What stuff?' asked Corelli, trying to sound casual but failing miserably.

'Well, like the other night, for instance, when Wayne said he'd like to—'

Leonard broke off, feigned a look of alarm.

'Oh, my goodness. I hope you gentlemen aren't thinking what I think you're thinking! I mean, it was just a joke! You surely wouldn't think . . .'

'We're not thinking anything, Mr Goldman. We're just interested.' Corelli took a notebook from his pocket. 'Wayne, you said.' He flipped over some pages and scanned a row of names. 'Would that be Wayne Hopkins by any chance?'

Leonard made his face into a scowl.

'Oh, now look. I feel just awful about this. It was one of those silly things that people say. I'm sure it didn't mean anything!'

Chapman nodded impatiently.

'Yes, of course. We just want to rule this person out of our inquiries, that's all. What exactly did Mr Hopkins say?'

'Well . . .' Leonard sighed. 'It was towards the end of my shift. Wayne came over to talk to me. I told him he'd have to spend most of the shift in the storeroom cutting up cheese. With a wire, you know – packaging it in shrink-wrap. He was in a c . . . cranky kind of mood.'

The detectives nodded.

'And?' prompted Corelli.

'And Veronica and Rick were up at the checkout, you know, fooling around a little. Wayne was watching them and he said . . . well, he said how he'd like to take that cheesewire and . . . and wrap it around Rick's throat.' Leonard gave the detectives a bemused smile. 'Of course, he was just making a joke.'

'I've heard better,' observed Chapman. 'He say anything else?'

'Uh . . . yes, sir. Something about Veronica.' He pretended to fidget uncomfortably in his seat, a method actor relishing his role. 'Something about . . . about cutting her up.'

Now Chapman could hardly restrain himself.

'Cutting her up?' he echoed.

Leonard waved a hand in dismissal.

'It's not how it sounds!' he insisted. 'What he said was something like, "Boy, would I like to cut me off a slice of that pepperoni".'

Leonard spread his hands in a gesture of supplication. 'See? Perfectly innocent. I think he has a soft spot for Veronica.' He pulled a face. 'I mean *had* a soft spot for her!'

Leonard noted with a twinge of satisfaction how Corelli's eyes narrowed ever so slightly, and how he made a surreptitious note in his little book. Poor Wayne, it seemed, would soon be in for the grilling of his life. Of course, he had a perfectly good alibi, since he was clearly working at Olsen's when the killings occurred, but that hardly mattered. The point was it would throw the police off course, turn their investigations away from Leonard, himself.

The two cops asked some more questions about Wayne. Leonard readily supplied the answers. Wayne was a bit of a loner, he told them. He had a beat-up old Chevy with a souped engine, and he liked to go driving into the late hours, out along the backroads, because he'd invented this game after watching a film called *Death Race 2000*, and the thing was, he awarded himself points for all the animals he knocked down. Fifteen points for a coyote, ten points for a rabbit, five for a dog, three for a cat . . .

It was all true, and it was exactly what the detectives wanted to hear. After another ten minutes of it, Leonard was fairly sure that he'd effectively sold them on the idea of Wayne Hopkins as the Wolfman. Now, he decided, it was time to introduce the second stage in his carefully prepared plan – Leonard Goldman, harmless nutcase.

He cleared his throat to get the detective's full attention.

'Lieutenant Chapman? I've been thinking about this case . . . and I kind of came up with a theory about it, myself.'

Chapman eyed him warily.

'Is that right?' he asked.

'Yes, sir. You see, I read the reports in the *Courier* and I noticed what Sheriff Wade said about the marks on the bodies. About the bites. He said it looked like an animal had made them.'

Chapman and Corelli exchanged glances.

'Sheriff Wade said rather more than he ought to have done,' growled Corelli.

Leonard could understand the man's displeasure. He knew that most sensational murders attracted more than their fair share of 'confessions' – sick people phoning in to claim responsibility in the hope of placing themselves in the spotlight, or injecting a little excitement into their drab lives. Withholding details about such killings helped to eliminate these phoney 'murderers', when their claims didn't match up to the actual facts. But Sheriff Wade had blabbed out all the attendant details to his friend Andy Dodd, and consequently Chapman and Corelli stood to be immersed in a welter of false trails. To complicate the matter, Leonard was about to offer them something very close to the truth, but in a form they would never accept.

'I was thinking,' he said quietly. 'Have you two gentlemen considered that the k . . . killings could have been done by a . . . a werewolf?'

Their faces were a picture. They sat there looking blankly at him, mouths slightly open. Chapman was the first to recover.

'Er . . . no, Mr Goldman. I guess we didn't think of that.'

'Oh, now, I know it sounds kind of goofy, but I've read a lot of literature on the subject and, believe me, there's plenty of documented evidence to suggest that such creatures do exist. If you like, I'll lend you some books . . .'

Corelli was trying hard not to smirk.

'That's real nice of you, Mr Goldman. We'll bear it in mind.'

'Oh, don't mention it. Usually I don't lend my books, but for something like this, well I think it's important that you follow up every lead.'

Corelli masked a grin with his hand and faked a cough. Chapman managed to keep his expression blank and now he was getting to his feet.

'Well, I think that about covers it, Mr Goldman. If we could just have that word with your mother before we go?'

'Oh, yes, sir, of course. Right this way. I'm p . . . pretty sure she'll be awake.'

He led them out into the hallway and up the staircase, the two cops looking around them as they climbed.

'Nice old house,' observed Chapman. 'There aren't many brownstones like this left in these parts. Been here long?'

'All my life. Mother moved here when she was first married. She's in her seventies now.' He paused at Mother's bedroom door and glanced at them sharply. 'Remember,' he warned them, 'she may not be quite herself. Sometimes, she can do and say things that are, well, pretty weird.'

Corelli smirked. 'I expect we'll handle it,' he said dismissively.

His tone prompted a sudden boiling of inner rage. Leonard saw a powerful image in his head: Corelli with his throat chewed ragged, his eyes wide and staring, his mouth hanging open, his immaculate fingernails dripping with his own blood as he fought to stem the tide of life. With an effort, Leonard pushed it aside, but stored it for enjoyment later. He rapped gently on the door with his knuckles. 'Mother? We have company. May we come in for a moment?'

He got no reply, so he pushed open the door and led the detectives into the room. He saw them wince as the stench hit them, and he noted that Corelli's knowing smile had slipped right off his handsome face. It took some getting used to, that smell.

Mother was awake. She lay propped against her lace pillows, gazing at the new arrivals thoughtfully.

'Mother, these gentlemen are detectives,' announced Leonard. 'They'd like to ask you some questions.'

Chapman gave Mother a reassuring smile and stepped closer to the bed.

'Mrs Goldman,' he began, 'I'm Lieutenant Chapman and this is my partner, Detective Corelli. We wanted to ask you—'

'Anything!' interrupted Mother breathlessly. 'Anything you want, Jerry. You know you only have to ask. I can't deny you when the heat's on you!'

Chapman looked puzzled. He glanced at Leonard.

'She thinks you're my father,' he said quietly. 'He died twenty years ago.'

'I see.' Chapman frowned. 'Er, Mrs Goldman, as I said, I'm a police officer. I wondered if you—'

'You want it doggy style, Jerry? You want me to take it in my mouth?'

Chapman gulped. He glanced sharply at Corelli, who was grinning again.

'Oh, I'm t . . . terribly sorry,' said Leonard. 'I did warn you.'

'Yes, well perhaps we'd better come back another—' Chapman broke off in alarm, his eyes bulging with shock. The old woman had pulled back the bed covers to expose her emaciated body. Her nightie was up around her middle, and her wide-open legs left nothing to the imagination. She shimmied her hips eagerly.

'Come on, Jerry, don't be shy. You ain't usually shy!'

'Jesus H. Christ!' croaked Chapman. He turned away, crimson with embarrassment. Leonard leapt to the bed and did his best to cover up Mother's nakedness.

'I'm sorry,' he gasped. 'I don't know what comes over her sometimes.'

But Chapman was already heading for the door, a sniggering Corelli trailing in his wake. Leonard followed them down the staircase, apologising profusely.

'She's really very confused,' he told them.

'Woman oughta be in a home,' snarled Chapman ungraciously. He was still beetroot red, and there were big drops of sweat on his forehead. Corelli was now clearly fighting an impulse to break into hysterical laughter.

107

'It's not her fault really. If you gentlemen would like to come back another time, I'm sure she'll be more herself.'

The detectives headed out of the front door without pausing. Leonard followed them on to the porch and threw in a parting shot.

'Don't forget, Lieutenant! If you want to borrow those books . . .'

Chapman said something that Leonard didn't quite catch, but judging by the scowl on his face, it was not a compliment. Already he was lowering himself into the passenger seat. Corelli, still grinning widely, was getting in behind the wheel. The doors slammed and the car took off up the street. Leonard watched until it had turned the corner and was out of sight. Then, smiling, he went back into the house. He was fairly certain those detectives would not be back to ask Mother any more questions; just as certain as he was that they had already filed him under 'H' for Harmless Fruitcake. A pity about Wayne, of course, but, after all, Leonard hadn't said anything that wasn't true. The kid would just have to slug it out for himself.

Leonard closed the front door and went back up the stairs to Mother's room. She lay there looking distinctly confused. Her wig had tilted sideways on her head, giving her a comical appearance.

'Where's he gone?' she asked plaintively. 'Where's Jerry?'

'He had to go out.'

'Oh dear. Is he coming back?'

Leonard moved to the bedside and straightened her wig, then patted her hand comfortingly. 'No, Mother,' he whispered. 'I don't believe he is.' He leaned forward and kissed her gently on the forehead, noticing, as he did so, the tear streaks that had eroded the white powder on her face. He settled her more comfortably against the pillows. 'You t . . . try to get some sleep now. I'll be up later with something for you to eat.'

'Drat the man,' said Mother. 'Always running off some place.' She sighed, closed her eyes. In an instant, her breathing settled to a slow, steady rhythm. Leonard moved silently to the door and went out, leaving it slightly ajar.

Back at his desk, he resumed his perusal of the *Dennings Courier*. 'We are looking for a cunning and highly intelligent killer,' Sheriff Sam Wade concluded.

Leonard smiled. It was nice to get a little praise for a change. He could get to like it.

Chapter Thirteen

Mark leaned back from the word-processor and sighed deeply. His spine was aching, his eyes were sore, and he felt like he'd been typing for hours. Glancing at his watch, he saw that indeed he had. He reached for his cigarettes, extracted one and lit it gratefully. He blew out a leisurely cloud of smoke.

Nearly there, he thought, with a genuine sense of surprise. His lycanthropic hero and his evil villain were currently slugging it out in a deserted opera house, surrounded by a full-bodied chorus of fantastical effects. Neither of them would emerge from the theatre alive. Another few pages, and his first draft of *Black Wolf 3* would be finished. That hardly seemed possible. He'd spent the last month working like a demon on the project, devoting every hour of every day and night to grinding it out, getting it done – getting it out of his way.

Strangely, it was his explosive argument with Sarah that had been the catalyst for this conversion to a new regime. He'd gone home that day and had set to work immediately, clear at last of the direction he wanted the novel to follow. Thereafter he'd become virtually a recluse. He'd turned down all of Brendan's invitations to debauchery, he'd cut his drinking to the occasional can of lager after a hard day's writing, and his only excursions had been regular walks down to the corner shop for a packet of fags, a sliced loaf and a bottle of milk.

He'd tried ringing Sarah a couple of times, and had suffered the indignity of having the phone put down on him. But he figured that when he rang her soon to say that the monkey was finally off his back, and he was ready to start work with her on *The Jumblies*, she'd quickly relent.

He eyed the telephone on his desk and decided to call her *now*, so as to give her the good news. Maybe they could arrange a celebratory meal for tomorrow night. He hit the '*save*' command on his keyboard and watched the chapter title shuttle safely on to the master screen. Then he picked up the phone and dialled Sarah's number. It seemed to ring for ages, and he was just on the point of hanging up when she finally answered.

'Hello?' She somehow managed to imbue that single word with an all-pervading sense of depression.

'Sarah, it's Mark. Look, please don't hang up on me again. I just want to talk for a minute, OK?'

A long, drawn-out sigh.

'Not much to talk about, is there?'

'I think there is. Listen, I'm sorry about the row we had, but Jesus, Sarah, it was over a month ago! I really thought you'd have forgiven and forgotten by now.'

'Well, you thought wrong, didn't you! Besides, you haven't exactly been trying very hard to make it up to me, have you? A couple of phone calls. Big deal!'

'Yeah, well I've been *busy*, Sarah. I've been . . .'

'Working on the book. So, no change there!'

Mark grimaced. 'All right,' he said. 'Maybe I have been using that as an excuse, I don't know. The thing is, I've about finished the first draft. Things'll just need a bit of tweaking after this, and then I reckon it'll be ready to send off.'

A long pause.

'So?'

'So then I'll be ready to start work on *The Jumblies*!'

'Oh, I got somebody else for that.'

'Who?'

There was a brief hesitation before she came back with a name, and meanwhile he figured she was lying.

'Roger Kidson,' she said at last.

'Who?'

'Roger Kidson. He's a children's author. Ellen Moran found him for me.'

'Never heard of him.'

'That's OK. He's probably never heard of you either.'

Mark sighed. 'Come off it, Sarah. You know perfectly well that's *our* book. I don't believe you'd get somebody else in to do it.'

'Believe it,' she told him.

Another long pause. He could hear static crackling in the background.

'Look, this is stupid,' he said at last. 'Why won't you give me a chance to make things up to you? I thought maybe we could go out tomorrow night for a meal or something. Celebrate me finishing this first draft. We could go to that new—'

'I've got a date tomorrow night,' she interrupted him. 'Sorry.' She put the phone down.

Mark sat there looking blankly at the receiver in his hand. For the first time it struck him that it really might be over. How stupid he'd been, letting this thing fester on for a whole month. He should have got in touch with her sooner. All right, so he'd *tried* to call her a couple of times, but that wasn't really enough, was it? He should have gone round there to see her, talked it out with her face to face. Instead, he'd opted to spend all his time on *that bloody book*. He slammed the receiver back on to its cradle and scowled at the monitor screen. He experienced a sudden, powerful desire to erase the disc the book was stored on; but, typically, that impulse passed away as quickly as it had come.

Like most writers, Mark was incapable of destroying work. The cupboards and storage boxes of his house were piled high with the writing he had produced over his lifetime. The essays and short stories that had been printed in his school magazine. The angst-ridden poems he had produced at university, when he was going through a doomed and pathetic affair with a girl who was, amongst other things, a Leonard Cohen fan. The hundreds of articles, reviews, criticisms and letters that had appeared in the wide variety of magazines and periodicals he had contributed to over the years. And, tucked away somewhere, his first attempt at a novel, a clichéd 'end of the world' story set in Arizona, loaded with 'meaningful' symbolism and peopled by stereotyped characters (he could see that now, but at the time he'd thought it totally original). Though it was unpublishable, he could not have destroyed it for the world. It occurred to him that writers were like squirrels, tucking away their nuggets of wisdom in the misguided belief that their words would be useful one day. But only ideas were recyclable. The trick was to find new ways of telling them.

The phone trilled, and his mood lightened as he pictured Sarah phoning back to apologise for her behaviour. He lifted the hand-set with a confident smile.

'Hello?' he said.

'Oh, hi. Is this Mark Tyler?'

Mark scowled. A male voice, deep, resonant, with a pronounced American accent.'

'Speaking.'

'Mark, this is Leonard. Leonard Goldman.'

Mark sat there, vaguely stunned. He hadn't thought about Leonard in a long time, hadn't received a letter in over a month now. He had assumed that his 'fan' had finally taken the hint. But now here was his voice, clear out of the blue, sounding as though he was only a street

111

away. Jesus, that was a bad thought.

'Where are you calling from, Leonard?'

'From home. It . . . it's a good line, isn't it?'

Mark tried not to let out a sigh of relief.

'How did you get my phone number?' he asked.

A puzzled silence. 'I've always had your number, Mark. It was on the headed paper when you first wrote to me.'

'Oh, yes, of course.' Mark felt foolish. 'So you . . . you just thought you'd ring, huh?'

'What else should I do? You don't answer my letters. I thought maybe, if I gave you some time to think about it, you'd realize you were wrong about that – and start writing back. But no letters. Nothing. Then I remembered the headed paper. I want to know what I've done *wrong*, Mark – to make you treat me so badly.'

'You haven't done anything, Leonard. I'm just . . . just too busy to write, that's all.'

'Well, then, that's easily solved. I can phone you! I don't mind paying for the calls. Say, just once a week to begin with. I could—'

'No, Leonard.' Mark was quickly becoming angry. 'I don't want you to call. I hate to be rude to you, but you make it very difficult to say this any other way. I have no desire to talk to you.'

'Gosh, Mark. I'm sure your other friends must call you up all the time.'

'You're not my friend though, are you?'

'Well . . . of course I am!'

'No, you're *not*! We've never met, so how can we be friends? Frankly, I have no wish to *ever* meet you. Do you understand what I'm saying? Let me put it like this: get off my back!'

There was a brief pause, punctuated by the sound of Leonard's heavy breathing at the other end, as though he was trying hard to figure this out. Mark thought about slamming the phone down, but decided to stay with it a little longer, to make sure that this time Leonard was thoroughly warned off.

'I . . . don't understand.'

'What don't you understand, Leonard? It's quite simple. I want you to stop bothering me, stop sending me those long, incomprehensible letters. I'm not *interested*, OK?'

'Are you sure you mean that? The first letter you sent me, it . . . it was so warm, so embracing. I felt a sense of our brotherhood.'

Mark lifted a hand to his face and massaged the bridge of his nose. He felt suddenly very tired and very irritable.

'Bullshit!' he snapped. 'That's all in your mind, man. I'm not an expert or anything, but have you ever thought about seeing a shrink? About getting some counselling – somebody you can talk to?'

'B . . . but I want to talk to *you*!'

'Why, for Christ's sake? Why me? What did I ever do to deserve this shit?'

Leonard said something under his breath that Mark didn't quite catch.

'What was that?'

'I said, "you wrote *Black Wolf*."'

'Oh, yeah. Well, at least you admit that much. The last I knew, you were claiming it was all *your* idea.'

'I was . . . angry. I guess I just got irrational. See, I've been trying to figure out what it was in my letter that turned you off me. Don't say that didn't happen. I know it did. Something happened: you were friendly at first and then, after my letter, you wrote back all formal like a solicitor or something, like it was a matter of business.'

Mark sighed. 'Maybe it was just a little too bizarre for me,' he admitted. 'Tell you the truth, I thought you sounded *weird*. So I made a decision not to write back to you. You can respect that, can't you? I mean, I offered you an easy way out. I told you I was busy and everything, but you wouldn't accept that. Oh no, you had to *push*, didn't you? So now we arrive at the real truth. From what I sense of you, I don't like you. And nothing is going to change my mind on that. I'm talking to you now only because I want to be sure that you fully understand the situation. Any more letters are going straight in the bin. Any more calls and I just hang up. Savvy?'

'I could *make* you talk to me . . .'

'What's that supposed to mean?'

'That's for you to decide.'

'Listen, sunshine, don't start making veiled threats. I don't respond to that treatment. Jesus, I don't even know how we came to be in this mess. If you had any common sense, it wouldn't have got this far. But now it has, and I'm warning you, back off!'

'You're being very foolish. I could have really helped you with Black Wolf. I have inside knowledge now. I've been where he's been.'

Mark felt a smile of satisfaction curving his lips.

'Is that right? Well, I'm afraid Black Wolf has his own problems right now,' he said.

'What do you mean?'

'I mean I'm just about to write him out, once and for all. Him and Star Child. In about fifteen minutes' time, they're going to go up in flames – along with Thaddeus Moon . . .'

'I don't believe you! You wouldn't do that!'

'Wouldn't I? Just wait and see, Leonard. Book Three's going to be the last anyone will ever hear of the whole Black Wolf clan. And, you know what? That's a good feeling!'

'No! no, you don't understand. That's impossible, because Black Wolf is *me*!'

Mark laughed. 'Well, that's tough, Leonard. You've got only about five pages left.'

'You wouldn't dare!' Leonard's voice was rising in volume now, distorting on the line. 'You wouldn't dare! You wouldn't dare!' he ranted.

'Get some help, Leonard,' concluded Mark. He slammed down the phone and made a two-fingered gesture at it. Then he leaned back in his chair, reached for his cigarettes, and lit himself another. He blew out smoke and rolled up his eyes to the ceiling. 'Crazy fucker.'

The phone trilled again, making him almost jump out of his seat. He snatched up the receiver and shouted into the mouthpiece.

'Leave me the fuck alone!'

Then he stabbed a finger on to the cut-off and left the receiver off the hook.

Cursing under his breath, he turned his attention back to his word-processor, and to the final chapter of *Black Wolf 3*.

Sarah stood staring at the handset in shocked disbelief. If that didn't beat everything! Gradually she'd started feeling guilty about the way she'd treated Mark earlier, softened up by what seemed the obvious sincerity in his tone. Finally, reluctantly, she'd swallowed her pride and returned his call – only to have him yell an obscenity at her and cut her off.

Right, she thought, *you little bastard. I don't need this.*

She slammed down her own handset and stalked silently back to her drawing-board, where a pencil sketch of Mortimer Rabbit was undergoing yet another transformation. *If only people were so easy to handle*, she thought wistfully. She took up her pencil and went back to work.

Chapter Fourteen

Leonard stood staring at the telephone, trying to register what he had just heard. He couldn't believe it. Mark Tyler wouldn't do that, would he? Destroy Black Wolf? Wipe out the single most important guiding light in Leonard's life? No, he *couldn't* . . .

Leonard lifted an arm to wipe his forehead on the sleeve of his shirt. There was a dull ache in his temples, and a vague nausea in the pit of his stomach. He felt sweaty, overheated, like he was maybe sickening for something. He had felt strange for the best part of a week now, as if his skin didn't fit him properly. Like he was changing from the inside.

He moved away from the phone and began to pace restlessly around his semi-darkened room, walking every now and then across to the window to stare listlessly down at the deserted lamplit street, then moving back to the jumble of books and papers that littered his desk. He had just finished a week's shift at Olsen's and had been yearning for some time off, but now that he had it, he could think of only one thing he wanted to do. But it was a bad thing and he had promised himself he wouldn't succumb to temptation again too soon.

Working in the shopping mart had become unbearable. He had stumbled through the last few weeks like a robot on automatic pilot. Bill Fernly had been brought in to replace Rick Devereaux on the late shift, and most of the employees considered this a change for the better. Veronica's position however, had not been filled, and Checkout 4 remained conspicuously empty. Apparently none of the other workers wanted to sit there: they thought it would bring them bad luck.

Over a month had slipped by since the killings, and the police hadn't been back to check on Leonard's alibi. Wayne Hopkins, however, had confided to Leonard that he had been given a thorough grilling. Since he had spent most of that fateful shift working on his own in the storeroom, the cops had come up with some half-assed theory that Wayne could easily have slipped out through the rear loading bay, collected his car from the forecourt, followed Rick and Veronica to the

115

Marsh, done the foul deed and got back to his post, all without being missed at all.

'Can you believe it?' Wayne had grumbled to Leonard. 'I told 'em who the fuck you think cut and wrapped near enough five hundred pieces of processed cheese? In the end, *that's* my friggin' alibi, man. A whole heap of cheese. Thank Christ I didn't goof off that shift, or they'd have me slammed up for sure!' Then he had frowned, shook his head. 'Can you believe my luck? Sayin' all that stuff about Devereaux the same night somebody offs him? Jeez!'

Leonard had been quick to apologize to Wayne for ever mentioning the matter to the police. 'They just kind of wormed it out of me,' he explained. 'I *told* them they were b . . . barking up the wrong tree.'

'That's OK, man,' Wayne assured him; but his eyes had held an entirely different message: hurt, bewildered – the expression of someone betrayed by a trusted friend. Leonard couldn't really blame him, but it had been in his own interests to give Wayne to the police. And wherever they were now looking for 'The Wolfman', it wasn't anywhere near Leonard.

But there was one big fat fly in his ointment. Leonard felt a growing urge to do it again.

It had started with his dreams. He found himself reliving the killings in minute and meticulous detail. The dreams always began with him again sitting in his car, waiting for his victims to emerge through the illuminated entrance of the mart . . .

From there everything unfolded in mesmerising slow motion. Rick's torn jugular spraying intricate crimson patterns from beneath his clumsy fingers . . . Veronica cowering white-faced away from her attacker's approach. And finally, Leonard's teeth would puncture her flesh . . . the rich, coppery taste of blood spurting into his mouth . . . And abruptly he'd wake then, his throat and tongue horribly dry, his penis erect and throbbing.

After a while, it wasn't just the dreams that bothered him. His fascination with blood was increasing. At Olsen's one night he found himself standing next to the meat counter, staring at a display of fresh liver – at the thick, dark blood oozing from it. He must have stood there entranced for quite some time before he came to his senses, and made himself move away, fearful that some workmate would notice him. But the incident left him with a powerful thirst that no tea or coffee or soda could pacify.

Driving to work lately, he had found himself watching the women walking on the streets. In the recent hot weather they wore skimpy clothes, vests and shorts, with their arms and throats left bare. Staring at their necks excited him till he had to force himself to look away. At night, alone in his room, he began to feel the urge to seek out another victim. He told himself repeatedly that it was too soon. The police were on the look-out and he would surely be caught this time. But the compulsion kept coming back to him, a hunger too powerful to ignore.

He knew exactly what it meant. He had known for years what it meant. He was becoming lycanthropic – just like Black Wolf before him. It was his destiny, and his body was now taking him further in the one inevitable direction. The first minor attacks and then the killings had been only the initial steps towards his transformation. Though he understood the inevitability, still he fought against it, afraid that he would make some mistake and the police would catch him, expose him, humiliate him. Make him a public laughing-stock, as he had once been before. But sooner or later, he knew he must succumb.

After a month of this continual battle against his developing appetites, he had felt himself approaching his lowest point of resistance. Then something really weird had happened.

There was an old painting hanging in the hallway outside Leonard's room, a grimy portrait of Mary the Madonna that was reputed to have belonged to his Polish great-great-grandparents. It had hung there as long as Leonard could remember, sad eyes staring reproachfully at anybody who came up the stairs. A few days ago, he noticed that something in the Madonna's face had changed. She was beginning to look more and more sorrowful, as though some terrible sadness had touched her. Her eyes appeared to be moist and rimmed with red, her lovely mouth was constantly turned down at the corners. She hadn't looked that way before, he was sure of it! He knew that it was crazy, impossible, yet every time he examined it, the changes were more apparent. It had got so that he was afraid to look at the picture any more. Yet, whenever he passed by it, he was aware that the Madonna's eyes moved in their sockets, following his every step. He could feel the weight of her gaze burning into his neck, and he knew that she was silently pleading with him, begging him to stay strong, not to succumb to this awful temptation eating into his very soul.

Tonight everything had come to a head. It was hot and humid again, on his night off from Olsen's. Mother had had a bad turn earlier that day, so he had asked Brenda to come back over that evening to tend to her. Brenda, who always had her eyes on extra money half reluctantly agreed.

Now Leonard angrily paced the room, his head throbbing, his throat raw with a powerful thirst. He had the mental impression of a transparent membrane stretched across the centre of his room, and of himself pushing through it, to a zone where everything was clearer. Then something seemed to snap in his head with an audible click. He threw open a desk drawer, took out the wooden box containing his killing teeth, and slipped it into his pocket. He went quickly out of his room and on to the landing.

The door to Mother's room opened, and Brenda stepped out.

'You got a minute?' she asked. 'We need t' talk.'

'Not just now. I have to go out.'

She glanced suspiciously at the cheap digital watch on her wrist. 'It's after ten o'clock. Where you going?'

'I need some fresh air. You wouldn't mind staying on for another hour, just to keep an eye on her?' He started down the stairs, without waiting for a reply.

Brenda followed him, intrigued.

'You seem to be in a powerful hurry, Leonard.'

'I need to blow away the cobwebs.'

'Yeah? Well, while you're out there, you'd better think about what you're going to do with your mother now.'

He glanced at her sharply. 'What do you mean?'

'I mean, she ain't at all well. I've done as much as I can, but her temperature's right up and I figure she needs a hospital. She's about as weak as a kitten.'

'You know she wouldn't stand for that. She hates hospitals!' He had reached the bottom of the stairs. He grabbed his denim jacket off the hall coat-stand and shrugged into it.

'Well, she might *have* to stand for it. I ain't no nurse. I can only do *so* much!'

'Yes . . . well, we'll t . . . talk about it later.'

He opened the front door and stepped outside, feeling the overpowering urgency of his thirst throb within him. He couldn't think of anything else right now – not till it was done and the thirst was satisfied.

But Brenda was persistent, shouting at him through the open door.

'Leonard, I don't think you realize how serious this is!'

'Of course I do! Now, please, leave it till I get back.'

He unlocked the door of the Camaro and climbed inside. When he switched on the headlights, he saw Brenda still in the doorway, peering at him with those shrewd little eyes, no doubt wondering where he was going at such a late hour. Well, let her wonder. He couldn't go on like this a moment longer. He started up the engine and pulled away from the kerb, heading for Dennings and whatever he might find to satisfy him.

No sense in going back to the Marsh; it was bound to be under police surveillance. Instead he headed into the town centre, towards the most public places, where nobody would expect the Wolfman to strike. Out on Highway 3 he noticed a cluster of automobiles parked in front of the Lazy Pig Bar 'n' Grill, a popular steelworkers' haunt. Through the open windows he caught a glimpse of bearded men wearing plaid shirts and baseball caps, arguing loudly over their pitchers of beer. He caught a snatch of music through the open window: Tammy Wynette backed by wailing steel guitars. She was singing something about how her man done her wrong.

He drove on into the outskirts of town, turned left on to the main highway, and cruised up to the main square. He pulled into a vacant parking space in front of the public library, its grey, three-storey building dark and deserted at this hour. Leonard switched off his headlights and sat still for a few moments, wondering what had compelled him to come here of all places. He glanced back over his shoulder – and then he remembered the park.

That was a generous name for the small island of greenery in the centre of the square; a rectangle of neatly trimmed privet hedges, a few weeping willows and mimosas, some carefully tended flowerbeds, and a couple of wooden benches, all arranged around a statue of a heroic-looking steelworker. It had been erected just after World War II, when the industry was still in its heyday. With the current situation in Dennings, the statue was a sour joke.

Leonard got out of his car, locked the door and moved across to the little park. At night it looked different. On sunny days old-timers liked to sit in the shade of the trees, playing checkers or simply watching the world go by. Between dawn and dusk the park was patrolled by a superintendent, who cleared away litter and kept the undesirable elements out. There'd been a furore recently when some discarded hypodermic syringes were found at the base of the statue. For several weeks, the town newspaper had muttered darkly about AIDS and hepatitis. Then the Wolfman killings had come along, and eclipsed all else in one fell swoop.

Leonard approached a secluded bench, and sat down in the darkness. He could hear crickets chirruping in the shrubs all around him. Glancing carefully around, he decided that he was well enough concealed from the street. The overhanging trees had plunged him into moon-shadow, and his head was barely above the level of the surrounding hedges. He, on the other hand, had a clear view all around. He settled down to wait.

Fate would decide who was to be next. If nobody came into this little park, then he would head home, frustrated.

A police car passed along a nearby street, its headlights briefly illuminating the foliage around him. He remained stock still as the car cruised on, around the square and out of it again. As darkness descended, the town clock struck the half-hour with a deep, resonant note.

Aware of a cold calm settling over him, Leonard waited ten, fifteen minutes. Then his ears caught a sound. The rhythmic thumping of feet on stone, rapidly drawing closer. He rose from his seat a little, craning his neck to see over the surrounding hedgerow. A figure was running directly towards him across the square. It was a young woman, lean and athletic, in jogpants and a white vest. Her hair was tied back in a ponytail, and even from this distance he could see she had a pair of Walkman headphones clamped to her ears. Since she was coming straight towards one of the openings in the hedge, she would have to run right by the place where Leonard was waiting.

He settled back into his seat and took the box from his pocket, smiling now. Taking out his dentures, he slipped the killing teeth into position, snapping the metal frames around his molars. He even ran his tongue across the biting surfaces to lubricate them. The footfalls were closer now, the urgent slapping of rubber on concrete. Leonard had time to savour the renewed sense of power that rippled through his body.

She came thudding into the open space by the statue, her breath escaped in shallow gasps, her face shining beneath a film of sweat. Leonard could now see her features quite clearly. She was a complete stranger.

A young woman shouldn't be out alone, so late at night, he thought with a twinge of mingled glee and regret. But he knew the type: stubbornly independent, and intent on proving that no man was going to frighten her off the streets. Well, some mistakes, once made, could never be rectified. Leonard remained where he was, perfectly still, as the jogger crossed the little square, her head down. This was going to be *so* easy . . .

And then the pager on his belt went off: a shrill, urgent tone that cut through the silence like a knife. Startled, he reached down to click it off, but it was too late. She had heard it even through the Walkman music pounding in her eardrums. She glanced up in alarm – to see him sitting there in the gloom. Her eyes registering panic, she swerved away as the tall figure rose from the bench. It flashed across his mind that perhaps he should abandon his mission. But then he recognized the expression on her face as she veered away – saw in her eyes that she had guessed who he was – and could describe him later.

He lunged at her and grabbed her around the waist, his superior weight making her stumble and fall. They hit the concrete in an ungainly sprawl, and he heard her grunt. As her headphones flew off, Leonard caught a snatch of tinny music: ZZ Top grinding through 'Gimme All Your Loving'. He scrambled over the prostrate form, his hands seeking her neck. But then she half-turned and pushed a hand hard at his stomach. And, where she touched him, an awful jolting shock pulsed through him. He released her neck with an oath, and rolled away, his body quivering.

She sat upright now, looking at him warily, and he could clearly see the device she held in her right hand. It was a pistol-sized electric prod, battery-powered, the kind advertised in certain magazines for 'personal defence'.

There was a moment of pure silence and uncertainty. Even the crickets seemed to stop singing. Leonard eyed the jogger, and she glared defiantly back at him. Now she was beginning to clamber to her feet, the prod held out in front of her like a gun. He could see that she was about to start screaming – and he began to panic at the thought of it. That's when he bared his teeth and growled, and he saw the terror register on her face. The scream died in her throat. Leonard, too, began to climb upright. As long as she held that prod on him, there was no safe move he could contemplate. But when she turned to run . . .

A light caught both of their attentions, off down a side-street. The patrolling police car coming back, its headlights lancing slowly through the darkness. Their glare reflected momentarily in the woman's eyes – a glimmer of hope for her. She broke and began to run for the car, and Leonard, desperate now, went after her. She darted around one side of the statue, an arm raised to attract attention. Knowing he had only this chance, Leonard threw himself headlong after her.

His outstretched hand found one of her ankles, bringing her down a second time, only a couple of feet from the gap in the hedge which would have guaranteed her salvation. She squealed, whipped around to stab the prod towards his face – but this time he was ready for her. He grabbed her wrist and twisted till the bone snapped. The prod dropped from her twitching fingers. This time she did scream, and he was forced to clamp his other hand across her mouth to stifle her as the cop car drew near, its lights illuminating the whole area where they lay. He pulled her back carefully behind the cover of the hedge. Her eyes were wide and filled with panic as she stared out from behind his hand. Now he could even hear the crackle of voices on the police-car radio as it cruised by.

He could hold back no longer; his excitement was too intense. He bit into her throat until his teeth locked behind the flesh, his body-weight crushing her to the ground. She began to buck and struggle, surprisingly powerful, but his mouth was tight on the puncture wound, sucking greedily as the hot blood spurted.

The police car had now cruised on, plunging them back into semi-darkness. His victim's struggles became even weaker as he continued to feed, and he could see that her eyes were already glazed. Now he uncovered her mouth and reached down with both hands to grip the hem of her vest.

In one swift movement, he released his hold and pulled the garment up over her head. He gasped, stared. She wasn't wearing a bra and her small but beautifully shaped breasts invited his touch. He had only ever seen women's breasts on film or in photographs; never in real life. He reached out one hand to touch them, but it was only out of curiosity. He was more excited by the spreading crimson stain on her white vest. He remembered to breathe and pulled away a little. The woman's hands and feet were still twitching, but to all intents and purposes she was dead.

It occurred to him now that something had happened just before he attacked the woman; something that had almost thrown him off course completely. He'd been sitting there on the bench, waiting for the woman to get close to him and then . . .

The pager! Oh God, his pager had gone off. That could mean only one thing. There was something wrong with Mother.

He got up quickly, then sat down on the bench. He took out a handkerchief to mop at his mouth and chin. Then he removed the killing teeth and replaced them with his regular dentures.

Leonard took one last look at his victim. Her vest was almost uniformly red now, and only one set of fingers still showed feeble signs of movement.

As Leonard pulled up in front of the house, he checked his reflection carefully in the rear-view mirror, scrubbing a spot of blood from the corner of his mouth. He had just reminded himself that Brenda was still on the premises.

Unlocking the front door, he went straight up the stairs. The Madonna examined him coldly as he went by, her face now set in an expression of stern reprimand. He could feel her eyes burning into him.

Once in the bathroom, he examined himself thoroughly in the shaving mirror. His shirt front was spattered with blood. He flung it into the washbasket. Now he took the handkerchief from his pocket, and began to unwrap his killing teeth.

With heart-stopping suddenness, the bathroom door crashed open. There was no bolt on the door since Mother first became ill and unpredictable.

Brenda stood there, wide-eyed, panicky. She registered him with an expression of surprise and curiosity. Clearly she had noticed the blood-drenched handkerchief in his hands.

'N . . . nosebleed!' he said. 'I had a damned nosebleed!'

Her eyes narrowed suspiciously, then widened again.

'I didn't hear you come in,' she began. 'I wanted to go to the bathroom . . .' She gestured vaguely at the toilet bowl.

Leonard thought she seemed a little dazed, out of touch with reality. 'Thank God you're here,' she concluded.

He stared at her.

'Is something wrong?' he demanded.

She nodded, then made the sign of the cross.

'Your mother,' she mumbled. 'It happened so sudden. One moment she was breathing shallow but, you know, still there. The next, I look down, and . . . she's gone. Just slipped away.' She shook her head. 'At least it was peaceful. If only you'd been there.'

'Mother?' Leonard stared at Brenda uncomprehending. '*Mother*!' Cramming the handkerchief into his pocket, he pushed frantically past the woman, slamming her against the wall.

He ran towards Mother's room – flung open the door.

She lay, as always, supported on her yellow pillows. But her face seemed to have sunk deep into them, almost as though death had made her heavier. The big Bette Davis eyes – like the garish red mouth – were wide open.

Leonard moved closer to the bed, moaning now, the tears brimming in his eyes. 'Mother,' he whispered. 'I'm sorry. I'm so sorry.'

A hand touched his shoulder, making him start violently. Brenda had followed him into the room.

'She's at rest now, Leonard. There was no pain, I tell you.'

He pulled away from her, sank down by the bed, threw his arms around his mother's body as if trying to hug the life back into her. An awful sadness hammered in his chest. With Mother gone, there was *nobody* to understand him. He was alone. He was abandoned. Suddenly, Mark Tyler's words came back to him: . . . *the last anyone will hear of the whole Black Wolf clan* . . . He was going to kill them *all* off. He must already have written Mother out. His threat was becoming real . . .

The belief hardened in his mind: it was too much of a coincidence. *Somehow* Mark Tyler had brought this about. His writing did have the power to influence real events, as Leonard had seen all so clearly. Now he had caused Mother's death, and clearly he wouldn't rest until Leonard and all his blood brothers had joined her. This had to be stopped. It had to be prevented.

'Where the hell were you?' asked Brenda, her limited concession to tact already exhausted. 'I called your pager ages ago. You sure took your time getting back!'

'I was just walking around,' snapped Leonard.

'You were just walking around, and you got a nosebleed?'

'Yes. Now, please, leave me alone.'

She scowled as she turned away and stalked out of the room, closing the door loudly behind her.

Leonard leaned over and planted a gentle kiss on his mother's powder white cheek.

'Don't you worry,' he whispered. 'We won't let *him* get away with this. He's going to pay, Mother. I promise you that. He's going to pay for every evil thing he's done to us.'

In the subdued light of the room, her red lips seemed to curve upwards the slightest fraction, until it seemed to Leonard that she wore an enigmatic smile. This he took as a sign of approval. He had her consent. He knew now what he had to do.

Chapter Fifteen

'What do you think of the place?' yelled Brendan.

Mark didn't hear him. The words were swept away by the aural blitzkrieg of sound and light exploding all around them. They had just staggered down the steps and into the club. According to Brendan it was the 'crucial' place to be once the pubs had closed.

'No use sitting at home and brooding over Sarah,' he'd told Mark. 'Time to show her you're independent. Time for a boys' night out!'

Brendan was still a fervent clubber, but Mark himself hadn't done this kind of thing since university, and he felt decidedly out of touch. This club was called 'Sun Daze', and was situated in Hampstead. Gazing down into the maelstrom of frantic colour that was the sunken dancefloor, Mark suddenly felt like somebody's grandad taken out for a birthday treat. Since when, he wondered, had club-goers become so young? The kids dancing dementedly beneath the strobing lights were barely into their teens. The boys favoured baseball caps, huge tie-dyed tops, baggy jeans or jog trousers, and multi-coloured trainers that made their feet look huge and clumsy. The girls seemed to prefer anything in lycra: leggings, cat suits, even hot pants, all worn with studded patent-leather belts and chunky accessories.

And the sheer energy with which they were dancing! Christ!

Mark could feel himself physically aging as he watched the dancers jerking and whirling in the lights. Behind them, on one wall was a giant screen, on to which was projected a series of seemingly random images. Mark recognized, in quick succession, a field of bright yellow sunflowers, an erupting volcano, the naked buttocks of a woman, white horses galloping through surf, an American Indian chief in full regalia, and what looked like the lower digestive tract of some large mammal.

He tried hard to focus on the music, but the five pints of lager he'd consumed earlier didn't help. All he could register was a pounding jack-hammer beat, a repeated keyboard phrase, a series of grunts, yells and squeals on deep echo. At key points in the music, the entire population of the dance floor would punch the air in unison, shouting

125

something that sounded like 'Do it' or 'Blew it' or 'Screw it'. Mark wasn't sure which, but it hardly mattered.

He became dimly aware of an arm around his neck, and then Brendan was yelling tenderly into his ear.

'Let's get a drink, shall we?'

He let Brendan guide him away from the ringside tables and across to a bar, which was lit by stark ultra-violet lights. As they neared it, they passed behind a perspex screen, and suddenly the music dropped dramatically in volume. Mark glanced around in surprise.

'Clever, eh?' enthused Brendan.

'A bloody relief. They call that crap *music*?'

'Hey, steady on! You're in imminent danger of sounding like your father.'

'I know, but really! And what's that smell all over the place? It's almost like Vick's Vapour Rub!'

'Got it in one. They like to rub it on each other when they're dancing.'

'Jesus, *why*? When I was a kid, that was my idea of torture.'

'I'm told that when they're on Ecstasy, it intensifies everything. You know what they say, don't knock it till you've tried it.'

'And *you* honestly come here a lot?'

'It's virtually my second home.'

The bar itself was crowded, and they had to locate a space to wedge themselves in. Mark eventually caught the attention of a tall black barman who looked like he'd escaped from the Harlem Globetrotters. He wore cycling shorts over rippling muscles. Mark ordered two beers, but Brendan countermanded it.

'Stow that!' he said. 'Give us a couple of Zombies. Large ones.'

The barman grinned, turned away.

'Come on, Brendan, we shouldn't be mixing our drinks . . .'

'Of course, we should! This is a lads' night out. And you've broken up with your girl, haven't you? So it's your duty to get totally shit-faced and cop off with the first skirt that comes within range of your dick.'

Mark looked doubtful. 'We had a bit of a row, that's all.'

'Oh, yes? And when was that?'

'Three days ago.'

'And have you spoken to her since?'

'I've tried, several times. But she just keeps putting the phone down . . .'

'Well, there you are. I know how these things work, squire. I've been there myself. She wants you crawling after her on your hands and knees, begging her forgiveness. So what do you do? Just the opposite

– that's what. You go out, have a good time, get yourself laid. Next thing you know, she'll be crawling after *you*!'

Mark was far from convinced. Brendan's past involvements with women had seemed a series of disasters.

The barman set down a couple of tall glasses filled with what looked like snow.

'Twelve quid,' he said matter-of-factly.

'Jesus!' Mark flashed an accusing look at Brendan, then fished a couple of notes out of his wallet. 'You know exactly what to order, don't you?'

'Hark at you, the big-time author!' Brendan took a sip of his cocktail and smacked his lips contentedly. 'You need to have something to spend all that money on.'

'And I can always count on you to provide suggestions.'

Mark raised his own drink and took a swallow. His first impression was that he *was* drinking snow – but then the lethal combination of rum and brandy struck him in the pit of the stomach. 'Shit!' he said.

'Quite.' Brendan was looking around now. 'There's some nice talent in,' he observed. 'Reckon we could be lucky tonight.'

Mark leaned his elbows on the bar.

'Are you kidding?' he reasoned. 'Have you seen the age of most of them here?'

'They're not all kiddiwinks, Marky. What about *her*?'

'Who?'

'Other end of the bar.'

Mark's eyes located a petite but predatory-looking punkette perched on a tall stool. She had cropped blonde hair, spiked at the front, and was wearing a basque top and mini-skirt in soft black leather. Her legs were crossed, revealing black silk stockings and a silver chain around one ankle. She might be in her early twenties, Mark guessed, but more than likely she was a year or two younger. She was undoubtedly a looker, her body lithe and nicely proportioned.

She seemed to become aware that she was being appraised, and glanced up so that her eyes met Mark's for an instant. She smiled at him suddenly and, embarrassed, he flicked his gaze away.

'*She's* a bit pneumatic, isn't she?' observed Brendan. 'What do you think then? Would *she* fill the gap in your life?'

Mark smiled sheepishly.

'Leave it out. Someone like that would never be interested in me.'

Brendan took another pull on his Zombie. 'She looks pretty approachable to me. Give her that old "famous novelist" routine and she'll be putty in your hot little hands!'

Mark shook his head.

'A relationship founded on that principle wouldn't have much chance, would it?'

Brendan groaned, buried his face in one hand. 'Who said anything about a relationship? What you need, my boy, is a little horizontal boogie, the old rumpy pumpy. You need to bury the purple helmet, coax the one-eyed trouser snake into action, make a coup-de-grâce with the trusty pork sword.'

'Yes, I get the general idea, Brendan. But I've never been interested in one-night stands. And there's a nasty little disease going around at the moment, you may have heard of?'

Brendan patted his breast pocket meaningfully. 'I came prepared. Never step out of the house without a packet of three.' Brendan drained his Zombie as though it was no more than lemonade, and motioned to the barman to replenish. 'And whatever the young lady is drinking,' he added, gesturing towards the punkette. The barman grinned, his perfect white teeth shining under the ultra-violet lights. He moved across to the girl and spoke to her. She glanced up at Brendan and nodded, then lifted a glass of champagne in a gesture of thanks.

'I can't believe you managed that,' said Mark quietly. 'The oldest routine in the book . . .'

'Yes? Well, let me tell you, it works every time. OK, since you're not going to take the initiative, stand back while I show you how incredibly easy it is to pick up a babe.' He took his new drink from the barman, ran his fingers through his hair, and advanced along the bar. Mark watched with interest. He couldn't hear what was being said, but Brendan was talking confidently and the girl was listening. Now she was nodding, laughing at some remark he'd made.

'Eighteen pounds.'

'Huh?' Mark turned to stare at the barman.

'Eighteen. Two Zombies, one glass of Moët.'

Mark nodded towards Brendan. 'It's his round. Why don't you ask him?'

The barman appraised the situation for a moment.

'He looks a little tied up.'

Mark grudgingly pulled some more notes from his wallet and handed them across the bar. 'God knows how these kids can afford to drink here,' he grumbled.

'They don't, mon. Drink fruit juice all night, maybe Lucozade for energy. Maybe take a little something to keep 'em buzzing.'

'Oh, you mean *ecstasy*?' Mark tried to look casual.

The barman nodded, leaned closer.

128

'Listen, mon, if you want anything like that, I can get it for you.'

'No,' said Mark, a little too quickly.

The barman turned disdainfully away to serve another customer, leaving Mark to gulp down the remains of his first Zombie and start on his second. It was already having a profound effect on him, giving a blurry edge of disorientation to everything happening around him. He hadn't even noticed Brendan and the girl come back over to join him. Suddenly their faces were right there in front of his eyes, smiling at him. He noticed that the girl had a wide mouth, lips slightly parted to reveal white teeth, a slight gap between the front incisors.

'Mark, allow me to introduce you to Kim.'

The girl was shaking his hand now, and he was astonished to experience a tingle of sexual electricity at her touch.

'Hello,' he said shyly.

'Hi.' She gazed at him with big green eyes, a smile playing mockingly around her lips. 'I don't think I've seen you here before.' Her voice was shot through with street-wise East End.

'Er . . . I just came here with Brendan.'

'Boys' night out?'

'That sort of thing.'

She was staring at him now, as though fascinated.

'Do you know, you've got lovely long eyelashes? Most women would give anything for eyelashes like that.'

Her attention was flustering him. He glanced at Brendan, hoping for some support, but his friend was merely watching the proceedings with a wry smile.

Now Kim had placed a hand on Mark's thigh. He could feel the heat of it through the fabric of his jeans, and couldn't help noticing that he was beginning to feel aroused.

'You, er, live near here?' he asked.

'Just up the road. Got a lovely apartment all to myself.' Now she was helping herself to one of his cigarettes. She stood with it in her mouth till he had the presence of mind to light it for her. She blew out smoke and held the cigarette in an exaggerated theatrical pose, like Bette Davis in *All About Eve*.

'Brendan was telling me you've just been through a bad time,' she said eventually.

Mark glanced over at Brendan, who was draining off the remains of his second Zombie. He made an exaggerated display of looking at his watch. 'Well, time I was making a move.'

Mark began to climb from the stool but Brendan pushed him gently back on to it. 'Now, don't you worry about me, Mark. You two stay here and get acquainted. I'll see you soon. Bye, Kim!'

Kim didn't even seem to notice his departure. As Mark watched, bewildered, Brendan threaded his way off in the direction of the exit. Kim was still waiting for a reply.

'I just split up with my girlfriend, that's all.'

Kim slid her hand higher up Mark's thigh, until a little island of heat nestled beside his testicles. He had to suppress a gulp.

'I know what that's like,' she said. 'A few months back, I split up with a guy. He was great – you know, very sexy, very good in bed. But he was so jealous! Didn't like me making too many friends.' She took a sip of champagne and slowly ran the tip of her tongue across her red lips. Mark could feel a stiffening in his loins.

'Friends?'

'Yeah. He couldn't understand why I needed them. So we split up and for a day or so, I felt really blue, you know?' Now she reached up a hand and traced a finger slowly down his chest. 'Then, what I did was, I picked up these two guys. Big, well hung . . . I think they said they was dancers.'

She had an abstracted air now, an innocent, almost girlish expression on her face. 'I took them back to my place. We all knew something was going to happen. I took all my clothes off, slowly, standing there in front of them. It was . . . like an act, you know? I enjoyed that. I enjoyed showing them the menu before serving up the main course. And then I just lay down on the bed and told them to do whatever they wanted . . .'

With an effort Mark turned away from her.

'I don't think I want to hear the rest of this story,' he said. He reached for his drink and took a large gulp of it.

'Oh, but I think you *do*,' she told him. 'Maybe not here though. Perhaps you'd like to see where it happened – would you, Mark? Would you like to see the bed where they did it to me? Huh?' She was very close to him now, nuzzling her mouth against his neck, sending white hot tingles of desire through him. He was nervously aware that he was now fully erect in a public place. He could see the barman grinning slyly at him, as though he knew.

'Listen, Kim . . .' Mark shuddered as her tongue probed his ear.

'I'm getting wet,' she whispered. 'My place is just down the road. You coming with me, or not?'

He nodded.

She smiled, stubbed out her cigarette, and drained her champagne in one gulp. Then she took his arm and led him through the crowd towards the exit. He was forced to hold his jacket in front of him to hide the bulge in his jeans. Away from the bar, the music swelled in volume again, and he glanced down to the sunken dancefloor where the kids were still bopping and grinding frantically.

Kim was climbing the stairs ahead of him. The sway of her hips made the black leather mini tighten regularly across her buttocks. And now they were strolling arm-in-arm down a deserted street, and they paused by a shop doorway so that he could kiss her. But it was *her* tongue that filled his mouth, *her* hips that ground against his. And now she was unlocking an anonymous graffiti-smeared door in what looked like an old warehouse building. She was leading him up a rickety wooden staircase. At the top, she unlocked another door, and they walked through into her apartment: a huge, open-plan room under a massive skylight, beyond which the black sky observed them indifferently.

Mark stood uncertainly in the centre of the room. It was the kind of place you saw only in American movies; stripped-pine floorboards, bare white-painted walls, a low futon-style double bed. A compact Japanese stereo system stood on the floor at one end of the room. Beside it stood a video camera on a tripod, and an untidy litter of cassettes. Off to the right there was a metal coat-rack on wheels, hung with a variety of rumpled garments, a stripped-pine chest-of-drawers, and one massive cheese-plant, huge serrated leaves reaching almost to the ceiling.

This was the only living thing in the room besides the two people who now turned to face each other.

Kim extended an arm to the wall, and hit a switch, plunging the room into darkness save for the combined beam of several spotlamps which converged on the white coverlet of the bed – giving it the look of a sacrificial altar. Now Kim moved across to the stereo and hit the 'on' button. The room filled abruptly with thudding, pulsing music, the kind they had played back in 'Sun Daze', the volume unnaturally loud for such small speakers.

She moved across to him and took his hand. Laughing, she pulled him across the room, towards the bed, licking her lips. He reached out for her but she twisted away from him, pushed him back so that he overbalanced and fell on to the bed. She came forward and sat astride him, began to remove his clothes. He kept reaching for her, but every time she pushed him away, as though determined to make him wait until she was ready. Once she had him stripped to the waist, she shuffled downwards and removed the rest of his clothes. Then she crouched there, watching him, evaluating his body, her eyes large like a hungry child looking in a sweet-shop window.

'Kim . . .' he said. She got to her feet, and an intense expression came to her, as though she was concentrating on the pulsing music. Then she began to dance, easing into the sound, gently at first then with more commitment, strutting and jerking her hips to the beat, wrapping her arms around herself, eyes closed, lips parted. Mark lay watching her, his body tingling. He felt supercharged, potent, about ready to explode.

Kim kicked off first one shoe, then the other. She danced a little closer, swaying her hips, moving in near enough for him to make a grab at her, then eluding him with a mocking laugh. Now she lifted her hands and began to untie the thongs at the front of her basque. It fell open, but she held it teasingly in place for a moment, then gave him a glimpse first of the left breast, then of the right. Now she eased it back from her and let it slide to the ground. She cupped her full breasts with her hands, reached up fingers and thumbs to probe her nipples, tease them erect. She tilted back her head, standing legs astride, closing her eyes, opening her mouth.

Mark gave an involuntary groan.

'Come here,' he pleaded with her. She watched him for a moment, like a Persian cat, flicking her tongue across her lips. Then she moved to the bed and settled down beside him. She ran the tips of her nails across his thighs leaving pale red tracks on his skin.

'Do you want to hear now?' she asked him. 'About what they did to me?'

He reached up one hand, pulled her to him.

'Yes,' he whispered savagely.

'And do you want me to show you what they did?'

'Yes. Please.'

She lay astride him, pushed him back on to the bed. She interlocked the fingers of her left hand with his right hand, and pushed it back to the metal railed headboard. Suddenly, he felt cold steel against his wrist and he tried to jerk his hand away, but it wouldn't move. Glancing up in alarm, he saw that it was now handcuffed to the rail. He noticed, too, that the rail was chipped and scarred with earlier transgressions. It was while he was staring at this that she repeated the trick: chaining his other wrist in place. She must have had the cuffs hidden under the pillows, he thought.

She sat back now, watching him with a triumphant smile.

'Now I can do anything I want,' she observed. 'Can't I?'

'Yes,' he said.

'I could take a knife and cut your throat.' She smiled sweetly.

He nodded, swallowed hard. At this moment, he wanted her more than he had wanted anything in his entire life.

'I could just see to myself, and leave you there watching couldn't I?'
'Yes!'

'Or I could . . . let me see now . . . what else could I do?'

He waited, sweating. She lowered her head, slowly, slowly and put out her tongue. She traced it along the line of his throat, across his chest and abdomen and down, lower, until she hesitated inches away from his throbbing penis, gazing up at him to savour his reaction. She turned her head and smiled across the room at the tiny dot of red light that was the lens of the video camera.

She didn't always film them, but she had a feeling about this one. Odd set-up. The other guy, posher but much more street-wise than his friend, coming over and telling her that his mate was depressed and here was fifty pounds if she'd show him a good time. Well, sure, good times were her speciality, as long as they were on her terms. But she wouldn't erase this tape, she'd keep it tucked away somewhere safe. Because she thought there was something familiar about this John's face. She'd seen it somewhere before, a photograph in a magazine or newspaper maybe, she couldn't really place it yet. But you never knew what might come up if you kept your eyes peeled.

She turned back and slowly, deliberately, she took him in her mouth. She heard him groan, the sound seeming to come from a long way away.

The tape ran silently through the camera, committing every move to memory. And afterwards, when she had bundled him unceremoniously out into the night, she would sit down and replay it, watch it through, trying to remember exactly where and when she had seen that face before . . .

Chapter Sixteen

Hot and uncomfortable in his sober black suit, Leonard followed the coffin slowly through the cemetery to the graveside. The day was sullen and overcast, but a powerful humid heat seemed to claw up out of the very earth, bathing Leonard in a sticky, clinging sweat from head to toe.

Beside him, Brenda too was dressed in black – though Leonard noticed that she hadn't gone to the trouble of washing her neck for the occasion. In addition to a blouse and skirt, she also wore what she had earlier described as her 'Paris hat'. This was an insubstantial scrap of velvet with a couple of black feathers protruding from it, the whole thing held in position by a pair of large steel pins, which crossed like rapiers in the wiry bun of her trussed-up hair. Leonard figured that the hat would probably have been considered very fashionable back in the Fifties, but now it made the wearer look like some rakish Robin Hood. Still, he concluded, at least she had made an effort, unlike the four coffin-bearers provided by the funeral director.

They were local men, Leonard knew their faces if not their names, probably ex-steelworkers grateful for any pin money they could pick up. But their suits were shabby and ill-fitting, one of them needed a haircut, another could have used a decent shave. Leonard winced when he noticed one man's hand resting against the polished wood of the coffin: his fingernails were ragged, and ingrained with the dirt of a lifetime. These men had never so much as met Leonard's mother, but what was he to do? She had no relatives left in the world, and nobody who could even be deemed a *friend*. They had all faded out of the picture years ago when she had first started with Alzheimer's disease.

The priest reached the grave and turned to watch the approach of the coffin. He, at least, had talked to Mother a couple of times. Father Paretski was the skinny young man who tended to the large population of Polish-Catholic worshippers in Dennings. He had taken up the post some five years back, and Leonard remembered that he'd called to see Mother a couple of times in his first flush of enthusiasm for his new

135

parish. Father Paretski had professed himself a 'go-getter' back then; he'd had big plans for Dennings, he envisaged making some radical changes. He'd outlined all this to Mother as he sat beside her bed, drinking coffee and nibbling cookies, while Leonard hovered nervously in the background, aware of the old woman's unpredictable behaviour. But she'd just lain there nodding and smiling, and everything had seemed hunky-dory. Then, just as Father Paretski had been getting ready to depart, Mother had casually invited him to climb into bed with her so she could administer a 'good relief massage'. The young priest had almost sprinted out of the door.

Now, after five years of ministering to the needs of the good citizens of Dennings, Father Paretski was no longer a go-getter. He was drawn and dour, walked with a pronounced stoop, and had the makings of a pretty spectacular facial tic. Dennings was like that, Leonard reflected. The thing was to get out before the town could stomp on your hopes, piss all over your dreams. Those that stayed, like Father Paretski, grew old and grey before their time. They got set in their ways, acquired a liking for shopping in convenience stores, and for television game shows like 'Wheel of Fortune'. They grew flabby and sedentary, and went around with sour expressions on their faces, ready to bite the heads off anybody reckless enough to cross them. Leonard had somehow managed to avoid all that but, then, he was more of an individual than most.

Father Paretski opened his Bible and began to read. The usual stuff. 'Man that is of woman born hath but a short time to live . . .' Man? Didn't they have something different to read when it was a woman that died? Maybe they did but Father Paretski just couldn't be bothered to turn to a different page.

The priest's thin voice rose and fell on the still air, and Leonard found his mind wandering. Earlier that morning, he'd received a call from Harry Benton, the family lawyer. Harry hadn't beaten about the bush. He'd got straight to the point.

'Well, Leonard, I guess it wouldn't be giving too much away to tell you that you're about to become a fairly wealthy man.'

'I really wouldn't know,' Leonard had told him.

'Hell, yes, son. That's about the size of it. You're the only beneficiary named in your momma's will. I may be jumping the gun a little but I don't mind tellin' ya, when you add it all up, the savings, the property and all the other assets, it comes to a pretty substantial sum. You got any idea how much?'

'No, sir.'

'Hmm. I figured not.' Harry gave a fruity chuckle. He was a tubby, red-faced man who sweated a lot and tended to affect an air of jollity; though everybody in Dennings knew that he'd been just plain miserable since his young wife had run off with a drifter six months ago. Rumour had it that he consumed a bottle of whisky a day and took seven different types of tablet for his nerves.

'Put it this way, Lennie-boy, if I was in your shoes, I'd go straight round to that mart you work at and I'd tell old man Olsen to stick his job where the sun don't shine, with the aid of a long broom handle if necessary!' He guffawed heartily at the very idea. 'I ain't sayin' it's gonna put you in the tax-exile bracket, but you ain't gonna have to work another day in your life, if you don't want to. Your ol' momma was a shrewd cookie, Leonard. She salted away a lot of dough over the years before she lost her mind, and never once went near it for herself. Now it's all yours, boy. Call around the office after the funeral and we'll make it all official.'

'Y . . . yes, sir. Thank you, sir.'

'Oh, and Leonard, if you need any advice about *investing* that money wisely, I'd be only too happy to help you out.'

'Oh, I bet you would!'

'What was that?'

'Nothing, sir. See you this afternoon!'

Leonard had been stunned by the call. Of course, he'd known there was *something* due to him on Mother's death – she had mentioned it often enough – but he'd had no idea it would be anything substantial. What use did he have for money, anyway? He had all the books he could read, all the videos he could watch. He already owned Bela Lugosi's writing desk, for goodness sake! He had no desire to trade the Camaro up for a racier model, he didn't smoke or drink, and he couldn't in any way be considered a gourmet. Besides, Mother was gone, and no amount of money could ever recompense him for the loss of her . . .

Father Paretski was still droning through the service. Now the hired hands were lowering the coffin awkwardly into the grave, fumbling with the ropes as though they had never performed this action before. It settled with a none too gentle thud, and two of the men exchanged nervous glances, smothering their laughter behind their hands. Leonard glowered at them and they lowered their eyes, their faces reddening, hands suddenly clasped in front of them in attitudes of sobriety.

Father Paretski ground on with the familiar ritual. 'Ashes to ashes, dust to dust . . .'

Leonard started as he felt a dig in his back from Brenda. He shot her a look of irritation, then noticed the barely perceptible nod she was giving him. He realized now that everybody was waiting for him. Leonard stepped awkwardly up to the grave, stooped to pick up a handful of earth and straightening up, he let it fall down on to the coffin. It seemed to make an inordinately loud crash as it struck the wood.

He flinched, moved slowly back to his original position. Now Brenda advanced towards the grave. Leonard watched as she stooped, noting with a twinge of disgust, the way her skirt rode up to reveal the grubby, yellowed slip she wore beneath it. She threw more soil into the grave, then stepped back, wiping her hand on her hip.

That's the last thing that sour-faced bitch will ever do for Mother, he reflected, not without a sense of satisfaction.

Then suddenly it was all over. The hired coffin-bearers were turning away, one man reaching for his cigarettes before he had taken so much as three steps from the grave. A couple of elderly gravediggers hovered impatiently in the background, eager to get the hole filled in.

Father Paretski stepped across to Leonard, smiling bleakly.

'So,' he said. 'That went well enough, I think.'

Leonard didn't know what to say to that. He was still feeling stunned by it all. He just stood there staring at the priest.

'And how are you bearing up, Leonard?'

'Uh. OK, I guess.'

Father Paretski nodded. He put a hand on Leonard's shoulder. 'It must have been a powerful burden for you all these years. There's few young men would have put up with it.'

Leonard shrugged. 'I guess I just did what had to be done.'

'He had *some* help,' added Brenda.

Father Paretski winced visibly, before turning his strained smile in her direction.

'Of course,' he said. 'Mrs Goldman was lucky to have had two such fine people to care for her during her last years . . .' He turned back to Leonard. 'You know, your dear mother was a devout church-goer before . . . before that terrible illness took her. I don't know if she's made any provision for us in her will, but when the time comes, I hope you'll remember our window appeal. We're currently way below target and . . . well, a fine obituary it would be to your mother, don't you think? A beautiful stained-glass window, perhaps with a little dedication plate, so everyone would know where the money came from.' He seemed to be waiting for a reply, but Leonard didn't intend to make any promises he wasn't ready to honour.

Don't give that holy roller one red cent of our money!

Leonard started in surprise. Had that been his own thought, or a sudden voice in his head? Just lately, he'd become aware of a voice that didn't seem to be his own, goading him, making suggestions to him. At first it had only come to him late at night, just as he was drifting off to sleep. But lately it seemed to occur at the oddest times.

He realized that Father Paretski was still awaiting a reply and he smiled pleasantly.

'We'll see,' he said at last.

'I've a christening in twenty minutes. Ironic, eh? As one door closes, another opens . . .'

He turned away and hurried off towards the church. The gravediggers, taking his departure as a signal, stepped up to the graveside and launched into their work, their spades crunching in the gravelly soil. Leonard watched them for a moment and considered how well they might dig with their spines broken, but forced himself to bury his rage for the time being.

He turned away and walked slowly towards the exit. Annoyingly, Brenda walked along with him, as though she had allotted herself the role of his companion. He indicated the black limousine waiting by the cemetery gates.

'The car will take you back to your apartment,' he told her. 'I think I'll walk.'

'I'll walk, too,' she told him. 'I figure we need to have a little chat.'

'What about?'

'Things.' They went out through the gates and Brenda leaned forward to talk to the uniformed driver through his open window. 'You can go now. We've decided to walk.'

The man nodded impassively. It was no skin off his nose. He started up the engine and the limousine purred away up the road. Leonard and Brenda turned right and headed along the sidewalk in the direction of Leonard's house, a distance of no more than half a mile.

'Well,' said Brenda. 'That's it, I guess. The old lady's gone and you're the master of the house. How's it feel?'

'I don't know. Kind of strange.'

Brenda nodded. 'When's the will to be read?'

'This afternoon. I'm going over to meet Harry Benton. He's got the details.'

'He need me to come along?'

Leonard shook his head. 'I'm the only beneficiary.'

'That a fact? Guess you're gonna be a wealthy feller, huh?'

'Guess so.'

'Thought about what you're gonna do?'

'Figured I might travel. I've always had this desire to visit England. There's somebody there I'd like to meet.'

139

'Yeah? Who's that?'

'Oh, nobody you'd know.'

They walked along in silence for some moments. Brenda seemed to
be chewing something over. Her face bore a glum scowl.

'And what happens to me?' she asked him at last.

'How do you mean?'

'You plannin' to keep me on as cook, cleaner, general dogsbody?'
Leonard frowned.

'Gosh, Brenda, I don't know. I hadn't thought of it. With Mother
gone, there doesn't seem much point, does there?'

Brenda sneered.

'Oh, so that's it, huh? After near on four years of tending to that old
woman, runnin' and fetchin' for her, sloppin' out her bedpans, that's
all I get! A pat on the back and so long, Brenda!'

Leonard shrugged. 'I . . . suppose when you put it that way, it
does seem kind of mean. Maybe I could come up with something. A
bonus . . .'

Brenda laughed unpleasantly.

'Get *real*, Leonard. D'you think after all that time I'm prepared to
settle for a handshake and a couple of hundred bucks?'

Leonard glanced at her warily.

'That seems reasonable to me,' he said.

Brenda shook her head, and the black feathers on her Paris hat
swayed from side to side.'

'Your mama wanted us wed, Leonard. She wanted somebody to
take care of you – or have you forgotten?'

'I haven't forgotten. But that's not something I'm prepared to offer.
And now Mother's gone, there's no reason to . . .'

'Oh, but there's *every* reason, Leonard! Every reason in the world.
You always did what your momma wanted when she was *alive*, didn't
you? If she hadn't died when she did, she'd have talked you round in
the end. She could have talked you into just about anything. But she's
gone now, and it's up to me to point out your duty.'

'My duty?'

'Sure. You owe me, Leonard. Hell, I know you ain't got no great
liking for me and, if it comes to that, there's no partic'lar reason I'd
want to be landed with a cold fish like you. But I do have a hankerin'
to be mistress in that ol' house.' She looked wistful. 'First thing I'm
going to do is get me a skivvy . . . put *her* through the kind of shit I've
had to suffer all these years.'

Now it was Leonard's turn to snicker.

'You're talking like it's a foregone conclusion!' he observed.

Brenda turned her head to give him that muddy-toothed grin.

'Oh, but it *is*!' she assured him. She slipped her arm through his, and he was too astonished to shake her off. She edged closer and he noticed that her breath stank of sauerkraut. 'You're gonna take me as your ever-lovin' wife, Leonard. To have and to hold, in sickness and in wealth!'

'What are you talking about?' he demanded.

'I'm talking about the night the old lady died. I'm talking about you, stood there in the bathroom with a blood-soaked kerchief, and something wrapped up in it. Something you didn't want me to see. A nosebleed, you said. Shit! I knew *something* was cockeyed but I couldn't figure it at first. Not till I read about that young woman killed in the town square. Paper said it musta happened around ten-thirty. You went out around ten after ten, and you didn't get back till near on eleven o'clock. Kind've coincidence, huh?'

Leonard stared at her in dismay, fear opening and clenching like a huge fist in the pit of his stomach.

'Brenda, you surely don't believe . . .'

'Then I got to thinking 'bout something the old lady told me once. 'Bout how you and that Veronica Nelson girl was havin' some kind of fling. Only, later, she said you'd had some argument and broke the whole thing off. At the time I figured it was all bullshit, but now I ain't so sure.' She rolled her eyes meaningfully. 'Bet the police don't know any of that? Bet they'd be real interested to hear about it, too!'

'That's ridiculous. Are you saying that you think I . . .?'

'I ain't saying what I *think*, boy. I'm saying what I *know*. You was in the wrong place at the wrong time, you come home all covered with blood and, what's more, you was friendly with that other girl that was murdered. Now it don't take a genius to know that puts you up to your neck in the brown stuff. If the cops was to get wind of any of that, they'd have you in custody so fast, your feet wouldn't touch the ground.'

Leonard frowned. He kept his expression blank but inside, he was close to panic. Brenda *knew*. She knew about him. He was going to be caught, exposed, humiliated.

'Who have you told about this?' he asked her.

She glanced quickly around as though nervous of being overheard.

'Nobody, yet,' she assured him. 'Oh, but don't go gettin' any smart ideas. I've thought this through, boy. I left a sealed envelope at my bank, only to be opened in the event of my death. I wrote it all down, Leonard. So don't even think about trying anything funny. It'll be in your interests to make sure that not one drop o' rain falls on my head.' She smiled, looked very pleased with herself.

Leonard kept his face impassive, but felt a sudden hopefulness. That part of her story didn't ring true: a sealed envelope at her bank. Who was she trying to kid? The woman had never set foot in a bank in her entire life; what little money she had was probably kept in a shoebox under the bed. This was some dumb line she'd copied from a movie. Coming from somebody else it might have been believable . . . but from Brenda Loomis? Forget it!

They were approaching the house now, and Brenda was gazing towards it eagerly.

'So what do you want from me?' he asked her.

'I already tol' you. Marriage.'

He glared at her. 'You'd still want to?'

'Surely I would! Think of it this way. If I shopped you to the cops, I'd like as get nothin' for my trouble. So consider this our little business arrangement. You keep out of my way, I'll keep out of yours. We'll have separate beds, separate rooms, whatever you want. Hell, you could divorce me after a couple of months and head off any place you like with half the money.'

'But you'd keep Mother's house?'

Brenda smiled. 'You got to understand, Leonard. It's everything I've ever wanted. All them years I worked for your Mother, I tol' myself that one day it'd be *mine*. When you've wanted something as long as I have, you'll try just about anything to get it. Whatever it takes. Even shacking up with a monster.'

They were drawing closer to the house, moving in beneath its shadow. The ancient facade seemed to tower over them. Brenda paused by the gate and stroked a hand over the paint-blistered slats.

'What's here for you, Leonard? Bad memories, that's all. Boy your age should be over in Pittsburgh, gettin' himself a bite of the cherry. Maybe if you'd gone there before this, you wouldn't have wound up in such a Godawful mess. There's a whole lot of crazies runnin' around in that place. You only have to look at the news. I figure a man with your interests could have himself a whale of a time there.'

'I just don't know what to say,' he told her. 'How do I know I can trust you?'

'You don't. But, then, life's a bitch, ain't it? And for that house I'd feed my own dead mother to the hogs.'

Scheming slut. I always knew she was poison. Again the voice piping up expectedly in Leonard's head. *If she wants to be in that house so bad, maybe we should just grant her wish.*

He nodded. He knew exactly what he must do.

'You'd better come inside,' he said. 'We'll talk some more.'

142

'Sure thing.' She glanced at him suspiciously. 'But don't you go gettin' any ideas now. Remember the letter.'

'I won't forget.'

He pushed open the gate and led the way up the path.

'It doesn't have to be such a bad thing,' Brenda told him. 'You should just look on it as a new beginning. But don't ever try and cross me, Leonard. I'd let you go down without a second thought.'

They climbed up on to the porch, and Leonard fumbled in his pocket for the keys, then unlocked the door. He opened it on to the gloomy hallway.

Brenda stood looking into the shadowy interior. She seemed suddenly less self-assured.

'Maybe,' she murmured, 'we could talk about this later. When you've had a chance to think it through.'

'It's all right,' said Leonard. He lifted a hand and, placing it carefully, almost lovingly, on Brenda's shoulder, he drew her gently inside.

The door closed quietly behind them.

PART TWO

Chapter Seventeen

It was only the third book-signing of Mark Tyler's career and, as far as he was concerned, that was already three too many. To him, this was the least attractive aspect of a writer's life: meeting his public. Gazing around the crowded interior of Winterson's Bookshop, Covent Garden, he told himself that at least he'd been spared the ultimate humiliation of *nobody* turning up at his launch party. Quite the opposite, in fact. Winterson's had a well-oiled public relations routine which took these 'meet the author' events very seriously. Consequently, such affairs were generally well attended. On this grey, chilly September afternoon, the shop was well filled with a fair crowd of horror fans, fanzine reporters, the odd press photographer, and even members of the general public who'd just wandered in to see what all the fuss was about.

Mark had already completed the ordeal of reading aloud a passage from his latest work, while his devotees sipped wine, munched vol-au-vents, and vainly sought suitable places to extinguish the cigarettes which they had defiantly lit up despite the proliferation of 'No Smoking' signs. Mark had chosen to read an atmospheric passage, rather than a full-tilt, all-stops-out horror sequence, mainly because there was some descriptive writing in it that he was rather proud of. Now he sat at a desk with forbidding stacks of his work placed strategically around him, fielding the final stages of a question-and-answer session, before everybody got down to the serious business of forking out the necessary wedge for his words of wisdom.

He scanned the crowd and spotted another raised hand.

'Yes?' he said.

A thin, bespectacled youth with shoulder-length hair, dressed in a camouflage jacket and a Metallica T-shirt, asked Mark to identify his influences, so he reeled obligingly through them: Ray Bradbury, Edgar Allan Poe, James Fenimore Cooper (always good to throw in a surprise no matter how tenuous the 'influence') and, of course, the obligatory nod to Stephen King, since nobody working in this particular genre could afford to ignore his current importance.

Brendan came over with a bottle of white wine and recharged Mark's empty glass.

'How am I doing?' asked Mark, ventriloquist-like, through clenched teeth.

'Totally crap,' Brendan assured him. 'Putrid.'

'Oh, well that's all right, then. Thanks.'

'Don't mention it.' Brendan moved back to his chosen spot next to the refreshment table.

Off to his left, Peter Maughan was doing his literary agent bit, chatting with the bookshop's manager whilst downing his eighth glass of white wine.

'Just wait'll you read the *next* one!' Mark heard him say, and he felt like laughing. He was still heavily involved in the fine-tuning on *Black Wolf 3: Moon Rising*, and Maughan had yet to see a single word of it.

A dumpy woman in a sober twin-set was now trying frantically to get his attention. He nodded to her, and she simpered like a little girl.

'Mr Tyler . . . Mark . . .' She coughed nervously. '*Black Wolf* draws much of its inspiration from mythology and legends, but transposes them into contemporary settings. I wondered what your own beliefs are?'

Mark was puzzled by the question.

'If you mean my religious beliefs, I'd say I'm an agnostic.'

'Umm . . . no. I mean do you *believe* in the things you write about? For instance, lycanthropy.'

'You're asking if I believe in werewolves?'

There was a ripple of polite laughter, and the woman's face reddened. 'Well, you write about them with such conviction, I simply wondered . . .'

'Yes, I do believe in them,' said Mark. He noticed a few astonished expressions in the crowd, and felt obliged to explain himself. 'Well, what is a werewolf?' he asked. 'A man who changes into a beast at certain times of his life. He develops a powerful lust for blood, and feels compelled to kill his fellow man. Look back through history and you'll find many like that. Peter Kurten, Ed Gein, Dennis Nilsen. Modern psychiatry has invented all kinds of words to describe their impulses: psychopath, necrophiliac, schizophrenic . . . one of the psychiatrists involved in the Nilsen case claimed that the killer was suffering from something called "Borderline False Self As If Pseudo-Normal Narcissistic Personality Disorder"!' Mark smiled, shook his head. 'In the Middle Ages, they'd probably have called him a vampire or a werewolf, which for my money is a damned sight easier to get a handle on.'

Another hand went up: an earnest, scholarly-looking man in a tweed suit. He had a grey beard and wore wire-rimmed spectacles.

'Ah, but with respect, Mr Tyler, it's a poor comparison. A lycanthrope is supposed to be able to change his *physical* appearance . . . to actually take on the aspect of a wolf.'

Mark nodded. 'True; and maybe there were killers who had that ability *in their minds.* Maybe the werewolves of old were simply psychotics who, by the power of their charisma, managed to make others believe in their shape-shifting abilities. Remember, those were more superstitious times. Now we have the cold light of science to work by, and yet no amount of research will ever fully explain why a man chooses to kidnap a baby, tear its heart out and eat it raw.'

There was a shocked silence. First to recover was the manager of Winterson's, who stepped forward to address the crowd in a voice that positively jangled with false jollity.

'Er . . . well, ha ha. I think, er . . . that's a jolly good place to leave the discussion. I'm sure Mr Tyler would appreciate a few minutes' respite before we proceed to the real reason we're here.' He gestured hopefully at the full table. 'Now, don't forget that, in addition to his latest novel in hardback, we also have large quantities of the first *Black Wolf* novel in paperback, so here's your opportunity to get signed copies for all your friends who couldn't make it here today. It just remains for me to thank Mr Tyler and his agent, Mr Maughan, for coming down to visit our shop for this very special occasion. Ladies and gentlemen – Mark Tyler.'

He clapped his chubby hands together and those who weren't clutching wine glasses, or cigarettes, followed suit. Mark leaned back in his chair and sipped at his wine. He took out his cigarettes and lit one up with confidence, being the only person in the shop who'd actually been supplied with an ashtray.

'Officially it's no smoking in here,' the manager had earlier explained. 'But, in my experience, people will just light up anyway, and I haven't yet met a writer who doesn't indulge . . .'

Brendan brought over more wine to top up Mark's glass.

'Tearing the hearts out of babies?' he observed. 'Leave 'em laughing, Mark. That's what I say!'

Mark frowned. 'Think I went a bit too far?'

Brendan shrugged. 'I don't think it will bother this lot.' He ran an eye critically over the crowd which was already forming up into an orderly queue in front of the table. 'They couldn't be anything but horror fans, could they?'

Mark studied them too, and had to agree. Some looked like perfectly reasonable people, though even the 'straightest' of them seemed to possess some small quirk that set them apart from the common herd; a pronounced facial tic, a startlingly unmanageable hair cut, trousers that ended a good three inches above the ankles, or a dress with a biliously garish floral design. And then there were the really *eccentric* ones. Check out that guy over by the hardback display, for instance: a tall gangling youth sporting a bright green Mohican haircut. He was wearing a long canvas rainslicker that made him look like a villain from a Sergio Leone Western, and beneath it his skinny chest was encased in a black T-shirt which bore the legend *Bela Lugosi Lives* in blood-red lettering.

'My Lord, it's a shame when cousins marry,' murmured Brendan none too quietly, and Mark was obliged to jab him in the ribs.

He still hadn't exactly forgiven Brendan for getting him into yet another godawful mess. Indeed he'd phoned him the very next day and bawled him out, calling him all the names under the sun, and warning him never to show his face in Mark's vicinity again.

But once his initial anger had died down, he had to recognize that Brendan, in his own pathetic way, had *meant* well. Of course, it was stupidly irresponsible . . . but, when all was said and done, hadn't Mark actually enjoyed his encounter with Kim? Hadn't it been genuinely exciting? He'd been hopelessly naive to accept that a complete stranger would succumb to him so quickly, so totally, unless she was a professional; thus much of his initial anger had stemmed from wounded pride at discovering how her favours had been purchased like any other commodity.

Brendan, meanwhile, had thought nothing of hiring Kim's services to cheer up his friend. Mark had always liked to see himself as the kind of man who would never avail himself of prostitutes; but, deep down, hadn't he had at least an inkling there was something fishy about the set-up? Turned on by the excitement, he had simply not allowed himself to think it through logically, so it seemed a mite hypocritical to protest too loudly. So Brendan had been cautiously admitted back into the fold.

Sarah hadn't been seen since the day they had argued so badly in Covent Garden, and his subsequent approaches had simply resulted in her slamming the phone down on him. Answerphone messages also remained unanswered. A couple of letters came back unopened, '*return to sender*' scribbled on the envelope in Sarah's distinctive handwriting. By now her continuing resistance to any advances had led him to one inescapable conclusion: she must have found out about Kim. How else could he explain her relentless hostility?

He knew that he ought to go round and confront her in person, to talk it over face to face, but whenever he was on the verge of doing so, some instinct made him abandon the idea. He was lousy at confrontations anyway, and this was not one to be relished. So it seemed that he had no choice but to accept that their relationship was really over . . .

'Mr Tyler?' He was recalled to the present by the bookshop manager's voice. 'Are you ready to start now?'

Mark reached into his breast pocket and took out his fountain pen. And it began. The press photographers stepped forward as he conversed with the first person in the queue. He was called Bernard, a computer programmer from Tooting Broadway, and Bernard had taken a day off work specially for this event. He was tall and thin, with wispy black hair and a goatee beard. He wore a shapeless grey anorak and a sweatshirt with a picture of Hannibal Lecter on it. He particularly asked Mark to sign his copy as '*To Bernard, my number-one fan, best wishes from Mark Tyler*'. Bernard had even printed this out on a piece of plain paper, to avoid any confusion. Then he also had a couple of queries which he hadn't had a chance to raise earlier . . .

Mark dealt with these as patiently as possible, but Bernard seemed to have a distressing amount of queries, and eventually Mark was obliged to point him in his agent's direction and turn to the next in line. Smiling inanely, Bernard stumbled away, clutching his signed copy close to his chest, as though it was some kind of treasure.

Next was Barbara, a diminutive woman somewhere in her sixties. She had fluffy blue-rinsed hair and a strand of pearls at her throat. She told Mark that she particularly enjoyed the sex and violence, and, oh yes, there were a couple of questions she'd wanted to ask him . . .

And so it went on, each successive fan approaching the table, proffering their copy, each one wanting a brief word with the author. 'I notice you mentioned Ray Bradbury earlier. Was *Something Wicked This Way Comes* a favourite book?' (It was.) 'Was that a reference to *Catcher In The Rye* in chapter six?' (It wasn't.) 'Are you aware that there's a heavy-metal band called Black Wolf in Canada?' (He was.) 'Would you like to listen to an idea I have for a novel?' (He wouldn't, thank you very much.)

Mark found himself inscribing his signature on a surprising number of books. It was heartening to see that, even in these lean and troubled times, people were still buying hardbacks. The end of the queue was still quite a way off.

Now the tall green-haired youth in the Leone rainslicker was stepping up to the table, a copy of *Black Wolf 2* clutched in his grubby hands. He grinned shyly at Mark, showing perfect teeth, and he handed over the hardback. Mark sat waiting for the man to say something, but he didn't speak. Mark then opened the book to the title page, and glanced at the youth expectantly.

'What shall I write?' he asked.

'To my number-one fan.' The boy spoke slowly, a strange dreamlike quality in his voice. He sounded stoned.

Mark wrote that down as requested, reflecting that this was his fourth number-one fan today.

'I'm a writer myself,' announced the youth unexpectedly.

'Oh, that's nice.'

'Yeah but like . . . poems, you know? They're like . . . really heavy poems about . . . about weird stuff. Like about dreams, you know, and . . . stuff. I thought maybe you might like to look at some.' Now he was fumbling in his pockets, pulling out scraps of paper, old bus tickets, crumpled sweet wrappers.

'Er . . . I'm afraid I don't really look at other people's work.'

The youth stared at him slack-jawed, for a moment.

'Eh?' he said.

'I don't really get the time. And, to tell you the truth, I don't know anything about poetry.'

'They're really good,' the youth assured him.

'I'm sure they are.' Mark smiled mischievously, pointed across the room to Peter Maughan. 'You see that man there? He's my literary agent. His job is to look at people's writing, and he particularly enjoys poetry. Perhaps he'd be interested.'

A slow grin spread across the youth's face, as the information was gradually absorbed into his brain.

'Yeah? Hey, thanks, man. I owe you one.' He picked up his signed copy, and headed in Peter's direction. In doing so, he revealed the next in the queue, and Mark's welcoming smile froze on his face. He felt like somebody had thumped him in the guts, and he was aware of his skin tingling as the blood drained from his face.

Kim stood there grinning insolently. She was dressed to kill in a black leather halter-neck, mini-skirt and motorbike hat, and was chewing a wad of gum. He could only sit there, mouth open in silent shock, as she stepped forward to the table and slammed a hardback copy down in front of him. Then she leaned her elbows on the table, and craned forward until her face was just inches away from his.

'I *knew*,' she began in a quiet voice. 'I knew, from the minute I saw you, I'd seen your face somewhere before. Took me a bit of time to put a name to it, though. Then I was in W.H. Smith's, and there was this big display right in front of me, with a photograph of the author – and who do you suppose it is? Said to myself, "Ah, right, *now* I've got you!"'

Mark made a desperate attempt at civility.

'Well, what a surprise to see you . . .'

'With my clothes on?' she ventured.

He winced. 'No, I was going to say, in a bookshop.'

'Oh, well I do like to read the odd page in between my clients,' she informed him brightly.

'I'm sure you do . . .' He was aware now that her presence was causing some interest in the queue behind her, probably because, in leaning over the table, her mini-skirt was revealing more of her than was generally acceptable in polite company. He hoped to God she was wearing underwear. *Hurry it up*, he told himself. He took the book from her hands and opened it.

'So, what would you like me to write?' he asked.

She chuckled unpleasantly. 'How about a nice big cheque?'

Mark blanched. He threw a desperate glance in the direction of the refreshments table, but Brendan was nowhere to be seen.

Probably hiding, Mark thought glumly.

'What do you mean?' he asked her.

'Well, I'm not really interested in books. I prefer to wait and see the video. I've got a great one back at my place.'

'Oh? I don't see . . .'

'I've got this film, see. It's a bit of a tits and bum movie, but I reckon it could be a nice little earner. And you know who stars in it? Me and you!'

Mark's eyes widened in disbelief. Then, in a horribly vivid flash, he remembered the video camera and tripod set up in her apartment. He'd been too drunk at the time to take much notice of it but, as far as he could recall, she hadn't gone anywhere near the damned thing. A bluff then? Or did she have some kind of remote control beside the bed? He felt suddenly like he needed fresh air, but he made a determined effort to call her bluff.

'I don't believe you,' he said simply.

'I can easily prove it. I made a copy, so you're welcome to borrow it.'

He considered this for a moment.

'All right, so what? Big deal! I'm a single man. I'm not in a position of authority, it's of no consequence to me who you tell.'

'No?' She seemed unconvinced. 'You sure about that? I was thinking of the tabloid newspapers. One of my friends is a reporter for the *Sun*, and he's always on the lookout for a juicy story. They love to get their teeth into somebody successful, you know. A celebrity. And what would all your adoring fans think of you, then?'

'I wouldn't particularly care,' he said.

'Right, then, we'll start with this lot here, shall we?' She began to turn away from him, clearing her throat as if to call for everybody's attention.

Mark panicked. He grabbed her by the arm and pulled her back around to face him. In the queue behind her, people were now exchanging puzzled glances.

'All right,' he whispered. 'You've made your point. We need to talk about this – but not here. Meet me afterwards.'

'Where?'

'There's a pub across the road. The Grapes, I think it's called. I'll meet you there at . . .' He glanced at his watch. 'At two-thirty. I should be finished by then.'

'You'd better turn up,' she warned him.

'I'll be there,' he assured her. 'Now, please, I'm rather busy.'

'You weren't too busy the last time we met,' she observed loudly. Then she gave him a broad wink, turned on her heel, and strutted back towards the exit.

Mark watched her in silent dread, registering the clicking of her stiletto heels on the tiled floor, the way her buttocks swung from side to side beneath the tight black leather. He suddenly became aware of how quiet it had become in the bookshop. The people still in the queue were staring at him. And though they couldn't have heard much of the conversation, it seemed to him that every pair of eyes held a knowing look – as though Kim's dirty film was already released, and was available in every video outlet in the country.

You dirty bastard, the eyes seemed to say. *We know what you've been up to.*

Mark cleared his throat. In the silence it sounded like a shotgun blast.

'Er . . . next?' he said hopefully.

Chapter Eighteen

Mark stepped through the open doorway of The Grapes and stood in the smoky interior, scanning the crowded tables for a familiar face. He could see no sign of Kim, and he asked himself if he'd missed her. He was, after all, over ten minutes late.

It had been a hell of a job getting rid of Brendan and Peter Maughan after the booksigning. Both of them had been in the mood for further alcoholic celebration, and naturally expected Mark to accompany them. Brendan had suggested a favourite watering hole near Leicester Square, so the three of them had started walking towards the nearest tube station. But, after a short distance, Mark suddenly announced that he'd left his notebook back at Winterson's.

'Important notes for the new book,' he explained. 'I'll have to go back for it.'

'We'll come with you,' suggested Brendan.

'No, don't be stupid! What's the point? You two carry on to Leicester Square. Maybe I'll catch up with you.'

'Maybe?' Brendan looked suspicious. 'Something wrong?'

'Tell you the truth, I don't feel too hot. Bit of a headache coming on. But that's no reason why you two can't enjoy yourselves.'

Brendan was still far from convinced. Then the penny must have dropped, because a knowing grin stretched across his face.

'You sly bugger!' he exclaimed. 'You've arranged to meet that Kim somewhere?'

'I told you, I left something . . .'

'At the bookshop. Yes, yes, we understand!' Brendan slapped Mark heartily on the shoulder. 'Christ, why didn't you just *say* you had something lined up?'

'Who's Kim?' Maughan wanted to know. 'Good God, Mark, not that half-dressed little floozie at the signing? You knocking her off or something? Ye Gods, what does young Sarah think about all this?'

Brendan chuckled.

'Naturally, young Sarah doesn't *know* about it,' he explained. 'She and Mark are no longer a going concern.'

'Since when?' Peter was dismayed at this news. 'Mark, you didn't tell me about any of this!'

'So? You're my literary agent, not my bloody counsellor. And there's absolutely nothing between Kim and me . . .'

'. . . except a very thin piece of rubber!' chortled Brendan. 'You give her one for me, old son! At the prices she charges, you can't afford this too often.'

Now Maughan looked positively horrified.

'Good heavens, you don't mean to say that she's a hooker?'

Mark could cheerfully have throttled Brendan. 'Peter, I promise you this is not how it looks.'

'But, Mark, you must be careful. You can't afford to . . .'

'I really have to go now. I'm late.'

He turned on his heel and hurried back along the street, aware of Peter and Brendan shouting after him, the worse for drink. He ignored them both and kept walking.

The Grapes was always a busy lunchtime venue, so the lounge bar was packed with punters. Mark scanned the tables and had a horribly vivid image of Kim, already pouring out her tawdry tale to a tabloid journalist. He pictured Sarah reading Kim's revelations in the morning paper. Beads of sweat popped on his brow, and under the tight collar of his white shirt. Where the bloody hell was she? Surely she hadn't already gone?

He was just on the point of giving up on the whole thing when he spotted her sitting alone on a wooden alcove bench, right at the back of the pub, where it was a bit less crowded. She acknowledged him with a brief wave, and he moved across the lounge to stand at her table. She waved an empty glass at him admonishingly.

'You're late,' she informed him unnecessarily. 'You're bloody lucky I'm still here.'

'I had trouble getting rid of some friends,' he said. 'Do you want a drink?'

'I'll have a Bacardi and Coke. A double.'

He turned back to the bar, where he ordered her drink and a double gin and tonic for himself. He kept telling himself to stay cool. If he kept his head, everything would be fine, and he'd soon get himself out of this mess. The worst thing he could do was to lose his temper.

He paid for the drinks and walked back to the table, taking a seat opposite Kim. Nervously he glanced through a gap in the rough wooden partition beside him, but the man in the next booth had his back turned. He wore Walkman headphones and was reading a newspaper, his head moving backwards and forwards to some unheard rhythm.

For a moment, though, neither had anything to say. Mark watched Kim as she sipped at her iced drink with those red, red lips. Then she sat back and ran the tip of her tongue around her mouth.

Mark felt a shudder go through him. Despite everything, he still fancied her, but that was a temptation he could no longer entertain.

'All right,' he said coldly. 'Let's get down to it.'

She glanced around, wide-eyed in coy surprise.

'What, here? In front of all these people?'

'Listen, I've had quite a day,' he said. 'So why don't you speak your piece, and I'll make my response. Then the two of us can get on with our separate lives – what do you say?'

Her mouth twisted in a grimace.

'You're very formal all of a sudden,' she observed.

'That's right. How do you expect me to behave with somebody trying to blackmail me? Or do you imagine this is all second nature to me?'

She shook her head.

'OK. Now, you said something about a video?'

'That's right. Real good stuff. Very hot, if you know what I mean. I've watched it a few times. It makes *Last Tango in Paris* look like a slow foxtrot in Morcambe!' She seemed to find this incredibly funny, tilting back her head to laugh out loud.

He sipped at his drink.

'And how do I know that this video really exists? That it's not just some figment of your imagination?'

She smiled. 'Like I told you before, I made you a copy.' She reached into her handbag and took out a large padded envelope. 'The quality's nowhere near as good as the original, but you'll be able to see that I'm not bullshitting. I suppose you do own a video recorder?'

He nodded, took the package from her, slipped it into his jacket pocket.

'Tell me, do you always film the clients you have sex with?'

'Only if they seem a likely prospect. I just had a feeling about you, and I suppose it's paid off for once.' She shrugged. 'It's nothing personal, you understand. Just business.'

'And what makes you think I'll be willing to do business? It's like I said, I'm not a married man, I'm not a politician or a high-court judge. Any revelation about me in the papers would probably just boost the sales of my books. So what makes you think I can be blackmailed?'

She laughed, unpleasantly.

'Because you're *respectable*, love. From the tips of your expensive haircut to the toes of your expensive boots. That night you were just slumming it for a change, you wanted to experience how the other half lives. But in the cold light of day you'd run a hundred miles to avoid being publicly linked with somebody like me. And of course you've got parents tucked away somewhere . . . maybe a nice respectable girlfriend . . . believe me, you wouldn't like *them* to know what you've been up to.'

He glared at her in silent resentment. Her assessment of him was frighteningly accurate.

'But it was all a mistake,' he protested. 'Christ, I didn't even know you were a hooker!'

She smiled. 'Who did you *think* I was, Julie Andrews? Face it, love, nobody is going to believe you on that one.' She patted him on the shoulder. 'I've got you over a barrel,' she said. 'You had some fun the other night, and your friend picked up the tab. Now it's *your* turn to put your hand in your pocket.'

'I wondered when we'd get around to this,' he muttered. 'All right, how much for the original?'

She took a large gulp of her Bacardi.

'I've never done this kind of deal before,' she told him.

'Oh well, that makes me feel so much better about it.'

'I mean, I've seen it in films and stuff, and people always get too greedy. They ask for some ridiculous figure, like a million pounds or something . . .'

Mark studied her in silence.

'. . . but I thought, no, you need to keep it nice and realistic, not too over the top. So, in the end, I decided what would be reasonable – and it was five thousand pounds.'

Mark stared at her.

'You have an interesting idea of what's reasonable,' he observed. 'Five thousand? Jesus!'

She pouted defensively. 'I think that's more than fair. According to *The Times* diary, you were paid £75,000 for your third book.'

Now it was *his* turn to laugh.

'What's so funny?' she wanted to know.

'You don't look like the kind of person who studies *The Times*!'

'Well, a girl can make the effort to educate herself, can't she?'

'Apparently so.'

He thought for a moment. Five thousand pounds was a horrifying sum, but thankfully not beyond his means. Maybe, all things considered, he was getting off lightly. He wondered wryly how his accountant

158

would react if he claimed it as research expenses.

'How do I know that this will be the end of it?' he asked her. 'Supposing you manage to blow the money in a month, and more copies of the video start appearing out of the woodwork?'

'I wouldn't do that. You have my word.'

He gazed at her for a moment.

'I may be a bit cynical, but somehow I can't help wondering if your word is enough of a guarantee.'

She hardened visibly.

'It's all you're going to get,' she assured him.

'I see. So much for the old myth.'

'Which old myth?'

'The whore with the heart of gold.' He leaned back in his seat. 'How and when will you require this payment?'

'Well, in cash naturally. And I suppose I could give you to the end of the week.'

'I misjudged you,' he said. 'You *do* have some heart, after all.'

'Saturday at one o'clock? I'll bring the video. You bring the cash.'

'I'll think about it.'

'Don't think, love. Just do it. I wouldn't particularly enjoy dropping you in it – but I wouldn't hesitate, if you crossed me.'

Her cool manner was beginning to irritate him. He felt his anger bubbling unexpectedly to the surface. He leaned forward across the table and grabbed her by the wrist – hard enough to make her gasp. He pushed his face up close.

'Has it occurred to you how often between now and Saturday you're going to be up at that apartment alone?'

She tried to pull free, but he was holding her too tightly.

'So?' she demanded between gritted teeth.

'So I might just come up there and take that video off you. And I might just break your bloody neck while I'm at it.'

She laughed in his face. 'Do me a favour. You and whose army?'

There was a long silence while they sat glaring at each other. Mark fought to get a grip on himself, and after a few moments succeeded in pushing his anger beneath the surface. He let go of her wrist and sat back, fumbling for his cigarettes. Lighting one, he blew out smoke, and then looked up at her.

She was smiling knowingly at him, massaging her wrist with her other hand.

'What . . . what will you do with all the money?' he asked her.

She grinned. 'Well, what do you think I'll do with it? Eat, drink and fuck it away, I suppose. Maybe score some decent drugs, I don't know.'

She gulped down the last of her drink and waggled the empty glass in front of him. 'I could use a refill,' she told him.

'Yeah? Buy one, then.' He stubbed out the cigarette and got up from his seat. 'I'm very choosy who I drink with.'

She sneered. 'Pity you're not more choosy about who you *sleep* with. I'll see you here one o'clock Saturday.'

He shrugged. 'You might.'

'You just be here,' she warned him. 'Or read about it in the *Sun*.'

'I take the *Guardian* myself,' he told her angrily.

He turned and headed for the exit, without looking back. She was right, he thought glumly: she did have him over a barrel. And he couldn't bear to have his dirty washing hung up in public view. But if he let her sweat it out till Saturday, it would afford him some small crumb of satisfaction.

He made for the tube station and rode to Leicester Square. In the pub he found his two associates on their fourth pint and their fifteenth dirty joke. They glanced up in surprise as he approached their table.

'That didn't take long,' observed Brendan. 'I assumed you were gone for the day.'

'Time off for good behaviour.' Mark gestured at the glass-littered table. 'Same again?' he inquired.

'No, it's my round,' Peter assured him. 'Lager?'

Mark shook his head. 'Straight whisky. A double.'

They exchanged looks beneath raised eyebrows, but Maughan got up and went over to the bar. Mark lowered himself into a vacant seat and took out his cigarettes. He gave a long, weary sigh.

'What's up?' asked Brendan. 'Did she give you a hard time?'

'You could say that.'

Brendan grinned. 'She's really something, isn't she?'

'Oh, she's a dilly.' He sighed again. 'Brendan?'

'Yes.'

'That first night you got us together. You knew she was a whore, didn't you?'

'Well, yes. She's got a certain reputation around the club. Tell you the truth, some friends fixed me up with her on my last birthday. Same trick as I pulled – didn't tell me she was a working girl. I assumed it was my new aftershave! Does she still do that business with the handcuffs?'

Mark nodded.

'See, I thought that if you knew in advance she was a hooker, you'd run a hundred miles. And I just thought, you know, she'd take you out of yourself.'

'Oh, she did that, all right.'

'I must say I'm kind of surprised that you're seeing her again. Tell me, now you're a regular, how much is she charging you?'

Mark studied Brendan in silence for a moment.

'You wouldn't believe me if I told you,' he said at last.

And then Peter came back with the drinks, so they dropped the subject. Maughan raised his pint of strong lager in a toast.

'To Mark,' he said. 'A young man we'll all be hearing a lot more about.'

Christ, I hope not! thought Mark. He raised his own glass and drank deeply, not wanting to think too much about the future.

Chapter Nineteen

Leonard followed her down the concrete steps into the draughty, neon-lit glare of the underground, keeping a respectable distance between himself and the woman. As he walked, he played back the recording he had made in the pub, marvelling at the crystal clear quality that emerged from his headphones. Despite the constant mutter of background conversation, the clinking of glasses, the muted thump of pop music from the jukebox, he could hear both their voices quite clearly. He'd purchased the equipment on impulse a week ago from a hi-fi shop on Tottenham Court Road. Since his initial intention was to keep Mark Tyler under surveillance, he figured it might come in useful. The equipment consisted of a Walkman Professional and a tiny directional microphone with an extending lead.

Things had gone surprisingly smoothly since his arrival in London. He'd been here nearly three weeks now, and had found accommodation in a place called Kentish Town – a location chosen because of it being close to Mark's home ground. It was a small basement flat in a quiet backstreet. He'd told the landlord that he was a drama student and the man had accepted two months' deposit without asking any further questions.

The book-signing had been a godsend, almost as though fate was guiding his hand. He'd spotted an advertisement by chance in the *Evening Standard,* and had seized the opportunity to get a first close look at the man who had now become his adversary. Leonard had taken considerable trouble over his own appearance. The day before, he'd purchased a tweed suit and a shapeless tweed hat. That night he'd streaked his hair and beard with grey dye, and as a final touch he'd added a pair of wire-rimmed glasses. Studying the result in his bathroom mirror, he tried on his various sets of special dentures to go with the outfit, finally deciding on a moulding featuring a prominent gap between the two front teeth.

He thought he now looked like an eminent professor, some ten or fifteen years older than he really was. He wasn't even sure why he'd gone to such trouble. Perhaps it was simply for the joy of play-acting, the desire to be somebody other than he was. But at the back of his mind was the conviction that he would be harder to identify if he wore a different face every time Tyler encountered him.

So it was in this same guise that he had asked his question about the nature of lycanthropy, and had obtained a signed copy of *Black Wolf 2*. The business with the girl was an unexpected bonus. Clearly he'd arrived at a crisis point in Tyler's life, and, though he wasn't sure exactly what was going on there, he resolved to find out more. After the book-signing he'd hung around and trailed Mark up the road with his two inebriated friends. He'd been obliged to duck into a shop doorway when the author unexpectedly doubled back towards the pub.

After that, it had been the easiest thing in the world to wedge the little microphone in a tiny gap in the wooden partition. He could record their conversation whilst monitoring it on his headphones. It was an interesting comment on contemporary society that a man could sit wearing headphones in a public place without causing the least curiosity in his neighbours.

That conversation had proved quite an eye-opener, and Leonard's mind was already working around ways of turning it to his advantage.

Now he followed the girl's swaying hips through the ticket barrier (he had already purchased a season ticket) and down a creaking escalator to the white-tiled sterility of a platform on the Northern Line. There he mingled with the crowd, keeping the girl in plain view, and trying not to watch her too openly. Film posters and advertisements covered the wall behind him, and a huge digital display informed him that the next Edgware train would arrive in one minute.

I might just come up there and take that video off you, Mark's voice buzzed like a tiny insect in Leonard's ears. *And I might just break your bloody neck while I'm at it.*

Leonard smiled. Now he realized exactly what he could do with that tape.

Warm, dusty-smelling wind came gusting out of the open mouth of the tunnel like a giant's halitosis. The platform seemed to shudder under his feet. Then headlights blazed out of the darkness, and a train swayed and clattered into sight, passengers sitting like pale waxworks in its lighted compartments. It slowed to a stop, the doors broke open with a hiss, and people spilled out on to the platform – the spaces they left instantly filled by others who had been waiting. The girl climbed aboard, and Leonard followed her into the same carriage. She took a seat, and he found a place diagonally opposite. The doors slid shut, the train lurched, and then moved off into the tunnel.

I take the Guardian *myself*, announced Mark's voice, and that was the end of the conversation. Leonard reached down and flicked off his machine. As he leaned forward, he looked down into the carrier bag at his feet, where the hardback copy of *Black Wolf 2* now resided. He shrugged off an impulse to examine it, warning himself that the girl might spot it and remember that he was present at the book-signing. He didn't want to approach her openly until he was sure she was near to her home.

When he lifted his head, she was looking straight at him, her eyes frank and knowing, a mocking smile on her lips as she chewed at a wad of gum. Flustered, he looked away, fixed his attention on an advert for a mouthwash, which was just above her head. It was in the form of a cartoon: a man chatting to a woman, unaware of the heaps of festering garbage stuck to his tongue. The woman wore a comical cross-eyed expression, as though about to faint. ARE YOU GIVING HER MORE THAN JUST YOUR OPINION? asked the headline; and the copy went on to explain why a daily gargle with Mintyfresh was absolutely invaluable if one wanted to make friends and influence people.

As they rode onwards into the shuddering earth, Leonard surreptitiously lifted a hand and breathed into his cupped palm. He sniffed sharply, but the result was inconclusive; he could smell only the skin of his hand.

He glanced at the girl again, only to find her still gazing straight towards him. Leonard shifted uncomfortably in his seat and directed his attention to the floor.

Several stops later on, the girl rose to get out at Hampstead. Leonard waited till she was out of the open doors, before getting up himself and following her. He moved with a small crowd along the platform, up another flight of steps, and out into the grey chill of the afternoon. For a moment he stood glancing this way and that, then spotted her hurrying away down the High Street.

He followed, weaving in and out of other pedestrians, in an attempt to keep her always in view. Then she turned down a side-street out of his sight, and he quickened his pace, fearful that he would lose her in the crowds. He swept around the corner, and nearly ran straight into her.

She stood waiting for him, hands on her hips, a defiant expression on her face.

'You've been following me,' she observed. 'What's your game?'

Dismayed, he stood there, his cheeks reddening. 'No, I . . .'

'Don't lie to me. You were givin' me the eye on the tube all the way home.' Her eyes narrowed. 'Come to think of it, you were at that bookshop too.'

He smiled sheepishly, nodded. 'Uh . . . yes, look. I saw you back there and I thought . . . you know . . .'

'You thought what?' She looked him slowly up and down.

'Maybe you were the kind of girl I could get to know.'

She sniggered. 'You're a bit forward, aren't you? It's only the middle of the afternoon! Now, supposing you was to come back tonight?'

'Uh . . . no. I have an appointment.'

She studied him doubtfully, taking in the tweed clothing and his scholarly appearance.

'Thing is, can you *afford* to get to know me? You're a Yank?'

'That's right. I'm over here on a lecture tour, and I'm missing my wife.'

'Ah, shame!' She made a sympathetic face. 'That's nice.' She reached out a hand and stroked his arm. 'Now then, love . . . Sorry, I don't know your name.'

'It's Leonard.'

'Leonard, right. You got money, Leonard?'

'Yes, mam.'

'And I do mean money – as in cash. No plastic, and definitely no traveller's cheques.'

'Cash, sure.'

'OK. Well, listen, Leonard. It *is* a bit early in the day for me, but since you've come such a long way, I dare say I could brighten up your holiday. Shall we say two hundred quid?'

'Two hundred pounds? That's rather expensive.'

'Well, I don't know what kind of girl you think I am!' she snarled. 'If it's some scabby old tart you want, you'd better look elsewhere.' She began to walk away, but he restrained her, putting a hand gently on her arm.

'No,' he said. 'I'm sorry. It really doesn't matter about the money.'

She turned back, smiling confidently.

'Attaboy! My flat's just down the road a bit. You won't be disappointed.' She linked an arm through his and led him along the street. She noticed the carrier bag in his hand and pulled it open to look inside. 'Bought one of his books, did you? You a fan?'

'Yes.'

'Wouldn't have thought an educated bloke like yourself would be interested in that kind of thing. What you lecturing on, then?'

'Er, folklore, superstitions – that kind of thing. Mr Tyler's books touch on some similar areas. And are you? A fan of his?'

'Oh, I'm more of a . . . business associate. I've had him several times.'
'Had him?'

She nudged him in the ribs. 'You know what I mean,' she said, looking pleased with herself. 'Oh, I could tell you some stories about celebrities. You get a lot of 'em in my line of work.'

'I g . . . guess so—'

'You should see somebody about that stutter,' she interrupted. 'How long you here, then?'

'Just a few weeks.'

'Well, don't you worry, love. I'm about to give you a holiday experience you'll *never* forget.'

Kim reflected that this might prove to be the hardest two hundred quid she had ever earned. She had been going through her dance routine for the best part of ten minutes now, bumping and grinding to the beat of the music. But the American just sat there on the futon bed, watching her with no more apparent interest than if he was watching an episode of *Dynasty*. He was still fully dressed, hadn't even removed his jacket, and was clutching the carrier bag in his lap as though it was some kind of talisman to ward off evil. She wasn't going to bother filming this guy – it would make pretty unspectacular viewing, and she was convinced he was just some hick from the sticks, well out of his depth in the big city.

She danced closer to him, unhooking the catch of her halter neck. Her professional pride was at stake now – she was determined to rouse him one way or another. She had evolved her dancing over many years, and it hadn't let her down yet. But this character was kind of slow; she was beginning to wonder if he was all there. No matter, she'd seen the stack of wedge in his wallet, when she'd made him pay for her in advance. Whether he enjoyed himself or not, there'd be no refunds.

She began to show him her breasts, cradling them in her hands, reaching up fingers to tease the nipples erect. Kim was proud of her breasts; they were round and full, and the dark brown areolae were unusually large. She swayed forward and offered them to him, meaning to snatch them away at the last moment, as he groped for them. But he didn't even move; just sat there watching her with those weird, tawny-brown eyes.

Gordon Bennett, she thought. *This one must be dead from the waist down.*

Kim then decided to abandon the dance, and adopt a more direct approach. At this rate she could be here all day. She clambered on to

167

the bed beside him, snatched his carrier bag and tossed it aside. Then she eased the jacket off his wide shoulders.

'Come on, Leonard,' she urged him. 'You Yanks aren't usually this shy.' She noticed he was trembling and she put it down to inexperience. On the hi-fi, one dance track segued into another.

'I'm a little nervous,' he admitted.

'Oh, there's no need. There's nothing to it.'

When she unbuttoned his plaid shirt and slipped a hand inside, her fingers recoiled, momentarily surprised by the pelt of thick black hair they encountered. Christ, he was covered in it! Funny how his body hair was jet black, while his beard was mostly grey. She wondered how old he was. She'd initially figured him for around fifty, but close up he didn't look anything like so old. Eventually she managed to tug his shirt off, then reached down to his waist, to undo the buckle of his thick leather belt. She nuzzled against his neck, probed his ear with her tongue.

'That's right, Leonard,' she whispered. 'Now you're getting it. Just like all the others I bring up here. Would you like to hear what they do to me? Would you like to hear what a bad girl I am?'

That did the trick. Abruptly, he was fully erect against her hand. With some difficulty she pushed him back on to the bed, easing his trousers down over his hips.

The music blared.

'Bad,' murmured Leonard. 'Bad girl.'

'Yes, Leonard. Well, you surely didn't think I was an angel? The thing is, I get hot and horny, and then I just have to give it away. I've been with them all. Every last one of them . . .'

'Tyler?' he whispered. 'You said you'd been with Tyler?'

'That's right. You want to hear how good he was, your hero? You want to hear about the things he did to me?'

She laughed, leaned close, ran her tongue around her red lips. They always liked the tongue; sometimes she figured it was all she needed to bring them off. She lay down on him now and slid one hand under the pillow to locate the first pair of handcuffs.

'Tyler was better than you,' she told him. 'Bigger. Harder . . .'

She clipped the handcuffs to the metal head-rail and took hold of Leonard's right wrist. She began to ease it towards the open slot.

Suddenly, Leonard realized what she was doing. He glanced up in alarm, saw the metal cuff, and reached across with his left hand to intercept her arm. She winced as his hand closed around her wrist like a vice.

'What's going on?' he demanded.

'Relax,' she advised him. 'You'll enjoy it.'

'You're trying to trap me!'

'Don't be stupid . . . just *trust* me. You'll like this . . . Leonard, what are you doing?'

Now he was pulling her own wrist closer to the cuffs. She tried to resist, but his strength was suddenly prodigious. In an instant, it was done. The cuffs clicked around her wrist and she was trapped. Staring at the closed cuff she lay there, bemused. She didn't like it this way around, this total abdication of power. The loud, sound-drowning music was making her feel edgy now.

'You pillock,' she yelled. 'It's not supposed to work this way . . . Now you'll have to get the key.'

He lay beneath her, breathing heavily.

'Over there, on the chest of drawers,' she prompted. 'There's a wooden box . . .'

He rolled out from under her all of a sudden, and the cuff bit deep into her wrist, making her gasp. 'Careful!' she howled. 'You've put it on too tight! Are you listening to me?'

He stood up from the bed – then sat on the end of it, rocking forward, his arms wrapped around his body. She rolled around on to her back with difficulty, and lay staring at him. From behind he looked like some huge ape. 'What the fuck are you doing?' she demanded. 'Get the key, will you?'

Without acknowledging her, he bent forward and began to unlace his shoes.

She was beginning to feel anxious. 'Leonard, are you OK? Listen, I didn't mean to upset you, or anything. Just get the key and we'll talk this over.'

Once he had his shoes and socks off, he started removing his trousers. Then he got to his feet and carried his clothes over to the chest of drawers. From his full erection she noted that he was very excited. The music was still pounding away, which made it difficult to think clearly.

'Look, turn that noise down, will you?' she screamed. 'I'm . . . I'm getting a bit of a headache.' She twisted her wrist in the cuff, but it was so tight that already she felt pins and needles in her arm. 'Please, Leonard, the key! My circulation's going . . .'

Ignoring her, he stood by the chest of drawers, holding a box in his hands. But it didn't look like *her* box – the one that held the key. Now he took something from it, and lifted it up to his mouth. Was he taking pills or something? She hoped to God he wasn't a junkie; they could be unpredictable.

'The music!' she yelled. 'Will you just turn it down! Leonard, what are you doing, for Christ's sake?'

The track reached the fade, and for a moment silence descended. He was still facing away from her.

'I'm changing,' was all he said.

His voice was strange, alien, as though his mouth was full.

'Changing?' she echoed. 'What do you mean?'

But then the next track thundered in, drowning out her voice: pounding drums, chittering synths, and a long echoing wail of feedback. It occurred to her briefly that she had never much cared for this track. It sounded like the howling of wild beasts.

Leonard turned slowly around to face her. He began to walk towards the bed.

Bastard's trying to frighten me, she thought. *The fucker'll pay extra for this . . .*

But what had happened to his face? It looked different somehow . . . the cheeks distended . . . the mouth pushed out into a curious shape.

'Leonard, pack it in!' she shrieked, and was dismayed at the naked terror revealed in her own voice. She didn't scare easily, but this was getting seriously weird.

Close to her now, he pulled back his lips and grinned at her.

Terror jolted through her at the sight – so overpowering that instinctively she tried to jump off the bed. There was a snapping noise from her wrist, agony pulsing up the length of her arm. She fell back, half on and half off the bed. Now he was reaching out towards her. She screamed, lashing out at him with her free hand. But he caught it easily and held her fast as he leaned over, his mouth wide open, displaying twin rows of jagged teeth.

And then his mouth was at her throat, his teeth locking deep in the side of her neck. She forgot the pain in her wrist as fresh agony blossomed like fire.

He pulled back briefly, and his face hovered before her, his eyes staring through a mask of blood. There was something trailing from his mouth, something red and for a confused instant she wondered where all that blood was coming from. Then she knew, and she opened her mouth to scream again.

But his mouth closed on her a second time. Suddenly, she couldn't breathe. Her windpipe was clamped, and she was horribly aware of the grinding of his teeth somewhere beneath her skin.

The world began to spin in a mad, red vortex around her head. Kim continued to struggle, but the strength seemed to be seeping out of her limbs. She was vaguely aware that her attacker had released his hold, that he was biting her again and again, biting her in a frenzy – her arms, her shoulders, her breasts . . . Now she no longer felt any pain. She was drifting away from reality on a cushion of air.

Her last thought was disappointment that this should happen now, just when she was making good. An image filled her mind: Mark Tyler with an attaché case full of money. She could see him as plain as day, standing in the smoky interior of the pub. He was looking at his watch, and now she could see the dial in extreme close up. The second hand was barely moving around the face . . . and seemed to be slowing down . . . even slower . . . hardly moving at all. And now, as her vision faded to grey, she was not surprised to realize that it had stopped altogether.

Leonard showered himself in Kim's bathroom, taking his own sweet time to be sure that he was perfectly clean. The temporary grey dye was running out of his hair and beard, but that didn't matter. Better that a grey-haired man had gone in, and a black-haired man came out. He took one of her toothbrushes and scrubbed his killing teeth spotless. He washed out the brush under the tap, wiped its handle with a piece of toilet paper, and put it back exactly where he had found it. He bundled up the towel, intending to take it with him. Then he studied his reflection critically in the mirror. He would look fine as soon as he put his regular teeth back in.

He strolled back into the main room where now a raucous salsa dance tune was blaring out of the speakers. He looked thoughtfully at the crumpled figure sprawled beside the bed, and was momentarily intrigued by how much blood there was. He could not remember biting her *all over* like that. Only the first bite – and the sweet coppery taste of her blood.

As Leonard dressed carefully, he kept gazing around the room to make sure that nothing was overlooked. Noticing the video camera, he went over to inspect it. The film chamber was open, but there wasn't a tape inside. He wondered where she had hidden the tape of her activities with Mark Tyler, then decided to leave that for the police to find. He looked slowly around the room for a last check. He had made sure to touch nothing in here – except the girl herself – and that could not be avoided. From the chest of drawers he retrieved his teeth and popped them into his mouth. The killing teeth, in their wooden box, he slipped into his trouser pocket. Finally he rolled up the bloodstained towel. He could get rid of that on his way home.

Now came the good part, the clever bit – the moment he had been relishing since he had first thought of it. Using a handkerchief, he removed the audio tape from his Walkman, wiped its plastic casing carefully and left it on the floor only a short distance from the bed, where even the most incompetent policeman couldn't miss it. Returning to the carrier bag, he took out *Black Wolf 2*. He opened it to read the inscription, smiling to himself.

> *To my number-one fan,*
> *best wishes*
> *Mark Tyler*

After wiping down the dust jacket with his handkerchief, he placed the book on the bloodied bedspread – not without a trace of regret. He'd enjoyed reading what little he had managed of the opening chapter. He would now have to buy another copy on the way home. Finally he picked up the carrier bag, put the rolled towel into it, and used his handkerchief to turn the handle of the door on his way out. He left it slightly ajar and went down the stairs, humming softly to himself.

Music was still booming out of the room, so he figured it wouldn't be long before somebody came to investigate.

Chapter Twenty

When the phone rang, Mark was sitting in his study reading a review of *Black Wolf 2* in, of all places, the *Guardian*. He was not feeling at his best. He had slept till midday and had finally crawled from his bed with a thumping hangover, to be greeted by the depressing sight of heavy rain hammering against his bedroom window. He'd trudged downstairs and breakfasted on coffee and aspirins, but hadn't felt up to working on the book. Instead, he'd elected to thumb delicately through the day's news. And there, to his considerable surprise, was the review of his latest release, which he settled down to read with interest.

It was not a kind review – on the contrary – but he had been frankly astonished to find it there at all. His favoured genre rarely made it into the pages of the quality papers. Indeed, he had long believed that it was only the Ian McEwans and Salman Rushdies of the world who were deemed worthy of inclusion. But there it was, in black and white, under the heading A TURKEY IN WOLF'S CLOTHING, a lengthy review by one Stephen Chamberlain (Mark had never heard of him) author of an academic tome called *Myth and Magic: The Horror Novel in the Twentieth Century*. Mark began to read – and his headache seemed to get worse.

In this second instalment of the unaccountably successful *Black Wolf* saga, Mark Tyler sets out once again to bastardise and trivialize the mythology of native Americans. While it is perhaps unusual for a best-selling novel to concern itself with anything other than the usual recipe of sex, violence and bombast, it has to be stated that Tyler displays only the most rudimentary grasp of his subject matter. The eponymous hero of the tale is that most banal of literary creations, a werewolf, but Tyler has cunningly tricked him out in the season's latest shades. With a passing nod to ecological issues, some passages about the genocide of the Plains tribes of North America, and by painting a vivid picture of the greed and brutality of the white invaders, Tyler has cleverly produced a marketable concept that is on the one hand designed to appeal to a 'right-on' audience, whilst on the other caters for the kind of audience that likes its gore poured on with a ladle. It is interesting to note that the other protagonists of the book – particularly the females – are relentlessly stereotyped throughout.

Tyler's 'wolf' is therefore a hybrid of dubious pedigree. The major emotion to be gleaned from reading these books is a kind of weary disgust that a writer as talented as Tyler (and it has to be admitted he *does* possess a taut, persuasive style) should choose to apply his gifts to so commonplace a subject. Clearly, there are many who will disagree with this view. The presence of this turkey in wolf's clothing on the bestseller list, only days after its release, is an eloquent testimony to the current lamentable taste of the reading public. One has to ask oneself the inevitable question . . .

Then the phone rang, and Mark never did find out what this inevitable question was. He grunted, put down the newspaper, and walked over to his desk to pick up the receiver.

'Hello, Mark Tyler speaking.'

'Oh, Mark, it's Peter—'

'Peter! Have you seen today's *Guardian*? There's a review of the new book. I was just reading it. They've really put the boot in. It's virtually a massacre!'

'Er . . . no, sorry, I didn't see that.'

Maughan sounded so unlike himself that Mark was forced to pay attention.

'Something wrong?' he asked.

'Umm . . . yes, well I just got a rather strange phone call.'

'So what else is new? You're an agent, Peter. You're supposed to get funny phone calls.'

'Mark, this is serious. It was the police!'

Mark frowned. 'Christ, Peter, what have you been up to now?'

'I haven't been up to anything. It was *you* they were interested in.'

Mark felt his stomach tighten. What the hell could this be about? Naturally, he thought first about Kim. Suppose she'd been blabbing to somebody, and they'd decided to bring in the cops? Christ, hadn't he already *agreed* to get the money for her? He was planning to phone the building society later that day to make arrangements . . .

'Mark? You still there?'

'Yeah, sure. What . . . what did they want to know?'

A pause. 'Well, basically, where they could get in touch with you. Your address and phone number. They talked to the publishers first.'

'Fuck!' Mark flinched, as though a jolt of electricity had just shot down the line. 'You didn't tell them, did you?'

'Of course I did!' Maughan sounded indignant. 'I felt obliged to. It's probably some routine matter, so I shouldn't worry.' Another pause. 'There's nothing you want to tell me, is there?'

Mark scowled. 'Of course not! Why do you ask?'

Peter sighed. 'Well, it's just that the officer I talked to . . . Inspector Judd, I think he said his name was . . . I was a bit wary of giving him your details at first, but then he came over all heavy, and said that this was a murder inquiry . . .'

'What?' Now Mark was aware of his heart thudding in his chest. He was beginning to get the most awful feeling about this. 'Peter, for Christ's sake, why do they want to talk to *me*?'

'Calm down. There's obviously been some kind of mistake. Or maybe somebody you know has been killed. I don't suppose you've heard from Brendan since last night? He'd had quite a skinful by the time he headed home. You don't think anything could have happened to him, do you?'

Mark was just considering the awful possibilities, when the doorbell trilled, making him start.

'Oh hell,' he said. 'There's somebody at the door!'

'I suppose that will be them. Keep calm. If you haven't done anything, there's nothing to worry about. Listen, phone me back when you've talked to them, OK?'

'Yeah, right . . .' Mark put down the receiver and tried to compose himself. A murder inquiry? Jesus, what the hell was going on? He went out of the study and into the hallway. Through the frosted-glass panel of his front door he could see two silhouettes. He cleared his throat nervously, walked to the door and opened it quickly.

Two impassive faces appraised him through a screen of falling rain. Neither of them wore hats, Mark noted. For some reason, he would have expected them to be wearing hats on a day like this. He did his best to keep his expression neutral.

'Can I help you?' he inquired.

The older of the two men smiled, but his eyes remained cold, mirthless. He had grey, crinkly hair, thin on top and plastered to his skull by the rain. His wide face was deeply lined. The kind of face that had witnessed too many bad things, Mark thought.

'Mr Tyler? I'm Detective Inspector Judd.' The man had a thick, Glaswegian accent. Now he was holding out a scuffed leather wallet, letting it flip open to display his ID. He nodded towards the man standing next to him. 'This is Detective Sergeant Maddocks. I wonder, could we step inside for a moment?'

'Well, I was working . . .'

Maddocks nodded. 'Knocking out the latest bestseller, are we? Don't worry, sir, this won't take long.'

Maddocks was a Londoner, judging by his voice. He was very thin, and fair-haired. He had pale, almost colourless eyes that regarded Mark from behind steel-framed glasses, and his wide, predatory mouth seemed fixed in a perpetual smirk. Those eyes could make a man very uncomfortable indeed, Mark decided.

'You'd better come in, I suppose. What's this all about?' He looked at them inquiringly, but they said nothing. 'Well, we'll go through into the study, shall we?'

They stepped inside, Maddocks closing the door behind them. The smell of their wet raincoats filled the hall as they followed him towards the study. Mark noticed that they hadn't bothered to wipe their feet, so were leaving wet footprints on the lacquered floorboards. He considered complaining about this, but quickly abandoned the idea. He didn't want to antagonise them. They entered the study and paused, looking around them, perhaps noting the word-processor, the stacks of manuscript paper, the large pinboard on the far wall with book-jackets and promotional clippings displayed on it.

'I'm a writer,' said Mark, trying to be helpful. 'But you already know that, don't you?'

Judd nodded. 'Oh, yes, we know all about that.' He gave Mark a look that surprised him – an expression of intense dislike. Mark felt quite thrown by it.

'Er . . . my agent just phoned me,' he stammered. 'To . . . to tell me you'd been in touch with him.'

'We're making inquiries,' said Judd. 'And it's come to our attention that you were a friend of Kim McAulay.'

Shit, thought Mark. *Here we go*. He affected a blank expression. 'Who?' he asked.

'Kim McAulay,' repeated Judd, slowly, stressing each individual syllable. 'She rented a top-floor apartment in Hampstead. We understand that you visited her there recently.'

'Never heard of her,' protested Mark. He hadn't planned to lie. It just sprang unbidden from his lips, and he instantly regretted it. He couldn't help noticing that Judd used the past tense.

'Maybe you knew her by another name, sir?' offered Maddocks. 'We know that she entertained a lot of, er, male friends at the same apartment. And you were one of them, weren't you?'

'I . . .' Mark's throat was suddenly very dry, as he tried desperately

176

not to panic. 'I may have . . . been there once,' he admitted. 'I'm sorry, but you're talking as though she's . . .'

'Dead, sir?' Maddocks nodded. 'That's right. She was found this morning – murdered.'

Mark stared at him, forgetting about any attempt to mask his expression.

'You're joking,' he said.

Judd smiled thinly.

'Wouldn't be much of a joke, would it, sir? Now, we thought *you* might be able to tell us how she came to be in such an . . . unfortunate situation.'

Mark almost burst into hysterical laughter. 'What makes you think I'd know anything about it?'

Judd sighed. He moved across to the sofa and sat down. He was watching Mark intently, as though expecting him to break down and confess. Once again, Mark registered that impression of intense personal dislike.

'Well, Mr Tyler, I have to inform you that we have in our possession certain evidence that prompts us to consider you a suspect.'

Mark shook his head in disbelief. A sense of profound unreality was rapidly overtaking him.

'You're making a mistake,' he insisted. 'I've never heard anything so preposterous. Never!' He felt physically sick now, a cold nausea churning in his stomach. 'All right, look, I admit I did know her. But I never knew her surname. That's what threw me. We met twice, that's all . . . no, it was three times.'

'Steady now,' Maddocks warned him. 'Which is it?'

'Three times. Once at a club in Hampstead, and we went back to her flat afterwards. And twice yesterday – first at a bookshop in Covent Garden, then later at a pub called The Grapes.'

Judd nodded. 'Go on.'

Mark licked his dry lips. 'Is it OK if I smoke?'

'It's *your* house,' observed Maddocks. He seemed amused by the situation, and Mark for a moment felt like telling him to get the fuck out of there – but of course he was hardly in a position to do that. Instead, he took the pack of Marlboros from the desk top and lit one. When he offered the pack to the two detectives, they shook their heads.

Mark took a drag on his cigarette and went on, aware of the ragged edge to his voice.

'The first time, we had sex in her flat.'

'We know that,' said Judd. 'We've seen the film.'

'The film?'

'Very athletic,' added Maddocks, waggling his eyebrows.

Mark glared at him. 'That was done without my knowledge,' he protested. 'You see, I just picked her up at this club, and the silly thing was, I didn't even know she was on the game.'

The detectives exchanged glances.

'Yesterday, when we met in the pub, she was trying to blackmail me. Said she'd go to the newspapers if I didn't give her five thousand pounds. I was going to do that, too . . .' He became aware that he was babbling, so tried to make himself speak more calmly. 'I was planning to phone my building society later this afternoon, to arrange to withdraw the cash . . .'

Judd frowned. 'But there wouldn't be any point, would there? You can't pay money to a dead woman.'

'I didn't know she was dead, did I?'

'Didn't you, sir?'

'No, I bloody well didn't!'

'Calm down,' Maddocks advised him.

'That's easy for you to say!' Mark looked pleadingly at Judd. 'You've got to believe me,' he said. 'I really don't know anything about this.'

Judd smiled sadly.

'Let me tell you what *we* know,' he suggested. 'We know that you had sex with Miss McAulay and that the incident was filmed. The video tape exists; that much is indisputable. We found six copies of it hidden in her apartment . . .'

'Six?' Mark was appalled. 'She swore there was only one.'

Judd shrugged. 'Blackmailers are not noted for their dependability. She'd have come back to you when the first of your payments ran out – and even you suspected there might be other copies. We know she said that you'd just have to take her word for it.'

Mark was astonished by this apparent insight.

'How could you possibly know that?'

'Oh, we know everything that was said between you, Mr Tyler. Miss McAulay seems to have had an obsession with recording information. We found an audio tape near the body. It contains a conversation, obviously between you and her, presumably in the pub you mentioned.'

'The Grapes. It's in Covent Garden.'

'Indeed. You may recall something else that you said. At one point you threatened to kill Miss McAulay.'

'I never said anything of the kind!'

'On the contrary, sir, I'm afraid you did.' Judd took a small notebook from his pocket and flipped it open. He read out what was written there: '"I might just come up there and take that video off you. And

178

I might just break your bloody neck while I'm at it."' He closed the notebook and slipped it back into his pocket. 'You can't argue with that, Mr Tyler. It's a straight transcript taken from the tape.'

'My God.' Mark moved across to the desk and sat down heavily in his chair. If he hadn't, he might have fallen down. He was trying to think logically, but his thoughts were like scraps of confetti blown on the wind. 'OK, yes, I *did* say that, but I . . . I had no intention of doing anything about it. I was just trying to frighten her.'

Judd nodded. 'And maybe you went back to her apartment, "just to frighten her". But things got out of control. Maybe you'd been drinking and—'

'No, no, I never went back there. I swear to you!'

Judd studied his own feet for a moment, as though embarrassed by Mark's outburst. 'There's one other thing, Mr Tyler. We found a copy of your latest novel right there beside the body. That's what put us on to you. It was inscribed "*To my number-one fan*". An odd thing to write to somebody who was blackmailing you, wouldn't you agree?'

Mark's mouth opened and closed with a dull click, but he said nothing. There was nothing he could say.

'So you see,' concluded Judd, 'we have quite a bit of evidence stacked up against you . . . enough to put you well and truly in the shit, I reckon. I think perhaps we'll go up to the station now, and talk it over in more detail. What do you say?'

'Are you arresting me?'

'For the moment we're asking you to come along and help us with our inquiries. If you have a solicitor, you might want to ring and ask him to meet you there.'

Mark felt stunned. He was only dimly aware of his eyes filling with tears. He felt lost, out of his depth, totally bewildered by the suddenness of this catastrophe.

'It's all a mistake,' he croaked feebly. 'I'm innocent.'

'Of course you are,' said Judd quietly. 'Everyone is until we prove otherwise. Now, sir, if you'd like to get yourself a coat? It's raining quite heavily.'

'We wouldn't want you to catch a cold, or anything,' added Maddocks.

Mark sat looking at the two detectives in quiet desperation. Now he became aware of the rain drumming rhythmically against the study window. He wanted very much to go back to bed, to fall asleep and wake up to find that this was all a bad dream. But he knew that wasn't going to happen. Not this time. He ground out his cigarette in the ashtray, and rose to his feet.

'I'll get my coat,' he said.

'And the solicitor?' asked Judd.

A streak of stubbornness surfaced amidst Mark's confusion.

'I've done nothing wrong. I won't need one.'

Judd shrugged. 'Suit yourself.' But he and Maddocks glanced at each other, their expressions knowing.

They reckon they've got me, thought Mark. *They think they can make this stick.*

He stumbled into the hallway to collect his coat. The detectives followed, staying close, as though half expecting him to make a run for it.

Maddocks stepped past him to the front door and opened it. Judd had been right. It was raining hard. Mark pulled up the collar of his coat as he followed them to the car.

Chapter Twenty-One

Leonard sat in the bus shelter across the street and watched through the rain-soaked glass as Mark Tyler came out of his house, flanked by the two detectives. He noted with satisfaction that Mark looked pale and nervous as he turned back to secure the front door.

Lock it, thought Leonard. *But you won't keep me out.*

The three men continued up the path, hunched beneath the driving rain, to where a pale blue Ford Escort waited for them. The driver had been smoking a cigarette, which he threw out of the window as his colleagues approached. The younger of the two detectives opened the rear door and motioned Mark inside, then climbed in after him. The older man slid into the front passenger seat. The car moved off along the street, and Leonard sat where he was for the moment, watching intently until it had turned a corner and was out of sight.

Now he studied Tyler's house. There was no sign of a burglar alarm – which made everything so much easier. He got up from his seat and glanced quickly up and down the street. It was deserted, most people either still at work or sheltering from the rain. Leonard crossed the road and went in at the gate. Without hesitating, he walked along the side of the house, and into the back garden. There was a high beech hedge badly in need of pruning, which offered him excellent cover from the view of the neighbours.

Approaching the back door, Leonard lifted a crowbar from under his raincoat. His gloved hands guided it to the gap in the wood beside the mortice lock and he braced himself, found a purchase, and levered back hard. The wood made an ugly, splintering sound and the gap widened visibly. He jammed the bar in further, and pulled back a second time, using all his strength.

The door exploded inward with a sound like a rifle shot, and he froze, glanced quickly around, listening for a challenging shout or sounds of movement beyond the fence. Nothing. Reassured, he pushed his way into the kitchen and closed the door gently behind him.

181

He stood looking around the silent kitchen, noting some dirty mugs and a cereal bowl with a puddle of milk in it standing on the draining board. Cutlery was stacked haphazardly in a plastic drainer, and on a small chalkboard affixed to one wall somebody had written the words WASHING-UP LIQUID! A black Habitat clock above the board was clearly in need of a new battery; its hands were stuck at a quarter to nine, and the second hand was making a rhythmic jerking motion just below the twelve, trying but failing to make it to the next numeral.

Leonard passed through into the dining-room, but found nothing there to interest him. He stepped through a doorway into the adjoining lounge. This was pretty much what he might have expected: a couple of low leather sofas, an expensive television and video set-up, and a state-of-the-art hi-fi unit. On a low pine coffee table, a small framed photograph caught his eye: the portrait of a young woman smiling enigmatically at the camera. Leonard picked it up and examined it carefully, wondering in awe if he was looking at the inspiration for Star Child. She was exactly the kind of girlfriend he would expect Mark Tyler to have: a slim, attractive woman with striking grey eyes. Perhaps he should look her up sometime. If the police decided to hold Mark for a while, she might be glad of some company.

Keep your mind on the task in hand, boy!

The voice, again an insect buzz in his ears, reminding him that he had a job to do. He put the photograph down and gave the room another cursory glance, though he hadn't expected to find much in here.

He proceeded out into the hallway and pushed open a door opposite. From his first glance he knew that he had found what he was looking for. This was Mark's study, the room where he did all his writing – the place where Black Wolf was born. For a moment, Leonard's old feelings asserted themselves. He felt like he was entering a place of sanctity, and would have removed his hat if he'd been wearing one.

Remember, Leonard. Remember what he's done.

He went first to the pin-board fastened to the wall and studied the various book covers, advertisements, reviews and artist's proofs that were affixed to it. Here was a clipping from the *Bookseller*: the Top Twenty hardback list, showing *Black Wolf* up there at number one. Somebody, presumably Mark, had circled it in red ink. Here, too, were photographs: a couple more of the girl whose picture he had studied in the lounge, and one of the same fair-haired young man he remembered topping up Tyler's glass at the book-signing. *Leaping Horse?* Leonard asked himself. Little matter. A friend of Mark Tyler's at any rate, and obviously a good friend to be displayed here on his notice-board. Leonard removed a small photograph of each, and slipped them into his pocket.

He moved over to the bookshelves that filled the alcoves on either side of the chimney breast. One shelf on the left hand side was clearly reserved for Mark's own novels. Here was *Black Wolf*, both in hardcover and paperback, its English and American editions. Here was a special bookclub edition, and here were numerous copies translated into half a dozen European languages. There on the end was the hardback of *Black Wolf 2*, fresh off the press. He noticed that Mark had left plenty of space on this same shelf, in anticipation of many more copies to come . . .

Man's got some disappointment comin' to him.

Leonard turned away from the shelves and approached the desk, the altar on which Mark Tyler plied his trade. An expensive-looking word-processor dominated much of the space, and beside it he found a real treasure: a thick stack of manuscript paper with the words *BLACK WOLF 3: MOON RISING* printed on the top sheet.

Leonard sat down at the desk and examined the stack with mounting excitement. He riffled the pages, lifted them to gauge their weight, and even sniffed them, flaring his nostrils to capture the aroma of paper and ink. This gave him pleasure so intense that it was almost unbearable, and he knew immediately that he would have to take this typescript away with him. So far as he knew, nobody but the author himself had read these words! To be the first other person to sample them . . .

For an instant, part of him wanted to return to the comfort and certainty of being Mark Tyler's blood brother, his number-one fan. It had all seemed so much simpler then. Adoration was such an easy emotion to deal with, almost like the simple security of childhood. This devious, flickering hatred that he nurtured now was far less predictable. But there could be no going back. He had been rejected, his advances spurned. New resolve flowed through his veins. Tyler no longer deserved such adoration, only contempt. And if Leonard found that what he read here corresponded with what Tyler had threatened on the phone . . .

Leonard forced himself to set aside the treasured pages, while he looked for other goodies. Here was a file of letters from various friends and acquaintances. He took a little time to leaf through the contents. Here was a loving little note from over a year ago, from somebody called Sarah, thanking Mark for the flowers and telling him, yes, she'd love to go to the theatre with him. Here was a more recent note from somebody called Brendan, apologising for 'dropping Mark in it the other night – but then, what were friends for?' Leonard smiled and copied names and addresses down on to a scrap of paper, using the author's own fountain pen.

Now here was a letter from Mark's agent confirming that a Mr Tom McBride of Ventona Productions was still expressing genuine interest in acquiring the film rights to the Black Wolf series. Maughan hoped he could arrange a personal meeting with one of McBride's representatives in the not too distant future. Leonard checked the date on the letter; it was only a few days old.

Leonard copied down more details, not wanting to take away the letters themselves in case their absence was noticed. Now, then, what about this metal box standing beside the desk, the key rather stupidly left in the lock?

Leonard lifted the lid and his eyes widened in delight. Computer discs! Apparently everything Tyler had ever written, neatly filed in a box. Right at the front was a disc labelled WOLF 3. He smiled, reached in – and was holding Mark's new novel in his gloved hand. He gloated over it. All that hard work. All that *grind* neatly contained on one piece of plastic! Could Leonard really be so heartless as to steal it? Could he really inflict this kind of pain on Mark Tyler?

Shit, boy! Sure you can!

He got up from the desk and made his way back to the kitchen. Under the sink he found a carrier bag to hold all his newly acquired treasures: the manuscript, the disc, the photographs, the addresses and phone numbers. He felt well pleased with his day's work.

Humming softly to himself, he slipped out the back door. He was pleased to see that the rain had subsided, and now a watery sun was doing its best to break through the clouds.

Mark sat at the table with the two detectives, Judd and Maddocks, and gazed blankly at the television that they had set up in the small, dingy interview room. He had been kept cooped up in here for hours already, the first of them spent by himself, chain-smoking cigarettes. Then he'd been allowed one phone call, using it to call Peter Maughan at his home to explain what had happened. After that the questioning had started in earnest, Judd aggressive and boorish, Maddocks playing it more sympathetically – just the way it was done on the television. The two men were painfully obvious in their attempts to trip him up on his story. Finally, in had come the video equipment.

'We're going to have a little film show,' Maddocks told him. He hit the *play* button on the remote control, and the screen lit up. Mark had known what to expect, but, even so, seeing it happening so blatantly on the screen, gave him a dull sense of shock. No lead-up, no preliminaries, it started suddenly. Just two naked figures grappling on a white bedspread. The action seemed to go on for ages . . . Now, the woman was handcuffing the man's wrists to the metal end-rail.

It was hard to accept that the man in the film was himself – and more so that the woman no longer existed. Mark turned his head to look at the detectives. They seemed to be enjoying themselves, both of them studying the screen intently.

'Is it strictly necessary that we watch any more of this?' asked Mark irritably.

'Come over all shy, have we?' said Maddocks. 'You must have realized that people would want to watch the film once you shot it.'

'I've already told you, I didn't *know* we were being filmed.'

'Mr Tyler, that's very hard to believe. You're telling us you didn't even notice?'

'Why would I? The camera was a long way from the bed, and she didn't even go near the thing. Maybe she had a remote control . . .'

'But isn't there a red light showing when it's recording?'

'I wouldn't have noticed. I'd done some pretty heavy drinking.'

Maddocks nodded at the screen. 'Not much evidence of that,' he observed.

Mark reddened. He now felt totally humiliated.

'Listen,' he said. 'Whatever you may think, nothing I'm doing there is illegal.'

'Perhaps it ought to be,' retorted Judd primly. 'Of course, soliciting for customers in a public place *is* a crime, but Miss McAulay is somewhat beyond our reach now.' Even as he said this, Kim turned and glanced knowingly towards the camera, as though she'd heard him. The effect sent a cold chill through Mark. 'Well, *she* evidently knew the camera was running.' Judd picked up a remote control from the table and aimed it, pressing a button so the screen reverted to grey static.

'It was just getting interesting,' complained Maddocks.

'Well, you'll have to take it home with you, Frank. Add it to your wee collection.' Judd glanced back at Mark. 'I can see that one's going to be popular with the lads. It's a pity you're not earning royalties on it, Mr Tyler.'

'Very funny,' snarled Mark.

'Who's joking?'

'Look, it's just something that happened. It wasn't planned in any way – at least not by me. Can't you see I was only the victim. She was setting me up for blackmail. That taped conversation confirms that much. It could have happened to anyone. It could have happened to you!'

Judd looked positively disgusted.

'It would *not* have happened to me, Mr Tyler! I'm a happily married man, and I haven't got the morals of a tomcat on heat.' He glared at Mark for a moment, making no attempt to conceal his contempt. Then he sat back and sighed. 'What *are* we supposed to think?' he asked. 'Everything points to you. The woman blackmails you, you threaten to kill her, and there's a personally signed copy of your book right there beside her.'

'That's puzzling me,' Mark admitted.

'Is it now?'

'Yes. I'm absolutely sure that I didn't sign a copy for her.'

Maddocks raised his eyebrows.

'But you've seen the book. You've already admitted that it was your handwriting!'

'Oh, I'm not denying that. But you see, I've been thinking about this. She *did* hand me a copy, but then she left without it. And you'll notice that the book doesn't have her name on it. It's just '*To my number-one fan*'. I must have written that five or six times yesterday, for various people. So I think one of them must have left it there.'

Maddocks smiled bleakly.

'Somebody at your book-signing, you mean?'

'It had to be.'

'Why would anybody want to do that?'

'To implicate *me*, I suppose.'

Maddocks glanced at his partner. 'I think he's just dreamed up the plot for his next book.'

Judd tapped his thick fingers rhythmically on the scarred surface of the table. 'So let's get this straight. You're suggesting that somebody else from that book-signing murdered Miss McAulay, and then left the book at the scene to get you dropped in the shit?'

Mark spread his hands in a gesture of hopelessness.

'I can't see any other explanation. If I'd killed her, do you think I'd be so careless as to leave all that incriminating evidence lying around?'

'Maybe you panicked.'

'No! It was put there deliberately.'

'But why, Mr Tyler? Why would anybody wish you harm? A fine, upstanding young chap like yourself?'

Again Mark was dismayed by that look of pure contempt, as though Judd nursed some personal dislike.

'I don't know – but imagine it this way. Kim comes to that signing, and one of the other punters notices her. Let's say he's seriously disturbed. You know the way she dressed: black leather, very revealing. The guy could have got excited by her. Anyway, it also happens he's a fan of my work. So he buys a book, gets it signed, and afterwards he hangs around. Maybe he follows us to the pub. Then, he trails Kim back to her place. It would be easy to get to her. She wasn't exactly the sort that discouraged strangers, was she? After he's killed her it occurs to him that, if he leaves the book behind, the spotlight is bound to fall on me. As it did.'

Maddocks eyed him scornfully.

'Bollocks!' he said. 'I hope to God your novels have better plots than that!'

'Well, I'm sorry. That's the best I can do! I've already told you that there are two witnesses who can vouch for me being in a pub in Leicester Square from three-thirty onwards. And I expect the landlord will remember me, too.'

'The landlord *does* remember you,' Judd admitted. 'Also Mr Maughan confirms that he was indeed there drinking with you. We haven't managed to get hold of the other chap yet.'

Mark glared at him.

'You've already checked with them? How long have you known?'

'I made the calls about an hour ago.'

'Then why . . .?'

'. . . are you still here? I'll tell you. Because our pathologist is still trying to establish the precise time of death. The landlord told me that you arrived at three-fifty-five p.m., not three-thirty, as you claim. A barmaid at The Grapes noticed you arguing with Miss McAulay, and says you left there at about ten minutes to three. By my reckoning, it's just possible that you could have dashed up to Hampstead, killed her and still made it back to your friends in Leicester Square.'

'Are you kidding? Covent Garden to Hampstead and back inside one hour? When did *you* last travel by tube?'

'It's a hectic schedule all right, but not impossible. Let's say you walked up to Tottenham Court Road station. The train to Edgware would take you straight to Hampstead. Miss McAulay's flat is a five-minute walk from the station. Then a train on the Northern Line going south would take you direct to Leicester Square. If our pathologist can establish the time of death somewhere within that hour, I'm going to nail your arse to the wall, Sonny Jim. And, believe me, nothing would give me greater pleasure.'

Mark studied Judd for a moment in silence.

'Is there any particular reason *why* you don't like me?' he asked. 'Or is it just my face?'

Judd sneered.

'No, it's not your face, Mr Tyler. It's your profession.'

'My *what?*'

Judd leaned forward across the table, and his eyes were now openly hostile. 'Let me tell you something. I've got a teenage son at home, and he's a mystery to me. A total mystery. I mean, there's a lad who's had every advantage in life, who's always been taught right from wrong. And he hasn't got a bloody clue. He's always bottom of the class at school. He has hair down to his arse, he wears a leather motorcycle jacket with the words "Iron Maiden" painted on the back and he listens to some Godawful racket called heavy metal. He's also addicted to trashy horror stories and comics. He keeps a whole collection of them up in his room.'

Mark frowned. 'I see.'

'No, you *don't* see! Let me tell you something, pal. If I went home tonight and told him who I'd spent the evening with, he'd be impressed, d'you know? He looks up to people like you. To him, you're Charles Dickens, William Shakespeare and Agatha bloody Christie all rolled up into one handy bite-sized chunk. But shall I tell you what *I* think you are?'

'I'm not sure I want to hear . . .'

'Well, that's tough, Mr Tyler, because you asked me a question, and I'm just getting into my stride. I reckon you're a nasty little man who writes nasty little stories for nasty little minds. *Horror?* Jesus Christ, some of us have to live with it every day of our lives. I've been on the force twenty-seven years and I've seen things that have made me weep. *Real* horror, you understand? And it bothers me that people like you are pedalling this stuff to impressionable youngsters who don't know any better. How many of 'em are gonna wind up imitating what they read in one of your books?'

Mark shook his head.

'There's no evidence that horror fiction contributes to . . .'

'Ah, go on away with your bloody evidence! I'm not impressed by statistics, Mr Tyler. You can make 'em say anything you want. But what I'm saying is this: in a world as grim and nasty as this one, why should anyone want to be reminded of it? Here . . .' He reached into his inside breast pocket and pulled out a manila envelope. He threw it down in front of Mark. 'Take a look,' he said.

Mark opened the flap and reached inside. He extracted a handful of colour photographs. He spread them out on the table top and examined them. They were photographs of Kim. She was hanging by one wrist from a metal bedhead. The chained hand was bent at an impossible angle. Her skin looked very white, and there was more blood than Mark would have thought possible. The open bites on her body were a lurid mixture of red and purple. There were some close-up shots of the bites, clearly showing the impressions of teeth marks. In one shot of her face, Kim was staring straight at the camera, her eyes and mouth wide open, a look of absolute terror etched into every feature. In that picture she didn't look dead. It was as though she was still looking up into the face of her killer and seeing him standing there in front of her.

Mark pushed the photographs away. He felt nausea churning in his stomach and he was dimly aware that his eyes were filling with tears. 'Oh God,' he whispered.

'*That's* horror, Mr Tyler,' snarled Judd, pointing a stubby forefinger at Mark. '*Real* horror. Not the kind of sick fantasies you serve up in the name of entertainment.'

Mark rounded on him angrily.

'What do you know about my work? You've never read one of my books!' He gestured at the photographs. 'And you . . . you think I'm capable of something like that?'

Judd got to his feet.

'That's it, Mr Tyler. Get angry, get indignant! You see, real life isn't like one of your stories. On the printed page, you can spot the monsters a mile off, but in real life these things are done by ordinary-looking people just like you and me.' He retrieved the photographs and put them back in the envelope. 'Now, I'm going to go and chase up those forensic results. And you'd better pray that they don't come out to your detriment.'

He stood there a moment longer, gazing impassively down at Mark, but his fists were clenching as though he wanted to strike him. A nerve in his jaw ticked rhythmically, betraying his inner feelings. Then he turned away and went quickly out of the room, slamming the door behind him.

Mark and Maddocks sat there for a long time in uncomfortable silence. It was Maddocks who spoke first.

'Do yourself a favour. When he comes back, *don't* offer him your autograph.'

Despite himself, Mark smiled ruefully.

'Did you know anything about that stuff? His son and every-thing?'

Maddocks shook his head. 'First I've heard of it. He doesn't talk

much to me about his home life. At least, not usually. He's definitely
got it in for you.'

'And what about you?' he asked. 'Do you think I'm guilty?'

Maddocks shrugged.

'I bloody well hope so,' he said. 'You're the only lead we've got.'

'Oh, that's great. You don't care either way, so long as you feel
somebody's collar?'

'Life's a bitch,' said Maddocks, and left it at that.

Mark took out his cigarettes and lit one up. He sat there, smoking
and waiting, trying not to think about the results of the forensic tests.
Time passed, maybe no more than ten minutes, though to Mark it
seemed more like an hour. He was just stubbing out his cigarette when
Judd came back into the room. It was obvious from the expression on
his face that things hadn't gone the way he wanted.

'You can go,' he told Mark glumly.

The old cliché was never more accurate: Mark really did feel as if
a massive weight had been lifted from his shoulders. He rose quickly
out of his chair, as though buoyed up by sheer relief.

Maddocks looked indignant. 'What happened?'

'They reckon she died between four and five p.m. They can't be any
more specific than that.' He glanced at Mark. 'That just about scrapes
you off the hook.'

'I tried to tell you—'

'Oh, don't try to get smart with me, sonny. I'm not convinced, not
by a long chalk. Forensic tests can be wrong; we've learned that often
enough. So I'll be digging deeper into this; you can depend on that.
We'll just say *au revoir*, shall we?'

Mark glanced at his watch. 'It's kind of late. I don't suppose there's
any chance of a lift home, is there?'

Judd scowled.

'No need for that, Mr Tyler. There's a woman waiting for you out
in the lobby. I understand she has a car.'

'She?' Puzzled, Mark walked out of the room. Maddocks went with
him to the desk, to collect and sign for his few belongings.

'See you soon, then,' said Maddocks, holding open the door.

'Not if I can help it,' he muttered. In the lobby, to his amazement,
he found Sarah waiting for him.

Chapter Twenty-Two

Sarah drove Mark in the direction of home, keeping the speed to a steady thirty, her gaze fixed on the road ahead. Beside her, Mark sat slumped wearily. He was smoking a cigarette as he gazed out at the shuttered shop fronts gliding by in the night. He hadn't spoken since they had got into the car, mainly because he didn't have the first idea what to say to her. From time to time he stole a sideways glance, trying to gauge her mood, but her expression told him nothing. He knew only that he was very glad to see her.

In the end, the silence became uncomfortable, both of them waiting for the other to start. It was Mark who finally took the initiative.

'Thanks for coming,' he said. 'I appreciate it.'

'It's the least I could do,' she assured him. 'Your agent phoned to tell me you were in trouble.'

'Yeah, well, it was very good of you.'

'Were you waiting for me long?'

'A couple of hours. They kept advising me to go home, but I wasn't having any of it.'

'How much did Peter tell you?'

'As much as he knew — which was very little. Just that you'd been picked up as a suspect in a murder inquiry.' She glanced at him warily. 'You want to tell me more?'

He frowned. 'I don't know if I should,' he said. 'I'm scared you mightn't want anything to do with me.' He studied the cigarette in his hand for a moment. 'I wouldn't blame you if you threw me out of the car now, and drove off.'

She looked puzzled by this.

'But they let you go, didn't they? I mean, surely it's a mistake?'

'Oh, I had nothing to do with the murder. But I . . . I *did* know the victim. A girl called Kim McAulay.'

Sarah shook her head. 'I don't think I've heard of her.'

'No reason why you should. I barely knew her myself. But the thing is . . . the awful thing is, I spent the night with her once.'

She glanced at him sharply. 'Not while we were going out?'

'No, it was only about a month ago, just after we split up. I . . . I went with Brendan to this club, and he introduced me to her . . .'

Sarah grimaced. 'Brendan! Oh, I bet he couldn't wait to get you off with somebody else, could he?' She must have sensed her old resentment bubbling to the surface, and she seemed to make an effort to shrug it off. 'Sorry,' she said. 'You don't like it when I get at Brendan, do you?'

He frowned. 'This time he really dropped me in it. The girl was . . . well, there's no polite way to say this. She was a prostitute.'

Sarah flinched, so abruptly that she nearly lost control of the steering. The car swerved sharply to the left, and she had to turn the wheel back hard to correct it. She fell quiet again for a few moments and he could sense her trying to exercise a similar control on her emotions. It was some time before she spoke again.

'Boy, you've obviously had a more eventful time than I have,' she observed.

'Sarah, I know it looks bad, but I swear to you, I didn't know she was a hooker.'

She laughed bitterly.

'Don't these girls establish their fee before you start?'

'Normally, yes . . . I mean, I suppose so. Christ, I'm no expert! But you see, Brendan fixed it all up beforehand. He paid this girl to come on to me, and I just thought . . .'

'You just thought you were God's gift.' She made a sound of exasperation, and he could see the dull spark of anger in her eyes. 'Bloody Brendan! Jesus, I don't want to be the one to say I told you so . . .'

He sighed, nodded.

'It wasn't the cleverest move he's ever made,' he admitted. 'And you can believe I've already roasted his balls for it.'

'My God, Mark, you realize that girl could have given you HIV or hepatitis, or any number of horrible diseases?'

'It's OK, we had safe sex . . .'

'Oh, marvellous! That makes me feel a whole lot better! You went off with a prostitute who wound up murdered, but there's no problem, because you had safe sex with her. Jesus, Mark, get real!' She turned to glare at him. 'Was she good?' she asked.

'What do you mean?'

'I mean, was she a good lay? Did she turn you on? Was it better than with me?'

'Christ, what kind of question's that? It was . . . it was *different*, that's all. And I assumed it was over between us two. If I'd thought for one moment that there was any chance . . .' His voice trailed away.

There was an awful silence after that. They were getting close to Camden Town but, having started on his confession, Mark was determined to tell the whole story.

'It gets worse,' he said.

'It couldn't possibly!'

'Yes it could,' he assured her. He told her about the video camera. He told her about the attempted blackmail. He told her about the tape-recording and the signed book found at the scene of the crime.

She listened in icy silence as he explained everything. Just as he was finishing up, she pulled the car to a halt outside his house.

'My God,' she said softly, 'it's a wonder they haven't locked you up and thrown away the key!'

'They would have done if they could have made it stick. But what frightens the shit out of me is that somebody's obviously trying to frame me.'

'You can't be sure of that. Maybe it's just a coincidence. She could have organized the tape herself – meaning to use it somehow.'

'The tape, sure. But the book, Sarah! I *know* I didn't autograph it for her. That means somebody at that signing session must have killed her, then left their autographed copy deliberately to implicate me.'

'Why would anybody take the trouble?'

'Opportunist maybe? Somebody decided that it would divert suspicion.'

She shook her head. 'It's all too much of a coincidence.'

'Well, how else do you explain it?' He sat looking at her imploringly. 'I've been over it and over it with the police, and the only theory I can come up with sounds so bloody half-baked. Jesus, I wouldn't believe it myself, if I was them. I'm innocent, Sarah. You . . . you do believe that?'

She gazed at him for a moment, then smiled sadly.

'Of course I do. You're many things, Mark – naive, irresponsible, sometimes downright bloody stupid. But you wouldn't harm a fly; I'm sure of that.'

'Thanks . . . I think!' He reached out impulsively and took her hand in his but she didn't respond to his touch. He let go of her and crossed his arms defensively.

'Yes, well, I guess this is where you bail out,' he said. 'I can't blame you. I really messed up this time, didn't I? I just wish we'd never had that argument.'

She nodded. 'Me too.'

'None of this would have happened, then. We'd have been stumbling along just the same as we always were.'

'Maybe.' She looked doubtful. 'Or maybe a split would have happened sooner or later. There were a lot of doubts in my mind. They were simmering away for months before everything blew up. Maybe I was looking for a little stability in my life – a little reassurance that I was more than just your occasional sleeping partner.'

'Oh, but you *were*. It didn't occur to me that you were unhappy with the arrangement. If you'd only said something. If you'd only let me know . . .'

'I tried, several times. But you were always so caught up in your books. I'd be going on about something, and you'd have that glazed look in your eyes – thinking about the next bloody chapter. And then that last time, when I returned your phone call? I intended to swallow my pride, open up to you, tell you all the things that had been worrying me. And what did I get? Only a right mouthful!'

Mark glanced at her, puzzled.

'I'm sorry,' he said. 'When was this?'

'It doesn't matter when it was, Mark. It's just a bit galling to be told to fuck off, when I'd just made the effort to—'

He held up his hands to still her.

'Wait, wait, hold it. There's something I'm not getting! You say I told you to fuck off? No way!'

'Oh, maybe it wasn't those exact words. You must remember – that night you called to say you'd nearly finished the book. So you wanted to go out and celebrate. I put the phone down on you, and then, later, I felt bad about it, so I called you back. Maybe you were drunk and you don't remember.'

'There's no way I'd have said that to you. Jesus, don't you realize there was nothing I wanted *more* than for you to call me . . .' He pondered for a moment, and then it came to him. 'Leonard!' he cried. 'Leonard bloody Goldman!'

She stared at him, uncomprehending.

'What are you talking about?'

'You remember that nut from America who kept sending me weird letters? He phoned me that night, started giving me all this shit. Eventually I slammed the phone down on him. Then, a few minutes later, it rang again. Well, I assumed it was him, so I shouted some abuse and slammed the phone down again.'

'Oh, come on.'

'No, really, I swear to you! I mean, Sarah, if I hadn't heard your voice, how could I know it was you?'

Mark slammed a fist on the dashboard. 'Leonard bloody Goldman! Jesus, I should have known. My life's been going steadily downhill ever since I got that first letter from him. It's like the guy's sole mission is to fuck up my life—'

He broke off in astonishment as he realized what he had just said. Looking at Sarah's expression, he could see that she had just registered the same thought.

'Jesus Christ,' he said.

'Mark, you don't suppose . . .?'

'I don't know. I mean, he's in America, isn't he?'

'No reason why he should be. He can get on a plane just like anybody else.'

'Yes, but he's a harmless nutcase.'

'We don't know that.'

'No and . . . now I come to think of it, that time we spoke on the phone, he made some kind of threat. Something about *making* me talk to him.'

Sarah touched Mark's arm.

'You need to tell this to the police.'

He nodded. He looked at her hopefully.

'You . . . you want to come inside a minute?'

She seemed to consider the question. At last she gave him a weary smile.

'Why not? I could use a cup of coffee.'

They got out of the car and walked through the gate and up to the front door. Mark unlocked the door and they stepped inside. As soon as he switched on the hall lights, he immediately sensed that something was wrong. There was a breeze blowing in from the kitchen and they could hear the sound of wood banging against wood. The two of them exchanged puzzled glances, then Mark led the way through. He switched on the light to reveal the damaged back door, swinging to and fro against its frame. They could see the splintered wood around the lock. The sight of it filled Mark with a cold dread.

'Burglars?' gasped Sarah.

'Maybe,' he said. But he wasn't convinced. He took her arm and led her back into the hall. He reached out a foot and pushed the door of the lounge back into darkness beyond. Switching on the light, he leaned cautiously in and studied the room. The television, video and stereo were enough to convince him that no ordinary burglar had been here.

Feeling suddenly vulnerable, Mark moved across to the fireplace and snatched up a heavy brass poker. Wielding it like a sword, he

195

stepped back into the hall and motioned Sarah behind him.

'You think he's still here?' she whispered fearfully.

He didn't answer. He ignored the dining-room, telling himself that, if his fears were well founded, there was only one room which would interest this particular intruder.

He pushed open the stripped-pine door of the study, and listened for a moment. Only silence. Mark reached out for the light, then stepped into the room, holding the poker ready to strike out at anybody who might be waiting there. That room, too, was empty. But as soon as his gaze fell on the desk top, he knew that something was missing. The place beside the word-processor, where the draft typescript had previously resided, was now shockingly empty. Forgetting his fear, he strode into the room.

'He's taken the bloody manuscript!' cried Mark.

Sarah followed him. 'Your new book?' she asked him.

'It's not a big problem, because I've still got—' He broke off as he noticed that the lockable metal box where he stored his discs had been left open. 'Jesus!' He went down on his knees to look inside it. Every disc but one was there: the one that mattered.

'Oh no,' he hissed.

'The disc too?'

Mark nodded. He stood up again, his face grim, then crossed over to a corner of the room. He lifted back the grey cord carpet to reveal bare floorboards. A short section of one board was loose. He lifted it aside, reached down and pulled out a small Perspex box containing several back-up discs. Then he let out a sigh of relief.

'For once my healthy writer's paranoia has paid off,' he observed. 'Remember how you used to laugh at me for this?' He returned the box to its hiding place and replaced the carpet, then he turned and looked at Sarah. 'Well, that about puts the cap on it,' he said. 'Who else but Leonard Goldman would be obsessive enough to break in here just to take a disc and a manuscript?'

She stood staring at him.

'Mark . . . does this mean that *he* killed the girl?'

'It kind of looks that way, doesn't it? Remember all that stuff in his letters about him actually *being* Black Wolf? I saw some photographs of the corpse. She'd been bitten all over. You could clearly see the teeth marks.'

Sarah's face drained of colour. 'Phone the police,' she whispered. 'Now.'

Mark went over to the phone and picked up the receiver. 'You understand why he's taken the manuscript, don't you? Because I told him that in the new book I intended killing off Black Wolf himself. In his own warped mind he probably thinks that that's as good as killing Goldman, too.' He dialled directory enquiries to obtain the number of the police station.

'It's late,' Sarah reminded him.

'Tough. Those bastards kept me up all night. Now it's their turn.'

'At least, you'll have plenty of evidence,' Sarah reminded him. 'I suppose you've still got all his letters?'

'I can do better than that,' he assured her. 'He sent me his photograph, remember? By this time tomorrow every policeman in London will know exactly what he looks like.'

Leonard set down the last page of the manuscript with a sigh of resignation. He had been sitting crosslegged in the threadbare armchair for hours, reading by the insubstantial glare of the Anglepoise lamp. His neck ached, his eyes were red and bleary, and a deep, fierce hatred was simmering inside him.

Tyler had been telling him the truth. He had carried out his threat, regardless of Leonard's pleas. The first major character to die had been the old whisky-drinking medicine man, Thunder Heart – viciously murdered by Moon, like a hog trussed for the slaughter. Next Leaping Horse was blinded with a hot iron, and sent, weak and helpless, to Black Wolf as a goad to lure him to his own doom. Later, in the blazing music-hall, the kidnapped Star Child had died, impaled on a crossbow bolt – the same weapon then mortally wounding Black Wolf himself. The last glimpse of him occurred as he fought with Moon up in the burning gallery, the two of them tearing and clawing at each other like wild beasts, as the flames moved in to devour them.

Leonard had read to the bitter end, hoping for some remission, some indication that Black Wolf at least would escape the holocaust. But, no, at the book's conclusion, the wind had blown the ashes of the music-hall into fine dust, and the townspeople searched through the destruction to discover the bones of two men fused together by sheer heat, their skeletal hands still clawing at each other.

Leonard got up from his seat and paced restlessly around the room. Then he reached a hand into the back pocket of his jeans and withdrew the computer disc. He carried it across to the open fireplace, and picked up a box of matches off the mantelpiece. He struck a match and held it against the corner of the disc. The plastic warped, bubbled, then caught light. Thick black smoke coiled up from the blue flame, and an acrid smell filled the room. Leonard leaned into the fireplace and tucked the disc into the grate, propping it upright so that the flames would eat up the whole of the casing.

He had thought that this destruction would give him an immense satisfaction, but still he couldn't settle. Still he had doubts. There might be other copies of the typescript deposited with Mark's agent or with his publisher. It was even possible that Tyler might have back-up discs hidden away somewhere safe. So Leonard couldn't be sure – not really sure – that he had prevented the publication of this abomination.

The disc flared with a hiss, as a bright yellow flame enveloped it. Gazing at it abstractedly, Leonard suddenly heard the voice again whispering in his ear.

Fight fire with fire!

And suddenly he knew exactly what he must do. He'd make Mark Tyler appreciate the true ramifications of his own – of their joint – imagination. He'd make him too afraid to even consider releasing this so-called novel. By the time Leonard had finished with him, Tyler would be only too willing to burn any remaining copies himself.

But now it was late, and Leonard was tired. He'd start again first thing tomorrow. He pulled off his clothes and went over to the single bed in the corner of the room. Switching off the lamp, he lay back and closed his eyes. Within minutes he was fast asleep – and dreaming of revenge.

Chapter Twenty-Three

Peter Maughan sat at his office desk reading that morning's edition of the *Daily Telegraph* with rather more attention than usual. Eventually he found a mention of the girl's murder tucked away on page two, a brief snippet simply relating that one Kim McAulay, nineteen years old, had been found brutally murdered at her upper-floor apartment in Hampstead. A man was helping the police with their inquiries.

Maughan breathed a sigh of relief. No names mentioned, thank God! With Mark's career poised at such a crucial stage, it was imperative that his name should not be linked with anything unsavoury, whether he was genuinely involved or not. Well, it seemed he'd been lucky. Nobody appeared to have discovered the suspect's name, and a call to the police station this morning had yielded encouraging news. Mark had been released last night, and gone home with a female friend. Presumably that was Sarah. Peter very much hoped that a reunion was on the cards. Mark evidently kept the wrong kind of company when left to his own devices.

Meg came into the office bearing two mugs of steaming coffee, and he smiled his gratitude.

'Just what the doctor ordered.' He folded the newspaper and threw it down on the desk top. Meg raised an inquisitive eyebrow.

'Anything?' she asked.

He shook his head. 'It merely mentions a man helping the police with their inquiries, but thankfully no name. He was released late last night, so even if the evening papers pick up on it there's nothing much they can say.'

'The *Mail* had pretty much the same story. He's been lucky.'

'Indeed.' Peter sipped at his coffee and gave a contented sigh. 'That's better,' he said. 'I barely got an hour's sleep last night, for worrying. God only knows how Mark must have felt.'

'Want me to give him a ring?'

Peter shook his head. 'Let the poor bugger get some rest. What's the point in hassling him? He'll get in touch when he's ready.'

Meg held her coffee in both hands and gazed thoughtfully out of the window. It was another bleak, chilly morning and, down below, the rumble of traffic, the blaring of car horns and the incessant chatter of pneumatic drills provided an irritating background for her reflections.

The phone rang, adding to the din, and she picked up the receiver. 'Hello, the Peter Maughan Literary Agency? Yes, who's calling, please? Oh, right! I'll just put you on hold for a moment, while I see if he's available.' She punched a button and glanced at her boss. 'Do you want to talk to Mr Al Schneider?'

'Al who?'

'Schneider. He says he's the new PA to Tom McBride at Ventona Productions.'

Maughan brightened. 'Put him on. I smell money!' He reached out a hand for the phone.

'Mr Maughan?' This is Al Schneider, personal assistant to Tom McBride.' A smooth transatlantic drawl poured out of the earpiece.

'Hello, there. But whatever happened to the lady I spoke to a few weeks ago . . . Rebecca Quinn?'

'Rebecca got a better offer. She's gone to Paramount.'

'Has she indeed? I must say, this is a wonderful line. You sound as though you're just down the road.'

'I *am* just down the road. I'm in London sewing up some rights to a TV mini series, and Tom asked me to call in for a chat about *Black Wolf*. We're now about ready to firm up our offer.'

'Excellent. Well, how long are you in town?'

'Just till tomorrow. But Tom's very keen to get this deal tied up.'

'I see . . .'

'There's no problem, I hope?'

'No, of course not. Only that it's not a great time for Mark Tyler. He's, er, very tied up with his new novel at the moment.'

'That's OK. I wasn't expecting him to be involved at this early stage. It's really just to talk over the terms of the contract.'

'Fair enough.'

'Trouble is, I'm flying out first thing in the morning, so I was hoping to drop by your office later this afternoon. What time do you stay till?'

'Around six p.m.'

'I hope I can make it in time.'

'No problem, I'll hang around till you arrive. Or perhaps you'd like to discuss things over dinner?'

A pause. 'Sounds good. My treat though, I insist.'

'I never argue about being treated. Well, I'll look forward to seeing you later on. I'm sure between us we can reach a satisfactory deal.'

'I hope so. Till tonight then.'

Peter put down the receiver.

'Sounds promising?' Meg observed.

'Ventona are ready to make an offer.'

'Did he mention a figure?'

'No. We'll talk it all through tonight. Once we're wined and dined, I'm sure we'll hit on a mutually agreeable sum. It's a three-movie package, remember.'

Meg frowned. 'I presume that means my presence won't be required.'

Peter smiled sweetly.

'Don't worry. I'll give you a blow-by-blow account, tomorrow morning.'

Meg chuckled. 'I love it when you talk dirty to me,' she said.

She went out of the door and down the stairs to her own office, where a disconcertingly thick manuscript waited for her perusal.

Mark paced impatiently up and down his study, while Detectives Judd and Maddocks sat side-by-side on the sofa, reading some sample pages from the collected letters of Leonard J. Goldman. It seemed to take them forever to get through a couple of pages apiece.

It had taken them an inordinately long time to get back in touch with him after his phone call last night. And, now they were here, they seemed, if anything, somewhat put out to discover that they had been called to what appeared to be a routine burglary.

Mark's mood wasn't helped by suffering a restless night. Sarah had headed off to her own place about two a.m., and he'd spent the subsequent hours either tossing and turning on his bed or experiencing bad dreams in which his house was infiltrated by scores of unseen prowlers with murderous intent. For the first time ever he felt nervous and uncomfortable in his own home, and that bothered him considerably.

Judd set down the letter he had been reading, and fixed Mark with a worldweary look.

'All right,' he said in that dour Glaswegian accent. 'So this guy is several butties short of a picnic, but I hardly see why you've dragged us out here.'

Mark stood staring at Judd in disbelief.

'I thought I explained to you, I think this is the man who broke in here yesterday . . . and also the man who murdered Kim McAulay.'

Maddocks smiled. 'What makes you think that, Mr Tyler?'

'You may need to read some more of his letters . . .'

'We're not exactly blessed with spare time,' Judd reminded him. 'Supposing you just tell us?'

Mark indicated the sheaf of papers on the sofa. 'This guy is an obsessive horror fan. He's focused in on the *Black Wolf* novels. When he first started writing to me, his letters were complimentary and obsequious, if a little over the top. But once I stopped replying, they became increasingly bitter and threatening.'

Judd spread his hands.

'So?' he muttered. 'He wrote you a few nasty letters. That hardly makes him a psychopath, does it?'

'No, but I don't think you appreciate the depths of his delusions. He told me that he believed he actually *was* Black Wolf – a creature increasingly drawn to feeding on human blood. I saw those photographs of Kim McAulay. Her body was bitten all over.'

Judd gave a grunt of exasperation.

'Please, spare me the amateur detective routine, Mr Tyler. All right, I can accept that this Goldberg character—'

'Goldman. Leonard Goldman.'

'I can accept that he might be a bit pissed off with you, but why would he kill a complete stranger?'

'Because he knew it would implicate me!'

'And how would he know that? Psychic, is he?'

Mark shrugged.

'Your guess is as good as mine. Maybe he's been watching me, waiting for his opportunity. Maybe he was there at the book launch . . .'

'Maybe, maybe! This is all supposition, Mr Tyler. We can't work from maybes. We need established facts if we're to build a case. The only facts I see here are that you've had a wee break-in.'

Mark buried his face in his hands.

'A break-in,' he groaned.

'Yes, that's exactly what it is.'

'And what kind of burglar steals only an unpublished typescript and a computer disc, but leaves a video and television absolutely untouched? Perhaps you can explain that to me?'

But it was Maddocks who chose to do that.

'You've acquired quite a reputation lately, haven't you? Articles about you in the papers, radio, television . . . that kind of thing?'

'Yes. So?'

'So your villains aren't totally stupid. They came into this room, saw the book covers and stuff on the board there, and realized they might be on to something bigger than a stolen video. It wouldn't surprise me if you got a call from them soon – holding your missing book to ransom.'

Mark clapped a hand to his forehead in disbelief. 'Oh, so now we've got a booknapper to contend with. Christ, and I thought you didn't deal in supposition. Doesn't it seem at all likely to you that both crimes were committed by the same man?'

'It doesn't follow,' said Judd, looking genuinely puzzled. 'Why would he want to take your manuscript?'

'Because, Inspector, in my new book I eventually kill off the character of Black Wolf. Goldman knew this. And since he's convinced he *is* Black Wolf, he may, in his obsessive fantasies, believe that I am deliberately trying to kill *him*. By destroying my novel, he'll then be ensuring his own survival. Don't you see what I'm getting at?'

'I see, but it still sounds like a load of nonsense to me.' Judd sighed. 'You said something earlier about a photograph?'

'It's right there with the letters.'

'Oh yeah, right.' Judd picked out the photograph and studied it for a moment. 'Lovely grin,' he observed. He handed it to Maddocks, who shook his head slowly from side to side. Judd glanced up at Mark. 'Well, there's no way this is our man,' he said.

'What makes you say that?'

The two detectives glanced at each other doubtfully. It was clear that they were reluctant to say more – but Judd eventually coughed up the information.

'This is just between you and us, right? The forensic pathologist has now established that our killer has large, misshapen teeth.'

'Forensics can be wrong. I heard you say that last night!'

'Well, true, but in this case I've seen the evidence, and I have to agree. The man we're looking for would have to have long jagged teeth – resembling those of a dog.'

'Or a wolf?' asked Mark, and saw Judd's eyes widen at the thought.

'Coincidence,' he murmured. But he now didn't sound quite so sure of himself.

'Something else you said the other night, Inspector. You'll forgive me if I quote you? "In real life, these things are done by ordinary-looking people just like you and me."'

Judd scowled. 'You've a good memory, Mr Tyler.'

'Occupational hazard. Who knows, one day I might need to include the character of a pig-headed, short-sighted copper in one of my novels.' Judd shot him a vitriolic glare, but he ignored it. 'Listen, you have Goldman's photograph. You have his address and home phone number in the States. Surely to God it won't hurt to make a few inquiries? What have you got to lose? You could even get your forensic people up here to have a look round this house.'

Judd nodded and glanced at his partner.

'Tell you what I'm gonna do, Mr Tyler. I'm going to take this wee photograph and this name and phone number here. And when I get a moment, I'll make some inquiries about this Goldman character. Just maybe, it's worth a shot.' He slipped the photograph and a piece of headed paper into his pocket.

'Waste of bloody time if you ask me,' said Maddocks.

'I didn't ask you.' Judd got to his feet, and Maddocks followed suit. 'But, if it sets our Mr Tyler's mind at rest, it's worth taking the trouble, isn't it?'

'And the forensic people?' asked Mark hopefully.

Judd sighed. 'I'll say one thing for you. You don't give up easy, do you? Aye . . . all right, I'll see what I can do. Could be some time before they're available though.' The detectives headed out into the hallway, and Mark followed them to the front door.

'We'll be in touch,' Judd told him. He opened the door and Maddocks stepped out. Judd was about to follow him, but hesitated in the doorway and turned back. 'Oh, er . . . one more thing, Mr Tyler. I suppose I owe you an apology . . . for the rough way I behaved at the station. I'm sure you appreciate I was only trying to do my job.'

Mark stared at him coolly. 'I would say that you somewhat exceeded your brief, Inspector. All that stuff about how I make my living, it really had nothing to do with the case.'

Judd nodded, smiled sheepishly. It was clear he was worried about the matter being reported to his superiors. 'No, I suppose not. Heat of the moment and all that. Still, no hard feelings, eh?' He reached out a hand, to shake.

Mark gazed at him thoughtfully for a moment. Then he took a step back and shut the door in his face.

Smiling, he strolled back to the kitchen to make himself a cup of coffee. Sometimes the pettiest revenge could be the sweetest of all.

Chapter Twenty-Four

Meg came into Peter's office at a little after six p.m., a large Jiffy bag containing the manuscript tucked under her arm. She glanced hopefully around the office as though suspecting that the glamorous-sounding Al Schneider might be hiding behind a pile of paperbacks.

'He's late,' she observed.

Peter nodded. 'You may as well go on home,' he told her. 'There's no reason to hang on here.'

She looked disappointed.

'I was hoping to get at least a look at him before I left. I mean, it isn't every day you get to see an honest-to-goodness Hollywood film producer.'

'Only a Hollywood film producer's assistant,' he reminded her, then glanced disparagingly at his wristwatch. 'Well, I'll give the bugger another ten minutes,' he decided.

Right on cue, the intercom buzzed. Peter and Meg exchanged glances.

'Halle-bloody-lujah!' said Maughan. He leaned over to the wall and pressed an intercom button. 'Yes?' he inquired.

'Al Schneider, Ventona Productions.'

'Come right in. Straight up to the second floor.'

Peter pressed the door-release button, then smiled at Meg. 'Looks like you'll get your wish after all.'

A few moments later, Schneider was bustling into the room, a tall rangy American with a neatly clipped moustache and an Armani suit. He had an expensive leather attaché case in one hand. He smiled as he reached across the desk to shake hands.

'Traffic was kind of hairy on the way here,' he apologised. 'Your taxi drivers are amazing. Guy didn't stop talking the whole way.'

Peter introduced him to Meg, who immediately offered to make coffee.

'Oh no, thank you. I'm cutting down. No more than two cups a day.' He slipped into the vacant seat, and set down his briefcase at his feet.

Maughan flashed Meg a meaningful look, which was an invitation to make herself scarce.

'Well, I'll be off then,' she announced lamely, not without a trace of regret. She would have liked to listen in and get the latest hot poop from Hollywood. Hearing it all second-hand from her boss the next morning just wouldn't be the same.

'You're not going to join us?' asked Schneider in a disappointed tone.

'No,' she told him. 'Back at my flat there's a piece of cheese on toast with my name on it.' She smiled sadly. 'It was nice to meet you, Mr Schneider.' She extended a hand and he stood up to shake it. She left the room and the two men could hear her footsteps going down the stairs.

'Pleasant lady,' observed Schneider.

'Oh, she's a treasure,' admitted Peter. He leaned back in his seat and smiled at Al thoughtfully. 'So, how did your miniseries work out?'

'Pretty good. Tom's keen on getting one of your best British actors for the lead role. We were originally hoping to tempt Anthony Hopkins, but, of course, he's red hot at the moment. Everybody's after him.' They heard the dull thud as the front door slammed.

Al leaned forward and picked up his attaché case. 'Now, before we go any further, Tom asked me to give you something.' He laid the case on the desk-top, and stood up so he could reach inside it. 'A little souvenir from New York,' he added.

Intrigued, Maughan stood up too. 'I love surprises.'

'Good.' When Al withdrew his hand, he was holding a heavy leather cosh with a flexible plastic handle. He whipped back an arm and hit the agent hard across the side of the head, just by his left temple. The ballbearings packed into the leather bag made a thunking noise as they rebounded off Peter's cranium. He jerked as though touched by an electric prod, and his limbs seemed to become rubbery. Then he collapsed, his outstretched hand clawing madly at the jumble on his desk, scattering telephone, files and papers, before he tipped sideways and hit the floor.

Leonard watched him for a moment, ensuring himself that Maughan wasn't faking. He prodded him in the ribs with the toe of one boot, but the agent didn't stir. For a moment, Leonard feared that he might have killed him too soon, but then he saw his victim's chest was rising and fall-ing. Good. Reaching into the attaché case again, he pulled out a length of rope. That he put to one side, then removed his jacket and threw it over a vacant chair. Squatting down, humming softly to himself, he began to remove Maughan's clothes.

* * *

Consciousness came back to Peter Maughan a little bit at a time. The first thing he was aware of was a sparking electric redness at the back of his eyes and a shifting wave of nausea undulating in his stomach. One whole side of his head ached with a dull throb of pain. Now his eyes opened but as yet, he was aware only of light, everything else was a blur. His next impression was rather startling. It was the sensation of his naked buttocks pressing against a hard, unyielding surface. He attempted to stand up but found that he couldn't. Something was holding him securely in place.

He let out a groan and tried to clear his thoughts. He'd been standing at his desk with Al Schneider, and then . . .

There was the familiar touch of his glasses, as somebody pushed them gently into position on his face. The world gradually swam into focus. He registered the shape of his desk and saw Al Schneider sitting at it, apparently waiting for him to come round. The man smiled warmly, showing his even white teeth.

Still disorientated, Peter smiled feebly back and then looked down at his lap. He was horrified to see his own body naked, tightly bound into a wooden captain's chair. Ropes encircled his thighs and his ankles, holding them in position. The shock served to bring him back to full awareness. He tried to move his arms, but they too were tightly bound to the chair. He struggled ineffectually for a moment – before relaxing with a gasp. He looked up at the other man again.

'You're . . . you're not with any film company!' he snapped. Immediately he felt rather foolish. It seemed a ridiculously obvious remark.

Leonard chuckled, but for the moment he said nothing. He was watching Maughan with interest, as though entertained by his predicament. Then he reached a hand up to his moustache and peeled it right off his face. Peter stared at him in disbelief.

'We don't keep any money on the premises,' he said, fighting hard to stay calm. 'You'll find a few pounds in my wallet. Please take that and go.'

Again the man said nothing. He simply studied his bound victim with those odd tawny-coloured eyes.

'Look, what is this?' demanded Peter. 'What do you want? I think you'd better untie me, right now!'

Leonard got up from his seat. Then he stepped around the desk to his attaché case. He reached inside it, and Maughan felt a jolt of pure fear kicking like a startled frog in his chest. The hands came out again, holding nothing more fearsome than a thick stack of paper. He turned away from the desk and came to stand directly in front of Maughan, holding the typescript out for him to inspect.

'What do you know about this?' he asked, and his voice was now different, the accent still American but much coarser – quite unlike the smooth drawl used earlier.

Peter stared at the typescript in surprise. On its top sheet, he could quite clearly see the title printed in large bold capitals: *Black Wolf 3: Moon Rising*.

'Good God,' he said. 'That's Mark Tyler's new book?'

The man nodded.

'Well . . . how did you get hold of it?'

'That's not important. Have you read it?'

Peter shook his head. 'No,' he said. 'It's not finished yet. But how did you get hold of it?'

'I took it.'

'Who *are* you? What's this all about?'

'I'm Leonard J. Goldman.'

Maughan frowned. That name meant *something* to him, but he couldn't place it.

'Well, now, look . . . Mr Goldman, don't you think you'd better untie me? I don't know what all this is about, but I'm sure we can—'

He broke off in stunned surprise as Leonard swiped him across the face with the manuscript, the impact rocking his head sideways, half dislodging his glasses. Shock and fear pounded in Maughan's chest. He was only just beginning to appreciate the full horror of his position.

'You *know* what it's about!' roared Leonard. 'You know *exactly* what it's about. I want you to explain this . . . this *pornography* to me!' He waved the manuscript in Peter's face, scattering stray sheets in all directions.

'But I told you . . . I haven't read it.'

'Of course you've read it. You're his agent. You p . . . probably collaborated on it. You've probably got your own copy tucked away somewhere!'

'No! No, I swear to you! I haven't read a word of it. What is it that offends you?'

Leonard moved his face up close.

'You really don't know?' he whispered, 'what he's trying to do to me?'

'I don't know what you're talking about.'

'He's trying to kill me. And he has to be stopped. He has to be deterred.'

Oh dear God, thought Peter. *He's a maniac. He's raving.*

And then he remembered where he'd heard that name before. Leonard Goldman. Mark had mentioned him. That series of screwy fan letters – each one weirder than the next. And now he was here, in Britain. Somehow he had got hold of Mark's new manuscript. This man was deranged: he was capable of anything. Oh, sweet Jesus . . .

Leonard was pacing up and down the office, slapping the residue of the manuscript repeatedly against his leg.

'He told me all about what he was planning. He was going to k . . . kill me off. The rest of it's right here in black and white!'

'That's awful!' Maughan decided to go along with him. It seemed the most prudent course. 'He can't do that. It's . . . unthinkable . . .'

Leonard came to a halt and turned back to stare at him with interest. 'Really?' he asked.

'Absolutely! It makes no sense at all. *Black Wolf* has been a resounding success. It has to go on and on. Don't worry, I'll see to it that it continues.'

Leonard was moving closer, staring intently. He reached out and gently readjusted Maughan's glasses. 'But you're only his agent. Do you have so much power?'

'Of course! He trusts me. He wouldn't write a word without my guidance.'

Leonard smiled slyly.

'If that's so . . .'

'It is, it is!'

'Then *you* must have guided him to write *this* filth!' He held the manuscript at arm's length. 'This must have been *your* idea.'

Peter's eyes widened as he realized his mistake.

'Oh no, I didn't mean that. He's done this off his own bat. There's no way . . . no way I'd advise him to do that. Never!'

Leonard frowned. He turned away and walked back to the desk. He put down the manuscript and began to unbutton his shirt.

'The part that really upsets me,' he murmured, 'is what Thaddeus Moon does to old Thunder Heart. That poor noble old Indian. To be treated like that – like some animal! I don't mind telling you, I cried when I read it. I *sobbed*!'

He removed the shirt and draped it over a chair. Peter stared in horrified fascination at the thick covering of hair on Leonard's back.

'What are you doing?' he asked.

Leonard ignored the question. He sat down in the chair and began to untie his shoe laces.

'A mind that can conceive of such a thing. That's a distorted mind. That's an evil mind.'

Maughan licked at his dry lips. He was now desperately afraid.

'Tyler has to be shown! We've got to make a stand.' Now Leonard was removing his trousers. The sight of his thick, hairy legs repulsed Peter.

'Please,' Maughan whispered. 'Can't we talk about this? Look, why don't we phone him up right now? What do you say? Phone him up and tell him we're here – and why doesn't he come on over for a chat, just the three of us? Shall we, Leonard? Shall we do that?'

Leonard was completely naked now. He didn't seem to be even aware of what Maughan was saying. He stood up and walked to the desk, where he reached into his case. Then he tilted his head to one side, as though listening to something.

'Yes,' he muttered. 'Yes, we have to do it.'

'Who are you talking to?'

The naked man didn't seem to hear the question. He was nodding away as though there was somebody else in the room with them.

'Leonard, please, we must talk about this. I beg of you! If we could just—'

Peter broke off, his heart in his throat, as Leonard turned back to face him. He was holding a Stanley knife fitted with a hooked blade, the kind for cutting linoleum. He walked back towards the trussed agent, his face expressionless.

'No!' Maughan thrashed his head from side to side, numb with the adrenalin jolting through his body. 'Please . . . please!'

When Leonard jabbed the hooked blade into Maughan's belly-button, the man lost control of his bladder. He was dimly aware of warm urine pulsing down his legs. He closed his eyes, and steeled himself for the next impact, but it didn't come. After a few moments, he dared to open them again – and saw a look of doubt on his tormentor's face. He saw how his powerful arm trembled as he held the knife.

Abruptly, Leonard seemed to think better of his original impulse. He jerked the knife free, and a thin trickle of blood coursed its way across the curve of Maughan's white belly. Leonard walked back to the desk, shaking his head from side to side. The bound victim remembered to breathe, his heart pounding so hard he thought he might be about to suffer a coronary.

Leonard was rummaging in his attaché case again. Then he lifted something to his face, and appeared to swallow it.

And then he turned around and came striding across with renewed interest, a savage grin on his face, the knife held ready. But Maughan just had time to register that the grin was different now: it was composed of twin rows of jagged doglike teeth. Then the blade was again in Peter's belly, and rising upwards, the flesh parting like a curtain. He grunted as the hooked blade ground agonizingly against his breast bone, and he found himself staring down in surprise as a mass of bloody viscera plopped out into his lap. He was astonished by all the colours. The shocking red he had expected, but there were also pinks, browns, and a deep, vivid purple. There was a terrible stench too, which was augmented as his bowels spasmed and emptied themselves. He sat watching in stunned belief as Leonard plunged his hands into this jumble of guts, and used his knife to cut something free. Maughan only vaguely registered the pain, and he noted how odd it felt to have his insides being manhandled *outside* his body.

Now Leonard raised the dripping liver in both hands and took a ravenous bite out of it. The blood squirting down his chin matted into the thick hair on his chest. He put out his tongue and licked his lips.

'Yum,' he said.

Then darkness drifted in, obscuring everything and Peter Maughan let himself drop into the void – grateful for the opportunity to escape . . .

Chapter Twenty-Five

Sheriff Sam Wade eased his lanky frame back in his office chair and crossed his hand-tooled boots on the top of his desk. It was a little after three in the afternoon and he thought he might get away with an hour's nap, if he was lucky.

Dennings was currently sweltering through an Indian summer and it was unseasonably hot for mid-September, the daily temperature still punching high into the 90s. The ancient electric fan, mounted on the wall above him, rattled and clattered, stirring the listless air without actually making it noticeably cooler, and Sam's game-plan for the day was to do as little as possible, thus conserving energy and maintaining a bearable body temperature.

It had been kind of quiet lately. Dennings had slipped back into its more usual mode after all that excitement over the 'Wolfman' murders. Chapman and Corelli, the two Pittsburgh cops sent down to conduct the enquiry, seemed to be getting absolutely nowhere with their investigations, a state of affairs that secretly delighted Sam. The two city slickers had been pretty snotty with him from the word go, berating him for shooting his mouth off to the local paper, and making it quite plain that they wanted him to keep out of their way. That suited Sam. He hadn't so much as clapped eyes on them for several days, and he certainly wasn't losing any sleep over it.

The door to his office opened and Marvin Grant, Sam's chief deputy, ducked his prematurely balding head into the room. Marvin was a thin, dour-looking individual with a mournful face and a long beak-like nose.

'Sam, there's a call for you out here,' he announced in his sleepy drawl. 'Reckon maybe you might want to take it.'

'Marvin, I told you, only real *important* calls!'

'Yes, sir. Well this is some feller name of Judd, speakin' from London.'

'You mean London, Ohio?'

'Nope, I mean London, *England*.'

'The hell, you say!'

'Feller says he's a cop. Wants to talk to whoever's in charge here.'

Sam frowned. 'Better put him through, I guess.'

Marvin nodded glumly and closed the door. Sam was impressed. He didn't think he'd ever taken a call from England before. The phone on his desk trilled and he lifted the receiver.

'Hello, Sheriff Sam Wade speaking. Can I help you?'

'I certainly hope so.' The line was surprisingly clear, which was more than could be said for the *accent*. What the hell was it, Scottish or something? 'This is Detective Inspector Judd, Metropolitan CID. I'm currently heading a murder inquiry, and it's been suggested to me that you may be able to help.'

'Really?' Sam swung his legs down from the desk and paid closer attention. 'Well, sure. Anything I can do, sir. Say, what time you got over there?'

'It's eight p.m.'

'Boy, you guys always work this late?'

Judd chose to ignore the question. 'I'm interested in a man who lives in your town – feller by the name of Goldman. Leonard Goldman.'

'Now, why would you be interested in him, I wonder? I hope nothin's happened to him.'

'I really wouldn't know. His name was mentioned, that's all. You know him?'

'Why, sure. Dennings is a small town, Inspector. I know just about everybody. But, er, did you say this was part of a murder inquiry? Goldman hasn't been killed or anything?'

'No. He's a potential suspect.'

Sam laughed at that.

'You kidding me? You ever met Leonard Goldman?'

'No, I haven't.'

'Well, 'scuse me for laughing, sir, but he's a great big quiet hulk of a feller. Why, until recently he was still living with his *mother*!'

'That's very interesting, Sheriff Wade. But, you see, he's written some letters to a man here in London, and I'd like to ask him some questions about them. I wondered if you could arrange that for me?'

Sam frowned. 'That'd be kind of difficult, right now. In fact, I'd say you'd have a better chance of arranging it yourself.'

'Sorry?'

'He's away on holiday. Been gone these three weeks or more, and I ain't rightly sure when he's expected back. Crazy thing is, he's gone to England. That's why I was askin' if something had happened to him. See, I know all about it because he phoned and asked us to keep an eye on his house while he was gone.' Sam registered the baffled silence on the other end of the line. 'Hello, you still there?'

'Uh, yes, still here. I was a little taken aback, that's all. Three weeks, you said? You, er, wouldn't know exactly where he was planning to stay, would you?'

'No sir. He didn't leave that much information. Talk locally is that he run off t' get married.'

'Married?'

'Uh yes, sir. He took somebody along with him. His housekeeper – lady by the name of Brenda Loomis. Seems she's had her sights fixed on ol' Leonard for a long time, and now his mother's dead, well, the poor devil prob'ly didn't have the stuff left to fight 'er off. Brenda's a reputation for being kind've bossy, you know?'

'I see.' Another long pause. 'But in your opinion, Sheriff Wade, this Goldman character is harmless?'

'Yes, sir, I'd say so. Fact is, he was checked out only recently by a couple of detectives here in Dennings, and they figured he was just a harmless 'centric. . .'

'He was investigated? For what?'

'For the "Wolfman" murders. Biggest thing that's happened in these parts in I don't know how long!'

'The "Wolfman" murders?'

Inspector Judd was beginning to sound like an echo.

'That's what the local papers called 'em, on account of the victims was all bitten around the throat. Goldman came under suspicion mainly 'cos he worked alongside two of the kids that was killed, but in the end there weren't nothin' in it . . . Inspector? You still there?'

Judd cleared his throat. When he spoke again, his voice was unnaturally calm, as though he was having to exercise considerable control to keep his temper.

'Sheriff Wade, you might be interested to learn that we've just had an identical killing here in London. A young lady apparently *bitten* to death.'

'Holy shit!' Sam sat upright in his chair. 'You ain't joshing me, now?'

'I can assure you I'm not! Just who exactly is heading up this inquiry of yours?'

'Not me, sir! Coupl'a detectives from outa town. Called Chapman and Corelli.'

'Well, perhaps I'd better have a word with them.'

'Yes, sir, sure! Only I don't rightly know how to get a hold of 'em just now. They don't check in with me that often.'

'That's some bloody circus you're running over there, isn't it?' Judd sounded like he was rapidly losing his patience.

'Sir?'

'Never mind.' Another pause, while Judd thought the matter over. 'This house of Goldman's. Perhaps, under the circumstances, it might be an idea to check it out?'

'Sure thing, Inspector. I'll get on to it right away, and I'll report straight back.'

'Do that, would you? That's if you can manage to *find* the place.'

'Don't you worry on that score, sir. 'Tween you and me, though, I'm still dubious about this whole thing. I can't see Leonard Goldman as no killer. That boy wouldn't say boo to a goose.'

'Just get back to me as soon as possible, Sheriff. I'll be waiting for your call.' Judd gave him a contact number, and then hung up. Sam tore the scrap of paper with the number off his pad, and slipped it into his shirt pocket. As he got up out of his chair, he was immediately aware of two islands of sweat beneath his armpits.

Godamned snotty sonofabitch, he thought. He hadn't missed the sarcasm in Judd's remarks. He opened the top drawer of his desk, took out his .38 pistol in its leather holster, and buckled it around his waist. It was beginning to look as though those two smug assholes from Pittsburgh had fouled up, after all. It occurred to Sam that it might be an immense feather in his own cap to be the one to solve this case behind their backs. After all, he could always play down the fact that the Scottish cop had more or less spelled things out for him. He could tell everyone that he had simply played a hunch – phoned up London after Goldman had announced he was going there. There had to be some way he could work this news to his advantage.

He put on his hat, opened the door of the office and went through the room beyond. Marvin was seated at an ancient manual typewriter, making out a traffic violation form with one hand and holding a battery-powered fan in the other. He looked up in surprise as Sam emerged from his inner sanctum.

'Goin' out?' he asked incredulously.

'Yeah. I'm headin' over to the old Goldman house. Shouldn't be gone long.'

'Ain't nobody there, Sam. He's away on holiday, remember?'

'I know that. I, er . . . got a hunch about the place, that's all. Figured I'd just see if it played out.'

'A hunch?' Marvin looked at him suspiciously.

'Yeah. Say, if those two detectives should radio in you, er . . . you might just tell 'em I'm out solvin' them murders for 'em.'

Grinning, he left Marvin to ponder that one, and he stepped out the front door. The afternoon sun struck him like a lead-weighted baseball bat.

Mother of God, it's hot!

He unlocked the door of his car and slid his rump gingerly on to the scalding upholstery. Quickly he opened all the windows. The interior of the car felt as dry and airless as an oven, and he was aware of his clothes already beginning to stick to him. He closed the door, started up the engine, and drove the short distance across town to the Goldman residence.

The old brownstone looked invitingly cool under the merciless blue sky. Sam left the car by the front gate and went in along the path and up the three steps to the front door. He peered in through the frosted glass, but couldn't see much. He stood back, surveyed the upstairs windows, which were all shut tight against the outside world. He went around to the back, and saw that a small window in the kitchen had been left open, but it was up high, out of his reach. He dragged a metal garbage bin under the window – that small effort wringing fresh beads of sweat from every pore. Then he clambered up on to the bin, reached an arm through the gap, and managed to hook his fingers around the old-fashioned latch on the main window. *Piece of cake!* he thought, as he levered it open. He clambered through the gap on to a work surface, and climbed down on to the stone-flagged floor. Sure enough, it was several degrees cooler in here, and it was a welcome relief to get out of the glare of the sun.

He glanced around the kitchen. Everything seemed to have been left neat and tidy, save for the presence of a wooden toolbox standing on the old oak table. A hammer had been left propped against the box, and several nails were scattered across the surface of the table, as though Goldman had been indulging in a few hasty chores before his departure.

Sam frowned. He went out of the kitchen into the long hallway, his high-heeled boots creaking on the ancient floorboards. Then he stopped, listened intently. He was aware now of a sound in the old place: a muted background buzzing. He tilted his head this way and that to try and locate the source, then he realized that it seemed to be coming from somewhere above his head. The staircase rose away on his right-hand side, and he moved on to the bottom step, turning his gaze up towards the gloom of the landing. Yes, the strange noise *was* louder now, like the distant buzzing of a chain saw. Puzzled, he unlatched the cover on his holster and took out the pistol. He began to slowly climb the staircase.

The buzzing grew louder with each step. Now it was not a constant drone: it rose and fell, rose and fell, as he made his slow progress to the top of the stairs.

As he headed out on to the landing, he saw that the noise was made by a great cloud of blowflies that, puzzlingly, were swarming around a picture on one wall. Baffled, Sam moved closer, and then his gut lurched as a smell of putrefaction reached his nostrils. He swore, removed his hat, and fanned the air in front of his face. This small movement must have disturbed the flies. They rose in a cloud, and Sam was now able to see that the picture was a portrait of Mary the Madonna, a familiar image that hung in countless Catholic homes in these parts. But Sam was puzzled by its eerie, three-dimensional quality.

The flies – buzzing, buzzing – started to resettle on the contours of the picture, obscuring Sam's view. He stepped closer and waved his hat to scatter them again.

His next thought was that this was surely the *homeliest* Madonna he had ever seen. The hair hanging almost in her eyes, the flattish nose, the wide, downturned mouth . . .

'Oh, sweet Jesus!' he whispered.

He had suddenly registered what he was looking at. Stepping back involuntarily, he nearly fell headlong down the stairs. He had just recognized Brenda Loomis . . . or at least that part of her face that had been neatly removed and nailed into position above the Madonna's shoulders. Sam felt his gorge rise. The blowflies were settling again, crawling into her nostrils, between her open lips, in and out of her empty eyes, to where the painted pupils peered out in mute supplication.

He turned away, a man with twenty years' experience of the horrors of the world, and went sobbing and stumbling down the stairs in search of a telephone. He found one in the lounge and dialled the operator with a shaking finger.

'Hello, Susan?' he gasped. 'This is Sam Wade! Honey, I need you to get me a line to London, England, quick as you can . . . yes, I know what time of night it is there. This is an emergency!' He was fumbling in his pocket for the slip of paper with Judd's number scribbled on it.

'Of course I'll hold! Oh, and, honey, soon as you get me the line, I want you to call Marvin at the office and tell him to hightail it out here to the old Goldman house. He knows where it is. Tell him to shake a tail feather. This'll sound real funny, but I don't want to be here on my own, at least not any longer than I have to!'

He stood fumbling for the scrap of paper, and that was when it struck him that, despite the heat, the sweat had dried on his body and he was shivering like it was ten below zero.

Chapter Twenty-Six

Mark was shaken roughly from sleep by the sound of a fist thumping repeatedly on his front door. He'd been dreaming, a vaguely threatening kind of dream, the details of which escaped him for the moment. He sat up, squinted at his bedside clock-radio. A little after ten a.m. He'd slept later than usual, having endured another restless night.

The knocking continued, a steady pounding. Whoever was down there clearly wasn't going to give up easily. Mark yawned, flung back the duvet. He picked up his towelling robe from the floor, where he had dropped it the night before, pulled it on and went blearily downstairs. It was only as he was approaching the front door that he remembered he should be careful; though he seriously doubted that Leonard Goldman would make his presence as obvious as this. Through the frosted-glass panel he could make out the silhouette of a single figure.

'Who is it?' he called out.

'Police. Open up!'

Mark scowled. Just what he needed, another visit from his friendly neighbourhood plods. He opened the door to reveal the unwelcome sight of Detective Sergeant Maddocks' pale countenance. The officer looked Mark up and down for a moment.

'Asleep were you?' he grunted.

Mark feigned surprise.

'My, that detective training certainly pays off.'

Maddocks grimaced. 'Save the sarky comments. I'm just here to collect you. Chief Inspector Judd has requested your presence.'

'Again? What's it about this time?'

'Search me. You going to get dressed or would you prefer to come along as you are?'

Mark peered reluctantly out into the grey, chilly street as though actually considering the suggestion. 'I'll get dressed,' he said at last. He turned away and Maddocks followed him inside.

'Got the kettle on?' Maddocks inquired. 'I'm choking for a cuppa.'

'Oh, *naturally*. I always make tea when I'm asleep.' He gestured in

219

the direction of the kitchen. 'Help yourself. I'll have a coffee – milk, no sugar.'

'But I don't know where you keep all your stuff,' protested Maddocks.

Mark began trudging up the staircase.

'Tea is in the jar marked "Tea", sugar in the jar marked "Sugar" and, eerily, coffee is—'

'Yeah, yeah, I think I've got the general idea.'

Up in the bathroom, Mark gave his face a wash in cold water, and dragged a toothbrush backwards and forwards across his teeth half a dozen times. His ablutions completed, he went to the bedroom and pulled on black Levis, a grey sweatshirt and a pair of Kickers. He went down to the kitchen and found that, against all the odds, Maddocks had managed to make him a decent cup of instant coffee. He sipped at it gratefully, aware of the caffeine kick-starting him into some semblance of alertness. Maddocks was gulping down his tea and, Mark noticed, was occasionally helping himself to some gingersnaps which he had presumably found in the jar marked 'Biscuits'.

'Those must be several months past their sell-by date,' he warned.

'Yeah? Thought they were a bit soft.' But Maddocks carried on pushing them into his mouth, just the same. He was eyeing the temporary DIY job that Mark had done on his back door by nailing several stout slats of wood across it.

'You're no great shakes at woodwork, are you?' he said.

Mark shrugged. 'It'll do until I can get in a professional. Joinery was never my strong point.'

Maddocks glanced at his watch. 'I must say I didn't expect to find you still in bed at this hour. Bit of a cushy number being a writer, isn't it? I started work at seven o'clock this morning!'

'Bully for you,' Mark told him.

'No, but seriously, is that all you do? Sit around at home and scribble down the odd line?'

Mark glanced at him sharply.

'Contrary to public opinion, there's a tiny bit more to it than that. If I worked on that principle, I'd probably publish a novel only every fifteen years.'

Maddocks seemed unconvinced. 'I've always thought about doing a book,' he said, 'about my experiences on the force. I could tell you stories that would make your hair curl.'

'I'll know who to come to if I want a cheap perm,' said Mark unhelpfully. He gulped down the remains of his coffee. 'Hadn't we better get moving?' He wasn't particularly anxious to see Judd's sour face again, but he figured anything was better than listening to the inevitable outline for a bestseller that Maddocks was about to unleash on him. If he had a thousand pounds for every time he'd suffered through *that* scenario, he'd never have to write another book in his life.

Mark collected his leather jacket from the hall rack and followed Maddocks out to the blue Escort.

'You don't drive, do you?' asked Maddocks.

'I'm afraid not.'

'Bit weird that, isn't it?'

Mark shrugged. 'Not really. Just haven't got around to learning yet.'

'Dunno how you manage in London without a car.' Maddocks threw open the passenger door, and motioned Mark to get in. He indicated a 'no smoking' sign fixed to the dashboard. 'Kindly take notice of that,' he said. 'This car is a smoke-free zone!' He walked around to the driver's side and climbed in behind the wheel. Mark had expected that they would drive in the direction of the police station, but instead Maddocks headed south towards the City.

'Where are we going?' Mark was puzzled.

'Relax. This is Sergeant Maddocks' Mystery Tour. It's a surprise.'

Mark shot a suspicious look at the detective, but clearly he wasn't going to learn any more from him, so he settled into an indifferent silence for the rest of the journey, staring sullenly out of the window at the ranks of traffic moving in a stop-start fashion into the grimy heart of London.

Eventually they turned into Tottenham Court Road, the grey air rank with petrol fumes. Exhaust smoke coiled low across the surface of the road, as if blindly seeking escape. It was long past the rush hour, but one wouldn't have guessed it. The pavements seethed with harassed-looking pedestrians. As they passed Warren Street tube station, Maddocks then hung a left on to Fitzroy Street.

Mark was about to mention that this was where Peter Maughan's agency was situated, when he noticed that the familiar entrance had been fenced off with strips of fluorescent orange tape. An ambulance and several squad cars were parked shoulder-to-shoulder on the narrow pavement, and a couple of uniformed men were guarding the doorway. Mark stared out of the window as Maddocks brought the car to a halt. He could feel a flood of anxiety rising within him.

'What's going on?' he asked Maddocks. 'What is all this?'

'Come on,' said Maddocks – which was no kind of answer at all. They climbed out of the car, and Mark followed the detective as he ducked under the tape and went into the building. On the stairs they had to squeeze past a couple of uniformed men coming down, who were carrying metal cases. As they gained the first-floor landing, through the open door of her office Mark saw Meg slumped in a chair, looking close to collapse. A young policewoman was sitting with her, trying to coax her to drink from a cup of coffee.

'Meg?' Mark hesitated in the doorway, gazing in.

She glanced up at him blankly, and he could see the streaks of mascara down her pale cheeks. Her eyes were misty behind the lenses of her spectacles. For a moment she didn't even seem to know him; then her eyes widened in recognition.

'Mark?' she whispered, as though unsure that it was really him.

'Mr Tyler?' Maddocks was beckoning to him from the next flight of stairs, but still he hesitated, wanting Meg to tell him what had happened. Then suddenly she was on her feet, shouting to him at the top of her voice.

'Don't go up there, Mark! You hear me? Don't go up there! You don't want to see that. It's horrible! Stay here with me, please!'

He shrank away from her, not so much because of what she was saying, but because of the naked fear on her face. Meg was always so reserved, so much in control; now she seemed like some lunatic.

'I went up to his office . . . I thought he'd come in early! I just walked in and . . . and . . .' Her voice metamorphosed into a howl of anguish. The policewoman had an arm around her shoulder now, and was easing her down into her chair, coaxing her in a low soothing voice. Mark backed out of the doorway and followed Maddocks reluctantly up the next flight, wondering what could have scared Meg so badly. Now he didn't really want to find out what had happened up there on the second floor.

There seemed to be a lot of people crammed into Maughan's office. None actually had the word 'cop' tattooed on their foreheads, but they didn't need to. It was clear in the way they dressed, the way they moved. A photographer was taking flash pictures of something that Mark couldn't quite see. Another man, wearing transparent gloves, was dusting down the edges of the desk with fingerprint powder. Two others seemed to be conducting a general search, though what they were looking for was anybody's guess.

Judd was stalking around in his raincoat, apparently directing the proceedings. He suddenly noticed the two newcomers framed in the doorway, and beckoned them into the room.

'All right, Harry,' he said to the photographer. 'That should do it.'

The man shot off one last frame, then turned aside, at last revealing the subject of his photo session.

Mark stared. His first impulse was to laugh. It looked as though Peter was the victim of some bizarre practical joke, the kind of thing that happened to young men at stag parties. There he sat, stark bollock naked, and apparently tied into his chair. It was vaguely unsettling to see an authority figure like his agent made to look so ridiculous. Mark registered the thin, bony legs, the coat-hanger shoulders, the toast-rack ribs. He seemed to be sitting there, gazing glumly down at some-thing that was piled into his lap – a jumble of discarded balloons and party streamers, some of which had trailed down on to the floor . . .

Then Mark realized exactly what he was looking at, and he had the immediate sensation of being punched hard in the chest. Stepping back with a gasp, he collided with Maddocks, right behind him.

'Steady,' he heard a voice say in his ear. Mark couldn't seem to control his breathing, nor the wave of nausea that bubbled up to the back of his throat. Now he was aware of the smell in the room: a mixture of faecal stench and raw meat. Groaning, he turned away and pushed past Maddocks, needing to get out. He made it outside to the landing, and leaned on the bannister rail for support, snatching deep breaths. Somehow he managed to stop himself from throwing up.

Somebody came out of the room to stand beside him.

'Better now?' asked Judd.

Mark turned to glare at him. 'You bastard,' he said. 'What was the idea of letting me see that?'

Judd's face remained impassive.

'I wanted you to see just exactly what you've caused, Mr Tyler. And I wanted to get your opinion . . .'

'Oh, yeah, I'll give you an opinion. You're a fucking sadist!'

Mark moved away from Judd, and fumbled for his cigarettes. 'No warning, nothing! That man in there . . .' He gestured at the doorway behind him. 'That man was a close friend of mine.'

Judd smiled grimly.

'I thought if Maddocks warned you, you might not have agreed to come here.'

'You thought right!' Mark put a light to his cigarette and inhaled deeply. After the initial shock, the full horror was beginning to hit him. He felt stunned to his very core. 'My God, what happened in there?' He gestured ineffectually, groping for the right words. 'It's like something . . . something in a butcher's shop.'

Judd moved closer.

'I'll tell you exactly what happened, Mr Tyler. Somebody cut Mr Maughan wide-open from belly to breast-bone and, as far as we can ascertain, ate part of his liver.'

'What?' Another mental punch. Mark took an involuntary step along the landing, as though trying to keep a safe distance between himself and the policeman. 'You're . . . you're sure?'

'Fairly sure, though we'll have to wait for the pathologist to confirm that.' Judd took a biro from his pocket and chewed on it reflectively for a moment. 'I'm not a gambling man, but I'd be willing to bet that this little display in here rings a bell with you. I wouldn't be surprised to learn that it's based on something in one of those penny-dreadfuls you write. Would I be correct?'

Mark inhaled on his cigarette. Then he bowed his head, nodded.

'And tell me, Mr Tyler, would this be the new novel? The typescript that was stolen?'

'Yes.' Mark eyed Judd wearily. 'There's a ritual killing performed by one of the characters in my story . . .' He shook his head, hardly believing what he was admitting to. 'Perhaps now you'll accept what I was trying to explain yesterday.' He pointed towards the doorway. 'Goldman did that. I'm convinced of it.'

Judd nodded. 'Well, that now makes two of us.'

This was a surprise for Mark. 'It does?' he gasped.

'Aye. See, after we talked to you yesterday, I decided it wouldn't hurt to make a few inquiries. So I placed a call to the police department in Goldman's home town. Dennings, Pennsylvania. I talked to the sheriff.' Judd was obliged to step aside for two ambulancemen carrying a folded stretcher. They moved past him into the room. Judd then went on with the story.

'You were right about Goldman being here in England. He set off on holiday three weeks ago. Dennings is the kind of place where everybody knows everybody else. The cheeky bastard even asked the police to keep an eye on his house. The neighbours believed he'd taken a woman on the trip with him. The theory was that they'd gone off to get married.' Judd leaned his elbows on the bannister rail, and gazed blankly down the stairwell to the ground floor. 'It seems they've had at least three unsolved killings in Dennings. The local press has dubbed them 'The Wolfman Murders' because all the victims were covered in jagged bite marks.'

'Jesus.'

Judd nodded.

'Anyway, Sheriff Wade promised me he'd go hotfoot up to Goldman's house and take a look around.'

Mark leaned closer. 'And?'

'And sure enough, a half hour later he returned my call. It seems the woman did not get to go on holiday. She was still up at the house – or, at least, *parts* of her. They found her torso in the bath, submerged in water. An arm and a leg turned up in a plastic bag at the bottom of a wardrobe. And her face . . . well, as far as we can understand it, her face had been recycled into some new kind of art form. They're still looking for the rest of her.'

'Maybe loopy Len took some with him,' said a voice behind them.

They turned to see Maddocks standing in the doorway, leaning against the frame. 'Sometimes people take a packed lunch when they go on a trip.'

Mark grimaced. 'You know, Maddocks, you're about as funny as a world famine,' he observed.

Maddocks turned to Judd. 'OK if they take the body down to the ambulance, guv? The backroom boys have finished sifting through the wreckage, and I'm about ready for some nosh.'

'Aye, all right. There's a decent café just down the street.'

Maddocks grinned and went back inside.

'How can you even think about *food*?' muttered Mark. 'Jesus, the smell in there.'

'You get used to it,' Judd assured him.

Mark nodded glumly. 'Well, at least you have a photograph of him. You could get that duplicated and sent out to the newspapers.'

But Judd was shaking his head.

'It's not quite as straightforward as that. I showed that photograph to Mr Maughan's assistant earlier, and she insists it wasn't the man who called to see him last night.'

Mark stared at him. 'She's positive?'

'Absolutely. Now I need to contact my new friend Sheriff Wade and ask him to fax me a photograph of the real Goldman. We're also going to take the lady to an Identikit artist, just as soon as she feels up to it.' Judd reached into his inside breast pocket and pulled out Mark's original photo of Leonard. Glumly he studied the man's clean-cut, handsome face. 'Whoever this is, it's not Leonard Goldman.'

'I guess that explains the business about the teeth,' said Mark.

'If only it did. It seems that Mr Maughan's visitor last night also had perfectly ordinary-looking teeth; and yet forensic were so sure that they would have to be pointed and doglike.'

'Perhaps he used something else: some kind of weapon that left similar marks.'

'I don't see how. They found saliva in the wounds: they were most definitely bites.' He sighed. 'Anyway, we'll just have to hope that Wade can get us that picture of Goldman soon. Once we know what he really looks like, then it'll just be a matter of time.'

The two ambulancemen came out of the room carrying the body on a stretcher. Mark backed away in alarm, slamming hard against the

225

wall in his eagerness to get out of the way. They had managed to fit Maughan into a body bag, but the corpse had retained its sitting posture, so the bag had a hunched, squarish look to it, and a bulge where one arm stuck out.

'They'll probably have to break the bones to get him laid out properly,' explained one of the men in passing.

As the two men squeezed past on the narrow landing, for several long moments Mark was obliged to breathe in a fainter echo of the stench he had encountered inside the room. He held his breath, aware of the blood draining from his face.

Maddocks came out of the office, rubbing his hands together. 'Right,' he said. 'Who's for sausage, egg and chips?'

Mark gagged. He made a dive for the bannister rail and retched violently over the stairwell.

Judd stepped forward and pounded him heartily on the back. 'That's the ticket, son. Cough it up! You should be used to this by now, you being the big horror writer and all.'

Mark hung over the bannister, his eyes streaming tears. For the moment he felt totally spent, and very, very apprehensive about the blurry darkness that waited for him at the bottom of the stairwell.

Chapter Twenty-Seven

Brendan was running for his life. He crossed the forest clearing at a frantic pace, and made for the cover of some bushes ahead. He was badly out of condition, and his heart was hammering in his chest by the time he reached them. He threw himself down and rolled sideways under the bushes, holding his pistol out in front to avoid dropping it in the mud. Icy water soaked through the fabric of his trousers, the shock of it almost making him cry out. He stayed in the cover, trying to control his breathing, and peered back along the trail. His instinct had been correct. Sure enough, somebody was stalking him. He caught a glimpse of a large figure skulking through the trees away to his right.

'OK,' he breathed. 'I see you, you bastard.'

He raised his pistol and drew a careful bead on the moving shape. At this range, he hadn't much hope of hitting his target, but, whoever it was, the man was edging closer – probably aware that Brendan was somewhere up ahead, but unsure of exactly where he was hiding. Now the figure slipped beneath the gloomy shade of a massive oak tree – and abruptly vanished.

Brendan swore beneath his breath. Carefully, noiselessly, he eased himself into a crouch and peered into the depths of the surrounding undergrowth. Nothing. He inched himself a little higher, craning his neck, ready to duck down again.

Movement off to his right! Somebody was now crashing through the undergrowth, making a charge! Brendan swivelled round, gun extended to fire, but still saw nothing – and then he realized that once again the weird acoustics of the forest had played tricks on him. The sounds had really come from *behind* him . . .

He turned, and the shot hit him square in the chest at almost point-blank range. It caught him off balance, and flung him backwards on to the grass. Brendan screamed as the impact sent trails of agony flickering through him. He could only lie there, groaning, as his assailant came towards him, pistol raised.

'You bastard, Deggsie!' roared Brendan. 'That hurt like hell!'

'Oh, stop moaning.' Roy Deggs lifted his goggles and stood admiring his handiwork. There was a bright magenta splash across the front of Brendan's green overalls, too generous a helping to be dismissed as a mere flesh wound. 'You're dead, Brendan. Off you go!'

'Bloody hell!' Brendan struggled into a sitting position and peeled back his own goggles. 'Some weekend this is turning out to be. I spent most of yesterday sitting in the dead zone, too.'

Roy shrugged in a 'those are the breaks' gesture. He had a thin, pinched face like a weasel. Not for the first time Brendan asked himself what he was doing here. Roy Deggs was an accountant who apparently earned disgusting amounts of money in the City. He often organized these paintball weekends for his 'friends'; indeed, it was suspected that was the only way he could entice people to spend time with him. Brendan wasn't amongst those 'friends' but he had been persuaded to come along by some who were, and he had thought it would be a good idea to get out of London for a while.

Since Peter Maughan's horrific death two weeks earlier, Brendan hadn't so much as laid eyes on Mark Tyler. The man had become a virtual recluse; and it hadn't escaped Brendan's attention that it wasn't too unrealistic to consider himself as a potential target, also. Over the last few days he had begun to suffer the eerie sensation of being watched by unseen eyes. Doubtless that was just paranoia, but suddenly the prospect of two days surrounded by a bunch of strapping males hadn't seemed as unsavoury as it might otherwise have done.

When Brendan had agreed to give it a try, he had not reckoned with Roy Deggs' uncanny skills in the paintball arena. The man obviously took the game extremely seriously. He owned his own rifle and customised overalls, he had a seemingly inexhaustible supply of ammunition, and was so adept at the art of camouflage that he could probably have re-fought the Vietnam War single-handed. How for instance, had he managed to creep into the cover of that tree up ahead, yet then suddenly reappear *behind* Brendan? And the guy was so disciplined, for Christ's sake! Last night, Friday, he'd been the first to retire to the dormitory, while the others had sat up drinking beer and telling jokes until the early hours. Then, at six a.m., Deggs had come marching into the dorm in his camouflage gear like some bloody sergeant-major, and had turfed everyone out of their bunks.

'Come on, lads, a hearty breakfast, and then off for the first game of the day!'

What had surprised Brendan most was that nobody else had complained about this treatment. On the contrary, they had clearly

revelled in it, as though each had a secret ambition to join the army.
Now here it was, barely eight-thirty in the morning, and they were
already on their second game of the day. The first had been a swift,
merciless massacre, from which Roy Deggs had emerged unscathed
and victorious. The guy never let up for a moment.

Even now, as Brendan watched passively, he was dropping into a
half-crouch, pulling his goggles back down over his eyes, as his keen
ears caught a rustle in the undergrowth.

'Shh! There's someone out there.' Deggs took some more
ammunition from his webbing belt to top up the feeder tube on his rifle.

Brendan lowered his voice to a whisper.

'Couldn't I just . . . you know, carry on with the game?'

Roy looked positively horrified. 'No. You're *dead*. Now get off to the
dead zone, and wait for the next round. Those are the rules.'

'Bollocks to the rules,' Brendan murmured, groping in his breast
pocket for his tobacco tin. He began to unhurriedly construct a
cigarette.

'And you can bugger off with that, too,' hissed Roy. 'The smoke
could betray my position!'

'Christ, it's only a game, Deggsie.' He rolled up the sleeve of his
overall to study a purple bruise on his forearm, the size of an apple.
'Look at that,' he grumbled. 'Shit, I nearly passed out with the pain.'

Now Roy seemed positively disgusted. 'I might have known you'd
be the one to whinge. God help you if you ever got into real warfare.
I only invited you because I needed to make up the numbers.'

'So, no change there then,' observed Brendan cuttingly.

Roy stared at him, not understanding. 'Look, I wish you'd just
bugger off back to the . . . shsh!' He ducked down again, looking off
to his left, where a thick screen of ferns was rustling.

'It's the wind.' Brendan licked his cigarette paper and lifted the
completed smoke to his lips. With a contemptuous flick of the hand,
Deggs knocked it out of his mouth. Then, dropping on to his knees and
elbows, he began to wriggle comically towards the ferns, his bottom
up highest.

Brendan dissuaded himself from firing a paintball right up that
swaying, bobbing target. Instead, he picked up his fallen cigarette and
examined it critically. It was too wet to light, so he started on another
one, glancing up occasionally to observe Deggs' progress. By the time
the cigarette was completed, Deggs was some twenty yards away,
peering into the ferns. Craning slowly up on to his knees, he took aim
at something he could apparently see in there. When he pulled the
trigger, there was an abrupt swoosh of air – then a corresponding grunt

from somewhere deep in the bushes.

'Got you!' exclaimed Deggs gleefully. He climbed to his feet and strode forward into the bushes. 'Come on, you're dead. I hit you fair and square!'

Brendan shook his head. He lit his cigarette and inhaled the smoke gratefully. The sooner he was away from this madhouse, the better. Somewhere in the undergrowth, Deggs was still remonstrating with his latest quarry.

'Look, I hit you. It's as simple as that. Now you've got to go off to—'

Something caused him to break off in mid-sentence. *Maybe he's been ambushed*, thought Brendan hopefully. If he got Deggs in the dead zone with him, he'd be able to tell him exactly what he thought about this paintballing weekend.

He rose to his feet and picked up his pistol and goggles, ready to head back down the trail towards the dead zone. He pushed the pistol into his belt and slung the goggles around his neck. When he turned back towards the bushes, he was suddenly aware of how terribly quiet it had become. An instant earlier, the glade had been full of the background melody of birdsong. Now it seemed suddenly, horribly silent.

The bushes ahead of him parted, and Deggs stepped out. He began to walk quickly towards Brendan, but there was something odd about his movements – a curious stiff-legged gait. The rifle hung uselessly in his right hand, and his left was clutched firmly to his throat. Behind the perspex goggles, his eyes were wide and staring.

Brendan stared at him, and then grinned. The opposition had clearly not succumbed without a fight. Deggs must have been hit in the throat; Brendan could see the magenta paint oozing out from beneath his gloved fingers . . . except that it wasn't magenta, it was a deep, dark red. And surely no pellet could contain *that* much paint? It was literally spraying down the front of Deggs' camouflage jacket and spattering amongst the vegetation.

'Roy?' said Brendan uncertainly.

'Gurk!' retorted Roy. A pink foam was bubbling from his lips. He removed the hand from his throat, and held it out to Brendan, as if for inspection. Now Brendan could see quite clearly the ragged hole in the man's windpipe, from which blood was squirting in a rhythmic pump action. Deggs, too, was clearly headed for the dead zone.

Finally Brendan had the presence of mind to react. He screamed and the cigarette fell from his mouth, trailing sparks down his overalls. Then he turned and ran off down the trail, his legs pumping madly beneath him, his feet slipping on the wet grass. Suddenly they shot out from under him, and he fell backwards with a thud that drove the breath out of him. For a moment he lay shivering abjectly, aware of the panic sweat oozing from his every pore. He glanced back at Deggs, who was now crawling on his hands and knees, making obscene bubbling noises. The bushes behind him parted as a pair of gloved hands pushed them aside.

With another gasp of sheer terror, Brendan scrambled to his feet and took off down the trail like a startled rabbit, his heavy boots slipping and stumbling over half-hidden tree roots. His first impulse was to head back to the familiarity of the dead zone but, after he had run some twenty yards, it occurred to him that he had been the first man 'killed' in this particular game, so there would be nobody else there yet. Better to make for the HQ, where the organizers could be found. He changed his direction, and plunged to the left, down a muddy slope, flailing his arms like a tightrope walker to maintain his balance.

Brendan reached level ground with an impact that jolted his spine, then he moved from mud back to grass, making better progress now. He ran flat out for several hundred yards, through a stand of saplings, holding one arm up across his face to protect it from whipping branches. He believed that he was heading towards the flat-roofed stone building that formed the company HQ, but when he emerged from the saplings, he could see only the denser reaches of Epping Forest unfolding before him, as far as the eye could see.

Brendan slowed to a halt, and just stood there, gazing slowly around. With a horrible, sinking sensation, he realized that he didn't have the faintest idea where he was. He glanced desperately this way and that, his heart thudding like a jackhammer in his chest, trying to make sense of what had just happened.

Somebody out there had killed Roy Deggs, had torn the throat right out of him. The thought made his stomach lurch into his throat. *Which way?* he asked himself desperately; aware that he was on the verge of losing his grip. His pistol was still tucked into his belt and he extracted it with shaking hands, popped a couple more paintballs into the feeder tube. He knew the weapon was next to useless, but the weight of it in his hands made him feel better somehow, and he told himself that if fired pointblank into somebody's face, a pellet would at least slow them down.

Fearfully, moving very slowly, he began to retrace his path through the saplings, stopping every so often to stare around, the gun held ready to fire. Away in the distance he heard somebody give a jocular cry, and for the first time it occurred to him to shout for help. There was a dozen of his 'friends' somewhere out there. But he immediately dismissed the idea: any noise would lead the killer straight to him. Brendan kept moving forward, through the last line of the saplings and into the thicker forest beyond.

Ahead of him, he recognized the muddy trail leading uphill to the place where Roy Deggs had fallen. He ran the tip of his tongue across dry lips. OK. That meant the HQ was in the *other* direction entirely; he needed to follow the trail off to his right. But he didn't much care for the risk of taking that exposed path, in full view of anyone who might come along. Instead, he stayed under cover, and crept through the tangle of bushes and brambles that edged the trail, moving parallel to it. He kept his gun poised to fire at anything that approached him.

He was doing all right, he decided. Move a few yards, crouch down, take a slow look around, then move again. Roy Deggs would have been proud of him . . . only he didn't much like to think about Deggs just now. Three steps forward, duck down, look slowly all around. Now again! If he stuck to this pattern, he'd soon be—

There was a sudden crashing in the ferns off to his left. He lifted the gun, fired instinctively – barely missed a large wood pigeon flapping up out of the cover of some brambles. The pellet swooped on past its intended target, and struck a tree in a startling splatter of magenta.

Brendan remained crouching. His heart thudded in his chest as he peered anxiously this way and that. Once again the forest seemed to have fallen into an eerie silence. Ahead of him the ground rose to a ridge, where at some time a huge elm tree had unearthed itself and tumbled headlong to meet the ground. Brendan ran forwards and threw himself face-down behind its fallen trunk.

When he raised his head to peer cautiously over the top of it, what he saw cheered him immensely. A couple of hundred yards away, down-slope through the trees was the grey stone wall of the converted farmhouse that was HQ. He was bound to find help there. There was a telephone, cars, other people . . .

Throwing caution to the winds, Brendan got to his feet and began to scramble over the fallen elm.

With heartstopping suddenness, a figure bobbed up from the other side of it – a hulking shape dressed in camouflage. Then a gloved hand grabbed hold of Brendan's lapels and yanked hard, hauling him over the trunk in a sprawl of arms and legs. He came down to earth with a jolt, and tried desperately to scramble away on his hands and knees. But something clamped around his neck with a force that made him wince. He was shaken like a rat, and thrown back against the tree trunk. His head struck wood with a dull clack and stars exploded behind his eyes. Then a heavy weight settled across his chest. He groaned – and opened his eyes.

A man was sitting astride Brendan, looking down at him. Brendan couldn't see much of the face. The hood of his attacker's camouflage jacket was raised up over his head and pulled tight with a drawstring. From behind perspex goggles, pale eyes observed Brendan with interest.

But what really drew Brendan's attention was the mouth – the lips pulled back to reveal bloody, pointed teeth.

The sight of those savage teeth rekindled the panic in Brendan's dazed mind, and he began to struggle furiously. A large hand dealt him a heavy swipe across the face, almost knocking him unconscious. He lay back, waiting, his flesh crawling at the thought of those misshapen teeth tearing into his throat. But the aggressor made no attempt to harm him further.

Brendan gathered his courage and stared up defiantly.

'What do you want?' he gasped.

The lips pulled back to reveal the jagged rictus of a grin.

'I wand to lib. Tell your friend, Marg, I wand to lib. You tell hib. I habn't fiddidged wid hib yed.'

'Tell him? But . . . but I thought you . . .'

'Goig to kill you? Oh no. Leabing Horze wadn't *killed.*'

'Leaping Horse . . .?' Brendan stared up at the big man in confusion. Saw him picking up the fallen pistol from the ground. Saw him check the firing mechanism. Then he was bringing the pistol around, to point it straight at Brendan's face.

'No! For God's sake, no!'

Again Brendan tried to struggle, but the powerful left hand clamped itself on to his forehead, pushing him back hard against the tree trunk, until he thought his skull would crack open. The gun barrel moved closer, closer, until it was only an inch away from Brendan's left eye.

'Please,' he whispered. 'I beg you—'

His eye exploded in a flash of red agony. He had never known pain like that. Somewhere, a long way away, he could hear screaming, a long high-pitched wail like a dying animal, and he thought to himself that something was being killed out there in the forest.

For an instant he was aware of everything, his blind, shattered eye, his twitching limbs, his gesticulating hands . . . and then he was gone, sinking down through a thick ooze, his ruined eye trailing tentacles of pain behind him. Through the bloody haze, he could dimly perceive the figure high, high above him, gazing at him with close interest, as though he could see Brendan lying down there beneath the forest floor.

Now the figure was leaning closer, a long metal tube coming towards Brendan's face, and at the end of it a huge round cavern which led upwards into oblivion. As Brendan watched fascinated, a blob of darkness detached itself from the cavern and began to spread out like a blanket – extending wider and wider until it seemed to cover his entire face. It moulded itself to his features, covering every inch of him, sucking the pain back into itself, and then there was only a blackness deeper than any he had ever experienced.

'Sleep,' said the blackness; and Brendan didn't feel inclined to argue.

Chapter Twenty-Eight

It was raining again.

Mark stood at the dining-room window staring blankly out at the back garden, a forgotten mug of coffee rapidly going cold in his hand. Over the past week since Peter Maughan's funeral, the weather had been unpredictable, the sun shining confidently one minute, the next obscured by landscapes of restless grey cloud. Mark hadn't been out of the house since. Even then, only a sense of duty had persuaded him to attend.

The service had taken place in Maughan's family village in Kent, and the weather had at least stayed clement for that. Afterwards, everybody had headed back to the victim's mother's house for the ritual of sherry and sandwiches. Mrs Maughan was a frail, white-haired little lady whose spacious semi was liberally sprinkled with photographs and mementos of her only child. Mark knew that this devotion had been requited. Peter had doted on his widowed mum and had taken every available opportunity to visit her, even taking her away on holiday with him. She was clearly devastated by his awful death, but was attempting to put a brave face on it all.

Mark and Sarah had not stayed there long. He felt particularly uncomfortable in the company of the other writers, the publishers and agents who were present, knowing that they would have all read the grisly details of the killing in the national press, and would be curious to learn more about the circumstances. The newspapers had dubbed it 'a ritual killing', but thankfully none had picked up on the fact of it being inspired by Mark's forthcoming novel. Not yet, at least.

As the view of the garden dissolved into a grey-green blur, Mark was obliged to raise a hand to wipe the tears from his eyes. He seemed unable to rid himself of the conviction that he was somehow responsible for what had happened to Maughan. He had always been opposed to censorship of any kind, and had often scoffed at those who suggested that his violent stories might inspire real-life atrocities. Now the knowledge that one particular scene had been re-enacted, blow by blow, shook him to his very core.

He knew now that he could never allow publication of *Black Wolf 3*. He would return the publisher's advance, tear up the contract, risk litigation if necessary. At this moment he even seriously doubted that he would ever write another novel. His agent, Peter, was dead – and how could he ever rationalise that?

'Are you OK?' Sarah's gentle inquiry made him start. She had been clearing away the remains of their largely uneaten lunch, and he hadn't heard her come up behind him. As he turned to her, she must have perceived the pain in his eyes, because she quickly prised the mug from his fingers and set it on the dining table.

'Oh, love,' she whispered. She put her arms around him, hugged him close.

If there was one consolation in all this horror, it was that Sarah had finally come back to him. He thanked his lucky stars for that. He didn't think he would have had the strength to get through alone. Over the past week spent together in the house, they had been learning to function as a couple again. The breach between them was gradually healing, and he knew now that he could never again afford to jeopardize their relationship.

She reached up one hand to stroke his face with the tips of her fingers.

'All right?' she asked him.

He sniffed, nodded.

'You know,' she said, 'it really *isn't* your fault.'

'Isn't it?'

'Of course not. Mark, you can't take responsibility for an obsessive aberration like Leonard Goldman. You might as well accept the entire blame for AIDS! This would have happened sooner or later – if not to you, then to some other writer, some pop star, or movie actor.'

'But it *didn't* happen to some other writer, did it? It happened to *me*.' He pulled away from her and turned back to look out of the window. 'Now Goldman's out there somewhere with that typescript, and who knows what he'll get up to next? Who knows what scene he'll choose to re-enact in his own sick way?'

'It's just a matter of time,' she assured him. 'The police now have his photograph, for goodness sake. They're sure to pick him up soon.'

'God, I hope so,' Mark said quietly. He himself had been shown the photograph of the *real* Leonard J. Goldman earlier that week. Sheriff Wade had come up with a copy of his passport photo, which was taken maybe six years ago. The square face was largely obliterated under a thick black beard and long hair, till the only distinctive feature were the

236

eyes which stared sullenly at the camera with brooding intensity.

Mark had compared this with the Identikit picture prepared to Meg's description of the sinister visitor. The latter showed a clean-cut, short-haired man with a totally unremarkable face and a neatly clipped moustache. The eyes, as she described them, were positively bland, gentle even – certainly nothing like Goldman's photograph. But that *had* to be Peter's killer. Police calls to Ventona Productions in Hollywood had proved that for them Al Schneider did not exist. Goldman was evidently adept at disguise, which thus rendered his passport photograph virtually useless.

There was a long silence, and he became aware of the kitchen clock ticking rhythmically, as the second hand attempted repeatedly to reach the next, higher notch on the face, then fell back again, defeated.

'You should get a new battery for that,' observed Sarah lamely. The clock must have reminded her of something, because she glanced at her watch and grimaced. 'I really must be going,' she announced.

'Do you really have to?' he asked her.

She nodded. 'I've got to get on with *Mortimer Rabbit*. I have to present the next batch of illustrations to Madam Moran next week, and it's still a long way from finished.'

'Couldn't you work at it here?'

She shook her head.

'Mark, I need to be in my studio, with familiar things around me. I can't work just anywhere. Besides, I'm planning my little field trip this afternoon . . .'

'What field trip?'

'I told you, I need to go to the zoo and sketch the wolves. To get a little inspiration for Mort's nemesis, Siegfried Snapjaw. She didn't think my original characterization looked menacing enough.'

'I don't like the sound of that.' Mark shook his head. 'You wandering around that open space all by yourself.'

'Hardly by myself,' she protested. 'There'll be *crowds* of people there. And now I know what the bloody man looks like, if I get so much as a glimpse of him I'll scream my bloody head off. Mark, I just have to do this work.'

He still wasn't satisfied, and began to pace up and down.

'But you can't be sure what he looks like,' he protested. 'I'll have to come with you.'

'Mark, no! I'm sorry, but how am I supposed to concentrate on my work with you lurking in the background like James Bond? I'll be *fine*. And I'm damned if I'll let that maniac bully me into hiding myself away.'

237

'You didn't see what he did to Peter. At least let me call the police and tell them where you're going.'

'*No!*' Her voice was firmer now, an edge of resentment creeping into it. 'I *couldn't* work under those conditions. Mark, I understand your concern for me, and I appreciate it, but life has to go on. I can't spend the rest of mine being afraid of every shadow.'

He bowed his head in capitulation.

'I suppose not,' he conceded.

She smiled, then squeezed his arm.

'What will *you* do?' she asked him.

'Me? Well, I suppose I ought to write . . .'

She brightened a little. 'Yes?' she prompted.

'I should write to the publishers, and explain why *Black Wolf 3* is a non-starter.'

She nodded. 'You're sure that's what you want?'

'Positive. I never had much enthusiasm for the idea in the first place, as you know, but . . . Peter talked me into it. If only . . .' He shrugged off the thought. 'I should have trusted my own instincts. I should have gone in another direction.' He seemed to recollect something. '*The Jumblies*,' he said. 'Remember that?'

'Of course. It wasn't that long ago.'

'No, I don't suppose it was. It just seems like years . . . you didn't really get somebody else to work on that, did you?'

She smiled, ruefully.

'No,' she admitted. 'That one was always *our* book. Maybe it still could be?'

It was more a question than a statement. He considered it for a moment.

'Maybe,' he said at last. But he sounded doubtful and she didn't press him on it. He would take time to come around to the idea. First, he had a lot of healing to do.

He saw Sarah out to her car, and watched her drive away. The rain had stopped and a feeble sun was doing its best to jostle between the clouds. Mark stood in the doorway, until the car was lost to sight. Then he stepped back into the house, bolting the door behind him. He walked along the hall to the door of his study, but he hesitated a while before going in. It seemed like years since he had last been in there.

He walked over to the desk, ran his fingers experimentally across the keyboard of his word-processor, and found it already coated with a thin layer of dust. Mark sat down in the leather chair and stared at his pale reflection in the screen of the VDU. Then he reached out a finger and punched the start-up button.

Opening the metal box that contained his start-of-day disc, he lifted it out and slotted it into the drive, watched the introductory patterns rippling and undulating across the screen. When the sequence had finished, he made another keystroke to create a new document, and a fresh page opened up in front of him, ready to receive his input. He raised his hands, poised over the keyboard. He sat like that for several moments, not moving, staring down at the keys in surprise. Then slowly he lowered his hands to the desktop.

He realized he didn't have the first idea where to begin. It was as if he had never written a word before in his life, as though the whole process was alien to him. He felt a flutter of panic within, and tried to shrug it off.

Of course you can do it, he told himself. He lifted his hands again and typed out two words. *Dear Adrian*. There they were, white on black at the top left-hand corner of the screen: *Dear* (an expression of affection) *Adrian* (Adrian Garner, his British editor). So far, so good. He hit the return and the cursor jumped down to the next line. Mark hit another key.

I. There now, good start, good start . . . What next? . . . *am sorry*. Hey presto, a sentence! *I am sorry*. My, but this boy had a gift for understatement! He groped mentally for whatever came next, and was shocked to discover that he didn't know yet, that his mental processes had not progressed that far.

This is ridiculous!

Well, what were the possibilities? I am sorry to tell you – I am sorry to *inform* you – I am sorry to *have* to inform you – I am sorry to be the bearer of bad tidings . . . Christ, what was he supposed to say! How did you even begin to tell somebody that what was once a promising and fulfilling career had suddenly turned into a crock of shit? I am sorry but because of something I wrote, my agent, a man I loved and respected, has been brutally and horribly murdered. Yeah, sure, tell it like it is, man! *I AM GUILTY!* Capital letters, underscored bold text? *Mark Tyler is guilty: he's the guy that got his agent killed*, anybody else like to apply for the vacant post? Come on, don't be shy, step right up, what are you afraid of, what's the worst thing could happen, somebody tears your fucking guts out? He realized with a dull sense of shock that he had been pounding the keyboard with his fists, that the screen had filled up with ranks and ranks of neatly-ordered gibberish. He sat staring blankly at the screen, wondering if he was losing his mind.

The telephone shrilled and he flinched so violently that he nearly fell out of his chair. He threw out a hand to grasp the receiver, and lifted it to his ear.

'Yes?' he said quietly.

'Mr Tyler? Inspector Judd speaking.' That familiar Scottish accent was about the last thing in the world he wanted to hear right now. He considered slamming the receiver down again, but for some reason he decided against it. Perhaps it was the grave, deferential tone in Judd's voice – the suspicion that, once again, the policeman had bad news to impart. Mark didn't say anything; he just sat staring at the jumble of letters on the screen. Incredibly, amidst all the lines of incomprehensible gobbledygook, there was something that resembled a word. WULLFBYT, it said.

'Mr Tyler? You still there?'

'Yes.'

'I'm calling from St Bartholomew's hospital. I think . . . well, I think perhaps you'd better get over here.'

Chapter Twenty-Nine

The Craft Village was a massive, three-storey Victorian warehouse in Highgate. Somebody had come up with the bright idea of dividing it up into units, and leasing them out to young tradespeople. Now it had the ambience of an indoor flea-market.

Leonard had discovered it a week ago, and had fallen in love with it instantly. Here, amidst this cornucopia of alternative medicine shops, second-hand bookstores and fancy-dress hire outlets, he finally felt as though he belonged somewhere.

As he strolled across the first floor of the complex, a variety of exotic creatures milled around him. There were goths in studded leather with shaved heads and amateurish tattoos; crusties in camouflage trousers, sloppy sweaters and greasy dreadlocks, invariably with a wretched-looking dog in tow; hippie chicks in long Indian-style dresses and sandals, their ears and noses pierced, their long hair vibrant with henna; heavy-metal freaks in motorcycle jackets and torn denims, each sporting a T-shirt exalting the name of their favourite band. And more, much more: men wearing make-up, women wearing Doc Martens, punks and cross-dressers, transvestites and junkies . . . In the midst of such a multitude of freaks, a guy wearing a long grey trenchcoat, a psychedelic T-shirt and a pair of camouflage pants did not cause so much as a raised eyebrow. Leonard felt like he'd died and gone to heaven.

Actually, he felt distinctly *odd* this morning. Light-headed and kind of floaty. At first he had thought he was coming down with flu, but then he reminded himself that he hadn't eaten a proper meal for days. Food just didn't seem to interest him any more. Also, he was finding it increasingly difficult to sleep. The voice in his head kept him awake till all hours, muttering and chuckling away, insisting that he must see his revenge through to its logical conclusion – that he must finally and incontrovertibly wreak his revenge on his betrayer, Mark Tyler. Then, perhaps, at last he would be able to rest . . .

He had come here this morning on a special shopping expedition.

On his last visit one particular window had caught his eye, and he had filed it in his memory. Sure enough, there it was now, sandwiched between an occult bookstore called 'Tarot' and an antique-cum-junk shop called 'Times Remembered'. It was a small, drab-looking place that lacked any kind of a name, but its window display explained all. Leonard paused to study its contents before going inside.

The shop had an interesting line in World War II surplus goods, though it seemed to concentrate mostly on Nazi memorabilia: flags with the swastika emblem, helmets, uniforms, medals and insignia. There were also a lot of plastic construction kits, their boxes depicting guns and tanks and motorbikes. But these items were just a sideline; what the shop really specialized in was weapons. Here at the front, for instance, was a display of knives; every size and shape of knife, from humble Swiss Army models to great big jag-bladed deerskinners. Beyond that there were reproduction Samurai swords, ninja death-stars, rice-flails, staffs and studded brass knuckles.

The rack of guns was, on closer inspection, something of a disappointment. Though many of them looked fearsome enough, they were merely reproduction weapons; nothing above a .22 air rifle was actually functional. As if to make up for this shortcoming, there was also a formidable selection of catapults – not the humble creations that Leonard had carved as a child, but sleek, dangerous-looking contraptions of glass fibre and chrome, each fitted with elastic the thickness of a child's finger. One model, 'The Black Widow', looked particularly lethal.

But Leonard wasn't interested in catapults either. Instead he let his gaze rise upwards to those beautifully constructed weapons that dangled tantalisingly from their wooden stocks in the very centre of the window.

Crossbows!

Leonard smiled. He knew it was fate that had caused him to look in this window a week earlier: fate pure and simple, as though some greater power had realized that soon he would be looking for just such a weapon. How else could it be explained? Had he gone out specifically to look for one, he would not have had the first idea where to start.

Leonard pushed open the door and went inside. The interior was cramped and gloomy, and held an unpleasant odour like damp clothing. A thin young man, clearly the proprietor, sat behind a makeshift counter. Leonard noted with distaste that he was eating a sandwich while alternately taking puffs at a cigarette. The man had very close cropped hair, and a faint discolouration of the top lip that might one day grow into a moustache. He was wearing some kind of uniform jacket, German army, and he grinned a welcome, displaying widely spaced teeth.

'Morning, sir.'

Leonard nodded, glanced at his watch. It was indeed a good hour before midday. As he approached the counter, he noticed a grubby paperback lying face-down: *The Rise and Fall of the Third Reich* by Albert Speer. The young man noticed him looking, and he took another enthusiastic bite of his sandwich.

'S'triffic!' he enthused. 'You read it?'

Leonard shook his head.

'I'm interested in crossbows,' he said.

'Yeah?' The proprietor perked up dramatically. He tossed the remains of his lunch into a cardboard box at his feet, stubbed out his cigarette in a tin ashtray, and wiped his greasy fingers on his khaki trousers, then he stood up. 'Well, let's have a look, shall we?' He stepped around the counter, strode across to the window display, and lifted down one of the weapons. For a moment he weighed it in his hands, then snapped it up to his eyeline and sighted on an imaginary target. Expelling air from between pursed lips, he made a noise to simulate a bolt speeding to its target. Then he chuckled, handed the weapon over to Leonard.

'That's the "Wildcat",' he said. 'It's a sporting target crossbow. European hardwood stock, alloy body. Got a velocity of 240 feet per second, and a range of 65 metres. Lovely machine. I tell you what, I wouldn't like to be standing in the way when *that* goes off!'

Leonard felt the weight of the weapon in his hands. It was surprisingly light.

'Could it kill you?' he asked.

'Mate, it would go in one side and straight out the other!' He seemed to find this idea very amusing. He threw back his head and laughed.

'Is this the most powerful one you have?'

The young man stopped laughing, and studied Leonard for a moment, his expression suddenly thoughtful.

'What you want it for?' he asked. 'Target shooting?'

Leonard considered his answer before replying.

'Hunting,' he said.

'Hunting what?'

'Big game,' said Leonard.

'Yeah?' The young man's eyes narrowed and he smiled dreamily. He retrieved the crossbow from Leonard's grasp and returned it to its place in the window. He then lifted down a bigger, chunkier weapon. This one had a tubular metal stock, Leonard noticed, and what looked like pulley wheels at each end of the bow. It gave an impression of sleek, deadly power. 'The "Demon Safari",' announced the man dramatically. 'This is the real McCoy: a trackless compound bow. Got an extended trigger mechanism, a velocity of 250 feet per second, an accurate range of 75 metres. Takes a 20-inch bolt.' He handed the crossbow to Leonard. 'You could do some real damage with one of these, mate.' He seemed quite excited by the prospect.

Leonard hefted the bow; it was heavier than its predecessor. 'How much?' he asked.

'Well, lemme see, now . . . I can do you one of those for three hundred pounds, cash. That would include the 4 x 32 telescopic sight, and I've a nice PVC carry-case which I'd throw in for nothing. You can undo the prod head here, and fold these arms back for easier carrying.'

Leonard was pleasantly surprised. He had anticipated it costing a lot more than that.

'And would I need a special licence or anything?'

The young man laughed unpleasantly. 'Mate, you just need to be at least seventeen. You *are* seventeen, I take it?'

Leonard felt vaguely shocked by this.

'You mean there's no restrictions. A *kid* could come in here and b . . . buy one of these things?'

The young man spread his hands in a gesture of helplessness.

'I don't make the law, do I?' He made an impatient gesture, as if dismissing the subject. 'Anyway, listen, I can see you're genuinely interested.' He glanced quickly around as though assuring himself that there was nobody to overhear him. 'Would you like to test it out?' he asked quietly.

Leonard shrugged.

'I guess so. But where?'

The young man motioned him to stay where he was. He walked quickly across to the entrance, slipped the catch across, and turned the OPEN sign around. Then he indicated a doorway behind the counter with the word STOREROOM stencilled on it.

'Come on through,' he suggested. 'You've probably been wondering why this shop is so small.'

He took some keys from his pocket and unlocked the door. He opened it, switching on a light as he went through. Leonard followed him.

He found himself standing in a second room, much wider than the first. It had been crudely partitioned off into six narrow target ranges, about thirty feet long. At the bottom of each lane, stood a painted wooden figure of an armed US marine. Each figure had a bright red target positioned over the heart, and the countless holes and abrasions around the bull's-eye bore testimony to some pretty accurate shooting. Leonard gazed around, noticing that the chipboard walls had been soundproofed with layer upon layer of egg-boxes.

'Wow,' he said, because he couldn't think of much else to say.

The young man smiled proudly. 'Built it all meself. Me and some mates. The minute I saw this big room, I thought this is what you've been looking for! I run a crossbow club, see, and it's not always easy to find a good place to practise. So we all put some money in, and came up with this.'

'It's remarkable,' said Leonard.

'Oh, it's a bit makeshift here and there, but it does us OK. We sometimes hold little tournaments here, put up a bit of prize money. 'Course, I have to be careful. If the landlords got wind of it, I'd be up shit creek, wouldn't I? They must wonder why it takes such a big storeroom to run such a tiny shop! Now, then . . .'

He took the crossbow from Leonard, put his foot into the stirrup, and pulled back the string with some considerable effort. 'It takes a bit of strength,' he explained. 'If you can't handle it, you can get what's called a goat's-foot lever to pull the string back, but it shouldn't be too much trouble for a big bloke like you . . .'

Now he was stepping up to the shooting position. He selected a long bolt from several standing in a rack, and slotted it in position on the crossbow. 'This is what we call a broadhead bolt,' he explained. 'Like a regular arrow, see? Now . . .'

He lined up the telescopic sight and made some minor adjustments to the focus. He seemed satisfied. 'All you have to do,' he said, 'is line up the target in the crosshairs, and very gently squeeze the . . .'

A whoosh of air, as the string flipped forward too fast for the eye to follow; and what seemed like a simultaneous thud as the head of the bolt buried itself in the bull's-eye.

'. . . trigger,' finished the young man. He lowered the crossbow with a satisfied smile, and handed it to Leonard. 'OK, let's see what you can do.'

Leonard took the bow and put his foot into the stirrup. He pulled back the string steadily, until it locked into position. He accepted the bolt that the young man handed him, and he slotted it into place. Then he stepped forward and sighted up carefully on the target. But he squeezed the trigger too quickly, so the crossbow bucked slightly in his hands. The bolt slammed into the wooden marine's forehead.

The young man laughed.

'That would have done the trick nicely, but you need to aim more for the chest.' He handed Leonard another bolt. 'Here, try again. You'll soon get the hang of it!'

'OK.' Leonard reloaded. He took careful aim at the target. He squeezed the trigger gently, and the bolt thudded into the outer ring of the bull's-eye. Leonard grinned in satisfaction.

'Nice one,' said the young man, slapping him on the shoulder. 'You're obviously a natural. Hold on a minute. We're running short of ammunition.'

He headed up the aisle towards the target, still talking over his shoulder. 'Give you a week's practice, and you'll be ready for your hunting trip. 'Course, it's different firing at a live target. Me and some mates did a bit of deer poaching a few months back. Some big estate in Scotland – we'd've had our bollocks cut off if we'd been caught. I was walkin' through the woods and I came face to face with this bloody big stag. I swear to God it just stood there and looked at me, and for an instant, you know, I just thought I wouldn't be able to do it. Then it started to turn, make a run for it, and I thought now or never, big feller – you or me. So I just sighted up on the fucker and let him have it. Took him right in the neck. Jesus, I never saw anything like that before. He went down like a stack of bricks, you know?'

The voice, coming unexpectedly out of nowhere, whispered in Leonard's ear. *Firing at targets is one thing. But what about people? You reckon you can do that?*

'Sure I could,' muttered Leonard. 'I guess . . .'

You guess? You don't sound certain. Maybe you should find out.

Leonard frowned. Then he nodded. Of course, you had to feel sure. He put his foot into the stirrup of the bow and pulled the string back until it locked. There were still two bolts in the rack at the firing line. He reached out and took one, slotted it into position. The young man was attempting to pull the bolt out of the wooden marine's forehead, twisting it with his hands to pull it free. It made a sound like bone splintering. Leonard knew exactly what that sounded like. Taking Brenda apart had been no easy matter.

The young man was still prattling on.

'Afterwards, when it was dead, I decided I wanted to take home a little souvenir, right. So I took out my knife and the others didn't think I'd do it, but what I did, I reached right in there and I cut off its—'

The man stopped in mid-sentence. He had turned back to face Leonard. He saw the crossbow aimed right at him, and all the colour drained out of his face. There was a brief silence before he managed to construct a sentence. Then the words came out in a angry protest.

'Hey, man, don't be fucking stupid! You never point a loaded weapon at somebody, unless you intend to use it!'

'I wouldn't argue that point,' said Leonard. He continued to stare down the sights at the young man. 'But supposing I *do* intend to use it?'

The other man laughed, but it lacked conviction.

'That isn't funny,' he said.

'No, it isn't,' agreed Leonard. 'Practice is what it is.'

'Practice?' The young man shook his head. 'Are you fucking crazy, or what?'

'An interesting question,' admitted Leonard, smiling. He squeezed the trigger but the damned thing kicked slightly to the left. The bolt went in through the fleshy part of the young man's arm, slamming him back against the wooden target.

Leonard tutted softly, annoyed with himself. He put his foot into the stirrup, and pulled back the string until it clicked into place. The man was still staring towards him, a shocked expression on his face, his mouth hanging open. A thread of scarlet pulsed out through a rent in his tunic, and ran down his transfixed arm. He let out a curious kind of gasp and attempted to move away from the target, but the bolt had pinned him in place. Now he lifted his free arm and began to tug ineffectually at the shaft, grunting with the agony it caused him.

Leonard slotted the last bolt into position.

'You were telling me before,' he said, 'about the deer. Something you cut off as a souvenir . . .' He sighted up on an imaginary bull's-eye around the young man's heart.

His victim made a last, desperate plea.

'Please, don't.' His voice was barely more than a whisper. 'Have mercy.'

'Like the mercy you showed that deer?' asked Leonard softly.

He squeezed the trigger, gently this time, and the bolt suddenly appeared as if by magic, sprouting from the young man's heart – the dead centre of the imaginary bull's-eye. He gave a convulsive jerk, his eyes widening in shock. He opened his mouth to scream, but all that came out was a slow exhalation. He stopped pulling at the bolt in his arm. His head flopped forward on to his punctured chest, and his body settled, hanging from the bolt.

Leonard grinned, pleased with the shot. He moved down the aisle to examine his target. A thick trail of blood trickled from around the shaft of the bolt, running down the young man's tunic. Leonard lifted a hand and put his index finger into the flow, allowed the blood to soak the end of it. Then he lifted the finger to his mouth and sucked thoughtfully. The sweet coppery taste made his belly rumble, reminding him of how long it had been since he'd eaten properly.

He considered staying on here a while longer, but almost immediately dismissed the idea. He had other calls to make, other purchases to attend to. Best to get them sorted out now. There wasn't much time left. Besides, it was good to keep a sharp appetite, the more to enjoy the culmination of the hunt.

When it was all over, then what a feast he'd have!

Leonard let himself out of the back room, switching off the lights behind him. In the shop, he selected everything he needed, in addition to the bow, from the shelves beneath the counter: twelve bolts, a telescopic sight – 4 x 32, the man had said – and the PVC carrying-bag. As an afterthought, Leonard selected a knife from the impressive display rack: a big, jag-bladed hunting knife. Zipping up the bag, he slung it over his shoulder, and let himself out of the shop, slipping the lock as he did so.

The CLOSED sign was still on display, and he figured it might be a day or so before anyone found the young man's body.

And by then it wouldn't matter anymore.

Chapter Thirty

Judd's phone-call had thrown Mark into a state of panic. He got out of the taxi and turned back to pay the driver. He pushed a couple of notes at the man, too anxious to wait for his change. Then he ran across the hospital forecourt and went in at the main entrance. As he passed through the sliding doors, he could see Inspector Judd waiting in the reception area, slumped in a plastic seat, a blank expression on his face. He glanced up as Mark approached, then got to his feet and indicated with a swift flick of his head that Mark should follow him. He led the way through a set of swing doors and down a passageway beyond.

'How is he?' asked Mark.

'Not good. Oh, he'll live all right, but the doctor says there's no chance of saving his sight.'

'Christ. How . . . how did it happen?'

'Seems he was taking part in one of these daft paintball games in Epping Forest. Bunch of silly arseholes running through the undergrowth playing cowboys and Indians. Our man must have caught him on his own. Fired paintballs into both his eyes at point-blank range. Made a right mess of them.'

Mark nodded. He felt he had reached the stage where nothing could shock him anymore. 'Witnesses?' he asked hopefully.

'Nobody saw a bloody thing. Except, presumably, one Roy Deggs, the game's organizer. He wasn't as lucky as your friend.'

Mark stared at him. 'I wouldn't exactly say Brendan was lucky.'

'No?' Judd shrugged. 'The other players eventually found Deggs lying in the forest with a big hole where his throat should be. I'd say he got the worst of it, wouldn't you?'

Mark didn't reply.

Now Judd was glaring at him accusingly. 'And now, Mr Tyler, I have the strangest feeling that you're going to tell me something more.'

'Oh yes? What's that?'

'I think that you're going to tell me that a similar blinding takes place in your manuscript.'

Mark let a deep breath out through clenched teeth.

'Yes,' he said quietly. 'I'm afraid so.'

Judd nodded. He looked almost pleased to hear this news. 'So it's as we suspected: he's following your story, blow for blow, trying to recreate all the gory details. Perhaps that knowledge could be useful to us. If we can forecast his next move, we can get there before him.'

'Perhaps.'

'OK, so what happens next?'

'In the story?'

'In the story.'

'Umm . . .' Mark was trying to collect his shattered thoughts. 'I think . . . yes, the next move would be the kidnapping of Star Child . . .'

'Who's that?'

'She's the wife of Black Wolf.'

Judd considered this for a moment.

'And which character was blinded in the book?'

'Black Wolf's chief ally, Leaping Horse.'

'Why do all these people have such stupid names?'

'They're Red Indians,' explained Mark.

'Oh, I see. And Indians have stupid names, do they?' Mark didn't answer that one so Judd continued. 'You told me that Leonard Goldman originally saw *himself* as Black Wolf. But now he seems to have cast *you* in that role.'

Mark nodded. 'It's his way of revenge. He wants me to *know* how it feels to be Black Wolf, now I've chosen to finish him off.'

'He dies in the new novel?'

'Yeah. They all die.'

'Christ! And people actually want to read stuff like that?' Judd stayed quiet for a moment, his brow furrowed in thought. 'Mr Tyler,' he said at last, 'do you have a lady friend? Because if you do, I'd be very worried about her.'

'I *am* worried about her! We talked about it this morning. I told her she needed some kind of protection, but she wouldn't listen to me. Insisted that she needed her independence.'

'Stuff that!' Judd took a notebook from his pocket. 'Give me her address and phone number. We'll assign somebody to keep an eye on her.' He handed Mark his notebook and a pen.

'She won't like this,' he observed.

'That's tough. She'll have to fucking well lump it. She'll be at home now?'

'She should be. Though she did say something about going to the zoo this afternoon, to do some sketching.'

'What, Regent's Park? Oh, that's very intelligent, isn't it? You might as well keep her tethered in an underground car park all night long!'

'She's very headstrong. I couldn't talk her out of it. She refused to be scared into hiding.'

'Well, let's just hope she doesn't get more scared before all this is over. I'll ring her place now, while you go and talk to your friend.'

Mark grimaced. 'Is he able to talk?'

'He's pretty zonked right now. They had to give him some powerful painkillers, as you'll appreciate. But he's conscious. I tried a couple of times, but I couldn't get any sense out of him. I'm hoping that a familiar voice might do the trick. We need to discover how much he remembers.'

They had now reached a side door leading off the corridor. Beside it, in an orange plastic chair, sat a uniformed policeman looking bored. Mark eyed the door apprehensively.

'I don't know if I *can* go in there,' he announced.

Judd turned suddenly and grabbed a fistful of Mark's jacket, his face gathered into a furious scowl.

'You bloody well *will* go in there, son! It's the least you can do. That poor sod is blind because of you, and we need your help.'

Mark pulled himself free of Judd's grasp.

'Why's it my responsibility?' His voice rose in volume as he began to lose control of his temper. 'Did I create Leonard Goldman? Did I bring him into the world?'

'No, but you nurtured him, you fed him with all that sick crap you pass off as entertainment. Just get in there and ask your friend if *he* feels entertained.'

Mark was prevented from answering by the sudden appearance of a middle-aged ward sister, who came out of the room and paused to peer at them disapprovingly from behind thick horn-rimmed spectacles.

Judd took out his wallet and showed her his ID. 'Sister, this man is a close friend of the patient. I'd like him to go in for just a few minutes.'

The nurse sniffed. 'Well, I suppose so. Just ten minutes, mind you. And I trust he'll speak to him a good deal more gently than he was to you.' She strode away along the corridor. Judd stared after her.

'Dried up old ratbag,' he muttered under his breath. He turned back to Mark, and indicated the door. 'Just get in there,' he suggested. 'I'll go and phone this girl.'

'Her name's Sarah,' Mark informed him testily.

'Aye.' Judd gave him one more meaningful look, and then moved off.

Left standing under the disinterested gaze of the seated policeman, Mark sighed heavily. At the door, he stood for several moments, gathering his courage. Then he turned the handle and went inside.

It was gloomy in the room, the curtains were drawn. Brendan lay on his back in the narrow bed, his head supported on a thick mound of pillows. His eyes were completely covered by gauze pads and bandages, and what little Mark could see of his face looked pale and drained of all vitality. His lips were slightly parted and the breath hissed in and out from between clenched teeth, as though taking considerable effort.

Mark wasn't sure if Brendan was asleep or awake. As he stood there uncertainly, looking down at his friend, the full impact of guilt finally hit him like a hammer blow. His legs buckled, and he had to throw out a hand to clutch the end rail of the bed to stop himself from falling.

'Brendan,' he gasped. 'Oh God, Brendan, I'm sorry.'

Brendan groaned, a low formless sound of suffering.

Mark fumbled his way across to the head of the bed, and collapsed into a chair. Instinctively he reached out and grabbed one of Brendan's hands, which was lying upturned on the covers. It felt cold and clammy, but Mark squeezed gently, and felt some response in the white fingers.

Suddenly, Brendan spoke, his voice slurred as though he was drunk.

'Oh, Grandmother, what big teeth you have!'

'Brendan?' Mark leaned anxiously forward. 'Brendan, it's me. Are you awake?'

There was a long pause as though his words hadn't connected. Then Brendan stirred, moving his head from side to side on the pillow, as though puzzled by his lack of sight.

'Mark?' he whispered. 'That you?'

'Yes, it's me.' Mark squeezed the hand again, hardly knowing what else to say. 'You're safe now,' he added miserably.

'Safe?' Another silence. Then; 'You got any fags?'

'What?'

'Fags. I'm dyin' for a smoke.'

'Well, I don't know if you're allowed to smoke, Brendan.'

'Fuck it. What they gonna do? Poke my eyes out?' He chuckled mirthlessly, and Mark felt his blood run cold. He had prayed that Brendan would not remember what had happened to him – or at least, might still believe that his blindness was a temporary thing. But he knew, all right, and there was no point in trying to bluff him.

Mark reached into his pocket for his cigarettes. Bugger it, he decided; he could use one, too. He lit two of them and held one out to Brendan. Then, feeling stupid, he had to insert it carefully between his friend's lips. For the first time it struck him how helpless Brendan was going to be, how *vulnerable*. That would surely be his darkest nightmare come true. Mark wondered if his friend could ever survive such a loss.

Brendan inhaled deeply, and blew out a cloud of smoke. He gave a sigh of contentment and then reached up to remove the cigarette from his lips. 'I needed this,' he announced.

Mark drew on his own cigarette. They smoked without speaking for several minutes. It was Brendan who finally broke the silence, in that curious sing-song tone.

'They tried to warn me that paintballing could be dangerous,' he observed. 'I just didn't listen.'

'Brendan—'

'Deggsie was killed, you know. He had a hole in his throat you could drive a truck through . . . You didn't know Deggs, did you?'

'No, I never met him.'

'Well, don't sweat it. He was a real arsehole, if you want the truth. Still, he didn't deserve to die like that.'

Another silence. Mark could almost picture Brendan's mind working, piecing together the small scraps of information available to him.

'It was Leonard Goldman, I presume?'

Mark nodded; then realized he'd have to speak.

'Yes,' he said. 'That was him.'

'A real charmer, that one. Told me . . . told me he wasn't going to *kill* me, because of what happened to . . . to Leaping Horse? That mean anything to you?'

'Umm . . . yes. Yes, I'm afraid it does.' Mark could hardly speak now. He was fighting a powerful urge to weep. 'It . . . it's the new novel, Brendan. The new *Black Wolf*. Goldman took the manuscript, and he . . . well, he's copying the things that happen in the story. First Peter, and now you . . .' He felt the anguish welling up within him. 'I . . . I couldn't have known, Brendan! How could I have known? Something like this, it . . .' His voice dissolved into sobs of misery.

'Here now, easy, easy!' Brendan's arm reached clumsily around Mark's shoulders, the hand stroking the back of his neck. 'It's not your fault.'

'But it is! Can't you see—?'

'Well, that's just the problem, mate, I'm completely in the dark about the whole thing!'

Mark stared at him in astonishment. Unbelievably, Brendan was chuckling.

'Oops!' he said, and waved a hand in apology, scattering grey flecks of cigarette ash across the bed covers. 'I'm sorry, I can't help it. It's the damned drugs they've put me on. I feel as high as a kite!' He paused to reflect. 'I bet it will all seem a damn sight less funny when I come down again.'

'How . . . how much do you remember?' Mark asked fearfully.

'All of it, unfortunately. Deggsie shot the bastard, you know.'

'Shot him?'

'With a paint pellet.' He giggled. 'I heard him grunt. See, he was dressed in the overalls, and everything. Deggsie thought he was part of the game . . .'

'Did you see his face?'

'No, not much of it. He was wearing goggles, but I noticed his eyes were a funny colour. Kind of a light orangey brown . . . No, khaki would be closer. And his teeth, Jesus! Like a fucking wild animal. They had most of Deggsie's throat still stuck to them.'

'I don't understand the teeth. In his verified photograph they looked normal . . .'

'So then he wears falsies?'

Mark stared at Brendan. Could the answer be as simple as that? Judd's line about forensics finding saliva and food traces in the wounds had made him think that they had to be the man's real teeth . . . but wouldn't false teeth produce the same effects? Yes, maybe they would.

'I think you've got something, Brendan!'

'Yeah, well don't worry. It's not contagious.'

'Brendan, please . . .'

'Joke, Mark, that's all! Anyway, the way I see it, maybe I got off lightly. Could be old Leonard's got something even more fiendish lined up for you.'

'That thought occurred to me. Do you remember anything else?'

'Only that he's a big motherfucker, built like the proverbial brick shithouse. He threw me around like I was a nine-stone weakling.'

Once again, Mark thought about that passport photograph of Leonard Goldman. It was impossible from a head and shoulders shot to get much impression of height and body mass. Nor could he show the photograph to Brendan and ask him to identify it.

Mark reached out and took the burned-down cigarette stub from Brendan's mouth, and crushed it under his foot.

Brendan suddenly yawned.

'I'm feeling pretty whacked. Maybe I should sleep now.'

'Of course.' Mark stroked his friend's head gently. 'Thanks.'

'For what?'

'For not blaming it on me.'

'How could I? That guy's totally nuts. He could have picked on anyone. It just . . . happened to be your turn.'

'Funny, that's more or less what Sarah told me.'

'Don't worry, sport. When I come down off this chemical high, I'm liable to get very bitter. Then I'll probably start blaming you for every little ache and pain . . .'

And then he was gone, slipping back into the drug-induced sleep from which Mark had summoned him.

Mark got up from the chair and stood looking down at his friend in silence for several moments. Brendan mumbled something, moving his head from side to side on the pillow as though plagued by bad dreams. It was hardly surprising under the circumstances.

Mark turned away and went out of the room, closing the door gently behind him. Immediately he heard approaching footsteps, and saw Judd striding toward him. His face was grim.

'She's not at home,' he announced. 'Or if she is, she's left her answerphone running. I've had to send a couple of cars up to the zoo to look for her.'

Mark nodded.

'You don't think there's anything to worry about, do you? I mean, he wouldn't try anything else so soon?'

Judd answered him with another question.

'What exactly is she doing up there?'

'Sketching something for a children's book. She wanted . . .'

'What?'

'She wanted to study the wolves for reference,' finished Mark quietly.

Judd frowned. 'I hope the only kind she sees are the four-legged variety.'

Mark flinched. Suddenly, a vision had filled his head. The poster for *Black Wolf* back at Peter's offices. That big, drooling mouth, with its jagged yellow teeth. He remembered now that the image had given him a strange sensation of foreboding the very first day he'd seen it. He hated to admit it to himself, but he was beginning to get that bad feeling all over again.

Chapter Thirty-One

The problem with the wolves was that they didn't behave as Sarah had envisaged. They didn't come slavering up to the chain-link fence, stripping their teeth and rolling their eyes at her. They didn't snarl ferociously and foam at the mouth. Instead, they stood in dejected little groups in the middle of their large enclosure, watching her suspiciously with tawny eyes. Every so often one of them would make a sudden, trotting foray around the perimeter, near the fence, tail between legs, nose snuffling eagerly at the ground. Sketching them was going to prove more difficult than anticipated.

It had been tricky enough finding their enclosure in the first place. It was tucked away in a quiet corner, away from the sizable crowds that wandered in and out of the monkey-house, the aquarium or the big cat enclosures. It seemed that few people were interested in watching wolves, and consequently Sarah had them pretty much to herself. Remembering how she had assured Mark that she'd be surrounded by crowds of visitors, she now felt a bit guilty. Moreover, she was beginning to think that this trip was going to be a waste of time. Wolves had such a fearsome reputation, but these creatures seemed positively timid, even comical – their tongues lolling out as though they were constantly grinning at some private joke. She had hoped to do some close-up facial studies, but had quickly abandoned that idea because they insisted on keeping such a respectable distance from her. Instead, she was obliged to make quick pencil sketches of them huddled in groups, using pencil crayons to get a suggestion of their grey-brown coloration . . .

'Beautiful, aren't they?'

The voice spoke from just behind her, startling her so that she almost dropped her sketchbook. She turned fearfully to look at the newcomer, horribly aware that he had spoken with an American accent. But she saw at a glance that this was not the man in the passport photograph. He looked much older, with piercing eyes and a grey beard and moustache. He wore a green waxed jacket, thick cord trousers and a shapeless tweed hat. He stood with his hands pushed deep into his pockets. He even grinned apologetically, showing white teeth that Sarah decided were a little too perfect to be real.

'I'm sorry,' he said. 'I didn't mean to startle you.'

'That's all right.' She straightened her sketchbook and went on with her work, remembering now that he had made some comment about the wolves. 'Beautiful?' she echoed belatedly. 'Well, I don't know. Maybe I was expecting something more exciting.'

The man leaned forward to glance over her shoulder, watching as she massed in the brindled greyish-brown coloration of a large male with the edge of a crayon.

'That's really good,' he observed. 'You're very talented.'

She smiled. Americans were always more forthcoming like this. An Englishman would never praise her work so openly.

'Thank you,' she said. 'But they're a bit too far away for my liking.'

'You'd like to put them in a smaller enclosure?' he asked, sounding a bit shocked by the idea.

'No, of course not!' She considered for a moment. 'Well, maybe just for half an hour, so I could draw them properly.'

The man sighed.

'They shouldn't be in cages at all,' he said wistfully. 'If ever an animal was made to run free . . .' He shook his head. 'In fact that enclosure is nowhere *near* big enough! In the wild, these creatures maintain home ranges of hundreds of miles.'

'Is that a fact?'

'Yes. And another thing, they don't deserve their fearsome reputation. Wolves only ever seem to get *bad* press. But a hungry wolf will carry food for miles to an injured friend, even in the middle of winter – even when it's near starving itself.'

'I didn't know that. You seem to be very well informed.'

'Oh, well, I ought to be. I'm writing a book about them.'

'You're a writer?'

'Uh . . . that's correct. Natural history. I've been working on this subject for two years now. I come here a great deal. Research, you see. I'm quite friendly with some of the keepers. So I daresay I could get you into that enclosure.'

'Really?' Sarah was doubtful. 'In with the wolves, you mean? But aren't they dangerous?'

'No, not at all. Not when you know what you're doing. I could go in with you, if you like. Tell you what, come along with me and we'll find somebody to organize it.'

Sarah frowned, shook her head.

'No thanks. I think I'll stay here . . .'

He stared at her.

'But . . . you were just saying you wanted to see them close up, weren't you? Come on, you'll be perfectly safe with me.' Now his hand was tugging at her sleeve, and she began to have terrible misgivings about him. She was also thinking about that Identikit picture – how it looked so different to the photograph. Was this man really so much older, or was it just his grey beard that gave her that impression?

She shook her head.

'Thank you but *no!*' she said firmly. 'I'd rather stay here, honestly.'

'What are you afraid of?' He was very close to her now. In fact he had her trapped against the wire fence.

'Nothing,' she insisted, but her voice lacked conviction. She was looking anxiously around for somebody who might help her, but realized with a sinking feeling that the two of them were quite alone.

'Maybe you're thinking I'm a wolf in sheep's clothing,' he murmured. He was staring at her now with those oddly intense eyes, and suddenly she became aware of their similarity to the many pairs of eyes that were watching her from the other side of the fence. She began to feel very afraid. She didn't want to acknowledge her fear, but it was there, blossoming like an ugly flower in the pit of her belly.

'Now look here,' said Sarah, desperately trying to keep from panicking. 'I don't know what you want but—'

'Forget it,' he snarled suddenly, looking off to his right. 'You can't do anyone a favour these days.' He turned brusquely and walked away from her, his hands back in his pockets.

Puzzled, Sarah glanced in the direction he had been staring. A policeman seemed to have appeared out of nowhere. He was walking quickly towards her, a concerned expression on his face.

'You all right, miss?' he asked.

She nodded, glancing back at the American, who was disappearing around the other side of the enclosure.

'That man,' she said. 'I think he—'

'We know all about him,' the policeman assured her. 'We've a couple of men waiting to pick him up just around the corner.'

She stared at him.

The policeman took her arm. 'Come on,' he said. 'I've been told to get you out of here.' He began to lead her away. She gestured vaguely at her artist's case standing beside the wire fence.

'Somebody else will fetch that,' he assured her. 'We can't have you standing around here when we tackle him. He could be armed.'

They walked quickly around the enclosure, in the opposite direction to the one the American had taken, and got on to the main path that led back towards the entrance gates. Now there were crowds of people about, and Sarah immediately felt more secure.

'Did Mark tell you where to find me?' she asked.

The policeman nodded. He seemed a bit nervous, scanning the crowds all around them as though expecting some kind of attack. 'We'll head straight out to the car park,' he announced. 'To get you out of harm's way.' He had a strange accent, she noticed now, a kind of broad cockney that was oddly familiar from somewhere.

Up ahead, in the crowd, Sarah saw two more policemen moving slowly towards them.

'Here's some reinforcements,' she pointed out.

'Yes, I see them.' He tugged at her arm and led her out of the main flow of the crowd, across to the edge of the path. There he stopped beside a large wire litter-bin. 'Just a tick, miss,' he said – and suddenly she remembered where she had heard the accent before. In the film *Mary Poppins*; it was Dick Van Dyke's colourful interpretation of the cockney accent, more Australian than English. The policeman took off his helmet and dropped it into the bin; then he quickly unbuttoned his jacket and did the same with that.

Sarah stood staring at him.

'What are you doing?' she demanded. Now he was pulling off his tie, and unbuttoning the collar of his white shirt.

'Quick change,' he muttered apologetically. Only it wasn't just his clothes he was changing. It was his voice, too. He snatched the sketchbook out of her hands and threw that also into the bin.

Before she could run, he clamped a powerful arm around her waist. His other arm reached under her coat and something sharp jabbed her in the ribs, snatching away her breath. She struggled to move away, but he held her fast, his tawny-coloured eyes burning into her.

'Now,' he said. 'Here's what we're going to do. We're going to walk very quietly up to the exit.'

His voice was now recognizably American. Sarah stared at him in disbelief; her whole body was rigid with terror. When she finally managed to speak, it was little more than a hoarse whisper.

'Oh no . . . no!'

'What's the matter, dearie?' He grinned at her, enjoying her confusion. 'Didn't you recognize me? Don't I look like my photograph?'

He pressed harder on the unseen blade, making her wince.

'Please . . . don't!'

'I'm not going to hurt you,' he said calmly. 'Not unless you make a noise, or try to draw attention. Then . . .' He gave the knife a suggestive twist, below her ribs. 'It's very sharp, and I'll use it if I have to.' He pulled on her elbow to draw her along with him. 'See, we're just a loving couple out for a nice stroll around the zoo. But now we're going to head straight on to those turnstiles – then out to the car park.'

When she tried to hang back, he gave the knife a small jab, and she felt the sting of its point cutting into her flesh. Sarah started walking, glancing desperately left and right. They were in the main thoroughfare now, with crowds of people moving around them, but she didn't dare call out.

'Just keep your eyes straight ahead,' he warned her. 'This knife may be only small, but it could open you up with one slash.'

They moved onwards, pushing through the crowds now as they neared the zoo exit. Random, unfocused thoughts hammered through Sarah's head, like confetti blown on the wind. She struggled to think logically, but fear wouldn't allow her to. What would happen to her once they were out in the car park? She thought about what he had done to Peter Maughan, and she felt faint, terrified that she might drop where she stood, thus impaling herself on that unseen blade. Up ahead, were the turnstiles leading out. Perhaps if she just screamed at the top of her voice?

Suddenly here came the two policemen again, approaching from the direction of the main gates. As they moved through the crowds, they were scanning each face they passed. The sight of them filled her with a strange mingling of exultation and dread. If only they recognized her, they could apprehend Goldman before he reached the exit . . . and escape. But supposing he used her as a human shield, or, in panic just cut her down with that knife? The policemen did not even look armed, so what could they do to help her?

'Keep going,' he whispered in her ear, steering her towards the turnstiles.

But the police were closer now. Sarah saw that each carried a small photograph, comparing it with the faces of passers-by. She felt like calling out, 'No, no, that's useless. That's not the face he's wearing now!' But the blade was still digging into her side.

And here was the turnstile . . . he was pushing her into it. It was narrow, so they had to pass through one at a time, forcing him to take the knife from her side for an instant. Desperately, she thought, Now! *If I scream now!* But then the blade jabbed into the small of her back, and she almost cried out with the pain. The turnstile began to click around . . .

'Excuse me, sir!'

The policeman's voice froze Leonard in his tracks. But he still had one hand on Sarah's shoulder, keeping her close. She held her breath, almost too afraid to move. She glanced back over her shoulder and saw that the young officer was studying Goldman's face, then glancing down at the photograph, as if trying to imagine the man in the picture without his thick black beard.

Then the policeman smiled, satisfied.

'All right, sir. Thank you.'

And he was rapidly moving away into the crowd.

Leonard turned back to face her, smiling confidently, as if amused that it had been so easy to fool the police. He gently increased his pressure on the knife, and Sarah pushed on through the turnstile and out into the car park beyond. There his arm closed around her again, steering her through the ranks of parked vehicles.

'What are you going to do to me?' she gasped.

'Use you as bait,' he said.

'I don't understand.'

'It's in the manuscript. Thaddeus Moon uses Star Child as bait.'

They paused by a van and Leonard took a key from his pocket. He began unlocking the door.

'You've got it all wrong,' she protested. 'I'm not Star Child!'

Leonard smiled. 'So?' he said. 'Nobody's perfect.'

He raised his hand, and there was some kind of pad in it, which filled her mouth and nostrils with a powerful chemical stench. As she tried to back away, he pulled her close, with an arm around the small of her back. Lifting her clear off her feet, he squeezed hard, driving all the air out of her lungs, so that she could no longer hold her breath, and was forced to inhale those sickening fumes. The car park around her seemed to shimmer like an apparition, then went whirling around her head in a dizzy, stomach-churning revolution. For an instant she thought she was a little girl again, out at the funfair with her friends, riding the merry-go-round as her head filled with blazing lights and raucous music.

Then everything melted, dissolved like hot candyfloss, went dripping down into a darkness she could no longer evade. Then she slept, with the foul taste of chloroform still in her mouth.

The old theatre was located in a deserted backstreet in Whitechapel. Few people ventured here, but Leonard sat a long time in the van to be sure that he would not be observed. It was late afternoon now, and everything was still going to plan. Today's schedule had been very complicated but it had all gone like clockwork.

Satisfied at last, he opened the door and walked round to the back.

He unlocked the rear doors, and hauled out the canvas-wrapped body, stooping briefly to drape it across his shoulder. Then he slammed the doors shut, and moved quickly across to the theatre's main entrance. Boarded over with slats of wood, at first glance it looked impassable; but he reached down for the base of a vertical plank from which he had previously spent several hours painstakingly removing the nails. It swung sideways, to reveal an opening beyond. Squeezing through the gap, Leonard carried his burden inside, and let the plank swing shut behind him.

He stood in darkness for a moment, savouring the odour of dampness and decay. Then he fumbled at the table where he had left candles and matches. Once he got a candle alight, he gazed slowly around the derelict foyer. Nobody had been here since his last visit some nights earlier.

It had been surprisingly easy to find the place. First a little time spent in a reference library, searching out the phone numbers of all the theatre preservation societies. Then, he'd phoned up several and spun a tale about being the location-finder for an American movie to be shot in London in the New Year. He was now looking for a deserted theatre in which to shoot some key scenes. Could the society suggest any possible locations?

No doubt scenting welcome dollars, they'd been only too willing to help out. From a short list of six, Leonard had quickly settled on this, the old Dominion Theatre. It stood in a suitably deserted location. Built in 1870, and shut down since the late 1960s, the Dominion had long ago been scheduled for demolition. But it was saved at the eleventh hour by a preservation order taken out by a group of theatre lovers, who then found that they lacked the funds to carry out the extensive repair work needed to make it into a viable venue. So here it remained, growing steadily more dilapidated.

In a decrepit upstairs room, he removed the canvas covers, and laid Sarah on the dusty floor, her back propped against a cupboard door. Next he checked her pulse and breathing to make sure that she had not smothered. In the poor illumination filtering down from a dusty skylight, he thought how very pretty she was. He reached out and traced the tips of his fingers across her cheek, then leaned forward to sniff at her hair, savouring the delicious scent of her.

Sarah moaned softly in her sleep, but did not stir. She was a long way from wakefulness yet.

Leonard tipped her towards him, in order to secure her hands behind her back with a length of rope. The warmth of her against his body excited him, but he had to exercise control, so pushed her quickly back against the door and tied her feet together.

Satisfied that she could not move far, he left her lying there and went off down a flight of stone steps, along a corridor, and passed through a set of swing doors leading into the darkened theatre.

Having relit his candle he then made his way through the tiered rows of mouldering seats towards the main stage. Going up the wooden steps at the front, he took great care in placing his feet, because on either side of him was the dark, open recess of the orchestra pit. Safely up on stage, he switched on the first of the six battery-operated lamps he had hired from a place in Wardour Street. These he had set up in a large circle around the perimeter of the stage. He still felt curiously lightheaded, realizing with mounting excitement that the culmination of all his plans was only a few short hours away.

There were still a few chores, though. A length of hemp rope lay coiled like a sleeping serpent on one side of the stage, and he still had to rig up the noose. Moving into the wings to locate the extending aluminium ladder, he carried it back to the centre of the stage and raised it up into the rafters, searching for a suitable point to rest it. A stout wooden beam, spanning the width of the stage, seemed the best place to secure it.

He thought he heard a movement behind him. Whirling around, he stared up towards the balcony. Was somebody up there watching him, sitting right in the same spot where he intended to wait for Mark Tyler?

'Who's there?' he gasped; and his voice echoed around the empty theatre.

No answer. Leonard hurriedly picked up a lamp and directed its beam towards the balcony, throwing a harsh glare on to the rows of empty seats. He ran the tip of his tongue across his dry lips. Things were getting very weird now. He was feeling spooked, and a strange woozy feeling was pulling at him deep inside. And something else was bothering him. For a moment, he was unsure of what it was, but then the voice spoke in his head, identifying the source of his concern.

It's the girl. She's a clever one and you can't ever trust the clever ones. Look what happened with the last girl you trusted . . .

Leonard considered this for a moment. She was tied up real tight, there was no way she was going to get free.

But it makes no difference whether she's alive or dead, does it? When Tyler gets here, she could escape. She could help him.

It seemed to make sense. Women could be devious; he'd learned that much. Maybe he should just go up there and kill her, right now. He could use a little more practice with the crossbow, anyway.

Sure. Go on Leonard. One less detail to take care of.

Leonard nodded. He could handle these chores later. He let the length of rope slip from his fingers and fall to the stage. Turning, he went down the steps and climbed the aisle to the exit, telling himself that it didn't matter what he did to the girl. It didn't matter at all.

Chapter Thirty-Two

Sarah emerged back into the light by slow degrees, as though surfacing from the depths of some dark lake. Her head swam with snatches of half-remembered tunes and half-glimpsed images. Nausea shifted in the pit of her stomach. Abruptly, the light clawed at her eyes and she let them open, blinking violently as her vision swam slowly and painfully into focus.

The first thing she saw caused her a jolt of pure shock. Goldman was crouching a short distance away, aiming a vicious-looking crossbow directly at her face. As she opened her mouth to speak, there was a whoosh of air, and something slammed into the hard surface behind her with a thud that made her wince. She was dimly aware of a warm liquid pulsing down her thighs, and she realized that she had just wet herself – something she hadn't done since she was seven years old. She tried desperately to move away, and only then realized that her hands were tied behind her back. Turning her head she saw that the bolt had missed her cheek by barely two inches. The feathered shaft was still shuddering from the impact, where it had entered the wooden door against which she slumped.

Leonard was smiling mysteriously at her.

'Practice,' he explained. 'I wasn't trying to hit you.'

She couldn't think of any reply, so she wept instead, the tears streaming down her cheeks.

Strangely, he just sat there toying with his crossbow like some oversized child who had been reprimanded by his mother – not even looking at her, as if waiting for her tears to subside.

Eventually they did, and she found herself gazing around at the unfamiliar surroundings.

It was a huge, dusty room, devoid of any furniture save for a pile of old wooden chairs stacked in one corner. She herself was seated on the bare floorboards, and light was filtering in through a dust-grimed skylight high above her. The place had the look of some disused institution, and it smelled damp and musty as though left unoccupied for years.

'Where is this place?' she ventured at last.

Leonard glanced up at her and frowned, as though debating the wisdom of revealing anything. Then he seemed to decide that it could do no harm.

'You're in a theatre,' he explained. 'This was the old green room.' He glanced around for a moment, as if in awe. 'Pretty neat, huh?' His strange, wide-eyed expression made Sarah wonder if he was on drugs of some kind. 'The place has been closed down for years. They say it's dangerous.' He stamped his heavily booted foot on the boards, and Sarah felt the whole extent of floor vibrate ominously beneath her. 'But those Victorians sure knew how to build,' he continued. 'This place'll be here till the 'dozers come for it.'

'Why have you brought me here?' she demanded, beginning to feel a little bolder.

'So we can be alone – just the three of us.'

She looked around, but there was nobody else in sight.

'Relax,' he advised. 'He's not here yet. He doesn't even know where to come.'

She remembered now. Something about 'bait'.

'He won't come here, if that's what you're thinking. You won't tempt him. At least, he won't come alone.'

'Oh yes, he will, if he cares about you.'

She considered this for a moment.

'And what happens to him when he does get here?'

He smiled again. Putting his foot into the stirrup of the bow, he pulled back the string until it clicked.

Sarah felt her body tense, her heartbeat speeding up.

'I've become pretty good with this bow,' he boasted. Again, she was reminded of a child: a bragging kid who thought he had one up on his playmates. 'I'm a real quick learner.'

He put a hand into his pocket and pulled out a large, red apple. 'An apple for the teacher. Remember that song? I used to like that one. I took an apple to my teacher at school once and you know what she did? She said I was creeping to her. Even the teacher didn't like me!' He laughed bitterly, turning the apple round and round in his big fingers. 'You remember, at school, reading about William Tell?'

He set down the weapon and crawled over towards her on his hands and knees. It was all too easy to guess his intentions.

'No, please,' she whimpered. 'Don't do it.'

'I'm a real good shot, honest,' he reassured her. He then reached out and placed the apple gently on her head, but immediately she tilted forward so it dropped into her lap.

He stared at her, and his expression was stern. 'Well, I guess I could just as easily aim for it right there.'

She searched his face for a hint that he was bluffing, that this was all a joke. But he seemed deadly serious.

When he picked up the apple and replaced it on her head, she did not shake it off a second time.

'Good girl,' he said, reaching out a hand to stroke her cheek. 'OK, Sarah, 'I want you to keep real still.' He slid over to his original position and picked up the crossbow. From a metal quiver affixed to the body of the bow itself, he pulled a long arrow-like bolt and slotted it into position.

He studied the target for a moment, then shook his head. 'Too easy,' he concluded. Moving back another ten feet, he squatted down again, and took careful aim.

Sarah sat very still, her flesh crawling with dread. She desperately wanted to close her eyes but found that she couldn't manage even that. Her entire being was focused on the lethal tip of the bolt, which seemed to be aimed right between her eyes.

She was suddenly, painfully aware of her own total existence; could feel her heart thudding in her chest, could feel the texture of the floorboards beneath her buttocks, was aware of every one of the million droplets of sweat oozing from all the microscopic pores on her body. The diverse odours of this dusty, forgotten room, clearly filled her nostrils, and from her own lap she smelled the overpowering stench of ammonia. As she held her breath, her head began to swim.

And then the door bucked behind her, as it was struck a powerful blow. The two halves of the apple tumbled to the floor on either side of her. She let out her pent-up breath in an explosion, and almost toppled forward.

Leonard was rising to his feet, a proud grin all over his face.

That was when Sarah became aware of the stinging sensation on the top of her head – and a warm, wet trickle coursing through her hair and running down her face.

He hurried over with a look of profound irritation. Kneeling in front of her, he pulled the bolt out of the door and threw it aside with a sound resembling exasperation. 'You must have moved,' he told her. 'I told you to keep still.' Only then did he take out a handkerchief and dab dutifully at the wound.

'Only a nick,' he assured her. 'Nothing to worry about. You know, I can't really afford to hurt you. Not yet. The voice said it made no difference if you lived or died, but that's wrong. It has to be like the book. I see that now.'

She winced as his large hands dabbed none too gently at the cut on her head. Sensing an opening, she decided to try for it. Maybe she could exploit the situation. She gazed up at him, trying to look her most vulnerable. Under the present circumstances, that wasn't difficult.

'Leonard?'

'Yes?'

'Leonard, I'm wet. I need to change my clothes.'

He frowned. 'I know, honey. I've got some things for you to p . . . put on, later.'

'*Now*, Leonard. I need to change now.'

He was leaning closer, one hand stroking her face again. 'I'm sorry, but you know I can't do that. You'll try to trick me, just like Veronica did.'

'Veronica?'

'Yes, she was . . . this girl. I would have done anything for her. Anything in the world. But she wasn't trustworthy. She fooled around behind my back.'

'I'm not like that,' protested Sarah. 'You could trust *me*.'

'Could I, Sarah? Could I really?' He put his arms around her and hugged her.

Sarah tried not to show her disgust. Close up, he smelled of stale sweat. But she could feel the strength in those big arms, and realized that it would take only a fraction more power to break her bones.

'Leonard,' she croaked. 'Please untie me. I need to change my clothes. If you could just untie me for a few moments . . .'

He released his grip and moved back a little. 'You've got to wait, honey. You know I hate to see you unhappy, but everything has to be perfect – like in the story. When he gets here, everything must be just as it was written. Then I can kill him.'

Sarah stared at him. The man seemed to be coming apart in front of her eyes.

He had his arms clasped around himself now, and was rocking gently backwards and forwards, his eyes staring out at something that only he could see. 'Yes, I'll kill him . . . then maybe we'll all be able to rest.'

She shook her head desperately.

'You don't have to kill anyone,' she protested.

'Oh, but I do! He's been bad, he deserves to die. And if you were bad, I would kill you, too. If you tried to trick me . . .' Now he was glaring, those tawny eyes bulging in their sockets. As if he had totally lost his grip on reality.

He suddenly lowered his voice, as if confiding a secret. 'I am Black Wolf. I have great powers.'

Sarah shook her head, terribly scared but determined to speak. 'No. Listen to me. You're not Black Wolf! You're Leonard Goldman. You need help. We can make sure you get it, if you'll just let me . . .'

'*I am Black Wolf!*' he roared, and she shrank back, terrified by the sheer power in his voice.

Now he was glancing at her slyly out of the corner of his eye. He was grinning triumphantly.

'Shall I show you?' he asked. 'Shall I prove that I'm Black Wolf?'

Fresh tears brimmed in her eyes. 'Please,' she whispered. 'Please stop.'

But he was already turning away from her, reaching into his pocket for something. He was leaning away, his hand to his face – making vile, slobbering noises.

Sarah waited in mute terror. When he spoke again, his voice had changed. She could hardly understand anything he was saying.

'Dob be afraid. I only wand to lub you.'

He turned back to her, grinning like a demon, and she screamed herself back into unconsciousness.

Chapter Thirty-Three

Inspector Judd helped himself to another slice of Mark's untouched Dial-A-Pizza. He took a generous bite from the end of it and chewed thoughtfully for a moment, his hunger seemingly as keen as when he had started on his own pizza, fifteen minutes earlier.

'Take my advice, Mr Tyler,' he said. 'Relax. Have something to eat. We could be in for a long wait.'

Mark thought how he'd like to take the rest of that pizza and cram it down Judd's throat. This had *already* been the longest wait of his life, it was nearly ten p.m. and there was still no word from Leonard Goldman. How was he supposed to relax, for Christ's sake?

As days went, this had to be the all-time stinker. If the shock of seeing Brendan at the hospital hadn't been enough to qualify it for that honour, the subsequent news about Sarah had clinched it. The policemen that Judd despatched to the zoo had come up empty-handed. They had found only Sarah's abandoned car, her discarded art materials and sketchbook and, most damning of all, a fake police uniform, crammed into a litter-bin. It was evident that she had been abducted, and it didn't require a massive leap of the imagination to work out who had taken her.

Judd, however, seemed smugly confident that they were now close to breaking the case.

'It's you he's after,' he'd told Mark. 'Like in your story, he's using the girl as bait. So sooner or later he'll get in touch, to tell you where he wants you to meet him. And when he does that, we'll be down on him like a ton of bricks.'

So, at Judd's insistence, they had returned to Mark's place and settled down there to wait. Judd's people had fixed an extra earpiece to the telephone in the lounge, connected to a cassette tape-recorder. There hadn't been enough time to install sophisticated tracing equipment, but Judd doubted that they'd need it.

'Bastard's sure to tell you where to go – isn't he? I mean, so far he's followed everything that's in your manuscript, so why would he change

273

his plans this late in the game? So he gives us an address, I make a quick phone call, and he finds himself with a SOFU team up his arse!'

'A what?' Mark had asked irritably.

'A Special Operations Firearm Unit. Those boys will take him out before he has time to turn around and *fart*.'

Mark had misgivings about that one, right from the first mention of it. Sitting there now, watching Judd munch his way steadily through a seafood deep pan with extra anchovies, he was all the more convinced that if Judd continued to be involved in this, Sarah was doomed. Earlier Judd had told him that he had a squad of ten 'professionals' geared up and ready to go at a moment's notice. Mark could picture it only too well: the noise, the chaos, the armed men storming Leonard's hiding place with tear-gas grenades and automatic weapons. All right, so they might be highly trained, fast and efficient, but Sarah could easily be dead within seconds. There had to be some better way.

He took a cigarette from his pack and lit it. Judd eyed him resentfully.

'Can't you at least wait till I've finished eating?' he growled.

'When will that be – next week? I've never seen anybody eat so much. Anyway, I'll do as I like in my own house.'

Judd sneered, threw down a piece of crust on to his plate, and wiped his mouth on a paper napkin. Then he gave a contented belch. 'Not bad,' he observed. 'A few too many of them salty things.'

'I happen to like anchovies.'

'Yes, but you didn't eat any of it.'

Mark glared at him resentfully. 'This may surprise you, but I don't have much of an appetite this evening.'

Judd sighed, leaned back in his chair. He had taken off his jacket and rolled up the sleeves of his shirt, revealing a crudely-drawn tattoo on his right arm that read '*Scotland Forever*'. He was now looking quite at home here, as though he envisaged moving in on a regular basis.

'I've already told you,' he said, 'I don't think he means to harm the girl. She's just the means to an end. He'll follow the story, like before.'

'Yes, but it's like I keep telling you: the woman *dies* in the book.'

'Aye, but not till this Black Wolf character gets there. Now, if we're interpreting this correctly, *you* are Black Wolf, right? So he isn't going to touch that girl until you show up. Only you aren't going to show up. My boys will do the honours instead.'

'I wish I had your boundless optimism,' Mark told him. 'If he so much as catches a glimpse of one of your people, he's liable to kill her before they get within range . . .'

'Och, you've no idea what you're talking about! These are experts,

Mr Tyler; the safety of hostages is their first consideration. They have all the latest technology on their side – nightscopes, laser-sighted rifles, body armour – and what's Goldman going to have? According to your book he'll be armed with a bloody crossbow. Jesus, it might as well be an elastic band for all the good it will do him!'

Mark inhaled deeply on his cigarette and blew out smoke.

'I don't think you actually appreciate what you're dealing with. He'll be expecting to see *me*. He's anticipating the kind of face-to-face confrontation that climaxes the novel. If you'd just let me go in there first . . .'

Judd shook his head.

'Don't even think about it, Mr Tyler. Let's leave it to the experts, shall we?'

'Easy for you to say,' snarled Mark. 'Sarah's just another statistic to you. It's no skin off your nose if it all goes wrong.'

They sat there in silence for a moment, glowering at each other across the table top. Then Judd laughed, shook his head.

'Look,' he said. 'I don't intend to sit here bickering with you all night. I've told you what's happening, and that's the way it'll be – like it or lump it.'

'That's the way it always goes with people like you, isn't it? Do it your way; you're right and the rest of the world is wrong.'

Judd shook his head.

'Not at all. But there are certain subjects of which I have considerable experience, and this happens to be one of them. And by that I mean *real* experience, Mr Tyler, as opposed to *imagined* experience, like in your books.'

Mark inhaled on his cigarette, blew out smoke.

'It's amazing how you can talk with such authority about my work, Inspector, considering you've never read a word of it.'

'I wouldn't lower myself to read trash like that.'

'But how can you be sure it's trash? Presumably your son must think it's worth reading . . .'

'You leave my son out of this!'

'Why?' Mark leaned back in his seat and studied Judd coolly for a moment. 'Bit of a sore point, is it? This son you can't do a thing with? This boy you can't make head or tail of? Tell me, Inspector, have you ever tried to *understand* him? Have you ever sat down and talked to him?'

Judd scowled.

'Of course, I have!'

'But on whose terms? On yours, I suppose. Ever thought about reading one of his books and discussing it with him? Finding a little common ground?'

Judd seemed to find this amusing.

'Do me a favour, will you,' he muttered. 'Stow all the psychological bullshit. It doesn't wash with me. That boy should have had a firmer hand taken to him when he was younger. My wife never believed in disciplining him, and the result is plain to see. There's a boy who cares nothing for authority, and who believes that the world owes him a living! He'll be leaving school in a year's time, and he hasn't a hope in hell of finding a decent job. Not that he cares, oh no. He's got this harebrained idea about becoming a . . .'

He glanced at Mark reluctantly.

'A what?' Mark prompted him.

'He wants to be a . . . a bloody writer!'

Mark threw back his head and laughed out loud. 'Well, good for him!' he observed. 'He might just do it, too. Wouldn't that just rub your face in it? A horror writer, I presume?'

'Aye . . . Stop your laughing. It's not funny!'

'Oh, but it is. It's priceless! He wants to be one of the things you hate most in the world. Isn't that always the way? You can bet that if I ever produce a son, he'll want to be a copper!' Mark let his laughter subside a little, before continuing. 'So has he done any writing yet? That's the kind of age I was when I started.'

Judd nodded.

'Short stories mostly. Absolutely sick. I couldn't begin to describe them.'

'But you *have* read them?'

'Yes. One or two of them. He writes them at school. His teachers seem to think he's got a real gift, but what I can't understand is why can't he write *positive* stories. Why must his imagination always run to morbid subjects?'

'The sleep of reason produces monsters,' murmured Mark.

'What?'

'Nothing. Listen, if it'd be any help, I'd like to read some of them. Maybe I could give him a little advice.'

'Oh, and he'd love that, wouldn't he? His hero offering words of encouragement! Thanks, but no thanks!'

'Jesus, what are you so afraid of? If the kid's got talent and it's something he actually enjoys, why be so down on it?'

'Because the world's a shit-hole, Mr Tyler. I don't want to see him build up his dreams and aspirations, only to have them thrown back in his face again. How many people ever succeed at writing?'

Mark shrugged. 'A few . . . but that's hardly the point.'

'I think it is. His chances are pretty remote, I'd say. There's only one piece of advice he needs, if he's to get on in the real world. The ones who succeed are the ones who get in with one quick punch.' He made his hand into a fist and stabbed it at an imaginary opponent. 'That's the advice I'd give to him.'

Mark opened his mouth to respond, but was interrupted by the shrilling of the telephone. Their argument instantly forgotten, the two men exchanged glances, got up from the table, and moved across to the telephone. Judd popped the ear-piece into position, switched on the tape-recorder, and motioned to Mark to lift the receiver.

He did so, and listened for a moment. He could hear the sound of traffic in the background, and realized that the call was coming from a public phone-box. Mark glanced at Judd and saw that he, too, had registered that fact.

'Hello? Mark Tyler speaking.'

'Hello, Mark. This is Leonard. I guess you were expecting my call.'

'Yes. How is Sarah?'

'Oh, she's just fine, Mark. Safe and well for the moment. Looking forward to seeing you.'

'You haven't harmed her?'

'No, she's fine.'

'Where is she?'

'You'll find out soon enough. I expect you've got somebody listening in, there?'

'No,' said Mark and hoped his reply didn't sound as unconvincing as he felt.

'Sure you have! They'd have made you play along with them. But listen, Mark, this is between you and me, right? I'll make you a promise right here and now. If anyone other than you turns up tonight, she's dead, Mark. You understand?'

'Yes,' said Mark grimly.

'Now I'm going to do it by the book. It's 10.45. I want you to go to Moorgate tube station. You know where that is?'

'Uh . . . yes.'

'There's a phone-box just to the left of the main entrance. I'll call you from there at 11.20. You'd better be there ready to answer my call.'

'Wait, that doesn't give me enough time to get there!'

'Then you'd better get a move on. And remember, I'll be watching you every step of the way. If anybody else answers that call, she's dead. Be seeing you.'

'Just wait a—'

The line went dead. Judd switched off the tape-recorder, his former confidence replaced by a look of exasperation.

'The devious bastard,' he muttered. 'He's not going to make it easy for us, is he? Well, let me see now. We'll just have to take you up to the phone-box with the rest of the team, and act on his next set of instructions.'

He took the handset from Mark, pressed down the bar, and started to dial another number. Mark reached out and pressed down the bar a second time. Judd looked at him indignantly.

'What the fuck are you playing at?' he snapped.

'You heard what he said. Only me.'

Judd sneered. 'And I told you, sunshine, stay out of it. *I'm* handling this.'

'He said he'll be watching me every step of the way.'

'Bollocks, he's bluffing you! How could he?'

'I won't take the risk!'

'You'll do what I tell you. Now, stop wasting time.'

'But we didn't finish our discussion, did we?'

'What are you on about?'

'You remember, that discussion we were having. Your advice to your son? Well, I've just decided to take it.'

Judd's eyes narrowed suspiciously, then widened as he suddenly realized Mark's intentions.

That was when Mark hit him, throwing his right fist into the detective's face with all his strength. Judd spun around with a grunt of surprise, and went down in an ungainly sprawl, one arm stretching out in an instinctive grab for the dining table. His fingers caught the trailing edge of the table cloth, dragging plates, cutlery, glasses, condiments and the remains of his pizza down on top of him. The policeman made a dull groaning sound and tried to lift himself up on to his arms.

Mark prepared to hit him a second time, but there was no need. Judd's arms buckled and he flopped down on to his face with a slow exhalation of air. Mark leaned over him, massaging the stinging knuckles of his own right hand. He prodded Judd with the toe of his boot, and got nothing but a low groan out of him. Now it was done, he could hardly believe he'd had the guts to go for it.

He glanced around for something to tie the detective up with.

Then, recalling scenes from some of his favourite movies, he pulled the telephone lead out of the wall and used it to secure the man's hands and feet. It wasn't as easy as it looked in films. The telephone kept getting in the way, and in the end he had to cut it off with a table knife in order to complete the job.

Then he rolled Judd on to his back, seized hold of him around the chest, and dragged him across the carpet to the sofa. He was just lifting him on to it, when Judd's eyelids flickered open. For a moment he lay there disorientated, looking up at Mark through half-closed eyes. There was a dark bruise blossoming on his jaw, and blood oozed from his bottom lip where he must have bitten into it. Then he tried to move his hands, and realized they were secured behind his back. Suddenly he was wide awake, and mad as hell.

'Tyler!' he roared. 'What the fucking hell do you think you're playing at?'

'I think it's called "assaulting a police officer",' said Mark grimly. 'One quick punch, you said, and I thought that was a cracker, myself.'

'Have you taken leave of your senses, man? Untie me *now*. That's an order.'

'Sorry, no can do. I asked you to let me try it my way, and you said no.'

'God help you when I get untied,' Judd warned him. 'I'll make you rue the day you were born!'

'I believe you,' said Mark. 'That's why I've tied the knots good and tight.'

'You bloody stupid moron! Just you wait, Tyler. Just you wait!'

Mark reached into his pocket, took out a handkerchief and stuffed it into Judd's mouth. It didn't silence him completely, but it helped to muffle the noise while Mark tried to explain.

'I can't take the risk of something happening to Sarah just because we disobeyed Goldman's orders. Look, I didn't enjoy hitting you . . .' He thought for a moment, shook his head. 'Actually, that's not true. I've been wanting to do that for quite a while . . .'

He suddenly realized that time was moving on, so he abandoned further excuses. Instead he went over to the chair where Judd's tweed jacket hung, and he felt about in the pockets. His hand came out with a bunch of keys.

'Since I'm in for a penny, I'm also going to borrow your car,' he announced.

Judd made some very strange noises around his improvised gag.

'Yes, I know,' agreed Mark. 'I've never learned to drive. But I've seen it done often enough, and this is an emergency. Let's face it, *you* drive, so how difficult can it be?'

Mark went into the kitchen, opened a drawer and pulled out a formidable-looking carving knife. This he slipped into his jacket pocket. He didn't know how much use it would be, but it was the only kind of weapon he was going to find in the house. Then he hurried back

279

into the lounge and switched on the television set. After a few moments, he was rewarded by the sight of two soccer teams chasing a ball around a pitch.

'There,' he said. 'FA Cup match. Something *you* can actually understand. Just lie there and enjoy it. I hope I'll be around to see you later.'

As he headed for the door, Judd was making those weird noises again. Judging by the tone of them, he *wasn't* wishing Mark the best of luck. It occurred to Mark that maybe it might go easier on him if he *didn't* come back from this alive.

He let himself out into the night, and hurried along the path to the spot where Judd's unmarked Escort was parked. Mark unlocked the door and slid into the driver's seat, assuring himself that he had watched Sarah driving a similar machine hundreds of times before; that he understood the principles, even if he didn't have hands-on experience. He pushed the key into the ignition, and got the car's souped up engine running.

OK, so far, so good. Now, clutch down, into first gear, touch on the accelerator . . .

Why wasn't he going anywhere? He pressed down further on the accelerator, and the rear wheels made a shrieking sound as they spun on tarmac.

Jesus, the handbrake!

He reached down to let it out, and the car shot forward at an alarming speed, straight towards a vehicle parked up ahead. Mark cursed and turned the wheel, a fraction too late, his front offside wing catching the other car's bumper with an ugly crunch. He winced, turned the wheel back again, and got out on to the high street, accelerating all the while, until he became aware of the engine producing a grating howl of protest.

Right now, change gear.

He stamped down on the clutch and tried for second gear, but found fourth instead. The gears made a hideous grinding noise, and the car shuddered as the engine began to falter. Mark kept his foot down on the accelerator, and the shuddering subsided as the speedometer rose above thirty. A car came screaming towards him on the other side of the road, horn blaring, and he realized that he was driving without lights.

Christ, which button is that?

He fiddled frantically with a lever on the steering column, and set the windscreen wipers squeaking across the dry glass.

No. How about this one?

He tried a lever on the other side, and was rewarded with a blaze of light which showed him that a column of cars up ahead was stopped at an intersection.

Startled, Mark stamped down on the brake so enthusiastically that the rear wheels went into a skid, and he had to fight with the steering to keep to his own side of the road. He managed to come to a stop scant inches from the bumper of the vehicle in front.

Right, back down to first . . .

He made the gear change, and sat there sweating. The heater was going full-blast, and he didn't know how to turn it off, but at least he'd managed to stop the windscreen-wipers. He wound down the window instead, and took the opportunity to glance at the digital clock on the dashboard. It was already 10.35 and he had a long way to go yet. He offered up a silent prayer that his hopeless driving wouldn't result in an accident en route. If that happened, Sarah would have no chance at all. For the first time, he wondered if he had made a stupid mistake. Maybe he really should have left it to the professionals . . .

The lights turned green, and the cars ahead of him moved on. There was no more time to think. He lifted the clutch and the car stalled.

'Shit, shit, shit!' he said. He turned the ignition, and the car lurched violently, then stalled a second time.

Still in gear, you pillock!

Behind him, a horn blared impatiently. He fought down his rising panic, slipped the gears back into neutral, turned the key again. The engine coughed, spluttered. He tried it a second time, and it fired.

OK, now into first . . .

The lights went back to red. He registered it, but knew that he didn't dare waste any more time. He pressed the accelerator, raised the clutch gently, and moved forward into the junction – just as other cars approached him from left and right. There was a cacophony of horns, screeching tyres, and lights filled the interior of his car. But he kept his foot down and sped onwards as, first, one car, then a second swerved to avoid him. Something clipped his rear left wing with a crunch that took out one of his lights, and he caught a glimpse of one driver mouthing obscenities at him as he was obliged to make an unexpected emergency stop.

Then he was across the junction and speeding down the road beyond, counting off the seconds as he drove eastwards – to where Leonard and Sarah were waiting for him.

He hoped he'd be there in time.

Chapter Thirty-Four

The digital clock on the Escort's dashboard stood at 11.18 as Mark coaxed the car through the light traffic approaching Moorgate underground station. It had been a nightmarish journey. He had run through red lights, stalled umpteen times and, most frightening of all, driven the wrong way up a one-way street, with cars swerving to avoid him all the way.

Somehow, he had made it. Now, to his left, he could see the illuminated brick entrance of the station. He scanned the area hopefully, and then spotted the bright rectangle of glass that was a phone-booth. That had to be the one! There was no other nearby.

There was no time to consider the niceties of parking, even if he'd known how to do it. Instead, he simply wrenched the wheel sideways, cutting across two lanes, oblivious to the blasting of horns from outraged motorists in his wake. He took the Escort half up on to the pavement, then stamped on the brake. With a shriek of protest the car slewed to an untidy halt at a 45-degree angle to the road, just as the clock's digital display clicked up another minute. Mark threw open the door and clambered out, leaving the keys in the ignition and the engine still running. As he ran towards the phone-box, he saw to his dismay that a man was opening the door and stepping inside to make a call.

'Hey!' Mark shouted. He hurried across the intervening space, waving his arms at the stranger. The man hesitated, half-in half-out of the box, staring at Mark over his shoulder. He was a big, surly-looking fellow in a donkey-jacket and heavy workman's boots.

'What's up?' he demanded.

'Emergency!' gasped Mark. 'An important call!'

The man looked distinctly unimpressed. 'That's tough.' He made as if to go into the phone-box, but Mark stepped forward, pulled open the door and reached out a hand to restrain him by grabbing the sleeve of his jacket.

'Oy! What's the bleedin' idea?' The man spun around to face Mark, looking decidedly pissed off.

'Please,' Mark begged him. 'Somebody's life depends on it.'

'Yeah?' The man opened his mouth for a suitable reply but, glancing over Mark's shoulder, he noticed a police car pulling up behind the illegally parked Escort.

'That yours?' the man wanted to know.

Mark shook his head. 'Never saw it before.'

The phone shrilled, making both of them jump. The man reached out to lift the receiver, but Mark, acting instinctively, pulled him back out of the booth by his arm, and flung him several steps across the pavement.

'I'm bloody well warning you!' snapped his victim, but already Mark had jumped into the box and grabbed the phone.

'Hello?' he said.

'You made it! Excellent!' Again, sounds of traffic in the background. The same public phone as before, Mark was sure.

'Tell me she's all right.'

'She's fine, Mark.'

'Let me speak to her.'

'Not yet, my friend. You've another journey still to make.'

'I'm listening.' Mark glanced nervously over his shoulder.

One of the policemen had stepped out of the squad car, and had walked over to the Escort. He was now peering curiously through the open door.

'It's now 11.23,' said Leonard. 'You need to go down into the tube station, find the Hammersmith Line, and catch the next train to Whitechapel station. According to the schedule I have, it leaves there at 11.27. It's the last train this evening, so I wouldn't miss it if I were you. I'm allowing you exactly eighteen minutes. When you get to Whitechapel, I want you to ring me. If I don't hear from you by 11.45, she dies.'

'How can I ring you, for God's sake?'

'When you get to Whitechapel, make your way to the main entrance and look for a very familiar poster . . .'

'Listen, I've only got six minutes to catch that train . . .'

'Don't miss it! Her life depends on it. You understand what I mean?'

'Yes, yes, of course . . . but please, don't—'

'We're wasting time, aren't we?'

The line went dead. Mark dropped the phone and stepped outside, noticing that the policeman had now crossed the pavement to talk to the man in the donkey-jacket. They were both looking over towards Mark with interest.

He began walking quickly towards the station entrance.

'Excuse me, sir! Is this your car?' called the policeman.

Mark shook his head and quickened his pace. He had less than six minutes.

The copper started to follow. 'Sir! Just a minute, please!' he shouted.

Mark began to run. Straight through the station entrance, weaving past a young couple just emerging. He glanced wildly around, then headed for the sign which indicated the Hammersmith Line. Uncomfortably aware of the uniformed figure in pursuit, he realized that, even with the best will in the world, there wasn't time to purchase a ticket. Rows of automatic barriers loomed ahead of him, and he ran straight for the nearest of them. Snatching a breath, he flung himself up on to the metal structure in an ungainly sideways vault, and went sprawling on to the other side of it. More by luck than design, he landed on his feet.

As he sprinted for the staircase ahead, another uniformed shape seemed to appear out of nowhere: an outraged ticket collector who had witnessed his transgression. The man made a grab at his arm, but Mark shouldered him roughly aside. The collector lost his footing and went sliding across the tiled floor, just as Mark gained the top of the staircase and plunged downwards, his heart hammering in his chest.

He suddenly reached level ground, the impact jolting his spine, then he angled sharply to the left and descended two more flights of steps, weaving past more leisurely-moving travellers, not daring to slow his pace.

At last he emerged on to the platform he needed. As he came charging through the archway, he saw a train already standing. Glancing to the left, he took in the illuminated sign: this train was heading for Whitechapel, and it was the last one that evening. Aiming himself at the nearest open doorway, he was still three yards away when the doors began to slide shut.

'Wait!' he yelled.

He lunged forward, arms extended, and just managed to intercept them. They shuddered briefly as he forced them back, then they sprang open again.

Mark staggered inside, gasping for breath. He moved straight across to scan the nearest route map, and assured himself that this train did indeed go to Whitechapel. There was a brief pause before the doors slid shut again.

Mark moved back to the platform side to peer out through the glass panels, half expecting to see a policeman signalling the driver to stop. But clearly his pursuer hadn't been as tenacious as Mark had feared.

The train gave a lurch and moved out of the station into darkness.

Mark slumped back against a metal partition and glanced at his watch. It was now 11.29. He had exactly sixteen minutes to make his next phone-call. But he didn't want to think about that too much.

The carriage was almost empty, but he remained in the door space, too anxious to sit down and rest. After what seemed an interminable time-span, the train pulled into Liverpool Street, and its doors hissed open again.

Loud football chants – and then a half dozen youths trooped into the carriage, obliging Mark to step back from the doorway. *Trouble*, Mark thought – big, gangly types sporting shaved heads and oversized boots. Instead of helping themselves to the empty seats, they grouped around the doors, occasionally looking at Mark with amused interest. He could smell the sour stink of beer on them and they were clearly in high spirits, sniggering away at some private joke. The nearest of them, a tall, skinny youth with acne grinned at Mark as the train moved out of the station.

'Spare a couple of bob, mate?'

Mark glanced up at him in surprise.

'What?' he said.

The youth affected a dumbfounded look – his mouth open.

'Wot?' he mimicked. He then glanced around at his mates, and was rewarded with snickers of laughter. Looking back at Mark, his expression hardened. 'Couple of bob,' he repeated. 'You know – ackers, mazoolah, dosh. Pay for me chip supper, like.'

'Sorry. No change.' It was Mark's habitual excuse, and usually that was enough.

But not tonight.

'That's all right. We take notes, don't we, lads?'

More laughter.

The spotty youth's mates were gathering closer now, enjoying this new game. Mark could see the dull gleam of stupid delight in their eyes.

Almost unnoticed, the train pulled into Aldgate East. The doors slid open on to a deserted platform and the only other occupants of the carriage got off hastily. Under different circumstances, Mark would happily have joined them, and waited for the next train. Only, tonight, there wasn't another train – and time was ticking away too fast.

One more stop, he thought grimly.

It was now very quiet in the carriage. Just himself and six oiks from hell. Perfect. Mark frowned, glanced at his watch: 11.33. Twelve minutes left.

Come on, he thought. *Let's go!*

The doors slid shut again, the carriage lurched, and the train began to move into the tunnel.

'Nice watch,' observed the spotty one.

'Rolex,' muttered one of his companions.

'Always wanted one of them.'

Spots was grinning savagely now. He gestured to Mark with one hand, indicating a battered old Casio digital on his bony wrist. 'Tell you what, I'll do you a swap.'

'Get stuffed,' Mark said calmly. He slipped a hand into his jacket pocket.

The youths exchanged surprised glances, then altogether made an oohing noise.

'Not very polite,' observed Spots, aping an aggrieved tone.

'Downright bloody rude,' said a mate.

Spots leaned closer, and Mark winced at the stink of alcohol on his breath.

'Tell you what, sport,' he said quietly. 'There's six of us and only one of you. If we decide to take your bleedin' Rolex, how you reckon you're gonna stop us?'

Mark pulled his hand out of his pocket, and showed them the kitchen knife.

'With this.'

They backed off a little with expressions of disbelief.

'Fuckin' hell!' exclaimed Spots, staring at the knife in dull surprise. 'Fuckin' hell,' he repeated, with a little more respect. 'You always come out tooled up, do ya?'

'Always,' Mark told him, trying to sound calm, though he was glumly aware that he was trembling from head to foot.

One of the other yobs made a move, but Mark whipped around to face him.

'Problem?' he asked.

The youth shook his head, and moved back to lean against the wall.

'He wouldn't dare use it,' sneered Spots.

'Don't bet on it.'

The routine shudder of the train changed to a new tone as it approached the next station.

'Stand back from the doors,' Mark told them. 'This is my stop.'

They stared at him uncertainly. The train was slowing now, as it emerged into light. White tiles and film posters flashed past the windows.

'Move back!' repeated Mark, gesturing at them with the knife. This time they obeyed, and he circled quickly around to put his back against the doors, his gaze flicking left and right.

'You're a fuckin' headcase,' observed Spots.

Mark didn't argue with him. Under the circumstances it sounded suspiciously like a compliment. As the doors parted, he backed out on to the platform. He stood for a moment watching the gang, the knife held out in front of him, convinced that the moment he turned away from them, they'd be on him like a pack of wild dogs.

The driver, glancing down from the top of the train, must have mistaken his lack of movement for indecision.

'You want this one, or not?' he called down.

'No!' Mark shouted back, a distinct tremor in his voice despite his efforts to conceal it.

The youths seemed to scent his fear: they took a step closer to the door.

'He's scared shitless,' observed Spots triumphantly.

Then the doors slid shut, and the train moved on. He could see their faces pressed to the glass, mouthing obscenities, their fingers stabbing frenzied V signs. Then the train moved into the tunnel.

Mark glanced at his watch. It was 11.39. *Only six minutes left!*

Mark turned and ran for the WAY OUT sign, pushing the knife back into his pocket. He pounded up a flight of stairs, raced across a deserted bridge, and descended again into the main station concourse, where he was confronted by a large black lady ticket collector. As he tried to run past her, she slapped a powerful hand on his arm, restraining him at the narrow barrier, so he was obliged to fumble for his wallet. He fished out a five-pound note and thrust it at her.

'I can't change this,' she grumbled.

'Keep it!' he told her. He pushed on through the barrier and halted in the main entrance, glancing desperately around. What had Leonard's instructions been? Something about a familiar poster?

But they *all* looked familiar: posters for theatrical events and films, adverts for chocolate bars, temp agencies and breath fresheners . . . Where was he supposed to start?

Mark moved hopelessly around the walls, checking them all out one by one – searching for anything that might give him a clue.

His last minutes were ticking away.

And then he saw it, the poster for *Black Wolf 2*, and he nearly let out a whoop of relief. Somebody had fixed a small sticky label over the glass – right in the O of 'Wolf'. Leaning closer, Mark noticed a local phone number written in a neat, precise hand. That was it, it had to be!

There was a row of phone-boxes nearby and, glancing at his watch, Mark saw that it was just coming up to time. He slid a hand into his jeans pocket, looking for change, and realized almost instantly that he had none.

Swearing under his breath, he ran back across to the ticket collector, who was now packing up for the night.

'Please!' he said. 'I need some change.'

She glared at him.

'Didn't you tell me to *keep* the change?'

'I know, but look – just enough to make a phone-call. Ten pence will do. Please – this is an emergency.'

'Can't you just reverse the charges?'

'No, listen to me.' His anger rising now. 'Godamn it, I just gave you five pounds! I only want ten pence, for Christ's sake!'

She made an irritated sucking noise through her teeth, then began to fumble grudgingly through the pockets of her uniform.

'All right, all right, keep your hair on.' Her plump hand then came out, clutching a couple of ten-pence pieces. Once she dropped them into his grasp, he turned and sprinted back to the poster, where he peeled the sticker away from the glass.

'Use to be people said "Thank you",' the woman shouted after him.

He moved to the nearest phone and lifted the receiver to his ear. No dialling tone.

'Jesus Christ!'

He jiggled the receiver to no effect, slammed the handset down, moved to the next booth. *Shit*! A card-phone. The third phone had been recently vandalised; its handset was missing entirely.

He ducked into the fourth, and final, booth, offering up a silent prayer as he lifted the receiver. He listened to a silence, so deep that it seemed to engulf him.

In that instant he told himself that it was all over. He had run the race and lost. Sarah was as good as dead, and he may as well just accept that fact.

Then some stubborn part of him rallied: would not accept this. He reached out a fist, and brought it down on the contact with a thud.

The line began to purr.

'Yes,' he whispered. He dropped in a coin and punched out the numbers with his index finger. As he glanced at his watch, his eyes widened, and he felt his stomach turn over inside him. It was 11.47. The time had slipped away – evaporated. He was going to be too late after all.

The phone began to ring – and sounded as if it was coming from the other side of the world. It rang twice . . . four times . . . six times . . . eight . . .

Please God, thought Mark. *Let him still be there. I'm only two minutes late. Please let him answer me . . .*

The phone rang twelve, fourteen times . . .

Come on, come on. You've got to be there!

Sixteen, eighteen . . .

And then the receiver was lifted.

'Hello?' It was Leonard's now-familiar voice, calm and mocking. Mark remembered to breathe. He felt hot tears welling in his eyes.

'Cutting things a little fine, Mark.'

'Sorry . . . I'm sorry.' Mark could hardly find the breath to speak. 'Is Sarah there?'

'Sarah's fine – so far. You *are* alone?'

'Yes, I swear to you.'

'Good. Well, here's what you do, Mark. Come to the Dominion Theatre in Standing Gate Street. It's no more than a mile from where you are now. A little off the beaten track, but I expect you'll find it OK. Sarah and I are going to be busy preparing things, right now. It'll be just like you wrote.'

'Please, you don't have to harm her!'

'That's kind of up to you now, isn't it? The show begins at midnight, Mark. That's when she goes on the chair. Be there or be square.'

'I can't possibly get there for midnight. You have to give me some instructions. I have no idea where this place is!'

'Then you'll have to use your initiative, won't you?'

'Leonard, no, wait!'

The other phone was abruptly slammed down. Mark stood gazing helplessly at the receiver. Then he turned his head to stare at the ticket collector, who was now padlocking the door on her little ticket hut. She saw him looking at her and she turned away, muttering to herself. He put down the phone and hurried across.

'Standing Gate Street?' he asked her. 'Any idea where that is?'

She shook her head.

'Think there's any chance of getting a taxi from here?'

'This time o' night? No chance, man. They's all up the West End, chasin' business. Look, I'm just about to close up for the night. Don't give me a hard time.'

'But I have to get somewhere. It's—'

'An emergency – yeah, yeah, I know.' She made that sucking sound again, then took a battered A-Z of London out of her coat pocket.

'Best I can offer,' she said. She handed it to him.

'Thanks!' He turned and ran for the exit, ignoring the howl of protest she flung after him.

'Hey, wait! I only meant for you to *look* at it!'

But he was out on to the street and running east, flicking through the index of streets as he went. In exactly twelve minutes time, Sarah was going on the chair.

Mark knew only too well what that meant.

He would have to be there, ready to catch her if she fell.

Chapter Thirty-Five

After spending so long tied up, Sarah found it difficult to move. Her wrists and ankles were virtually numb. Leonard had brought a small battery lamp into the dark room, and it threw a harsh glare on to his face, but she saw that at least he had normal teeth again. Had she imagined that nightmare earlier?

Most of the day, she had heard him working downstairs, and occasionally the sound of his voice as he held mumbled conversations with himself. At one point she thought she heard him leave the building, and she had then thrown herself into the task of rubbing her tied wrists against the edge of the door-frame. But, as far as she could tell, she had made no impression on the rope whatsoever.

Leonard seemed strangely excited now, in a weird, childlike way. As soon as he had untied her, he handed her a package wrapped in tissue paper and urged her to open it, like it was her birthday and this was a special present he had bought for her. She tore it open with clumsy fingers, and found that it contained an expensive-looking white silk negligée, very demure, ankle-length, with an elegant lace bodice.

She looked at him uncertainly.

'Put it on,' he urged her.

She glanced around for a place to change, but the room was bare. He continued to stand there, watching her eagerly.

'Hurry up!' he said.

She turned her back to him while she undressed. She had expected to keep her underwear on, but he urged her to remove that too. As quickly as possible, she slipped the garment over her head, and shook it down to her ankles.

'Turn around.' His voice was hoarse, as though he was aroused, and she felt terrified that this was some kind of prelude to rape. But when he approached her, he only stroked her hair and said that she looked beautiful.

'I picked this out special for you,' he told her. 'I wanted you to look your best tonight.' He glanced at his watch, as though reminding himself of some schedule. Then he picked up the lamp and nodded towards the exit. 'This way,' he said, sounding more businesslike now. 'Everything's ready.'

She went out through the doorway, stumbling along on numbed feet. Beyond the door, an ancient mouldering staircase led down into darkness. Sarah felt nervous about the safety of the stairs; they creaked and sagged beneath her as she went down.

Leonard moved beside her, holding the lamp out in front of them to light the way. A scuttling black shape ran up the damp-stained wall beside her head, and Sarah drew back with revulsion.

Leonard's hand closed on her shoulder.

'Spider,' he said quietly. 'Big feller, too. I used to be afraid of spiders. Then I was cured.' He took his hand from Sarah's shoulder, and crushed the spider with a careless sideways swat. When he took the hand away, he noticed a smear of blood on it. He put out his tongue and licked at it experimentally, then smiled again that dreamy smile.

Sarah felt her gorge rise. She moved on down the staircase, and he followed. At the foot of the stairs they turned right into a long corridor, and walked on to a set of swing doors. Leonard pushed them back, and ushered Sarah into the room beyond.

She saw that they were in an old theatre. Ranks of mouldering seats angled downwards to a bare stage, which was brightly illuminated by a circle of big battery-operated lamps. It was so damp and cold that Sarah could feel her breath clouding.

Leonard took her arm and guided her down between the rows of seats, down to the foot of the stage. Now that she was closer, she could see that a chair had been set out in the very centre of the stage and, more disturbingly, that a rope noose was suspended above it, its other end rising up into the gloomy darkness, out of her line of vision.

She glanced at Leonard fearfully.

'Don't worry,' he told her. 'Stay calm and you'll be fine.'

Taking her hand now, he led her up the short flight of steps and on to the stage. On either side there was a drop down into the dark recess of the orchestra pit. The ancient wooden steps bowed alarmingly beneath their combined weight.

Then they walked out into the glare of the lights, and Leonard set down the lamp. He indicated the chair.

'Climb up,' he suggested.

She shook her head.

'No,' she whispered. 'You can't make me . . .'

'Climb up and stand on it!' His voice, more threatening now, echoed around the theatre. He reached behind him and pulled a big, jag-bladed knife from his belt, waving it threateningly. She moved to the chair and noticed that it had only three legs: the right front leg had been removed. She glanced at him again, baffled.

'It's a kind of game,' he told her. 'All you have to do is keep your weight to the back. Then it's easy. Go on, you can do it.' He glanced at his watch again.

Carefully, she eased her weight on to the chair. She found that he was right. If she kept her weight to the rear left-hand side, the chair remained upright. But she would only have to lean forward a fraction to upset the balance.

Now Leonard was pointing to the noose.

'Put it around your neck,' he commanded.

She stared at him for a moment, then shook her head defiantly.

'If you're going to kill me, you'd better just get on with it,' she told him. 'There's no point in playing these sick games.'

'I'm not going to argue with you,' he growled. 'Now p . . . put the rope around your neck!'

Sobbing, she did as she was told.

'Pull it tight, or I'll kick the chair out from under you!'

She reached up and pulled the noose down until it fitted snugly around her neck. The action caused her to shift her weight slightly, and the chair began to tilt. She flung her arms out desperately and managed to steady herself. She waited, afraid to move so much as a muscle, while he stood below her, his hands on his hips, gazing up into her face.

'You look p . . . perfect!' he observed. 'Just as I pictured it.' Moving over to one of the lamps, he altered its position slightly, to throw more illumination on to the white silk of her negligée.

'The first thing Mark will see when he comes through those doors,' he explained.

'Mark is coming?' she whispered.

'Yes. He'll be here. I warned him to come alone. You'd better pray that he does.' He turned and walked away from her. He went down the steps and disappeared into darkness.

'Leonard?' she called, her voice echoing in the still, chill air of the ancient theatre. 'You're . . . you're not going to leave me here like this?'

She tilted her head round to see him, and once again threw herself off balance. The chair wobbled precariously, threatening to tip forward. Sarah extended her arms and leaned back slightly to compensate, aware of her heart thudding in her chest, the thick rope rasping against her neck. Despite the cold, she was sweating.

She wondered how long she could remain standing like this, before her already numb feet betrayed her. She snatched a breath and listened to the enveloping silence. For a moment she thought she heard footsteps, but they seemed to be coming from somewhere up above her.

'Leonard?' she hissed at last. 'Where are you?'

'Don't worry!' His voice startled her, coming from a point a short distance above her head. 'I'm watching you. It won't be long now.'

And then silence descended, deep, heavy, overpowering. Sarah tried to keep very still. Her eyes were beginning to grow accustomed to the darkness that lay beyond the pool of light in which she stood, and for the first time she realized how big this place was – how *empty*. A slight movement overhead caught her attention and she saw that Leonard was sitting up in the balcony. He was looking down at her, smiling fondly.

He stooped, and Sarah heard the rattle of metal as he picked something up and cradled it lovingly in his arms. The crossbow. My God, he was going to wait up there for Mark!

'Yes,' she heard him say. 'She *does* look lovely, doesn't she?'

He was staring at her now with an expression of rapt concentration, waiting for the show to begin.

Chapter Thirty-Six

Mark came running down the road like a madman, his breath
shuddering in his throat, his heart thumping against his ribs. Despite
the chill, his clothes were sticking to him. The streets were deserted
apart from the occasional vehicle passing on the main road. Every sign
he encountered told him that he was near to his destination; but he
seemed to have been going round in circles for the last ten minutes.
Finally, when he had begun to despair of ever finding it, he stumbled
across a narrow turning on his right, little more than an alleyway. He
must have passed by it more than once or twice, but this time he
noticed an ancient rusting sign up above his head. Standing Gate
Street. He turned and plunged into darkness.

Twenty yards or so further on, the alley opened on to a cobbled
street. The crumbling walls of ancient warehouses reared up on either
side of him, swallowing him and his echoing footsteps.

A theatre up this forgotten back alley? Was it possible? Up ahead of
him he saw a solitary rectangle of light, a phone-box, looking oddly out
of place on this street where time seemed to have stopped still. He ran
to it and ducked inside, mainly to have a look at his watch: 12.12. Sarah
had been up on the chair for twelve minutes, for God's sake. Already
he might be too late . . .

On impulse, he glanced at the extension number on the phone dial,
and recognised it as the number he had called from the tube station.
So he had to be very close.

He came out of the box, stood looking around at the gloomy brick
facades that surrounded him. One building appeared to be derelict, its
doorway and windows boarded over. He raised his eyes and above the
entrance he saw the word DOMINION etched boldly over a curved
arch. He crossed the road and approached the short flight of stone
steps that led up to the door. The words PROPERTY CONDEMNED
featured prominently on the slats of wood in big red letters. But Mark
noticed that one of the vertical planks nailed across the front entrance
had been prised away, to reveal an opening beyond. It could be his

imagination, but he thought he perceived a faint glow of light from within . . .

He reached out a hand and pulled at the slat. It hinged easily to one side, revealing a gap that was easily big enough to step through but, despite everything, he hesitated, fearing that somebody might be lying in wait for him.

He eventually took a deep breath, and pushed through the gap.

He found himself in a gloomy foyer, an interior lit only by a few candles. The building had evidently been splendid in its heyday, but all that remained now was mildew and decay. In front of him lay the ornate facade of the box-office, constructed from elaborately-carved mahogany that was now festooned with cobwebs. To his left a once magnificent staircase led upwards to the enveloping darkness of the balcony. A yellowed poster on the wall beside him bore witness to the fact that this theatre had drawn its last breath as recently as the 1960s. Mark recognized the names of television sitcom stars from that era – appearing in a children's pantomime. Over in one corner, heaps of broken seating and rusting lighting fixtures framed a doorway, and above it was a jagged hole in the ceiling where part of the upper floor had fallen in.

Mark glanced around, not sure of where to go next. Then his eye was caught by a poster further along one wall, brightly illuminated by a strategically-placed candle. As he moved towards it, he saw that this was a new addition: the paper almost shockingly white and clean, the lettering crudely scrawled with a thick, black felt-tip pen. He stopped to read.

NOW SHOWING
for one night only
LEONARD'S REVENGE
or, The Death of Mark Tyler.
Seats available in the
STALLS ONLY

Mark frowned. He slipped a hand into the pocket of his jacket and pulled out the carving knife. He examined it doubtfully, wondering what use it could be. If only he possessed a gun. Up on the wall, beside the poster, an ancient wooden sign indicated the direction of the stalls.

Mark turned to follow the painted arrow. Rounding a corner he saw a set of swing doors ahead, with two small circles of glass set into them. As Mark neared the doors, he became aware of a source of brilliant light from within. He pushed one door open a fraction and peered through the crack – knowing already what he would see.

The seats angled sharply downwards to the stage. In the very centre, Sarah was standing on a chair, a noose tied around her neck. She wore a long, white nightdress, and Mark could see that her face and hair were soaked with perspiration.

He went inside, closing the door gently behind him. He moved forward a little until he could see the edge of the balcony jutting out above him. That was where Leonard would be waiting for him – with the crossbow. It was uncanny but this was exactly like the place he had pictured when he wrote that scene. Goldman had chosen well.

Mark remembered the stairs he had seen leading up to the balcony, so considered retracing his steps. Perhaps he could sneak up there and catch Leonard by surprise . . . But then he looked back to the stage, and realized that Sarah couldn't afford the time that diversion might take. She was swaying slightly from side to side on the chair, as though she might faint at any moment. Her eyes were closed and her lips were moving, repeating something over and over. Perhaps she was praying.

Mark began to creep closer, hoping to get her attention without alerting Goldman to his presence. He kept glancing up to make sure that he was out of sight to anyone sitting in the front row of the balcony. Maybe he could get around to the side of the stage – then run out and cut through that rope before Leonard sussed what was happening . . . In the book, Black Wolf achieved his objective by making a superhuman leap. But Mark was only human, and would need something to stand on. And by the time he dragged out another chair, he'd be dead meat.

There had to be some solution . . .

It was just as he was debating this problem that Sarah opened her eyes and saw him approaching the stage. Shock registered on her face, and she opened her mouth to yell a warning – leaning slightly forward. Suddenly, horribly, the chair began to overbalance.

Mark watched it happen, and for an instant he was frozen to the spot with terror. She waved her arms in a frantic attempt to regain her balance, but this time she had gone past the point of no return.

The chair tipped forward.

The sight of it galvanized Mark into motion. There was no time to think of anything else. He began to run towards the stage – all else forgotten as the chair slipped out from under Sarah's bare feet. He saw her wild-eyed stare, saw her hands grope frantically at nothing.

The chair fell and Mark ran, moving out from beneath the protective shadow of the balcony. And now Sarah was falling, and he could sense somebody above and behind him, but he dared not hesitate, for the rope was now tightening around her neck, her eyes bulging in shock.

And Mark was pounding up the staircase, across the dark void of the orchestra pit . . .

It was the rotten step that saved him. It collapsed beneath his foot like a damp twig, and pitched him headlong on to the stage – just as the bolt flew across the intervening space. The metal head grazed his back, and flew on to bury itself in the pulpy floorboards. He landed heavily, rolled, the knife still clutched in his hand, and he twisted around to see where Sarah was hanging. Except she wasn't hanging. She was still falling. And the rope was trailing after her, pulling debris with it; chunks of damp plaster and the length of thick beam to which it had been attached. The ancient wood, rotten to the core, had snapped under Sarah's weight.

She hit the stage feet-first, and sprawled sideways. Down she went in a tumble, dust and rubble raining all around her. Mark registered the look of dull surprise on her face. She had really expected to be dead.

'Sarah!'

He reached out to her, and she extended a hand. But then fire flickered through his left thigh, and he felt an impact as something thudded into the floorboards. He glanced down in astonishment, to see that the bolt had pinned his leg to the stage. He cried out, more from shock than from pain, as he attempted to move, and felt the rigid wooden shaft jar through his leg – and then he thought he might pass out from the agony of it. His hand spasmed and he dropped the knife, without even noticing.

Suddenly, Sarah was with him. She was tugging at the bolt, her expression dazed, the length of rope still trailing from her neck. The bolt came free from the wood but remained pinned in his leg. The impact made Mark gasp, and he sensed, rather than saw, a movement in the gallery above him. He flung his arms around her, and threw her to his right, rolling instinctively across her and onwards towards the front of the stage.

Another bolt thumped into the place where he had been lying an instant before. As Mark rolled further, he glimpsed, ahead of him, the dark forbidding rectangle of the orchestra pit. And, as his back connected with the floorboards, he threw Sarah over again. He didn't know what lay down there in the darkness, but it must be preferable to taking their chances up here in the merciless glow of the lights.

They rolled over a third time, to the very edge of the drop.

As they teetered on the brink, Sarah tried to resist, but he clung to her tightly, and forced his body into one more irresistible roll.

They fell into blackness – and seemed to fall forever before they hit the bottom.

Chapter Thirty-Seven

They landed on something soft and yielding, but the impact still jarred the breath out of them. There they lay in almost total darkness, letting their breathing settle back to a less frantic rhythm. A little light filtered down from the opening ten feet above their heads and, as their eyes adjusted to the gloom, they could see that they had come down on heaps of old black curtain material, mildewed and rat-eaten. They listened for a moment, but there was no sound from up above.

'We can't stay here,' whispered Mark. He pointed into the pitch darkness ahead of them, the sub floor beneath the theatre. 'Should be a way out there someplace . . .' He tried to move but the head of the bolt snagged against a fold of cloth, making him gasp as pain spasmed through his leg. He sank back again and gazed down at the bolt, where it jutted out of his thigh.

'We'll have to get that out first,' he told Sarah grimly. 'You'll have to do it.'

She was removing the rope from around her own neck, and glanced at him apprehensively.

'No way,' she said.

'Sarah, you've *got* to!' He turned back to look at the opening above. They were still too exposed for his liking. 'Otherwise we'll be stuck here like a pair of sitting ducks.'

She frowned. Moving to kneel beside him, she took hold of the bolt's wooden shaft with both hands. She then prepared to pull it back through, but he restrained her with a hand on her shoulder.

'The other way,' he warned. 'If you try and pull that head through, I'm liable to pass out from the pain. Just do it quickly, and don't stop till it's out, even if I beg you to.'

'All right.'

She shifted her hands to take a firm grip on the bloody arrowhead, which protruded a few inches from the front of his thigh.

'Ready?' she asked him fearfully.

He nodded.

301

She took a deep breath and began to pull.

The scream welled up inside him like a pool of boiling, black tar, and he had to clench his teeth to keep it from spilling out of him. Only a low, formless groan escaped him as Sarah drew the twenty-inch shaft through his leg. It came out with a soft plop, and blood squirted across the piles of curtaining.

Mark shuddered and fell back with a sigh. His face was drained of all colour, and he had trouble hanging on to consciousness. Hearing a tearing sound, and looking up, he saw that Sarah was now ripping a long strip of fabric from one of the discarded curtains. She tied the material tightly around his leg, and its black fabric instantly turned a dark glossy red.

'You're bleeding like a stuck pig,' she observed. 'You really need to—'

She broke off at the sound of footsteps moving across the stage, just above their heads.

'Christ!' hissed Mark. 'Let's move!' Fear jolted him back to total wakefulness. He took Sarah's hand and pulled her over into darkness, one arm extended in front of him to probe the way. His injured leg felt useless beneath him, and he wanted to scream every time he put his weight on it. His groping fingers eventually encountered items of stacked furniture ahead of them. He hesitated uncertainly, felt to the right and the left, but the barrier continued on each side. Cursing beneath his breath, he fumbled in his jeans pocket for his cigarette lighter. Above him, the footsteps had stopped. He could imagine Leonard peering down into the orchestra pit for a glimpse of his quarry.

Got to risk it, he thought. He flicked open the lighter and spun the wheel, igniting it for just a second, then dousing it again. The brief flare of light was enough to show him that in the darkness he had drifted to the left, and was trying to find a way through a solid wall of stacked, ancient wooden filing cabinets. The exit lay towards the back of the room, flanked by heaps of old equipment and furniture long rotted past any usefulness and a uniform grey beneath layers of dust and cobwebs.

'This way,' he whispered, and tugged Sarah forward again, using a hand to steer them along the row of filing cabinets. They had gone only a short distance when he heard a new sound behind him. Whipping around, he saw a dark shape drop down through the gap from the stage above. It hit the pile of curtains, raising thick swirls of dust, and crouched there, staring into the darkness. A trick of the light illuminated the figure's eyes as two dots of brilliant white.

Mark felt Sarah's sharp intake of breath, and he slipped an arm around her to give her the courage to keep from crying out.

The figure began to move, and there was a metallic rattle as Leonard raised the crossbow.

Mark felt the hairs on the back of his neck prickle, and he began to push forward again with great care. When his toe brushed against something unidentified, it caused a loud clattering noise. In the silence of the orchestra pit, that sounded like a gun shot.

With an abrupt hiss of air, something fanned Mark's ear in the darkness. Then came a loud crack, as the bolt struck some unyielding surface and careered off, clattering against wood and stone before smashing against the end wall.

Now, thought Mark. *It'll take him some time to reload.*

Pulling Sarah after him, he started to run blindly, keeping the fingers of one hand trailing across the reassuring surface of the filing cabinets. It struck him suddenly that this was how it must feel for Brendan now, plunged into a darkness from which there was no escape.

It couldn't be far to the exit now . . .

His foot struck something obstructing the walkway, and he fell, bringing Sarah down on top of him. His injured leg connected with the object, and pain exploded through him, making him cry out involuntarily. Redness flickered through his head and sparks fizzed like firecrackers behind his eyelids. He lay still, hanging grimly on to consciousness, and was only vaguely aware of another bolt whizzing over his head. That lodged in something up ahead with a jarring thud.

Mark tried to calm his jolting nerves and thudding heart. He put a hand back to touch Sarah's face, and she responded by grasping his hand and giving it a gentle squeeze.

I'm getting a little tired of this, he thought.

He released her hand and felt around the object that had brought him down: a wooden chair. As he eased himself carefully upright, helping Sarah back to her feet, he was aware of footsteps advancing slowly towards them. With a flash of hope he wondered if Leonard had finally run out of ammunition.

Putting his hands on Sarah's shoulders, he pushed her firmly past him, towards the exit. Then he turned back and groped for the chair, and took a firm grip on it. Listening intently, he gazed back towards the faint illumination at the far end of the room. For the first time, he enjoyed a slight advantage, as occasionally a darker shape moved between himself and the light, and he knew that this was Leonard approaching.

Come on, then! he thought. *One shot. That's all I need.*

Leonard was close enough now that Mark could hear his heavy breathing, and the scuffling of his boots on concrete. A metallic rattle revealed that he was still carrying that damned crossbow. Mark tensed himself, raised the chair slightly, holding back until the last possible moment so as to be sure of making contact with his target.

Then, unexpectedly, Leonard spoke – and Mark nearly jumped clean out of his skin.

'M . . . Mark? What are you doing?'

Mark said nothing. He waited.

'I know you're there. I can *smell* you. You can't surprise me. I can see you.'

Mark fought down a desire to run.

Bullshit, he told himself. He can't see any more than I can. Sweat was pouring from him now, making his hands slippery on the chair. But he didn't dare adjust his grip.

Leonard took another cautious step forward.

'I've got another three shots left. At this range, I can't miss!'

He's lying, thought Mark. *If he had more shots, he'd use them.*

'Mark? Where's the sense in fighting me? This is your destiny, so give in to it. I promise I don't want to hurt the girl.'

Trying to get me to speak – betray my position.

'She could still walk out of here alive, Mark. But *you* have to pay for what you did. Everyone must pay for their sins.'

What the fuck's he talking about? Come on, one more step. Just one more step.

'Mark, are you listening to me?'

As Leonard took another step, Mark swung the chair with all his strength. It connected with something solid, shattering completely, and leaving Mark standing empty-handed.

But he was rewarded by a howl of pain from his target, and the clatter of the crossbow skittering across the smooth floor. Then something heavy fell, knocking over a stack of furniture. Mark turned away, and pushed Sarah roughly ahead of him.

'Go!' he shouted.

They made for the exit, and quite suddenly they were through a doorway, and had emerged into light: a faint, muddy light streaming down from a tiny overhead window, but enough at least to let them see where they were going. A narrow corridor stretched ahead of them, and at the end of it a wide flight of stone steps led up to a door marked EXIT.

Mark almost yelled with relief as they stumbled towards the steps. Sarah started up them, and he followed as best he could, dragging his injured leg painfully.

Sarah turned to look back anxiously, but he gestured her on.

'You go on,' he told her. 'Get out in the street and shout for help.'

She pounded barefoot up to the top, grasped the locking bar on the exit door, and tried to lift it upwards. But it was stiff with age and rust, and nothing happened. She put both hands to the task but couldn't make any headway with it. She turned to look imploringly at Mark.

'I can't—'

Then she broke off, her eyes widening in horror, staring over Mark's shoulder, down towards the foot of the stairs.

Mark turned slowly around.

The figure crouching there looked hardly human. It was the first time Mark had properly laid eyes on his tormentor, and he felt fear and shock jolt through his veins.

Leonard was stripped to the waist: a big, powerful man, heavily muscled around his arms and shoulders. Like his quarry, the struggle through the orchestra pit had plastered him with filth from head to foot. He stared up at Mark with tawny, wolfish eyes, and blood ran from a fresh cut on the cheek, where the chair had struck him. But worst of all, he was grinning – revealing twin rows of jagged fangs.

And now he was moving further up the stairs, crawling on his hands and knees like some hideous mutation. A low, guttural growl rose from the back of his throat: saliva was running down his chin.

Mark backed away up the staircase, clutching the banister for support, limping on his weakened leg. Behind him, Sarah was still desperately trying to force the exit doors open.

The creature crept closer.

'Marg,' he hissed. 'Tibe to die.'

Trying to back up another step, Mark tripped suddenly, and half fell backwards.

Leonard's eyes focused on Mark's unprotected throat. Then he leapt forward, his big hands outstretched for his victim's shoulders, his hideous teeth bared. The weight of his attack slammed Mark back hard against the stone ridges, and pain hammered through his thigh.

He threw up his hands to claw at his attacker's face, gouging at it with his thumbs, while pushing back the massive head to hold the snapping jaws at bay, only inches from his throat.

Leonard howled, twisted away, then threw a punch that caught Mark on the left temple and made his head spin. He got a knee under Leonard's chest, and pushed up hard, causing him to slide down a few steps.

As Leonard toppled, Mark caught sight of a leather sheath hanging from his belt – the handle of a knife offering itself. He flung himself on to Leonard's back and grasped the handle, pulling the knife out just before he was thrown off. Mark tumbled down several steps himself, skinning knees and elbows, but still managed to retain his grip on the blade. He came to a halt halfway down the flight, lying on his side.

As his attacker hurtled at him again, Mark lashed out with the knife and cut a deep slash across his opponent's stomach.

Leonard roared with pain, and reeled back. Seizing the chance, Mark made another lunge with the knife, Leonard stepped quickly aside, but seized Mark's outstretched arm, and sank his teeth into it.

Mark threw back his head and screamed. Never had he experienced pain like this. The knife dropped from his twitching fingers and clattered on to the stone. With his left hand, he desperately threw a punch into the man's face, but even that didn't seem to deter him. His teeth were locked on Mark's arm, and he would not relinquish his grip.

Frantically Mark rained blows on Leonard's face, then he dug his fingernails into the man's cheek, tearing away strips of flesh. In a desperate last effort, he pushed a finger into his oppressor's eye, and rammed it home to the knuckle.

Leonard opened his jaws to bellow his agony. He dropped to his knees, clawing at his face, then fell sideways and slid down the stairs.

Gasping with relief, Mark began to crawl back up to the top, where Sarah waited, frozen in terror.

But suddenly, unbelievably, Leonard's arms were around Mark's neck, wrenching him backwards with a force that threatened to snap his spine. As Mark lost his grip on the smooth stone, the two of them went tumbling down the flight of steps, locked together in their mutual hatred.

Mark hit the bottom first, and Leonard came crashing down on top of him, driving the last breath out of his body. Mark could only lie there, the world spinning slowly around in a great, dizzy circle. But Leonard was pulling himself up now; he was getting wearily to his knees. Strangely, his one good eye was bulging, as if in surprise. He lifted his hands to claw at his mouth. Saliva ran down his chin, and Mark saw that there was blood intermingled. Then he heard the noise coming from him: a coarse, ragged wheezing sound, as he dragged the air in and out of his lungs. As Leonard's lips curled back, Mark could clearly see that the false teeth had come loose in his fall, and were now lodged at the back of his throat.

Realization dawned on the man's shattered face. He must have sensed he didn't have long, for he turned his full attention to Mark, his hands extended. The huge fingers closed around Mark's throat and began to squeeze with an irresistible force – till Mark felt his head was going to burst. He reached up with his good arm and tried to prise one of the hands away. His empty lungs began to ache, and he sensed a black void opening beneath him.

Then suddenly another face rose into Mark's vision. Sarah behind Leonard's shoulder. For a crazy instant, Mark thought she had come to watch him die.

Then she lifted her arm and he saw the big hunting knife. Gazing down with an expression of calm hatred, with all her strength she plunged the knife down between the madman's shoulderblades.

Leonard howled in pain and surprise. His body jolted as she pulled the knife free, and his hands opened convulsively – releasing his grip on Mark's throat. The big man twisted around and got unsteadily to his feet. Mark's relieved gasping now mingled with Leonard's, as though they were somehow sharing the same lungs.

Leonard staggered slowly towards Sarah, reeling like a drunkard. She retreated back to the steps and began to climb them, the knife still held threateningly out in front of her. She now looked completely terrified, as though she had just realized the enormity of what she had done.

Leonard's face had turned a deep, ugly purple, and red bubbles formed on his lips. His ruined eye was streaming fluid. He came to a halt, and though Sarah was standing a few steps up from him, their heads were now on the same level. His wide chest rose and fell spasmodically, and he uttered a low, despairing sound. He lifted his hands as if in supplication.

Mark lay watching them, unable to move even a muscle. There was still immense power in Leonard's arms, and even now they were reaching out to enfold Sarah, to pull her towards him.

She lifted the knife a second time.

For an instant Leonard seemed surprised; then his expression seemed to soften into something resembling acceptance of his fate. Then she drove the jagged blade downwards into his chest – pushing it in to the hilt. Now her expression had become one of savage hatred. Wrenching the knife out, her arm came down again and again, raining blows. And Leonard just stood there like some great, dumb brute, gazing at her with what looked like undying devotion.

And then, at last, he sank to his knees, gave a long convulsive rattle, and pitched forward to lie at Sarah's feet.

She let the bloody knife drop on to the steps, and stood totally still for a few moments, staring down at the fallen man. Then she stepped carefully past the body and went to Mark. She put her arms around him and buried her face in his chest, but she wasn't crying. Just stunned, and totally detached from reality.

After a while Mark pulled away from her and looked at her questioningly.

'Sarah?' he whispered. 'Did he . . .?'

She shook her head.

'No, he didn't hurt me,' she said. 'I think . . . in a weird way, I think he liked me.'

Mark felt waves of fresh pain rippling through his body.

'Phone box . . . just across the road,' he croaked. 'Get out and . . . call the police.' Dizziness swam through his head, and he fell back with a groan. He could hear the soft sounds of her feet on the stairs and, a few moments later, the crash of the exit door as she finally forced it open.

Mark lay still, feeling his functions shutting down one by one. His enemy was lying only a short distance away, his head twisted at an odd angle. Leonard's one good eye was wide open, and staring straight at Mark. The fallen knife lay a few inches away from his outstretched hand.

As Mark watched, the fingers of that hand began to twitch. Mark's last thought, before he drifted into unconsciousness, was that the bastard was going to get up and come at him again.

The trouble was, he was now too tired to care.

Epilogue

Mark was lured downstairs by the smell of frying bacon. First he collected a pile of mail from the doormat, then strolled through into the kitchen, where Sarah was preparing breakfast. It was a cold January morning and she'd risen half an hour earlier to light the solid-fuel Aga stove. It was now throwing out a delicious heat.

Mark was surprised to find Brendan already up and about. He was sitting at the pine table dressed in a towelling bathrobe and what he called his 'Stevie Wonders': a pair of wraparound black shades. Mark took a seat opposite him and began to leaf through the mail, sorting it into two piles: one for items that looked interesting, and the other for junk mail and bills.

'Morning,' he said. 'Sleep OK?'

'Like a baby,' Brendan told him. 'I woke up screaming every ten minutes. Do those sheep bleat like that *every* night?'

Mark smiled.

'You get used to it,' he said. It was heartening to see Brendan more like his old self. He'd turned up for the paperback launch of *The Jumblies* in London, the previous night, and it had been Sarah's suggestion that he should come and spend a few days at their cottage. It was months since they had spoken to Brendan, and they were both pleasantly surprised by his newfound cheerfulness. They could use a little of that; the months following the death of Leonard Goldman had proved difficult to say the least.

As for Brendan, it was hard to believe that it was already sixteen months since he'd lost his sight. He'd spent a good year of that time sunk into a black depression from which nobody could retrieve him. But now, at last, he seemed to have come to terms with his disability, and was even learning how to exploit it. Mark had watched him at *The Jumblies* launch, chatting up a young woman. Within ten minutes, Brendan had obtained her name, address and phone number.

Sarah brought a bowl of cornflakes to the table, and sat down beside Brendan. 'Your starter,' she announced, tucking a serviette into the front of his bathrobe. Mark watched, incredulous, as she began to feed him, spooning the cereal tenderly into his mouth and pausing each time to wipe any dribbles of milk off his chin with the corner of the serviette.

'There's really no need,' Brendan told her, between mouthfuls. 'I *can* feed myself, you know.' But he didn't protest very loudly, and it was clear that he was enjoying the attention.

Mark smiled, remembering the time when Sarah had not had a good word to say about his friend. Since encountering the horror of Leonard Goldman, she'd become more forgiving, and more motherly. For a year now, she and Mark had been trying for a child, and looking at her with Brendan made him wonder if they hadn't just acquired one. He felt certain that Brendan's stay would last considerably longer than a few days, but he didn't mind that. It was remote out here in the wilds of Kent, so they didn't get many visitors. Even though he was beginning to enjoy a little solitude, it would be nice to have a different face around.

Mark turned up an envelope from the American publishers of *The Jumblies* (it had been renamed *The Thrifties* over there), and he opened that one straight away. You never knew: there might be a cheque in it.

But there was no cheque inside; just a compliments slip and another sealed envelope. 'The enclosed was sent to us here in New York for forwarding,' he read.

He examined the envelope thoughtfully. It was addressed simply to *Mark and Sarah*, suggesting the familiarity of an old friend, the words scrawled in a thick, black felt-tip pen. Mark frowned.

'What have you got there?' asked Sarah, still spooning cornflakes into Brendan's mouth.

'Don't know,' said Mark. 'The American publishers have forwarded a letter from . . .' He glanced at the postmark. 'From New Orleans.'

'Probably a fan letter,' observed Brendan.

There was an uncomfortable silence. Mark held the letter out to Sarah. She took it from him and glanced at it without interest. Then she put it down on the table top, while she fed Brendan the last of his cereal.

'There,' she said. 'You're in the clean plate club, Brendan.'

'Thanks, Mum.' He grinned. 'Don't suppose there's any chance of you helping me with my morning bath, later?'

She smiled. 'No chance whatsoever.' She got up from the table and took the letter across to the Aga. She opened the door and pushed it inside, on to the hot coals. It crumpled, blackened, ignited with a whoosh. She closed the door, and went to check how the bacon was doing.

Mark realized he had been holding his breath. He exhaled slowly and went on with sorting the mail. Amazing how long it took for old scars to heal. In damp weather he still got stabbing pains in his arm, where the porcelain fangs had gouged deep, and an occasional spasm in his thigh where the crossbow bolt had pierced his flesh. Worse, though, were the recurring nightmares, in which he was stalked through a pitch-black room by something with tawny eyes and jagged white teeth.

He wasn't going to speculate about what might or might not have been enclosed in that letter. Like the others, he was doing his damnedest to forget.

The kettle came to the boil, with its shrill whistle.

Sarah turned from the stove to look at him.

'Tea?' she asked. 'Or coffee?'

Mark smiled. These days, he wanted all his decisions to be this simple.